THE SWORD

Albert Daniels

The Sword by Albert Daniels
Copyright © 2019. All rights reserved.

ALL RIGHTS RESERVED: No part of this book may be reproduced, stored, or transmitted, in any form, without the express and prior permission in writing of Pen It! Publications. This book may not be circulated in any form of binding or cover other than that in which it is currently published.

This book is licensed for your personal enjoyment only. All rights are reserved. Pen It! Publications does not grant you rights to resell or distribute this book without prior written consent of both Pen It! Publications and the copyright owner of this book. This book must not be copied, transferred, sold or distributed in any way.

Disclaimer: Neither Pen It! Publications, or our authors will be responsible for repercussions to anyone who utilizes the subject of this book for illegal, immoral or unethical use.

This is a work of fiction. The views expressed herein do not necessarily reflect that of the publisher.

This book or part thereof may not be reproduced in any form, stored in a retrieval system, or transmitted in any form by any means-electronic, mechanical, photocopy, recording or otherwise-without prior written consent of the publisher, except as provided by United States of America copyright law.

Published by Pen It! Publications, LLC
812-371-4128 www.penitpublications.com

Published in the United States of America by Pen It! Publications, LLC

ISBN: 978-1-950454-97-6
Cover by Donna Cook
Edited by Rachel Hale

Promise:

That which has been is what will be,
That which is done is what will be done,
There is nothing new under the sun.

Ecclesiastes 1:9

Contents

Contents 5
Prologue 7
2254 BC 9
3124 AD The Finds 15
The Match 55
The Stolen Mower 107
France 149
Spain 169
The Wedding 189
Saint George and the Dungeon 203
Johnson's Place 219
The Drone 249
Barb's Illness 271
Jane's Announcement 321
The Proposal of the Anothen 325
The Stolen Sword 347
Author Bio 357

Prologue

In days of old before Knights were bold
Long before guns were invented;
A Sword was forged and in the hilt;
Time changes were cemented.

The war raged on and thousands died
And very few lamented;
The water roared and covered all;
The tool was buried in it.

The sword was lost, buried deep;
The story did die with it.
The legend goes that Arthur rose;
To rule and reign due to it.

The tale lingered but few believed
Of power strength and might;
Until one day it showed up again;
Just to end things right.

© Albert Daniels a.k.a. Daniel A. Breithaupt 2019

2254 BC

"Do you see that dust plume?" bellowed the general to the terrified towns people huddled in horror as they looked over the horizon.

"Is that not just a dust storm?" fearfully shouted one of the men from the crowd.

"It is a storm all right," announced the wicked warrior, "The last storm you will ever see. Now bring out all of your jewelry, gold, silver, and precious stones, and pile them in this bag. If you cooperate, I promise you will not get hurt. You have heard about what has happened to the others who refused to do as they were asked and lost their lives!" he shouted with his sword in the air. "Lay down your weapons and join our side for we are taking over the world."

"How can we fight this monster?" asked one woman to another.

"It can't possibly be as bad as we have heard," asked a petite but bold beauty as she hid the knife in the folds of her dress.

"You saw how Eber returned," reminded the first, "When he left his hair was brown like yours. When he returned eight days later it was as white as snow."

"What could possibly scare him so much?" asked the younger.

"He said it was the strong, swift, and sharp."

"How strong can it be with so many of us?"

"Eber said he could not see the killer only the killed." replied the older woman.

The younger thought about this for a few moments, "Then what chance does anyone have?" she slowly removed the sharp object from her skirt and dropped it in the bag.

"Smart move," said the general, "Will you accompany me on my exploits?" he invited with a leer.

"I have a family," she said wishing she had not been so hasty in surrendering the blade, "I will stay with them."

"Suit yourself." he growled as he picked up the bag and rode off.

* * *

The cloud grew closer at such a rate that had never been seen before. Within moments all the townsfolk lay slain in the streets having been dragged from their houses. One young woman had hidden herself in an attic closet, missed by the assassin. She had her young son with her hoping to start the family again with him. Desperate times...

The dust settled after a few hours and she busied herself dragging the bodies off to a pile on the lee side of town.

"How can I bury all of these bodies before the disease of their death destroys me?" She headed out to the farm she knew of a few miles out of town. There she found only four dead and buried them in a common grave a good distance from the house and barn. There was one cow and her calf in the barn that was missed by the assassin that had roared through.

"Thank you stars in heaven!" she rejoiced at the find and returned to town to collect what little she had left. A small brass cup was used as a milk bucket to gather some for her and the child. The calf helped himself to what he thought was needed. A few months later she thought things were looking up and life would be hard but not totally impossible. Then it started to rain.

"What is this?" she asked her son. A fine mist was falling from the sky in the early morning. By noon the rain was coming down in sheets.

"This has never happened before!" she explained to her boy, "What is happening?" By mid-afternoon she heard a roar in the distance although the water from the sky did not produce lightening. Looking off to the east all she could do was stand there and wait frozen in horror as the wall of water approached.

"Where do I hide now?" she pondered, "The mountains are almost a thousand miles from here." Before long the rushing torrent had taken her and all that was left in a three-hundred-foot tsunami. It took less than twenty-four hours to catch up with the villain with the instrument of terror.

* * *

World conquest was finally within reach. The manufacture of the sword clenched all power into the hands of he who wielded it. It would only be a matter of weeks till the wealth and population of the world would be under his control.

A mist was falling but it was thicker than it was an hour ago. He heard the sound from behind. Turning he saw the wall of water rushing faster than anything could ever outrun. The crest was churning humans, animals, and trees like a baker tossing dough. Many were already dead but there were a few that were still holding on to life.

"Were they the fortunate or unfortunate?" he pondered aloud, but not for long. He drew the sword with his right hand. With his left he grabbed onto the neck of the horse. He timed out as far as he thought safe and the horse bounded over houses, towns, and lakes as it headed west in front of the rushing water.

"I heard there is a coast with mountains in this direction!" he hollered to the steed, "If we can make it there, we may be able to ride this thing out."

It didn't take long to adjust to get the next jump as he rushed to the coast. He traveled so fast the sun seemed to stand fixed in the sky. He calculated he was traveling at the same speed as the sun around the earth but not nearly as far out in orbit.

There was a farmer and his cattle below, so he slowed down and quickly rode up to the man.

"How far to the coast?" he asked.

The man turned fully startled. "Where did you come from?" he asked the rider with the drawn sword, "I can see for miles and I did not see you approaching."

"Never mind that," he threatened with the sword close to the man's throat, "How far to the coast?"

"Eight days if you have a fast horse." answered the horrified man. "Six if you can get a fresh horse every four hours."

"Thanks." replied the warrior and turned back west.

The herdsman glanced at his flock to make sure the villain had not taken any as he passed through. He turned to watch the rider fade into the distance, but he had already disappeared. Looking around he asked himself, "Where did he go?"

Eight days eh?" the warrior mumbled to himself. Quickly he did the calculation. "Then I could be there a few hours real time." he mulled over the idea. "It could be a little dangerous, but I need to get to the coast before that wave of water."

He timed out farther and the horse was now jumping twenty miles each leap. In normal time he would be galloping about twenty-eight miles per hour. At one hundred to one he could make it to the coast in less than one-hour real time.

The mountains appeared and approached fast. He timed down, and the horse was a little more comfortable with the three-mile leaps.

"Good." thanked the rider, "These mountains are a number of thousand feet high. That tsunami was only about three hundred feet. Hopefully it will calm down enough to be able to escape." He pushed the horse unto higher elevation.

Lots of animals and many humans had ascended higher thinking they would be safe. At fifteen hundred feet he stopped and let the animal rest. He lashed the sword to his belt and sat on the east side waiting for the water to come. It took two more days then he could see it coming. The water picked up everything. Great clumps of trees were being rolled together like someone making a giant snowman as the wave roared across the landscape.

"I wonder if I'm high enough?" he thought as the wave crashed into the base of the mountains. All he could hear was the roar of the flood taking everything in its path. The water circled around the base of the mountain then the level crept up. The mountain started to shake and quake. The horse spooked and took off. What good would it do now? The earth started to dissolve under his feet, and he fell into the pit of sloppy mud. Dying was somewhat quick but not painless as the muddy water filled his lungs.

The body was carried for miles by the raging currents. In a few days it had bloated. The corpse floated to the surface and the hemp strap that held the sword began to rot. He was carried back to the plains and in time the string let go, dropping the sword into the depths. Down it fell into the mud and finally ended up between two pieces of granite that were being covered with silt as the waters receded.

Over time the stories became legends and finally were dismissed as mythology then forgotten about completely. It was left in the mud for thousands of years until, once more, it was needed to perform the consequences for a race of people who could not distinguish wrong from righteousness, rewards and responsibilities.

The sword surfaced to reveal the true nature of the heart of all of humanity.

3124 AD
The Finds

Ply Gallant was someone who did not handle boredom well. His teachers in grade school whispered to the next class guardian, "Make sure you keep this one occupied! Try not to do it with just busy work." Some even handed over a list of his current interests.

At sixteen, after graduation from high school, he applied for a four-year electrical apprenticeship and was immediately accepted due to his math and science marks. By the time he had finished he found that it was barely sufficient stimulation to keep his curiosity in check. He got his journeyman papers, worked in the trade for a few years, saved most of his money, then looked for something else to satisfy his appetite for adventure.

Ply found the fascination of caves would fill the void for a time. Gathering experience for a number of months, he worked himself up from one cave to another and finally he applied at the big one. His electrical skills made him a prime candidate but all he wanted to do at this time was tour and learn about caverns.

By the age of twenty-two, he had been given the coveted position of giving tours in one of the longest and deepest caverns in what had been known as the North American Continent. The program offering to read maps and promote safe spelunking skills he found delightful.

Ply was five-foot-ten inches tall with thick light brown hair. He kept it neatly trimmed, square at the back and just off the ears. He liked the 'kiss curl' that showed up a few weeks after a trim, so he waited longer than usual till the next cut. He tanned easily with his olive colored skin that came from his distant German heritage. He was skinny as a kid but filled out a bit as he exercised and tried to keep his body in shape. The cave wasn't doing much for his tan nor his body tone.

Okay, he decided to himself one slow Tuesday afternoon, *What else is out there where the boredom won't wear off quite so fast? There is so much to learn and so much to discover.*

He was getting weary with the same old routine day after day, month in, month out, and was seriously contemplating a new endeavor, when, early Thursday morning, he felt a slight breeze coming from what everyone thought to be just a hole in the rock partially filled with water.

Tour guides instruct from parts of the cave that were just, the-other-side-of-the-line, so to speak than the paying customers. The clientele viewed from the best place to see what was being explained. The tourists had the better view but the employed had the opportunity to see the attraction more than once. This usually was needed to get a better appreciation of the site. No one had taken much notice of the breeze seeing that the maps had not shown anything exciting on the other side. That evening there was a fairly good rain and the next morning the breeze was not there.

That's funny! thought Ply as he passed the water hole with each tour. *I wonder why a breeze came out of that place yesterday?* he pondered as he gave tours on the Friday before his vacation.

I hadn't planned to do much but watch a bunch of movies, eat a lot of junk food, and surf the net to see about "opportunities". I sure need a change from this humdrum job. A vacation from this place seemed like a good idea but now other possibilities were crawling around in his mind.

There had been a great earthquake and torrential rains that brought a flood more than eighty years earlier in the area that was once known as Central United States. Thousands of new caves had been discovered since the "uncovering", as the locals referred to them. The "Midwest" was rearranged with an unfortunate loss of life. Some of the ancient cities were destroyed. Most of the population was now much more spread out so the destruction was horrendous, but the loss of life was confined to about a two-hundred-mile radius of the area affected. About ten miles from the "destruction zone" there was limited damage. For the most part it seemed repairable. Due to the fact that so much progress had been made in the forecasting of earthquakes and weather patterns all, but the foolishly stubborn had fled. Death had been curbed but not eliminated and had once again performed its horrifying deed.

Thousands of trinkets and hundreds of priceless antiques had been discovered that had been buried in the distant past. Hidden rooms and caverns had all been mapped and explored. At least, that's what everyone had been told. Once the explorers, professional spelunkers and geeks had been satisfied with the haul and the mapping, the caves were turned loose to the public for commercial use. Some of the more interesting caves had opened for tours but only after thoroughly searching by radio-scope the entire areas up to one-hundred feet from the habitable and research-able limits.

An entire month off with nothing to do just might land me in some sort of trouble. Not that he had a police record, but he had a few good warnings due to his titanic curiosity. *Trespassing after hours is not conducive to keeping a job even if it is a little on the repetitious side, and a lot on the monotonous side,* he thought. Looking around again on his final Friday tour he shone his flashlight towards the cameras confirming his suspicion.

The water hole was just out of sight of cameras on each side. There really was not much in the cave to steal but, once in a while, some kids from homes in the area would sneak in to carve their initials in some of the stalagmites. That was a little obvious as the next morning tour came through. Their action made it fairly easy to catch the culprits.

"If a breeze came from that hole in the rock then there must be an outside entrance on the other side of that wall. Vacation may not be so dull after all." he whispered to himself.

Saturday afternoon he headed back to the caverns to have a look at some of the radio-scope maps that were made of the area. Most of these were kept in an office for those who had an extra dose of inquisitiveness about caves.

"Good afternoon Mr. Pierce. I would like to look at some of the maps that have been made of this cave if I could please."

"No problem Ply. Looking for something to spruce up the tour with?"

"That could very well happen." he responded as he was led to the door of the room where they were kept. Ply studied the maps and memorized what had been found and recorded. *Not much there according to the maps,* he said to himself.

Closing time was six o'clock. At about ten minutes to, he wandered back to the water hole and sat quietly as the lights were turned off. He had brought all his gear with him stuffed into an old high school sports bag.

Let me see if I can get through without all this gear, he mused as he set down the bag. He stripped down to a sweatshirt and track pants. He tossed his clothing into the bag then wrapped it all in a large plastic Ziploc Bag.

There, he said to himself. *That should keep things dry until the other side*. On the first try through the hole his sweatshirt caught on a sharp protruding rock.

Try not to panic, he told himself. Wiggling back, he banged off the sharp rock with his spelunking hammer and picked it up and took it topside inside the tour cave.

On the second try he cleared a lot of sharp edges as he passed to the other side. It took another few minutes to clean the fallen rock from the bottom of the tunnel. He tossed all the rubble on the other side in the unexplored new-found area. It took a full two minutes catching his breath before he tried again.

Let me practice this a few times just to get the hang of it.

Four successful attempts later and a bit more banging off snags he was ready to bring his gear through. This time he was through the hole and out the other side in about fifteen seconds. He shone his light around and found a long, curved corridor stretching in two directions. He changed into dry clothing leaving the wet hung on a rock to attempt to dry.

"Not much luck of it drying here with all the moisture in the air." he said.

With his back to the water hole, to his right the corridor elevated for a while then made a long sweeping curve to the left. The other direction it seemed to be headed in a downward angle curving gently to the right and he chose that to follow. Tying a string to a rock he dropped it back into the pool, so he could find his way back if his lights were lost. Sliding his hammer into the hook on his belt and grabbing the light, he started walking down the hall. He could see why there was no interest in this part of the cavern. Nothing special; no colors, no large rooms, only a slender hallway and endless dripping of water. After a little more than a hundred and fifty feet of the gentle curve to the right the hallway turned sharply to the right.

This is why the scopes did not show anything past this point. He shone the light and saw that there was a blank wall about fifteen feet from the turn. A slit in the rock just to the left on the wall seemed a little too small to get through but it widened closer to the ceiling.

No harm in looking, he thought and climbed up and shone the light through the opening.

No ceiling visible here, he said to himself and crawled into the hole.

The floor was about three feet down and the room was very

large. He pushed the ball of string through and followed it to the floor. Flashing his light around to quickly survey the surroundings he was surprised at what he saw.

"Wow! The colors are amazing." he quietly breathed.

Off to the right were stalactites and stalagmites that glistened in the reflection of his light. In front of him there was something that reflected his light a little differently. At times it appeared that there were two lights shining and other times it seemed that there was only one. He crouched down and looked closer at the reflective surface. Gently touching it, it rippled.

"Water?"

He knew not to drink it. There was a sample bottle in his kit on the other side. He retrieved his gear and stole a sample of the liquid to look at later through a microscope. He dared not stir up the body not wanting to attract any attention. *Who knows how deep it is and what could be living here.*

The 'lake' bordered on a very steep shore about sixty feet to the other side. This side there was a slight pebble beach slope that gradually fell to the water. Off to the left there was another corridor. Not wanting the string to touch the water he buried it under some lose stones and headed toward the passage.

Another long dark descending path to no place, he thought. He had seen about enough and was ready to turn back. Maybe he would try the other direction from the pool he entered through. Flashing the light one more time down the sloping corridor expecting to see nothing but a dark cave something glittered in the distance.

"Wait," he thought out loud, "Are there gems down here?" *Have I been missing something all this time?*

He flashed his light over the ceiling of the cave looking for shiny objects. *Nothing seems to be here.* Dropping the beam back to the sloping corridor he said softly, "But there certainly is something there."

Remembering that excitement can make one careless he was even more cautious in the approach to the glittering object. Watching for loose stones and slippery spots he gradually inched his way as things got a little steeper until about fifteen feet before the shiny piece. There seemed to be something stuck in the rock in the ceiling. Even getting close to it, the shape made it hard to figure out what was actually there. As he studied it, he noticed a small round ball that was some sort of metal that was attached to...

What on earth is this?

With his hammer he gently chipped some of the gravel from around the ball. There was a piece of metal attached to the ball. He chipped a little more. An eight-pound rock fell from behind the object just missing his foot.

"Whoa!"

Quickly, he stepped out of the way as a flow of loose gravel fell from behind the fallen rock exposing metal. He covered his face with a dust mask as a plume gathered from the falling material. He backed down the corridor a little but noticed a crevice about fifty feet from the dust cloud. His heart skipped a beat as he was thankful again for his spelunking training. Shining the light down the hole he could not see bottom.

"Man, that's deep!"

He picked up a stone about the size of his fist and dropped it into the hole and started counting. When he got to four with no sound, he stepped a little closer to the dust plume. At seven seconds he heard a gentle clatter then a faint splash. Shining his light, a lot more reverently into the crevice he noticed that the sides were very smooth.

"This must be an ancient shaft from something... or maybe not so ancient." he concluded half under his breath.

The dust had settled somewhat, and he went to examine the glittering piece. As he drew near his eyes widened.

"It looks like a handle to a knife."

Again, very carefully, he tapped the rocks and more fine gravel fell from the handle exposing about two inches of a blade.

"Is it a sword?"

The blade was about thirty millimeters wide and about six millimeters thick at the center and tapered to what appeared to be very sharp edges. The little that he saw appeared like new under the flashlight.

How did this get down here?

He scraped away the gravel with his knife but found the blade of the sword stuck right into the granite. He grabbed the handle and gave a gentle tug, but nothing moved. He tried to pull it again, but it did not budge. He dropped his hand from the object.

It sure is in there tight.

Grabbing it again, it did not move at all. He quickly let go.

If this thing is old, I don't want to break it.

Studying it once more he held on and tried to slide the device out of the rock, and it seemed to wiggle a little.

"Did it move?" he questioned out loud as he dropped his hand. Not that he was worried that someone might be listening. He grabbed the handle again and quickly tried to move it in any direction.

Nothing.

He held the sword by the handle and pulled. In a minute it seemed to move just a small amount.

Good, he thought, *It's getting loose.* He took his hand off to rest. A few seconds later he tried again, and the sword seemed tighter than it had been at first.

There must be some loose rock up there that falls back in after it moves.

Again, he grabbed the handle and pulled to no avail. Shining his flashlight on the handle he noticed that it was not rusty at all.

"Wow," he said, "That thing looks brand new. How could a brand-new sword get way down here without the cameras catching any action?"

As if to answer his own question, he realized that there must be another entrance to this part of the cavern. He shut off his light and listened for a full two minutes. Nothing but the dripping of water in the distance and absolute darkness.

If there was another entrance close, it was either well concealed or around a lot of sharp turns, he thought. *That shaft would prevent anyone from coming from that direction.*

As his eyes got used to the darkness, he glanced up at the hilt of the weapon but still saw nothing.

Why should I expect to see anything in such blackness?

Ply had been in the darkness numerous times. Part of the 'tour' was to allow the visitors to experience the full darkness of a deep cave. He had learned to sense the crowd as to how they might react in the blackness. Unfortunately, there are some guests that cannot tolerate the 'ink' as well as others. He taught himself to time the crowd and to make sure the lights were turned back on before difficulties arose. Thankfully he was schooled by others not to push their patience.

One guide thought he could let the patrons stay past the

tolerance level of the least able to endure the darkness. After someone was punched, the lights came on and the guide quickly finished his last tour. Since then the instructions to the guides had been strict. There was a blackout on the 'lights off' policy for about three months until the furor died down. The darkness was gradually re-established in short duration for the first few months till the media quieted down about the 'chamber of horrors' as one reporter publicized the incident.

He was not afraid of the darkness but being sunless in an unfamiliar part of a cave gives an eerie feeling that cannot readily be explained. Turning on the flashlight with the lens pushed against his jacket, he let his eyes grow accustomed to the light in small doses. He shone the light around and down the corridor in both directions to confirm his hopes that there was no one there. Caves with swords stuck in the ceiling can fertilize overactive imaginations. He lifted his hand to the hilt and felt the metal.

What kind of metal is this?

It seemed to be like stainless steel, but the luster was brighter. Perhaps it was just the light. He rested his hand on the grip and was surprised at how comfortable it felt.

Man, this feels good.

He moved his fist to warm up the handle and the sword moved a little. Slowly he pulled the sword out of the rock as if he was sliding it from a sheath. He shone his light on the blade and it appeared a mixture of reds and blues that he could barely describe.

How come...

He moved the beam up to the rock and was confused to see only a small slit.

Where is the hole for the blade?

He placed the point to the crack in the rock and slid the sword back into the rock all the way to the guard. Astonished, he let go and the armament stayed in place. Stunned, he looked at it for a short period, then grabbed the sword to pull it out but it stayed fast. Letting go quickly, he backed away not believing what he had just witnessed. He moved quietly till he was out of sight of the instrument then ran as fast as the terrain would allow him up to the lake. Winding up the string, he went in feet first and dropped to the floor of the long hallway. He quickly returned to the pool and stood to catch his breath. He had to mentally calm himself down so not to get stuck crawling to the other side. Resting for a few minutes as he changed into his wet clothes and re-packed the bag into the plastic, he tried to think about what had just happened.

It just doesn't make any sense at all.

Leaving the string and the tools about three feet from the pool he grabbed the light and lowered himself in and exited the caverns.

* * *

That night he had not a little trouble getting to sleep. He pondered how the sword let loose of the rock then grabbed on again after being slid into it so easily. After a few hours of nervous tossing he got out of bed, made a sandwich for a snack then slept lightly till about five-thirty AM. He awoke with a start having dreamed of ancient battles against horrifying beasts and every time the frozen sword gained the victory. He lay in bed with the blankets pulled up close as beads of sweat gathered on his brow. Suddenly he threw back the covers.

"The frozen sword." He said a little too loudly.

He paced the room trying to recall all that had happened in the darkness the night before.

Frozen, he thought to himself, so no one would hear.

Living alone made talking to oneself a little more socially acceptable. How he thought, was out loud.

"When I first grabbed it, it stayed there because it was cold. As I rested my hand on the hilt it warmed up a little and wiggled."

He paced around the room a few more times.

"When I let the handle warm up it came out of the rock."

He doubled back around the small apartment.

"When I slid it back into the rock and let go it stayed as the handle cooled and I could not get it out again until it warmed up."

Over and over again he mulled the action in the corners of his mind.

Why?

All day he pondered why and at about two in the afternoon he decided he had to return on Monday.

By four o'clock Monday afternoon, he could hardly wait to get back. The moments dragged but a little before six he was allowed into the cave and quietly walked to the pool. No one around and no one suspicious so he submerged through the opening to the other side and cautiously made his way to the instrument in the ceiling. As he approached, he kept all his senses alert. He studied the ground to see if anyone had come from the other direction or if there were any other prints but his own.

Nothing! There it was just as he had left it. This time he approached the sword with a much different attitude than he had previously. Almost afraid as to what might happen, he stared at it for what he thought was too long.

"Get a grip Ply!" he muttered to himself.

His self-encouragement did little to stem his apprehension. Slowly he lifted his hand and touched the cold metal. He tried to slide it out with one finger. As before nothing moved but the bending of the finger. Wrapping his hand around the hilt he pulled and tugged to no avail. He let his hand rest until the metal was warm then he slid out the glittering instrument into his light.

Studying the eighty-centimeter blade he noticed that it might be very sharp. He gently touched the edge with his finger and cut himself. He held the cut tightly closed and counted slowly to thirty. Opening his fingers, he noticed that there was no more pain. He licked the excess blood from his hand and realized that the finger left no evidence of damage.

"This thing must either be magic or some new technology. It is so sharp when I cut myself the wound is so clean that it heals almost instantly. How on earth did it get down here?"

Moving it through the air and it seemed to make a low rumble. Holding it still he was confused by what was happening. Again, he shone the light around to see if there was anyone watching. No one.

"This thing is so light," he spoke, "Almost no weight at all. What is this made of?"

He pretended to be in a fight with one of the wild beasts of his dream and as he moved the sword it slashed and rumbled through the air. Lancing and charging he pretended to cut the beast in two. The blade seemed to do exactly as he wished. With a final lunge he struck the imaginary beast and took off its head.

He danced a victory dance waving the blade in the air until a twenty-pound piece of rock fell from the ceiling. Instantly he backed away and shone his light up to the ceiling of the cave noticing the slits the sword had cut and the hole in the rock in the shape of the piece on the floor.

Silence gradually settled as the echo of the fallen rock bounced around the cavern dying out in the distance. He let the weapon slip from his grip and the blade sunk into the granite right up to the guard. For long moments he stood there trying to comprehend what just occurred. As he reached for the hilt slowly wrapping his hand around the metal, surprised at how quickly it cooled, he warmed the metal and drew the instrument into the air.

Cautiously, he moved the sword to the piece of rock that had fallen and moved the blade. It slid effortlessly through the rock leaving the granite cut in two on the floor.

He carefully inspected the blade to discover perfect smoothness, straight lines with no chips, dents, or even scratches.

Immediately he felt as if someone was watching.

"Who's there?" he yelled drawing the tool into position. Nothing but the reverberation of his own interrogation. It was gone but there was something, or someone.

What on earth is this thing?

He slowly looked around in the cave and noticed a part of rock that stood up from the floor. He sliced through the rock. He cut a small stalactite and watched it tumble to the floor. Thrusting it into the rock wall he cut a hole into the wall and watched the rock fall to the ground at his feet.

He looked around for a part of the wall of the cavern that looked solid. He flashed the light around and found that there seemed to be a corner behind a stalagmite. He shone the light behind it and mumbled, "Hmm."

The corner was almost invisible from either direction. The rock curved just enough to present an optical illusion to anyone passing but gave a perfect hiding spot if one was needed. He crawled around the heavy formation, pierced the rock and cut a small hole close to the floor of the cave. It was just large enough to crawl into and dug it about eight feet deep. Sliding the sword into the rock at an angle he cut the pieces into gravel. Turning upwards he carved a small room in the granite up and over to one side.

What will I do with all this rubble?

He gathered up a few pieces and carried them over to the crevice and threw them in. He listened, and it seemed like forever before they thudded and splashed at what might have been the bottom. The floor of the cave was pretty rough and steep, so he cut a road with steps into the floor so his way to the crevice would be level and easier to travel.

I better make the road go past the entrance to the hiding place as not to generate ideas if visitors ever show up.

He cut the road past the small room right to the mouth of the entrance by the lake. Making a sack out of his sweatshirt, he filled it with the gravel and dumped the small stones down the shaft. It took over two hours to clean up the mess. The water did not cease to splash proving that the pool was not the end of the gravels journey.

"This also is a mystery!" he said and remembered a mine shaft that had been allowed to fill with water, so scuba divers could enjoy the depths.

"Maybe it is just where the water table levels at this spot." he decided.

Turning back to the room he had just dug; he shone the light in from the outside. It appeared to be just a hole in the wall. One had to go in to see that there was much more to the room.

"It needs a door,"

Crawling into the entrance feet first he slid the sword into the ceiling about six inches inside the entrance. Sliding the weapon into the rock right up to the guard he cut a slit into the rock about thirty inches deep. Holding the blade straight he moved his hand from one side of the tunnel to the other. This time the material was cut with a fine slit. Removing the instrument, he did the same about two inches deeper into the cave. He cut four-inch slits on a slight angle at each end, so the door would fall easier. Admiring the work, astonishment again overcame him. He set the sword down flat side to the floor and waited for five minutes for the handle to cool. He tried to cut the rock with the cold metal but nothing and still no scratches or chips from the metal. The sword was very different than anything he had seen or even heard of.

Scooting out of the entrance he warmed up the tool again and pushed it into the rock about sixty centimeters above the roof of the entrance. Not wanting to leave much evidence he moved the blade inside the rock cutting the door lose but leaving only a small hole above the entrance.

With a loud thud the rock slid from the ceiling to the floor sealing the small room.

Now how hard is it to push the door back into the place from which it fell?

The rock weighed about two hundred pounds and he could not lift it while he was laying down. He was thankful he was outside the room when the door closed.

"This might take a little more thought." he said too himself.

"What if I make a door a little thinner so it is lighter, and have it slide side to side instead of up and down?"

With a short inspection he decided it might be possible. "The existing door is much too heavy," so he chopped it up and dumped it down the well.

After cutting a sliding door and setting it in place, he glanced at his watch and noticed it was almost one-thirty in the morning.

"Yikes! It is that late already? Time sure flies when you are having fun." He wrapped the sword in the dirty sweatshirt and proceeded to the lake.

When he arrived at the slit, he cut a narrow zig-zag-stable doorway, so it was easier to get in and out. He left the rubble in a pile by the side of the new door.

"I'll have to bring a large towel next time to carry that stuff to the well," he noted, "Or a couple of those cloth shopping bags."

He wrapped the sweatshirt around the blade and maneuvered it through the pool without warming the handle. Again, he left through the non-alarmed emergency exit at the far end of the cave. He was thankful that he had gained enough time and trust to find out about this special exit. There was no way to get in, but one can get out if problems arose like a fire or a gas build up that may necessitate a hasty exit. This was why he had to wait until just before closing time to get back into the cave. The last two cameras were just before and just after the water hole that led into the other part of the cave. If he refused to use his flashlight until after the first bend past the last camera, he could escape unnoticed. Having worked so long giving tours he often thought he could give a tour blindfolded. This is the second time he had proven he could do so.

There was a non-alarmed panic bar on the emergency escape, so it was not a problem to leave but if anything was left behind it had to wait until the next open day to retrieve it.

All of a sudden, I am very tired, he thought.

The emergency escape was a little more than a quarter mile

from the end of the tourist section of the cave. The escape door led into another small cave. The mouth of the cave faced away from the door, so it was not seen from outside the cave. With the emergency exit emptying into the second cave at an angle one had to get almost to the door before it became visible. The emergency exit faced a blank wall of the second cave about twelve feet from the door keeping out snoopers. Few knew of its existence. Covering the door with artificial rock on the cave side deceived even the most curious.

He retrieved his car from hiding, loaded the stuff in the trunk, and headed home.

* * *

Arriving home, he glanced at the clocks in the house.

"How come the clocks are different from my watch?"

He noticed it with the outdoor time marquees but thought that they were usually off by a few minutes but by two and a half hours?

"All the clocks in the house were within range of the outside timepieces. My watch must be going bad. Maybe it just needs a new battery." he mused. He reset the watch and then showered and went to bed.

The next morning, he thought he might shave with the new blade. *If it is sharp enough to cut rocks it is sure to be sharp enough to cut beard stubble.*

He was so excited about the idea he didn't even take off his night shirt.

This might be a little tricky with such a long blade.

Picking up the sword and unwrapping it from the sweatshirt he grasped the handle and once again he was fighting wild beasts from ancient days. Dragons and lions appeared in his mind and with precision and swiftness he lay all the creatures that appeared before him, slain.

"No victory dance in the apartment." he said to himself.

When he arrived at the bathroom door, he looked for a reflection in the mirror, but the room appeared empty. He walked right up to the sink and looked but all he could see is the door ajar behind him. Setting the sword on the vanity, as he let go his reflection and the sword appeared in the mirror. He touched the blade of the sword and nothing happened. They were both reflected in the glass before him. Looking out of the corner of his eye he picked up the instrument by the handle and watched as he and the sword disappeared from view.

"How am I going to shave with this?" he muttered to himself. He set the instrument on a towel and dug a razor out of the drawer. While he shaved, he wondered about the invisibility factor.

"What is this thing that makes me invisible in the mirror? Am I invisible to everything and everybody while I am armed with the sword?" In the middle of the shave he picked up the sword and looked in the mirror. As the handle warmed his reflection disappeared. He set the sword down and picked it up again this time touching only the blade. The reflection remained.

So, this is how it works. He carefully grabbed it by the blade and tried to shave a small patch of hair from his arm. He could still see himself in the mirror. Carefully dragging the blade across his arm, he felt practically nothing but noticed that the hair was being removed very effectively.

"I think I will wait until I know a little more about this thing before I try to shave my face."

His arm reddened then started to bleed where he cut the hair. Then it bled a little faster. He reached for a paper towel to blot the wound but soon the entire towel was soaked red.

"Oh no!" he stammered. "What have I done?"

He wrapped his arm with paper towel five or six times and dug out the first-aid kit. He put a tourniquet above the wound and tied a tight mulch-padded bandage around the wound occasionally loosening and re-tightening the tourniquet to allow a little blood flow.

"Good Grief! I am going to have to experiment with things other than myself. Now what am I going to do? I can't go to the hospital it will involve too much explaining. With this thing in the wrong hands it could cause havoc and put the owner in control of... of what... and how much?"

Again, he pondered on the possibilities of what the owner of this instrument could do.

"With this toy, could the Ruler be overthrown?"

He grabbed the sword by the handle and squeezed it tightly warming it up quickly. "Who is there?" he shouted. No answer but his own echo throughout the apartment. He ran around the small quarters looking for the intruder, but he was gone. *I could have sworn someone was watching.* He thought. *I just may have to guard my tongue a little more with this toy in my possession.*

He looked at his arm. The bleeding was under control. That solved that problem for the moment. He took off the tourniquet to see if the wound would hold the pressure and thankfully the bleeding had stopped. Again, he was thankful for his first aid training. He wrapped a clean towel around the apparatus, hid it under the bed and went out for a long thoughtful walk.

* * *

Crogg Park was a little more than a half a mile from his front door. He liked to go there to walk or jog. With exercise, he could think a little clearer away from the clutter. If an idea popped in his head, he would have time to consider it more before implementing it by walking to and from the park. Today was no exception. The paved blacktop track was bare of pedestrians save for himself. This gave him time to not just think but talk quietly to himself.

"I need to be able to transport the sword without anyone knowing about it. How do I do his?" he whispered as he jogged along.

Remembering some of the old movies showed machine guns hidden in violin cases he wondered how the sword would fit.

"It's not as if one can dismantle it. How about a guitar case? That would mean he would have to buy a guitar. What a waste of money for someone who doesn't play."

After an hour of weighing options, he went to the ATM and drew out three hundred dollars. He had to go to the city to get a half decent guitar and not be noticed. Back home he showered and changed clothes. He drove to the commuter lot and took the train.

* * *

"I need a small inexpensive electric guitar and a hard-shell case please." he addressed the owner of the small store.

"Anything in particular you would like to play?"

It never crossed his mind that one had to test drive an instrument!

"It's for a nephew who is learning to play, and he needs a hard-shelled case, so things don't get battered up on the bus to school." he lied. "I really do not know much about them and have a very limited budget, but his birthday is soon, and I would like to surprise him with a small set."

In a few minutes they settled on a used child's instrument and a hard-shell flat case that was a little battered but would be perfect. There was an extra pocket in the case beside the neck for picks and a tuner. He paid for the purchase and took the train back to the car.

The ride home gave him time to think again. With the case on the kitchen table he unwrapped the blade and warmed up the handle. He cut the corner of the case and left the covering on one side as a hinge. Then he slid the blade into the hardened Styrofoam to a depth of about eight inches and dug a hole to fit the hilt. Sliding the sword into the foam was not a problem. With a little more digging and testing the sword fit snugly into the bottom of the case. With a few tries it was easy to slide the sword in and out without having to warm it up. He attached some sticky Velcro to the inside of the door to hold it closed. A little paint job on the case made the door in the corner almost invisible.

If I take a few strings off this thing I could always say that it is in the trunk so it can be repaired. I just haven't had the opportunity to do so yet seeing that the only place to get it fixed is in the city.

That night he watched the news while devouring pizza and soda. Channel seventeen had often been commended by many as the most reliable of the 'new' stations that had arisen. Within the last generation or so a new attitude had taken over. Distrust had surfaced about the Leader that had been in power for so long. Many of the new networks had proven to be broadcasting 'invented news' as Seventeen put it. So far, Seventeen had been able to keep its credibility. Unlike other networks, it showed the best news stories at the end of the broadcast. This kept the viewers tuned in to the end. That was the philosophy behind the action but sometimes it backfired, and a few refused to tune in till the last ten or fifteen minutes.

This night the big story was about some wild dogs that had terrorized a small town about twenty miles away. Things had been so peaceful for so long guns were no longer needed, and the world had ridden itself of explosive actuated weaponry, until recently.

"The animals had been traced to the condemned barn on the old Whopplehorst farm." announced the TV anchor.

"Wild dogs? This world really is going to pot!" With that, he locked the outside doors and went to bed.

He lay there for a few minutes thinking about the dogs eating chickens and pets and even killing children. As he thought he remembered that he became invisible in the mirror.

"Why am I not tired?" he mumbled.

"If I park about half a mile from town by that old barn, I may be able to get to the pack without being noticed."

Getting dressed quickly he set the old guitar in the trunk, turned to get into the car and thought that he may need this thing sooner than expected. Sliding it onto the seat beside him he placed the car into gear and moseyed towards the old Whopplehorst homestead.

Just prior to his arrival he doused the headlights and drove up behind the barn. To his surprise, five rabid dogs met him snapping at the tires. He shut off the engine and sat but the animals kept jumping on the car and barking.

"I don't think I can open the door to get out."

He removed the tool from the case and warmed it up. He kept the other hand on the metal door handle. Within a few minutes the dogs had settled down and returned inside the barn.

Is it because they can't see me or the car? he thought to himself.

He wore lined thick jeans and had high top boots with steel toes. On top he had a leather vest under a long-sleeved thick leather jacket. He donned a black motorcycle helmet and a high temperature Kevlar glove on the hand that did not use the sword.

Better safe than sorry, he encouraged himself.

He touched the metal on the door handle and the dogs stirred.

"It would be better if I could deal with them in the moonlight than in a dark barn."

One by one, three of the five came out to inspect, looked towards the car and walked back to the barn. He opened the car door and got out not letting go of the door to the vehicle. He stood back a bit and slammed the car door which brought all five of them running. They circled the car barking.

Wow! They can't even see me.

He plunged the blade into the side of the big one as it ran past and heard a yelp as the animal rolled in pain. The movement of the creature helped tear a large gash into its side. Retracting the blade, the other dogs headed back to the barn. As the large one lay dying he stabbed it again, ending his misery. He tried to pick up the dog with the sword and throw him into the brush, but the blade just cut through the animal. With the gloved hand he picked up the pieces and threw them behind the foliage.

Walking around the car he remembered that the dogs seemed to be running but they moved very slowly. *Not until I stabbed the one did the one that was pierced move at the same rate I did. So, my time frame changes compared to theirs?*

Once again, the car door was slammed and the four came running. With the weapon preheated it was almost humorous to see the mutts bounding into the air barring the foam flying from their faces. He did not really like killing the dogs but the fact that they were rabid and had killed humans...

The first one out the barn was within reach. One by one he took out the wild animals. When it was all over, he sank the sword into the dirt, fell to his knees, and wept.

He felt that someone was watching. He still had hold of the hilt and he quickly walked over to the car and touched the metal placing the vehicle into the same time frame as he was. A few seconds later the sensation left him. This time no questions were raised.

With his hand on the car he pondered who it was that was making themselves known as he employed the sword. The impression did not leave him as he carried the beasts behind the bushes. It was still dark, and things were starting to cloud over, so he warmed the sword and dug a common grave. He wiped the blade on the grass and returned it to the case. Slowly he drove home sick at the deed he had done. He stuffed his clothes into a large plastic bag, showered, and then fell into a fitful sleep of rabid dreams.

That morning he awoke with the tragedy still on his mind. He lay in bed thinking about all that happened the night before. Once again, he questioned what this toy was, where it came from, and who it was that knew of the trinket.

I just may have to go to the library and do some research.

He found little information save a story in the mythology section about a king of England and France in the early centuries

A.D. who pulled out a magic sword from a rock and established his reign with it. All the immorality and vengeance of the tales were of little importance to Ply. There was little information on the weapon and what ever happened to it. The name of the sword of Arthur was 'Excalibur'. He found that the word was actually Celtic and meant strong belly or voracious. The remaining research seemed fruitless except the fact that pulling a sword out of a rock is not a new phenomenon.

As usual, he spoke to himself, *that which is misunderstood is usually put down to hocus-pocus and relegated to the realm of superstition.* Searching for Merlin the magician did little to advance the understanding.

After a number of hours at the library, he was ready to rest and flopped down on the couch to catch the news with the standard fare of soda and pizza.

"This diet just might get old," he mumbled to himself, "And me along with it!"

There was little to say about the dogs seeing that they did not terrorize anyone today. They did mention the dangers of rabid animals around and how easily it spreads if someone is contaminated by one. Normally it takes being bitten but if saliva from an animal was exposed to an open cut the outcome could be the same.

"An open cut?" he sat up startled. As fast as he could he rolled up his sleeve and tore off the bandage to the scrape on his arm mowed by the sword the day previously.

"Nothing?" He stared at it for numerous long seconds than started to scratch it not believing that the wound had healed perfectly. He flopped down on the couch in bewilderment and fear of what hidden powers this thing had.

"The only way to really curb the rabies is to burn the habitat of the animals when they show their faces again." blurted the tube.

"Burn their habitat? I am the only one who seems to know where that is." He thought of all the other dogs in the area that might get infected, then of the kids that might have to go through the treatment. He tried to sleep but his conscience was not yet seared enough to allow this wickedness to happen. At one-twenty-five in the morning he got dressed, donned the black jacket, threw the bag of contaminated clothing in the trunk retrieved a few gallons of diesel fuel from the garage and headed for the old barn.

The house was about five hundred feet from the barn and the

slight breeze was from the direction of the house. The property had been up for sale for almost two years and there was little evidence that anyone had been around. Going into the barn he saw the broken boards where the animals entered the structure. The place had been pretty well emptied of all the equipment that farmers used when the W's ran the place. All the kids had sold whatever they could and moved out of the area. Things other than farming had caught their attention and lured them away from the work and patience of planting and harvesting. There was a pile of dry straw and hay in the far corner where the beasts bedded and thought it might come in handy. Donning a pair of Mylar surgical gloves, he wove a braid of the grasses together he made a long string. He laid it out from the stack and every foot or so dropped a bit of fuel on the wick.

"This will give me some time to escape." he thought. He poured the rest of the catalyst around the inside of the edifice, lit the fuse, dropped the gloves, and the soiled clothes from the previous night to be burned and left. The barn had been unused for years and the condition was deplorable. "Even if the place was sold," he mumbled to himself, "I doubt the barn is in good enough shape to be usable." As he glanced around, he noticed that most of the wall boards had shrunk letting in too much wind. "Not to mention the contamination of the rabid animals." he consoled himself.

The fire departments were busy with a three-alarm warehouse blaze in the next county so the old Whopplehourst barn burned to the ground leaving very little evidence save traces of diesel fuel here and there.

At home he washed up again with some very strong Lye soap. The warm water from the faucet hissed; reminding him of the horrible deed he had done.

Once again, he returned to a sleep of uncommon nightmares.

* * *

There seemed to be little to think about at this point in life but what the attributes of this instrument actually were.

"Breakfast? The usual I guess."

Dry cereal and milk seemed to have various promises, but, cereal, soup, sandwiches, and pizza did not add up to a balanced diet.

He thought of other available possibilities.

"Getting a house maid is out of the question. Getting married is even farther out. Who would put up with all this silliness of killing dogs and burning barns all in the middle of the night? Man, this superhero stuff is not all it is cracked up to be. Sometimes the bland is a lot less exciting but never as much fun. I just may have to learn to cook."

The thought settled into his mind.

"Horrors!"

As he ate, he pondered about what he had learned.

"Apparently, this thing speeds up my personal time frame."

A few bites later, "How much can it speed it up?"

Mulling it over brought forth ideas of how he could test such a thing. "What is there that I could test this with without putting myself in too much danger?"

(Munch, munch,)

"I need something that will shoot at me but what if I miss and it gets to me first?"

(Munch, munch,)

"Not a pretty picture."

(Munch, munch, munch)

"What do they have that shoots balls?"

A few more seconds of slight mental and physical activity, namely, lifting the spoon to the mouth.

"A baseball thrown at ninety miles per hour could really hurt, but a tennis ball? Hmm. A tennis ball could still hurt but perhaps I can adjust the speed of the machines."

(Munch, munch,)

"There is a tennis club in the next county."

Dumping the dishes in the sink he realized, before too long it would take either paper plates and plastic spoons or time at the sink. Procrastination was in order. The present curiosity took precedent. With the guitar case and sword in the trunk he noticed that there were not a few cars in the lot at the courts. He walked in and found an employee working at a kiosk.

"When is a good time to practice when there are very few people around?" he asked the girl.

"Two in the afternoon is usually pretty quiet." she responded.

"What kind of machines do you have and how do they work?"

"Just load up the rack, set the speed you are comfortable with, and push the start button. It's really pretty simple."

"May I look around and see what's in use?"

"Sure, most of the courts are in use so there is lots of opportunity to see what we have available."

"Thanks." he responded. Leaning over a little closer he admitted to her with a stage whisper; "I am really quite terrible at this and would like a time when there is practically nobody here."

"Just between you and me," she whispered back leaning one elbow on the counter surface but still about three feet away from him, "There are lots of people quite terrible at this. Either you are very humble, or you have lots of company."

He winked at her and thought to himself, *Cute, I wonder if she cooks and does dishes*. Then mentally kicked himself for jumping to such a chauvinistic manipulative conclusion. "I will look around and then we can talk."

She smiled back at him as he turned towards the courts.

Ply hung around for about an hour watching the machines pitch balls and the customers bat them about. Some were pretty good and set the machines to throw in various directions, so they could move about the court like in a real game. The attendant behind the desk was correct about a few of the others.

Returning to the kiosk, "How much does it cost to rent one of those machines?" he asked.

"Do you need a court or just a room to bat the balls in?" she probed.

This brought forth another opportunity that he did not notice in his tour.

"Can I see a room like that? What are they like?"

"They're not unlike squash courts. No windows, no distractions, just hard smooth walls to bat balls in. Squash and racquetball are in a cool season for some reason, but we could put a machine in there, and no one would see you."

"That certainly sounds appealing. Where are they?"

"I've got a break coming up. Why don't I show you around?"

"Sure." he acknowledged with a pleasant smile.

She grinned back, grabbed the keys, and headed for another part of the building. They passed the courts and made a short left turn down a narrow hallway.

"In here is where the other courts are." she informed him.

"This is an older part of the building that has not been renovated so there are no bathrooms or soda machines. If you need one, they aren't very far."

The hallway had a high ceiling and the lighting was sparse but sufficient. She opened a small door to their right, turned back to turn on the court lights and stepped inside. Ply followed.

"The light switches are on the outside to keep the walls smooth." she said. *And to keep them from getting smashed up by people sizzling balls at them,* she thought but did not voice to the new customer.

The lighting was recessed, high and guarded by Plexiglass keeping the ceiling to one plane. The room was a twenty-foot square with fifteen-foot high ceilings.

"This just might work." he said.

Looking around he did think that the room was too old to have cameras. The need for the devices only came back into vogue in the last thirty years and this seemed much older. Any cameras would have to be wireless or cabled to somewhere.

Why would they need them in here? he thought.

"How many machines can you get into a room like this?"

She turned to look at him with one eyebrow raised, "We can probably get five but the best anyone has done so far is keep two busy at three quarter speed and he went to Wimbledon. What have you got planned?"

Oh, Oh. thought Ply. *Keep your head straight and don't give anything away.*

"I have a new toy that I need to test, and I guess I'm just a little obnoxious about its capabilities." he said and swallowed nervously.

"Okay, let's start with two." she suggested, a little exasperated at the gall of the young man.

"Sounds great." he returned with a bead of perspiration forming on his brow.

Having that settled, he promised he would return about two when things were a little quieter.

On the drive back home, he stopped at a sporting goods store and purchased a cheap racquetball racket.

This might give her the impression that I haven't a clue what I'm doing.

Arriving at home, he packed his large sports bag with a

number of things, as well as the guitar case and a change of clothes.

He showed up at five to two and was ushered to the change room. She went back to her duties and he walked to the squash court, walked around it once and dropped the bag in the corner. There were two ball tossers to his right, other than that, the room was empty. He flipped the lights off, stepped inside, and shut the door. It was pitch black but that wasn't something that he wasn't used to. He allowed his eyes to get accustomed to the light, but it was still very dark after five minutes. He closed his eyes, opened the door and turned on the lights. He turned out the lights and closed the door with him inside. The binoculars were ready, and he quickly glanced around the lights as the phosphor on the fluorescent lights cooled.

"Good," he thought, "Just enough to see if there are any hidden cameras in the lights."

The canisters for the lamps looked empty. Having thought about it all morning, he wondered if the young lady might just make a surprise appearance with the two machines going. He moved the sports bag to the other side of the door from the throwers to partially hide the bag from view. Arranging the guitar case, he left it inside the bag and open if he needed to get the tool back inside quickly and set the racket beside the bag. He spent a few minutes getting acquainted with the ball tossers. There were instructions on the top which were pretty simple.

"Let's start with just one machine." he whispered to the walls.

He removed the sword and warmed it up. Batting the balls at one every three seconds got very dull. He set the sword against the wall, adjusted the tosser to full speed, and had no problem keeping up.

"OK, this is much too easy."

He set both machines on full speed and flipped the switch. It was fun to bat the balls at such a rate but found that he could adjust his timing, so the projectiles crawled through the air. Returning to the desk he asked the girl her name.

"Jane." she replied, showing very nice teeth and an attractive smile.

"Ah, Jane, is there any opportunity to get more machines into that room?"

Her jaw dropped, and she asked, "Why?"

"I'm having too much fun with these toys." he replied.

"Do you want them right now?"

"Is it a problem?" he asked gently.

"We have three tossers available, but it will take some time to get them moved."

"Can I help?"

"I, I guess." she stammered half amazed and extremely curious about what was going on in there.

"It is rather quiet here and nobody has an appointment for an almost an hour seeing it is only quarter after two. I'll take my buzzer so I can hear the door and we will get you some more equipment."

As they moved to the room where the tossers were, Ply followed behind and looked at his watch.

Two-thirty-one he thought. I'll have to make sure I take into account the time changes next time I get into this kind of situation.

It took over half an hour to set up the three machines with the oversize ball racks.

"Do you have enough balls to fill these racks?" he asked.

"Perhaps." she said wondering if he was able to handle what these gadgets could throw at him.

They only found enough to fill the racks to a little over three quarters full.

"I don't have authority to open any new packages and we have used all the balls that are available so what you see is what you get." she informed him dryly, but her curiosity was a little more than obvious.

"This will have to do."

"Can I watch?" she asked excitedly.

"I'm sorry," he replied, "I am testing unpatented material and I am unable to allow anyone else to see. Can I walk you back to the kiosk?"

"Okay." she said, considerably disappointed.

He left her at her kiosk but the curiosity in her eyes worried him.

"Man, girls sure make things complicated." he muttered to himself as he turned the final corner, he checked to be sure she was not following him. Not seeing her, he climbed into the room and pre-warmed the sword. With the instrument in his hands he touched the start button on each machine and batted the balls. As the handle warmed up the balls slowed like rush hour traffic and shortly, he was convinced that he needed a greater challenge. He had time to watch the door to the court and after half of the balls had flown, he noticed it start to open. In his time frame he had enough room to get the sword into the case, close it, and grab the squash racket from the floor.

"Are you Okay?" she called, running to his side as he cowered in the corner getting showered by the balls flying around the room.

"I think this was a little too overconfident."

"I'll bet." she replied.

* * *

They started to clean up the balls, but Ply had found out what he needed. He noticed there was one half of a ball on the floor and turned to Jane.

"I can get these if you need to get back to work?"

"I might." she fibbed, having noticed another half in the piles.

He took her by the arm and said, "When I have finished, I will let you count the balls, but I might want a few for souvenirs. She rolled her eyes and faked a laughed as she made her way out the door. Ply closed it behind her.

Man," he mumbled to himself, "Girls sure make things complicated." He collected all the balls and loaded them into the trays but found three that had been sliced. "I'll have to buy a can of four to replace these." he said to himself.

"Where am I going to dump them?"

When he told the attendant, he was ready for the inspection, she led the way silently.

As she walked Ply noticed she had almost perfect posture. Her pony-tailed dark blonde hair fell just above the bottom of her shoulder blades and waved teasingly at him from her slender but physically fit five-foot ten frame. It wasn't that he had not seen a woman before but something about this gal was a little different.

"Whoa there horsies." he mumbled quietly under his breath.

"Do you have horses?" she stopped and turned looking at him with surprised interest.

"Ahh, no." he replied sheepishly. *Well, yes actually, but probably not the kind you are thinking of.* He thought to himself as she returned to the lead to the court.

"Seventy-five balls here, twice, three times, four, here but only seventy-one here. "What goes?" She interrogated the obnoxious newcomer.

"I did say I wanted to keep a few for souvenirs."

"Ya got time to help me put these things back? It is always easier with two." she coaxed.

"Sure, if you would like."

"I would like." she smiled.

They packed up the machines and he paid for the rentals and an extra set of balls to replace the four that he kept. As he turned to leave, she said,

"Are you coming back some time?" Too late, she held her eyesight, but realized the statement might be a bit forward.

He paused and turned to respond. No rings on any fingers so she is either in limbo or between boyfriends but not necessarily available.

"I did find out all I need to know at this stage." he answered.

She brought her line of vision back up and scrutinized his face. Her mouth said "Oh", but her eyes said, "No you haven't!"

He turned to leave and after taking a few steps, she asked, "How did the balls get slit?"

"Uh, they got jammed in the machine?"

"Right." She goaded with a suspicious smirk on her face.

He smiled at her and left but she got the picture that he just might be back but not to check out tennis ball tossers.

Dumping his bag into the trunk he groaned, "Man, pretty women sure make things complicated."

At home he wrapped the sliced balls in a separate bag and dumped them into the kitchen garbage.

"No need to make it too obvious I'm trying to hide something."

The left-over ball he kept on his nightstand by his bed as a souvenir. That evening he fared his usual pizza and soda and thought to himself, "Pineapple on the pizza is probably not sufficient fruit and veggies for the week! That Jane is becoming more of a temptation than I am willing to admit. I wonder if she can cook spaghetti?"

That night the news was bland about traffic accidents and kids in pre-school, so he turned it off early and crawled into bed.

"Tennis balls shooting at eighty miles per hour is a whole lot different than bullets at five hundred feet per second. Air rifles range at about a quarter that, I just might try something in the morning."

The next morning, he made an attempt at employing his cooking skills.

"I do have some eggs in the fridge." He grabbed the frying pan, turned on the stove top and slid them from the cooler. Cracking the egg over the hot pan his nostrils were hit with the odor of rotting death.

"Yuck! Now I remember why mom told me to always crack the eggs over a bowl." Dumping that one in the garbage he rinsed out the pan and cracked another over a bowl to the same smell. He checked the egg carton and notice that the best before date was nine months passed due.

"Well no wonder!" He pitched the eggs, dumped them in the outside trash, and dug out the milk and cereal.

"Hello, Jane?" he called to the walls in his apartment, "Can you cook spaghetti?"

After a meaningless munching of 'Dreary-O's' he returned to what might be a little more dangerous than the tennis balls. With string and a lever, he rigged up a mechanism to shoot an air rifle. There were some hooks over a doorway that he draped a number of blankets over as a stop for the projectile if the need arose. He warmed up the sword, stepped on the lever and pulled the 'BB' with his bare left hand right out of the air.

He set the sword on the floor and sat on the chair just to absorb what had actually happened. He gathered all the stuff up, put it away, and went for another long walk. This time it wasn't just to think but to get a little lost in wonder.

Three hours later the 'breakfast' had worn off and it was time to arrange for some real nutrients.

"I am going to need some more money sometime soon." he thought. "The caves are just not going to generate enough to test the parameters of this thing. I do have some in savings. I better transfer some into my checking account, so I have some available."

* * *

After a purchased warm sandwich, a thorough cleaning of the kitchen, and a transfer at the bank, it was time to see what was available where there were real guns. He opened the door to the Police shooting range and was met by a very large uniform.

"Are you authorized to enter?" he harshly asked.

"What do I need?" voiced the young man as he quickly glanced around the inside of the building.

"If you don't know, then you don't belong." gruffed the bully as he shouldered the intruder back onto the sidewalk.

Happy to make your acquaintance, pondered the assaulted.

Back on the road he thought that he had seen enough to get inside and have a look around while 'under cover' so to speak. Half a mile down the road there was a strip mall with an ice cream shop that was usually busy this time of year. He parked the car by the employee vehicles off to the side opposite the shooting range. When the coast seemed clear he checked for cameras. Not seeing any he opened the trunk, warmed up the sword, became invisible and closed the back of the jalopy.

Fifteen minutes later, by his watch, he was at the door of the range. It took some waiting, but the door opened to let one out and Ply slipped in. He found a place where traffic was light so not to get bumped into.

That would be just too exciting.

The lanes were empty until the targets were checked and replaced. All the 'pigeons' were set for firing, but no one was up to bat. He checked the lanes and found three at twenty-five yards, three at fifty yards, two at one hundred yards and one at three hundred yards. The deep one had ten bales back of the target.

"Now what would they use the thousand-foot range for?"

He glanced toward the firing position and found a fifty-millimeter cannon on a tripod with its snout pointed to the dirt.

If they load that up, I will certainly get my practice in, he gulped.

Someone started shooting at a fifty-yard lane with a thirty-eight. Ply immediately adjusted to the speed of the bullets and walked over as they hit the target. He batted a few onto the ground. He backed away and looked around at what was behind the shooters. Above their heads there was a mezzanine with bales of straw and foam used to stop the projectiles behind the pigeons.

I wonder... While still holding the sword, he removed the Kevlar glove from his left-hand switched hands, placed the right-hand Kevlar on and grabbed the blade like a baseball batter bunting a ball. Looking at the projectile he stepped into the path and bunted the bullet into the straw with the flat side of the blade.

The shooter stopped a little curious as to why the target was not registering the rounds. He checked to see if he had run out of bullets, but the gun did fire. The clip was still more than half full, so he punched it in and shot again. Ply bounced the metal up into the straw and this got the shooter a little more than curious.

The fifty-millimeter cannon sounded, and the sword adjusted to that. He watched as the first bullet fly past then slow to a crawl as it struck the target. Arriving at the lane he noticed the shooter did not move his finger from the trigger.

So, it is in automatic mode, he thought to himself. He waited almost fifteen seconds before the second projectile emptied from the muzzle. As it meandered down the lane, he wondered how long it would take to get to the one-hundred-foot mark where he was standing. He slowed down a little which sped up the metal in the lane. As it approached his side, he slowed it to a crawl, quietly raised the sword and sliced the metal lengthwise as it passed by.

"This is going to cause some confusion if there are more holes in the target than rounds fired." he mused. As the third approached he slowed it to a crawl and reached out with his un-gloved hand to catch it, but it was too hot to touch. He moved the sword and ricocheted it into the sand. It sank deep seeing it was not within his own time frame. With the gloved hand he picked the next one from the air and set it into the sand to cool. He dug the blade of his own weapon into the sand to keep the spent bullet in the sword's adjustment of space and waited as a few others sauntered by, picked up the cooled slug, he adjusted his time frame and batted the next ten to the floor. This brought all the occupants of the place to investigate what was happening on the long range. Ply stepped back into the previously occupied fifty-yard lane, picked up two of the four, thirty-eight bullets that were in the dust, and watched them all herd to the far end of the range. With the sword in motion mode he ran up to the desk, placed the spent thirty-eights and the one fifty caliber missile end up on the registration desk and left as those outside came in to check on the excitement.

He spent one hour in his time but the clock on the wall of the range had only registered twenty minutes. He trotted back to his car, checked for John Q. Public, loaded the sword into the case and drove home contented with the afternoons work and in wonder at the magic of the new-found contraption.

* * *

The next morning Ply, once again, lay there thinking about the way things were going.

This thing could get me into a lot of trouble. I've already killed dogs and had thoughts of eliminating criminals, but the justice system is still working well enough at this point. Things are getting a little bogged down with the recent rebellion against the Leader but certainly not to the point of vigilante activity.

He tossed around a bit, got up, dressed, wolfed his cereal, brushed his teeth, and went for a visit to the tennis courts.

The place was swarming. Dozens of people were milling about. The place was packed but confusion did not reign. Everybody seemed to be doing something or ready to do it. He spotted her at her kiosk.

"Hi, busy day."

"It sure is." she replied, not appearing disturbed at his arrival even in the midst of the mob. "This sale has been planned for months in conjunction with the sale of tickets for the state tournament in the city next month."

"What time do you get off?"

He picks the busiest day of the season to ask for a date and there is no way I can escape, she brooded.

"Normally at five but I don't think I can get out of here till after seven tonight."

"Can I help?"

"Help in what?"

"Whatever is needed."

"They aren't even thinking applications today with this herd."

"Can I buy you an ice cream on your break?"

"No breaks today."

"When do you eat?"

"I have a couple of sodas, energy bars, and some fruit here at my kiosk."

"So, by seven you might be ready for more than ice cream?"

"I don't think it will take that long."

"Look, I can't cook spaghetti, but I know a nice place that does."

"That sounds like fun already."

"So, I'll pick you up at seven?"

"Better make it six if you don't mind waiting around for a few minutes."

"I'll see you then." he grinned and left.

* * *

At five-forty-five he returned to the courts to find the place desolate. The place was empty with only one car in the lot out back. As he approached the vehicle Jane got out and walked towards him.

"What happened?" he quizzed.

"Things started to cool down about three thirty. By ten to five there were only six customers left. After my clean up and handing in of the cash, I managed to escape by twenty-five after."

"I am so sorry I made you wait."

"I couldn't wait inside seeing I am not authorized to lock up, so I just waited here in my car. I'm starving."

"Here is my phone number so this won't happen again," said Ply as he rattled off the digits and she entered them in her own device, "Is it safe to leave your car here?"

"Why not?" she responded.

Ply figured it was too early in the relationship to expound on the horrors of the rebellion, so he placed his car into park and got out to assist her to the other side of his chariot. He was very thankful he had a chance to clean out some of the junk food trash that was the previous passenger. He did manage to vacuum the old horse but now he wished he had got the car detailed because French fry droppings need a little more than suction.

"The Maserati is in the shop." he joked.

"Oh really?" she flatly replied as her nose curled at the grease attempting to dry that was ground into the carpet, leaving him in confusion of whether she really knew what he was talking about as he hurried to the driver's side of the car.

"How long have you been working the tennis circuit?" he coaxed hoping to get her to talk to break the ice a little.

She looked his way, a little surprised at the terminology he used and said, "I played for a while but could only get so far. It seems that my gifts are not quite good enough for a career in the sport, but I do appreciate a good game once in a while. It's always fun to spar with one who can eventually do much better than I and I have had a chance to play some of the great's but that was before they went onto stardom.

"Really? When did you start playing?" he asked as headed for the highway.

"I got my first racket when I was about five and have been hooked ever since."

"Five?" he gulped. "I promise I will not be a challenge to you."

She looked over at him with recognition and a bit of humor twinkling in her eyes, "I probably saw that on the squash courts the other day." the corners of her mouth lifting at the memory.

No reply from the accused. "How often are the courts busy like this?"

"Like today? Usually only two or three times a year but lately there seems to be a lot more interest. Three years ago, this would happen twice a year, but this year it is already the third time. What is it you do?"

"I, ah, work as a tour guide in one of the large caves in the next county." he boasted.

"A cave guide?" she asked with an inviting grin.

Perhaps I managed to impress her, he thought.

"Then there is no Maserati?" she queried.

Whoa, he gulped to himself. "No, that was supposed to be a joke."

"Have you ever seen one?" she inquired.

"At the car shows I attend once in a while. I saw one on the highway once doing about five miles per hour less that the limit. Why would anyone want to spend all that money on a vehicle that can never reach its potential legally?"

"Status, I suppose." she belittled.

"So, everybody thinks you are super rich but only demonstrate that they don't have enough sense to spend their money wisely?" he responded. "How come you know the name, Maserati?"

"I dated a guy who had one for a while. Well, I dated him for a very short while. I don't know how long he had the car."

"You dated a guy with a Maserati?" Gloomily he looked around at the heap he had and wondered if she was really in his league.

"Easy Ply." she calmed him. "Guys think they impress girls with their cars and some of them are impressed but not this one, at least, not anymore. If someone has to work for what they have it makes them a better person. He never had to work a day in his life for anything he had. With his natural talent for tennis he won a lot of money and spent it just as you said, very foolishly. He was a boiled sprat as the dyslexics say. He got everything he wanted all the time and never had to put out an ounce of effort on anything he did not know how to do. It didn't take long for me to just hate it. He was handsome, talented and likable enough until he didn't get his own way then then look out world."

By this time Ply was wide eyed, staring straight ahead, keeping the speed limit and sounding like a giraffe, saying nothing!

"No, I'm not out of your league." she continued. "Real women are not looking for all the money in the world, just a man who will love them and protect them when it is necessary. Even to the point of needing protection from themselves."

Man, he thought to himself. *Pretty girls that are really smart sure make things complicated. Or is it just reality that is settling in?*

"You said you can't cook spaghetti," she quipped attempting to keep the conversation going, "Why not just throw the stuff into a deep pan of boiling water, set the timer, and rinse?" She glanced his way and waited for a response.

He took a quick look to acknowledge her question and noticed large soft almond brown eyes with what appeared to be very long lashes. He quickly returned his sight to the road wondering if the lashes were really hers or just attached for the moment. *I'll check when we stop at the restaurant,* he thought to himself.

"Well!" he said, "There is question number one answered. I sometimes get distracted. Once I tried to cook that stuff but got sidetracked by a movie I was watching."

"And?" she asked after a short time of silence.

"I left the burner on high."

"For how long?"

Until all the water boiled away, the bottom of the pan got red hot and melted the pasta right into the metal. I had to recycle the pot seeing I could not get it clean."

A look of mirth meandered across her face then she broke into a wide smile. "Why did you wait so long to check things out?"

"I was getting hungry, but the movie was so good, and then the smoke detector went off."

The smirk vanished from her face and concern took over.

"Was there a fire?"

"No. I dumped some ice into the pan and after it bounced around for a while then pan was cool enough to put water into it."

"Ice?" she questioned.

"Yeah. Water would likely bounce right back into your face with the temperature of the bottom of the pan being red hot so if you put a little ice it, it just bounces around until things are cool enough to take cool water. The water from the ice boils very quickly but only a little at a time letting the metal cool in a hurry and not endangering much as it happens," he paused for a second or two, "Often the ice will warp the pan, but it was already wrecked."

The single eyebrow raised again.

"Just simple physics." he exclaimed.

She turned and looked out the front windshield. *Why is this guy just working in a cave?* she wondered.

"You recycled the pan?" she asked. "Wasn't it wrecked in the meltdown?"

"It sure was. All you have to do is re-melt the pan, drag off the sledge, and the metal is just about as good as new."

"Just about as good as new?"

"When you pull it out of the earth and smelt it down it is in the best condition it will attain to. After it is smelted again, it loses a little of its properties that make it what it is. Just Newtonian thermodynamics. All things tend to degenerate with time and use."

She could not handle the curiosity any longer, "How come you are working in a silly cave if you know all of this stuff about physics?"

"Just a hobby. I really do not know what I really want to do 'for the rest of my life'." he said and quoted the air with his index fingers not lifting his hands from the wheel. "What are you going to do with yours?"

"I want to meet someone who will just sweep me off my feet, place me on the back of his white horse, slay the great dragon with his magic sword so we can live happily ever after in the castle the dragon inhabited." she recited with a gleam in her eye.

He sat there staring straight ahead and thinking, *Well I've got the white horse,* glancing around at the remains of a vehicle that had seen the best part of life under the hands of someone else. *I guess time will tell if I sweep her off her feet.* He refused to admit the encounter with the magic sword. *How much did she actually know?*

He pulled into the parking lot of the restaurant, stopped the car and ran around to open her door.

"Chivalry?" she beamed delighting in the action.

He took a smiling glance at the eyelashes and found out they were real. *Wow,* he thought, *I know girls who would kill for a pair of those.*

* * *

Dinner was in a quiet spot in the back booth of the restaurant. A small incandescent lamp above them gently lit her soft features and he found himself about to make a very dangerous tumble. He let her talk and was amazed at the places her tennis had taken her. She did not seem to regret the fact that it did not take her to stardom. There were lots of stories about those who had 'arrived' only to crash into severe disillusionment of not only their abilities but also of life itself. Others had demanded recognition and acceptance thinking their talents gave them entitlement to fulfill their own foolish desires.

He tried not to 'vacuum-up' his dinner but still finished before she did. He watched her eat and listened to her talk then he paid for the meal and drove her back to her car.

"What part of town do you live in?" he asked.

She looked at him again and wondered about his intentions.

"I am a little nervous about you driving the highway at this hour with the trouble that is starting to arise. Could I follow you to your turnoff?"

"Okay." she said hesitantly.

He again jumped for her door. He swung it open and announced, "Your wish is my command."

"Thank you." she quipped with a mischievous smile wondering if the knight with the white horse would soon return.

What is that snicker about? he thought to himself. He waited until she was out and closed his car door behind her and walked her to hers. She stood beside her vehicle waiting for his next move.

"I, ah, don't have a key." he replied.

Removing her key from her purse she unlocked her car.

He pulled the door open and bowed deeply. "Thank you for a most enjoyable evening. I have no recollection of ever having such a good time."

Just a wee bit confused she slid into the seat and rolled down the window. "It has also been an evening of joy for me." she replied nervously resulting in a bit of awkwardness.

As he backed away a few feet from the car, she rolled up the window and started the car.

Huh, she thought, *Not even an embrace? Maybe I was a little too forward.*

Ply scurried over to his rattletrap and followed her two cars behind. As she turned on her blinker, he pulled up beside her, honked to get her attention, waved and drove off to the next exit to turn around.

Hoof in mouth Jane, she scolded herself. *He seems like a nice enough fella, but I wonder what I did this time to scare him off. Oh well. I guess it's back to the courts on Monday.* Her thoughts paused for a moment, "Not that I'm expecting a proposal on the first date." she audibly scolded herself.

Ply thought about the date all the way home. She isn't drop dead gorgeous, but she sure is attractive enough, he mused.

"She is smart but doesn't seem to be a baccalaureate type, at least she doesn't advertise such an attitude. And she seems to know what she wants in life. She doesn't seem to mind a little excitement by the way she traveled with her tennis. I fill the role of knight by being male. I have the horse in this beat up old clunker that has some white left on it."

He quietly drove for a few minutes.

"Does she have enough spunk to handle the magic sword?"

* * *

"I challenge you to a tennis match!" whispered Ply to the young lady at the Kiosk.

"Oh come-on Ply." she sarcastically replied, backing off into the center of the circle. "I saw you in the racquetball courts."

"Okay, tell me what you saw."

"You were huddled in a corner cowering from all those balls that were flying about. You looked like an imbecile who was about to be swallowed by a brontosaurus." she recounted as she tossed some sweatshirts from a box into a bin.

"Good. Then I succeeded."

"Succeeded in what?" she questioned as she turned to face him, "Showing me that you were a little less that what you thought you were?"

"Okay, beautiful one. Not only are you very attractive but you are also smart but this time I tricked you into what I wanted you to believe. Let's review and see if you can find some missing clues?"

"Okay." she said, a little taken back by being called beautiful. "You came to the court wanting to test something or other. Asked if you could have five ball throwers, of all things, and the next thing I find is you cowering in the corner with a racket ball racket with a million balls in the air. Now you want to challenge me to a tennis match?"

"Brilliant. Now think about what you just said. Repeat it back to me, slowly, right from the first."

"You came into the courts wanting to test something..."

"Stop!" he interrupted.

There was a moment of silence and she looked at him with a sudden moment of recognition. He looked at her and invited her to continue in her thoughts as he raised his eyebrows.

"What was it you wanted to test? Was the racket ball bat just a rouse to lead me astray?"

"And you fell for it hook, line and sinker! And am I ever glad you did. If you found out about it then, I don't know what I would have had to do."

"What was it you tested?"

"Let's put it this way. I think I can help you improve your game."

Again, the single eyebrow rose. *I have not seen this guy lie to me before. He is a little sinister... and I hardly know him,* she thought. "Okay. Where and when?"

"We need a private court where we will not be seen, where there are no cameras, and where there is no chance that we will be observed by anyone at all."

"You're kidding!"

"I, young lady, am as serious as cancer."

"Why are you letting me in on this little invention of yours?"

"It's not my invention. I, ah, found the toy in a cave."

"In a cave?" she urged, eyes and the corners of her mouth pulling back into a grin at the suggestion.

"I told you I work in a cave and I found a hidden passage and found this 'toy' in the passage."

She thought about what had happened in the last few months, then finally stated, "Okay. Let me talk to some of my friends. A few of them have courts in remote places and I will see what I can do."

There was just enough curious mischief in her eyes to urge him on, so he told her of the secret water hole entrance but none of what was behind it.

The Match

Jane arranged to 'borrow' a court in the mountains for a weekend. She didn't like the situation, but her curiosity got the better of her. One of her sparring partners had gone on to stardom and built a lodge with an indoor court about six years ago and the novelty had mostly worn off. It seemed delightful to have your own indoor tennis court a hundred miles from nowhere but who else would want such a thing? As a result, it had sat for about nine months without a soul to clean or air the place. Thankfully it was tight enough to keep out the critters and almost all the dust. The owner called the cleaning service to make sure the place was livable just after Jane made reservations.

Ply picked her up from work at five complete with hot piz za. Once again it had been a busy day and she had devoured most of her share before they were halfway there.

"Did you bring the food?" she asked, mouth still chewing a chunk hoping he had not forgotten.

"Just what you wanted plus a jug of milk and large bag of cereal for me to snack on when I get bored or hungry. Not that I think you are in the least bit boring. I brought some physics books to help with the explanation of what we are actually playing with."

"Physics books?" she droned, "How absolutely de-light-full!"

"If you don't think so now that's fine. If you think so later that's also fine but I have noticed your curiosity and perhaps it just might spark. What's with that eyebrow?"

She frowned a little being caught once again in her distracting mannerism and dropped the inquisitive look.

"You said that the rooms have multiple beds?" he asked. "And each have metal doors and lock from the inside?"

"Yeah, and there are twelve rooms. Well twelve bedrooms," she announced having swallowed most of what was in her mouth. "I don't really know how many rooms there are in the place."

"Twelve bedrooms?" He glanced in her direction in curious surprise.

"Six beds in each room, watch the road will ya, and there are three others that are pretty much honeymoon suites. Some of her friends were married."

"And how many will be there this weekend?" he asked.

"Just the two of us as far as I know. You said this was a top secret what-ever-it-is you have."

"I sure hope I am doing the right thing." he sighed.

She backed her body against the door and window as far as her seat belt would allow and questioned with the single raised eyebrow, "Two unmarried people going to a secluded resort all by themselves for a weekend is the 'right thing'?" She questioned and quoted the air with her fingers.

"I hope I have proven to you my integrity." he appealed. "It appears so because you have agreed to do such a thing with someone you have only known for six months."

"These last six months have spoken to me in such a way I do believe I can trust you." she returned. "Besides, I think I can take care of myself, unless he has a gun and when they did, you rescued me you still did not take advantage of me. I think you have proven yourself trustworthy."

"And I think you have proven yourself by not telling anyone about the encounter."

The incident he was speaking of was when she had a delivery to make in a rebellious part of the Area of the Cedars. In a dark block with high buildings she found herself caught by two men who crowded her into an alley. She had a little money but the tennis equipment she was carrying was worth fifteen thousand dollars. They pulled out guns and were about to use them when the bullets were deflected into the dirt. Then the men started shooting each other. When the excitement was over, Ply came around the corner. It was still all a bit of a mystery.

She made her deliveries, but Ply was right there to protect her if need be. Thankfully, all he had to do is keep himself invisible. The receiver of the goods was an executive of a small company and wanted new tennis equipment thinking it would improve his game. It did to a small degree but not enough to go professional. He had paid for the stuff on his credit card hoping he could cancel the payment because the delivery girl had been robbed. He was considerably taken aback when she showed up at the door a little disheveled but still in one piece.

Ply made no more comments seeing that the toy would do much of the explaining. They pulled off the highway and hit the mountain road and Ply noticed the third car back turned the same direction.

"Hey Jane, are you sure there is no one else coming up here with us?"

She turned and saw the vehicle gaining on them, "I was told we would be alone. There are numerous lodges and villas in this part of the state and most of them are separated by rather large properties and high fences."

About three-quarters of a mile before they turned off, the trailing car disappeared onto a side-road. "I sure hope that is not a bad omen." he worried out loud.

"The court is indoors so unless they break in, we should be fine."

"That is a comfort." he responded.

"Don't worry, things will work out just right. I think this is our turn here on the left. That's the fire number."

They turned down a freshly paved roadway marked 'Private Drive'. The branches of the tall trees practically covered the road. They had just turned colors seeing it was early fall and the two felt like they were driving into a tunnel of the most beautiful maples and oaks. Ply slowed down so they could enjoy the view as the tires crunched over the acorns on the pavement. The road wound around for more than half a mile. They approached a large stone wall and slowly passed through the twenty-foot archway and there it was.

"Wow!" He exclaimed, "This place is monstrous."

The front wall of the property was fifteen feet high and two hundred and fifty feet long. There was an archway twenty feet high by twenty feet wide right in the middle of the wall. The driveway was only fifteen feet wide so there was a little dab of grass each side of the pavement. They drove into the front yard. The castle sat back another quarter mile on a forty-five-degree angle from the wall. They stopped at what they thought might be the front doors. An entrance way of two double doors was set back ten feet from three story tall porch pillars. The doors were three feet wide and ten feet tall. It looked like all four would open leaving an entrance of twelve feet wide by ten feet high.

"Yikes." proclaimed Jane. "She warned me, but I had no idea."

They just sat in the car for a few minutes then she said, "Let's see if the drive goes all around the house. The sun has not quite set, and we won't have as much an opportunity until morning once it is dark." They drove on and sure enough the pavement circled the mansion.

"The place seems to be in excellent shape save the grass being much too long." commented Ply. "I wonder if she has a riding mower?"

"Isn't the grass a little tall for a rider?" She inquired.

"You could be right," he mused, "Look, there's an outbuilding. I wonder what's inside?"

"Barb said there were a few out buildings for various purposes but it is getting dark. Besides, you didn't come here to do all her chores!"

"Are you paying her for the use of the premises?" he asked.

"No." she whispered as she leaned into the back of the seat slightly drooping her head.

"Then would it not surprise her if a little work were done while we were here?"

"That sounds like a good idea. When are we going to practice my game?" The ambition in her voice surprised him.

"How soon can you be ready?"

"In about fifteen minutes." she said, eyes bright with excitement and face beaming.

"I want to look around a bit before I show you my toy, just to make sure." he stated as he drove a little farther around the estate. As they circled, they noticed a hole in the fence.

"It appears that the fence is in need of some repair. Let's have a look."

As he drove over the grass for a closer inspection something moved. Suddenly a huge buck jumped in front of the car and out through the hole in the fence.

"Whew. That's all it is." she rejoiced falling back into the seat.

"Yeah," said Ply, "But that buck did not cut a hole that size in the fence."

Jane had a ring of keys that she pulled out of her purse and they headed for the door of the structure. As she moved toward the lock, she noticed that it was already unlocked. It just looked closed from a distance.

Wait a minute," said Ply, "I did not want to show you this till later but we might have to get serious. If there is someone there, I do not want to get them angry by seeing someone sneak up on them."

Jane was about to yell but he gently muffled her voice with his hand.

"If there is someone here, I do want to catch them. You must follow me precisely. I will not hurt you, but you must promise to trust me."

She nodded her head with eyes wide. *Why did I ever get myself into this mess?* she thought. *He seems to be a lot stronger than I noticed and he is too quick for me to handle. What have I done?*

He hurried her to the back of the car and Ply dug out the old guitar case. "You must hold my hand and you will not get hurt. I don't know what will happen if you let go. As long as you touch me you will be as I am, but if you let go, I will become invisible, so you must hang on tight."

"Invisible?" she gulped.

"I will explain later."

He grabbed onto her right hand as he drew out the sword and her eyes widened even more. He let the trunk lid down slowly but did not latch it. He adjusted their time frame and they moved toward the structure. She did not notice the time difference and when they got to the door Ply slowed down just long enough to flick on the light. There was movement in the back of the room.

Ply took a step forward, but Jane held back. Ply nodded his head to encourage her. She had never seen such courage before, so she went into the building with him.

They crept into the large room and saw a shadow move on the other side of a doorway. Ply kept the sword in front of him as they approached the intruder.

A porcupine waddled away from the light but other than the spiked resident, the room seemed empty. Ply dropped to just above normal time. There were oil marks on the concrete floor but no machinery. All that was there was two well used push mowers, an old weed whip leaning up against the wall, an air compressor under a workbench, two, one-gallon plastic gasoline containers and three five-gallon Gerry cans.

"Let's have a look around." suggested Ply and they walked

through the building turning on lights. Most of the rooms seemed empty. The floors were dusty with numerous footprints and tire tracks, but no one was there.

"This looks suspicious," said Ply, "We had better do a quick scout around the property and see if there is anything else amiss."

"Do we take the car?"

"No. At this point walking is much faster."

This only confused the woman but at this point she was willing to see what Ply had in mind.

They prodded the intruder out, doused the lights and properly locked the shed and walked briskly around the house to see the other buildings. By their time-frame it took almost an hour, but the sun did not move at all. There was enough light to see the outside and make access to all they found. All the doors of the house were secure. There were no windows jimmied nor broken. It was only the one out building that had suffered loss.

"Okay," he instructed. "Let's get the car and put it in the garage attached to the house. If you drive, I will walk behind you with the toy if it is needed."

Once inside the house, the instrument was cased, and the call was made to the owner and the police. The police arrived, and it was determined that the lawn tractor and perhaps a few other instruments for property maintenance had disappeared.

"That might explain the hole in the fence." said Jane.

"Exactly," replied the officer, "We will send someone out tomorrow afternoon to take pictures and casts for the footprints. Seeing that the house is alarmed, and the maintenance shed is not might be the reason there has been no intrusion in the main building." he observed. They bade farewells and then they left.

Before the officers came, Ply explained to Jane the time change that happens in the manipulation done by the holder of the sword. They both had to adjust their watches but the clock in the car was still accurate to 'normal' time.

"I sure hope this is enough excitement for one evening," expressed the young lady in a tired tone, "It is about time for a snack and some shut-eye." They ate then headed up stairs.

"Keep your door locked and don't answer to anyone unless it's me." and then he whispered in her ear a code word so she would know it was him. Her perfume gently tickled his nostrils. *What on earth is happening?* he scolded himself and quickly regained his composure.

"Hopefully things will be quiet. There seems to be nothing here that is not in many of the other estates in the area." she encouraged.

"Except that this place has been empty for nine months, not to mention the outbuilding being behind the house, so the lights from it would be difficult to see with the trees behind the fence and the grass so deep. I'll leave some downstairs lights on, so any visitors might be discouraged from entering. If you hear anything just call my phone and talk quietly. If I need to come in, I will be invisible, but you will see me once I am inside."

The night proved to be uneventful. She woke up, quietly showered, dressed, then slowly opened her door to see if he was up. Immediately she was hit with the odor of bacon, eggs and toast. She roared down the stairs.

"Wow, I thought you couldn't cook!"

"I guess I never had enough motivation," he replied, "I hoped that this might get you out of bed a little earlier. I want to get to the lessons and the game before the authorities show up. The last thing I need is to have them understand the implications of what this toy can do."

"Is it really that wonderful?" she probed, seating herself at the breakfast table in front of the large window.

"I think it is a whole lot more dangerous than even I can imagine." He stopped there refusing to add any more comments until his understanding of the instrument had been explained to her.

"Let's go then," she responded, "We can eat on the run."

"No," he responded, "Let's sit down and eat a good breakfast and I will explain some of the principles that I think may be the reason this does what it does." He opened the physics book and started reading and explaining how he figured the principles worked in the acquired toy.

"Aren't you going to eat?" she asked with her mouth half full of eggs and toast.

"I already did about half an hour ago. I waited until you got up then started to cook your breakfast." He read and explained for about half an hour exhorting her to continue to eat because they had a full day ahead of them.

61

They rinsed the dishes then stuck them in the dishwasher.

"Let me show you how I found out some of the properties of this thing." he instructed. "Last night we had to reset out watches back because our personal time changes according to the parameters of the sword. As our time frame changes, we become invisible. That is why I wanted to walk around last night and not take the car. Walking proved to be much faster. While the sword is warmed the time frame of the user changes according to the desire of the user. I am not sure exactly how it works but it seems that our brains help decipher the time change. Let's go in front of the mirror and I will show you."

He demonstrated to her by the large mirror in the front foyer the same way he was shown. It did not take long, but she had to sit down for a few minutes.

"You mean last night we were invisible to anyone who came on the property?"

"Exactly."

"We had to adjust our clocks about an hour. How much did we age?"

That question took him aback. "I'm not sure but I expect that we age in the time that we are in, not in real time."

"So, if we do a lot of this, we will get a lot older, a lot faster?"

"That may be the way it works." he responded.

"How fast do I want to die early?" she asked herself. "Last night took one hour off our lives."

She pondered the situation and the physics for a few minutes.

"Wait a minute. We are told that it is appointed unto man once to die..."

"So?" he questioned.

"If God has appointed a time for us to die that may not make a difference whether we do it quickly or slowly."

Now it was his turn to raise the eyebrows. "You seem to be catching on to this thing."

"Okay," she agreed, "Let's get on the court."

While she dug out her racket, he scouted the house a little more with the sword and found nothing out of the ordinary, as much as 'out of the ordinary' can mean in a castle with so many rooms.

Each door had a brass title-plate glued to the front at eye level. The room he slept in last night had a title of *San Jose, Costa Rica*. The one across the hall that Jane stayed in was titled *Paris, France*.

In *San Jose* the room was eight sided. One entire wall was papered with a mural of a tropical beach. The sand was a blonde/white with driftwood protruding from the beach in a scattered number of places. Not a soul was to be seen nor any footprints of human description. A large sea turtle was making her way back to the ocean after burying eggs twenty feet behind her. At the far end of the beach was a river and a rocky shoreline.

Across the room was a mural of the *Mercado Central de San Jose*. People were selling and buying in a crowded market scene with every description of persons displayed in the photo. One lady was haggling over a price that she thought was too much. Men were setting out wares for whoever needed them. A butcher was behind a screen chopping up some animal with an ax as people were in front of the counter purchasing meat for the day. Many people were just walking past the forty or so booths that each had a different scene happening. Off to one corner there was a man who seemed to be just taking it all in enjoying a cool drink from a waxed heavy paper carton in the early morning sun. The shadows were a little long reminding the viewer that it was still the very beginning of the day. The angle of the shot was apparently taken from across the street and a few floors up from ground level.

One of the other walls had a picture of a rain forest with a waterfall giving the varied flavor of different parts of the country.

Ply found titles on all the doors. *Johannesburg, South Africa*; *Berlin, Germany*'; '*Sidney, Australia*'; '*Barcelona, Spain*'; '*Madrid, Spain*' *Toronto, Canada*... All the doors were locked so Ply could not get in but promised himself he would get Jane to give him a tour.

There were sitting rooms scattered along the hall with a large fireplace in each and even a small theater with about thirty seats before a large one-hundred-and-twenty-inch video screen right in the middle of all the commotion.

In thirty minutes, his time and ten hers, he met her on the court. They volleyed for a few minutes to get warmed up and then he tapped the ball on the other side of the court she was playing on. She had to run to get there but did retrieve it. After a few minutes of catching returns, she asked, "Is this all that toy of yours can do?"

"How fast do you want me to return the serve?"

"As fast as you can." she teased remembering the incident in the racket-ball court.

He stared at her for a few seconds then said, "Okay".

She served the ball at a steaming rate, but the sword adjusted time, so it crawled through the air. He smacked it back so hard it left a skid mark on the court one inch inside the line, burst against the wall with a loud 'pop', then floated behind her and landed at her feet a pile of mashed rubber. She just stood there with her jaw dropped somewhere towards Australia.

Just as fast he adjusted his time to hers and said, "How's that!"

She tried to compose herself and replied, "Why don't we just volley for a while, so I can get my game back?"

"Sure."

That they did as Ply sped up just a bit to push her a little and she caught most of them. After about fifty minutes she called it quits for a rest. "How come you're not sweaty?"

"My time frame changes so I don't have to work at most of this stuff. I just bunt the ball back in the accelerated time frame and you get to chase it."

This got the girl thinking as walked to the net, "Can we switch places?"

Ply never thought about this side of the offer. As she hopped the net he said, "Try not to touch the blade. It is unimaginably sharp. When I first found it, I touched the blade once and it cut my finger so quickly I did not even feel it."

Her hand slowed as she reached out for the device and a serious look came over her face. "What exactly can this thing do?"

"I don't know its full potential yet."

She glanced at the dead ball on the edge of the court and then gently grasped the hilt of the sword.

"If you use anything but the flat of the sword you will slice the ball," he cautioned. "Remember the chopped balls at the clubhouse." Nevertheless, it took a few expired spheres to get her used to the swing of the thing.

After another half an hour, Ply was the one who was sweaty, and she was fully amazed.

"We better get cleaned up before the cops get here." He exhorted.

In forty minutes, real time, they had showered, dressed and had a light lunch. There was a knock at the door and two plain clothed officers presented their ID's and the four proceeded to the back building. Castings and pictures were taken. One officer decided to follow the faint tracks through the fence. They led about a quarter mile to a side road on the neighbor's property. "I guess that's the end of that trail." he muttered to himself.

"When can I fix the fence?" examined Ply to the officers.

The three looked at each other. "Hold off till we get some more information if you could please." stated the shorter of the two.

"What more information do you need?" asked Ply.

"We need measurements and distances from here to the road and we can't do it right now." grumbled the bigger uniformed man attempting to impose his authority on the youth.

"Okay," backed off Ply holding his hands up with his palms to the officers, "I did not mean to pressure or impose."

"You're catchin' on kid." returned the cop.

In an hour they were finished with their questions and investigation. They left promising to get to the bottom of the case, but their body language gave no clues to the confidence or ambition of the patrolmen. The name and number of the owner was given to them and then they left. Ply made a mental note of their names and badge numbers and wrote them down after they had gone.

"Well!" spouted Jane. "I suppose that ends that!"

"Not necessarily." he lured.

"What do you mean?"

"Let me think for a bit. We may be able to find where this stuff has been taken if it has not already been sold."

"I am NOT a detective!"

"Well, you haven't been, but I saw the gleam in your eye as you played with that metal 'racket'." he reminded her. "We may not get all the stuff back, but we might be able to catch the thief."

"What is wrong with you? Are not the police on the job?"

"Did you see the look of confidence and desire to catch these crooks on the faces of those guys that left? They actually seemed aggravated that they had to spend a Saturday afternoon on the job. Besides, I didn't like the way they refused me permission to repair the fence." Then he wondered if they were hiding something.

"What's your plan?"

"Let's get together with the owner and find out exactly what is missing."

"She won't be back for a month. She's in Toronto."

"Hmm, that may be too late."

"We can call her and find out exactly what was there."

They made the call, but the owner was unable to answer her phone, so they left a message to have her call back.

"I guess that will have to do for the moment." he replied.

Ply paced around the front room for a few minutes then said, "Hey gorgeous, we need to talk."

"About what?" she said.

"About us."

Once again, the eyebrow manifested its maneuverability.

"I am getting very interested in you, like a whole lot more than a friend."

"Go on." she coaxed crossing her arms being a little cautious as to where the conversation was going.

"I really did not mean for all this to happen so soon, but it seems that we have been thrown into this together by something much bigger than either of us."

"I agree." she said cautiously, arms still tightly folded, the fingers of her left hand tapping her right forearm.

"I wanted to get to see how you reacted to the sword and when you wanted to play with the toy, I thought it might be time to form some sort of partnership."

"A partnership?" she responded in a surprised voice, dropping her arms and planting her hands on her hips with a questioning look.

"Well, I would like a little more than just a partnership."

"Just what exactly are you after Mr. Gallant?" she interrogated in a somewhat disgusted voice.

This isn't going very well, he thought. By now they were standing a few feet from each other. "I was wondering if you would be willing to marry me?"

"Marry you?" she burst out. "That certainly is a little more than just a partnership!" She announced thrusting her arms out to her sides. She paced around the room twice then looked at him and thought about it for about fifteen long seconds.

"What took you so long?"

"Whew!" he breathed, "Okay, when?"

"What do you mean when?"

"How long does it take to get married?" he queried, "I've never done this before so what do I have to do?"

"Oh, men!" she exacerbated, "When do you want to do this?"

He looked into her eyes, "What fun. Our first fight. When do we get to kiss and make up?"

She threw her arms around him and kissed as she never had kissed before.

"Okay, okay, I need to calm down." he blurted and gently pushed her away, but not very far.

"How is that for a yes?" she beamed. Dropping her arms, she said, "First I need some answers."

"You already said yes," he reminded her, "What answers are you looking for?"

"How did you know I went to the far side of the city with all that expensive equipment?"

"That is the question?"

"The first one."

"I went in to see if you wanted to take in a movie and there was a different girl at the kiosk. Hoping you had not quit, I asked where I might find you. She said you had to make a delivery and when I found out where I immediately drove out there and parked on the top of the hill to watch for your car. I have zoom video on my phone so once I spotted your car, I could check to make sure it was you. You were in the passing lane, so I hopped onto the freeway and stayed about three cars behind you. I had the sword in the front seat and when I jumped out, I locked the car, fired up the sword, and followed you trying not to bump into anybody. You know all the rest."

There was a knock at the door.

"You get that." she instructed, "I'll get the sword and if it is not a problem, I will emerge from the library without it." She ran to set the library door ajar then zipped up the stairs.

Ply answered the door to a rather disheveled middle-aged man who said in somewhat of a panic, "Did you lose all your lawn equipment?"

"Who needs to know?" asked Ply a little curious at the forward question.

"I saw the cop car leaving your place and wondered if they had hit you also."

"Hit by what?"

"It must be a gang then. All the places within a ten-mile radius have lost some very expensive lawn tractors." he stated as he walked into the foyer.

"And who are you may I ask?" Ply asked standing between the man and the door.

"Oh dear, excuse me. I am the custodian for a few of the mansions that are in the area. I get to cut the grass, plant flowers, keep the places in shape. I know most of the other maintenance men in the area and once a month we get together to share ideas and information about the 'richies' that own all these palaces. Are you the new custodian for this place? Here is my card and my number. We meet the first Monday of the month but lately we have been getting together once a week with all of the stuff that is disappearing."

"Okay," said Ply, glancing at the card, "Come in and sit down and tell me about it."

The gentleman told of some of the equipment that had disappeared in the last few months and Ply stood in the middle of the room and listened. He felt a puff of air on the back of his neck and figured it was Jane in ready with the sword. "Hey hon." he hollered and turned his head towards the library.

In a few seconds her head popped out from the library doorway, "Yes?"

"Could you get some coffee ready for me and our guest, Mr. Johnson?"

"Abe Johnson," blushed the gentleman, "Like the outboard motors but just a little too far removed from the money." he stated. "I think we need a private investigator."

"A private investigator? Are the police not doing their job?" Ply questioned.

"They may be." reassured the gentleman, "They just don't seem to be very interested in the case."

"I might agree with you there. Are you aware of any rewards that might be granted if the case is solved or even if the material is returned?"

"Oh yes. Many of the victims have put up money. So far the reward is up to ten thousand dollars but not all of the owners have yet been notified seeing that the crimes have happened so recently."

"I do know of a P. I.," suggested Ply, "but we will need a little more information before we contact him. When is your next meeting?"

"Seeing as another robbery has taken place, we just might meet Monday."

"We are only guests here and we do not know how long it has been since the equipment disappeared from this property. We will get in touch as soon as possible. Is there any opportunity I could attend the next meeting?"

"We have been meeting at *Robert's Cafe* in town about seven in the evening."

"Good, I will see you there."

They shook hands and the man left.

"What are you doing?" whispered Jane, "I have to be back at work on Monday."

"I know, but I don't, so I will take you home tomorrow and come back here and live unobtrusively for a while."

"I don't think you have permission!"

"We'll ask when the owner calls back. We don't have to tell her about the sword, but I think if it means a return of her property and the 'rental fee' could be the payment of me using the house. And I will cut the grass!"

"With what?"

"With the decoy I am about to rent, and I will clean up those oil spots in the outbuilding."

"And with exactly what are you going to pay for all that with?" she interrogated.

"Let's just say I have a rich uncle."

"A rich uncle?"

"Well, not exactly rich, but I do have an uncle."

With that the phone rang inside the house.

"A land-line?"

"She has her own phone system inside the castle."

"Hmm," he mumbled, "I wonder what other little surprises she has in store?"

"I'll – bet – you - do!" She fired back. Jane talked with her friend for about ten minutes then hung up the receiver. "She says she is glad she called. The house is set up, so the police are immediately called if the door opens without her authority with the burglar alarm system. Now that she knows you will be here for a while, she will reset the thing, so you might be left alone."

"Another surprise."

"Yes," admitted Jane, "Apparently you're not the only one with them."

"I should hope not!" he replied with a twinkle in his eye.

Her returned look seemed to say, "Who? Me?"

Jane told Ply about the equipment that was previously in the shed. He recorded it in his phone.

* * *

Sunday Ply took Jane back to her car at the tennis courts. She returned to her parent's house and he to the old apartment to get a few things and then to the castle.

Monday morning Ply thought about what he could do in cleaning up the yard.

"All I have is this old weed whip." he muttered. "I could clean up around the buildings and the fence line." He had worn old clothes in preparation for outside work. He cooked himself a good breakfast and headed out back. At about eight-thirty he arrived in the back building and set the weed whip on the bench. There were some tools in the drawers of the bench, and he managed to get the whip apart enough to clean it out with some of the gasoline then blow it out with the air from the compressor. He reassembled the machine, filled the tank on the whip with gas from one of the gas cans, pulled the cord and it fired up.

"I might as well start right outside here." he said.

He cut a swath about eighteen inches from the walls of the building and circled the structure rather quickly. With the hole in the fence he cleaned up both sides of the back fence making it a little easier to keep the fence clean. He found some thin rope and tied the fence open, so he could mow when he had the opportunity. The police told him not to repair the fence but tying it back temporarily he didn't think would do any harm.

At one-thirty he had his large cup of cereal and a soda just to keep him going. By then he had cleaned up around all the back buildings and most of both sides of the fence line. He was getting tired by three o'clock so he cleaned up the whip, reloaded it with string so it would be ready for the next time, and set the gas can that was empty by the door, so he could fill it when needed.

He drug himself upstairs to his room, showered and lay down for a short nap.

"I better set the alarm, so I don't miss that meeting." he admonished himself.

* * *

At six-twenty Ply showed up with a Bluetooth sticking out his ear. It was tied to his cell phone that had a three-hour record time, so he might have to excuse himself but only if the meeting went too long. Ply waited in his car just out of sight and watched speaking to the recorder who arrived and when. He did not know the names of the men but gave the recording their description and videoed them as they entered the building. Parking more than a block and a half away allowed him some invisibility but kept things in good focus with the zoom on his phone.

Abe Johnson was the first one there at twenty minutes before seven. Ply got a good facial shot of Johnson as Abe walked into the cafe. *I wonder who else will show up,* he thought to himself. Ply waited until about five to before going in. Mr. Johnson had his back to the door and was doing something on his tablet when Ply addressed him.

"Good evening Mr. Johnson."

He turned in his chair with a start, "Oh, hi. I didn't hear you come in."

Ply noticed that he quickly closed the app he was involved in on his tablet. Abe rose to shake hands with Ply.

"So how much equipment has disappeared?" asked Ply.

"Well, that depends on how much is missing from your property." he returned.

"I think just one at the moment. If any more is missing, we will have to add it to the list."

"Then that would make twelve."

"Is there any way I could have a copy of the list?"

Johnson looked at him for a moment. "I don't see why not but I have pretty much everything under control."

"If I'm going to get a P.I. then I will need the list, but it is up to you..."

"Not a problem" interrupted Johnson. "Here, I'll send it to you."

"Why not just bring it up on your tablet and I can take a picture or it." Ply did not want Johnson to have his number. If he had Ply's number, he could find out where Ply was using GPS. Ply didn't think that was really any of Johnson's business yet.

Johnson was not pleased with the response, but he could not think of a reason to refuse the youth. He dug out the list and Ply took a picture. He expanded the list by spreading his fingers and counted.

"I only got nine. Are there a few I am missing?"

Johnson picked up his tablet and brought up the other three. Ply pixed them and said thanks as someone approached from behind them.

"What we got here?" asked the newcomer, "A new victim? Hi, I'm Gerry Walters." he stretched out a strong worn hand.

"Ply Gallant." greeted the youth. "I'm at the Cully place."

"She got hit too. I'm not surprised. Never nobody there; and who is supposed to be cutting the grass? It is almost ten miles deep!"

"Guess I get to do it now." grinned the kid. Five more men walked in and gathered around the table. They all sat and ordered snacks or dessert and drinks as the waitress showed up. She left to fill the orders and Johnson introduced Ply to the group.

"This is Ply Gallant from the Cully mansion." stated Johnson. "He has met Walters..." they introduced themselves counter-clockwise around the table.

"Waters."

"Seaboam."

"Olson."

"Gabriel."

"Gillette."

Ply looked around the table at the expression of the men seated.

"How come it is taking so long to find any of this machinery?" started Olson. "It has been three years since some of this stuff went missing. What's the hold up?"

"How are you going to trace a machine that nobody knows where it is?" informed Johnson. None of them have tracking devices and it seems almost impossible to catch this rascal in the act."

"And I suppose you have lost one also." griped Seaboam looking at Ply.

"Yes, I have." agreed Ply. "I have a model number but no serial number yet. Mr. Johnson has suggested we have a private investigator look into the matters seeing as the police are not getting very far. I happen to know of one..."

"What's that gonna' cost?" interrupted Gillette. "We're spending our own money on replacement machinery and we haven't much, if any, to hire," and he almost spat out the words in disgust as he wagged his head, "a private investigator."

"I know of one who just might work for the reward money so none of you will be out any more than it is already costing you." announced Ply and the faces at the table relaxed somewhat. The waitress showed up with a large tray and handed out what each had ordered.

"And just who is this P.I. that you know?" interrogated Johnson.

"My uncle is an ex-investigative policeman. He used to work in New York on the city streets until he got shot at too many times. Thankfully his Kevlar saved his life, but his wife was thinking this was happening all too often and a bullet to the face was just around one of those corners, so she talked him into quitting and buying a farm. It didn't really take much. He was brought up on a farm and loved it more than anything until he met his wife. She loved the city and talked him into moving there but once she realized she could have him come home in a bag one night she settled into the farming life pretty easily."

A glimmer of hope seemed to cross the faces of most of those at the table.

"As chair of the committee I should be the one who decides when it is necessary to get someone from the outside." interrupted Johnson. "I think it would be better if we contacted someone that we knew rather than hiring someone just out of the blue."

"You could very well be correct." agreed Seaboam. "With this uprising that has been developing lately we do not want someone from the other side getting involved with this mess."

"Okay then," concluded Johnson, "We will table the matter until the next meeting. Any new business?" Everyone seemed to be satisfied for the moment.

"Meeting adjourned!" finalized Johnson. "The next meeting is scheduled for one month from today unless anything else turns up."

"Or disappears!" corrected Gillette.

After the meeting Ply got to know some of the other maintenance men of the area. He devised a plan that he might get to know some of these guys without the stuffiness of a formal meeting and invited himself over to help in some of the two-man chores that were needed once in a while. Glenn Olson was the first to accept help as he was putting an extension on his shed. Plans were made for Ply to arrive about nine in the morning on the next day.

At nine sharp Ply drove up to Olson's place. "Good morning son. Had anything to eat?"

"Yes sir, I have had breakfast. What is it we need to do?"

"Outside walls are a bit of a challenge all by yourself. I am glad you offered." Mrs. Olson arrived at ten-thirty with hot drinks and some cookies. They sat for a few minutes while Ply gobbled cookies and the three of them enjoyed hot chocolate.

"Man," mumbled Ply with his mouth full, "This is the best hot chocolate I have ever tasted!"

Mrs. Olson blushed, finished her drink, and the two went back to work.

They worked till one in the afternoon and then Mrs. Olson called them in for lunch. They washed and were seated then the lady brought out mashed potatoes, roast beef, gravy, green beans, corn-on-the-cob, peas, carrots, and whipped yellow squash.

"We don't get a lot of help around here and we can't pay you much, but we can give you a pretty good feed."

Ply looked at all the food then Mr. then Mrs. Olsen. "I've never seen a spread like this before. Except maybe at Christmas, and then maybe only once or twice."

It took more than forty-five minutes to quietly eat and talk. They took a short walk around some of the buildings then got back to work. All three walls went up and most of the roof trusses were placed and fastened.

"If you can come back tomorrow, we just may be able to get some of this roof on." Mr. Olson invited.

"What time would you like me here?" Ply asked.

"Nine would be fine."

"I'm not really busy if you want me here earlier." stated Ply.

Olson looked at the ground then said, "I usually start about six and the wife calls me in between seven-thirty and eight for breakfast..."

"I think I can do six if I get breakfast." said Ply thinking of the feast he recently devoured at their table.

"Great, we'll see you in the morning."

Wednesday, they got the metal roof on and all of the metal siding by about six o' clock in the evening. The tin was up but not fully fastened so Glen had a few days' work to finish but the heavy stuff was done.

"Thank you for the opportunity to enjoy your friendship." Ply stated as he shook the hand of Mr. Olson. "That was a good workout."

"Thank you for all of your help. That went a lot faster than I ever expected." commented Mr. Olson.

Ply arrived back at the castle and fired up the weed whip. He decided that the fence-line could use some more work and trimmed for about two hours.

"This grass is really deep." he said. "It is going to take hours to cut this stuff even with a good strong rider. I wonder..." He looked around and a lot of trees separated the next property from the back of the castle. He put the whip back into the shed and went up to his room.

"If I use the sword to cut the grass, I can probably get it all cut in about thirty minutes. But then how do I get rid of the grass?"

He called Mr. Olson.

"Glenn Olson speaking."

"Sir, this is Ply from the Cully residence..."

"Good to hear from you already. Need more work?"

"Not at the moment." replied Ply. "What I do have is a problem."

"Anything I can help you with?"

"That I was wondering. I have about twelve acres here of grass that is from three to four feet deep and I wondered if you wanted it for the taking?"

"How open are the fields?"

The gate is twenty feet high by twenty feet wide but it's an archway. There are some trees in the back, but the front is pretty well open. How big is your machine for harvesting hay?"

"I may have to come over and have a look."

"I am planning to leave in the morning to see my uncle who is the P. I. but I'm not leaving till just before eight."

"If I get there at about seven-thirty in the morning can we go over it together?"

"Sure, I'll be packed up and ready to go by then."

"Great," agreed Mr. Olsen. "I'll see you then."

* * *

Ply decided to do a little more whipping prior to having a late supper. He had done most of the back and figured he could get some of the front done before it got too dark. The fence at the front was a fifteen-foot high wall about three feet thick stretching along the entire two hundred and fifty feet of the property.

"Wow," he thought to himself, "This girl must have made some real money in this game. Either that or she still owes a bundle."

As he whipped, he noticed that the wall was almost perfectly straight. He passed the end of the wall and something seemed a little out of kilter. He took a step back and aligned his sight along the side and noticed some of the bricks seemed to be slightly out of place. The angle of the sun showed the shadow of the protruding bricks. They were all at the same height about five feet off the ground and evenly spaced apart. He finished whipping and then paced off the uneven rocks. At about twenty-five feet each there was a square rock that sat out from the others about one half of an inch. At the end of the wall he tried to see if any were loose. With a little wiggling he removed the brick and found a large cavity behind the stone.

"Hmm, I wonder what this was designed for?" There were three, two-inch PVC pipes, one in the back, and one on each side of the cavity.

"I can see why there might be two but three?" he questioned to himself. He carefully slid the rock into the slot and proceeded down the wall to inspect the next. Same thing. Assuming that all of them were similar he walked to the last one and found three pipes in a deep cavity.

"Why would there be an entrance on each end?" He picked up the weed whip but could not get the oddities of the wall out of his mind.

"Why does she have all these facing the outside of the property?"

Searching the house, he found one locked door in the basement at the front of the house hidden in a closet and figured that this is where the pipes must end up. It appeared that the door went to a room under the front porch.

While eating dinner, he glanced at the list of missing mowers. He noticed that most of the equipment was good quality stuff, not that he was a connoisseur of lawn tractors, but he had seen some advertising. He looked up the pricing of the models that had disappeared and entered pictures on his phone.

"Whew." he breathed, "I can see why a thousand bucks would not be too much as an incentive to get some of this stuff back. I wonder how much this stuff would sell for as 'experienced machinery'?" He looked up a few dealers and found that there were three in this state and four in others.

"Only seven dealers of this brand of equipment in all the Northern Continent? This might be a little easier than I first thought." He added the list of dealers to his phone and thought about how he could get to each of them.

"The closest one is only two hours away from my apartment. This might be a good place to start. And not too far from Uncle Jack's place." With that he called his relative.

* * *

Jack Morgan married Ply's aunt when Ply was five years old. It was a formal wedding but small enough not to break the budget for the next thirty years. John Morgan was kind, gentle, and fairly large; six foot-four weighing in at two-forty-five with a three percent body fat. Farming was his first love. Then he met Naomi Elizabeth. It took two encounters. The first quite by accident; the second was planned like a fox chasing a rabbit and the love of the field was suddenly relegated to second place!

"Morgan Farms." came the response on the other end of the line.

"Uncle Jack, this is Ply how are you and that lovely wife of yours?"

"Ply Gallant, what a pleasant surprise. She is just as wonderful as ever. What kind of excitement are you up to now?"

"What prompted you to say such a thing? When have I ever

been involved in anything exciting?"

"Well let me think. How about the time you tried to flip right around the top of the swing..?"

"Then there was the time you and some of your friends got trapped on the cliffs as they started to crumble. Some friend had to let you down with a rope."

"Then there was..."

"Okay, Okay, I get the picture, and yes there is a little more excitement, but I might win a reward on this one."

"Enough to retire on." teased the older gentleman.

"Not quite yet but maybe enough to keep me fed for a few more months. I was wondering if there was any help you needed around the farm for a day or two? I still have some time off and am getting a bit bored."

"How soon can you get here?"

"How about tomorrow about noon?"

"That bad, eh? Okay we will have something we can pop into the microwave when you get here."

"I just might show up early." drooled the younger.

As soon as he hung up, he called the owner of the mansion from her land line and was surprised to get her.

"Hello?"

"This is Ply Gallant. I have been here in your castle with Jane and need to inform you that tomorrow morning I will be gone for a few days."

"What time are you leaving?"

"I hope to be gone by eight in the morning and I should be back by noon Friday."

"I'll set the alarms."

"If I could ask one more thing?"

"Yes."

"If you could put my cell number into your phone so if anything happens, I can get hold of you a little easier?"

There was a five second pause then, "The four-one-six number?"

"That's it." he replied. "How is the game going?"

"Oh, win a bunch and loose a few. Helps keep me humble."

Ply tried to hide his gulp but almost heard the smile from the other end of the line.

"Jane tells me you play a little also."

"Only against those who do not leave me lost in love."

"She is pretty good isn't she. She turned down a tournament from a broken heart and never really got back into the game. Quite a shame. She might have gone somewhere."

"She is getting to the place where she might be on my 'no spar list'." uttered Ply.

"I should be back by the end of the month. Maybe the three of us should get together." stated the star.

"I think Jane and I would like that very much."

"Let me know how things go."

"I am going to have to rent a machine to do the lawn, so the place looks a little more occupied."

"The grass has not been cut?"

"It is four feet deep plus, in some places. I figure I might as well cut the grass as a gift of appreciation."

"Well thank you that is very nice of you." encouraged the owner. "Please keep me informed as to what is happening there. I will get back to you soon if I am unable to answer immediately."

"Will do, oh by the way, this is a nice place you have here."

"Thank you. Do keep me posted."

"Safe game."

"Thanks, goodbye"

* * *

Early Thursday Ply was up with his usual bachelor breakfast of milk and cereal, had the car packed, and met Glenn as he pulled up right at seven-thirty. Ply locked the door at quarter to eight just to make sure he was out of sight when the alarms were set.

"Wow." stuttered Glenn. "This place is a mess... I mean," he corrected himself, "the grass."

"I was wondering if you wanted the feed for some of your animals?"

"Hop in and we can drive around." invited Glenn.

Ply climbed up beside his new friend.

"The grass looks good for feed I just wanted to see if I could get some of my equipment in here. I might have to bring it in in two loads seeing as the gate is only twenty feet wide. You said there is twelve acres here? It sure looks like a lot more than that."

"The house takes up almost an acre and a half." responded Ply. "Some of the trees in the back will prevent you from getting all the back but I figured maybe you could get as much as twelve acres pretty quickly."

"How soon do you want this done?" asked the guest.

"I don't think there is a real hurry." stated Ply. "I'm going to see if I can rent a mower and get some info on the stuff that was stolen but I'm not in a hurry."

"When are you planning to be back?"

"I hope to be here sometime tomorrow afternoon."

"So," pondered the farmer, "If I can get most of this stuff cut and bailed by Friday, you'll be happy?"

"I'd be more than happy, and I could help with whatever when I got back."

"Well let's see what we can do. Feed isn't cheap these days and a free field is always welcome. If nothing else gets in the way I can probably do it."

"Wow. That is wonderful." stated Ply. "I'll get back as soon as I can."

"Don't rush and make sure you get all the information you need." encouraged Mr. Olson.

"Thank you, sir!" shouted Ply as he hopped out of the truck and into his old white jalopy. "I'll see you sometime tomorrow."

Glenn waved the kid off as he passed through the gate to get his harvesting tools ready to work.

* * *

Jack Morgan watched for dust down the long driveway and at eleven-thirty-five the dry road started showing plumes. Liz got some leftovers ready from the fridge and set in in the microwave, so it was hot on the table when Ply came in the door.

"Wow," declared the younger of the three, "Do you know something I don't?

"We do assume that you probably haven't eaten very well in the last six months." quipped his aunt glancing at his thin frame.

"There have been a few times where I have had more than just pizza and cereal, but not much more than a few." he stated remembering the feasts at the Olson's in the last few days.

"So, what brings you out here in such a hurry?" asked his uncle.

"Jack, let the poor kid have something to eat. Look at him! He is half starved to death." interrupted Liz.

"I'm sorry." apologized the elder. "I could at least wait until his mouth was full."

"Please," stated Ply, "Not while I'm drinking." He set down the large glass of raw milk and swallowed. "I am a private detective."

"What?" laughed his Aunt. "Now what have you gotten yourself into?"

"I met this girl..."

"It's about time." blurted the lady.

"Liz," exhorted Jack, "Something has happened, and I think we need to know..."

"When is the wedding?"

"Ahh, we haven't yet decided on a date..."

"There now!" crowed the woman. "I knew it was finally going to happen. What else could be more important?"

"Please sit down, honey, and have a cup of coffee."

"Ply is getting married." she sputtered. "I don't need any more stimulation! What does she look like?"

"Well," started Ply, "She is about your shape and size..."

"Is she rich?" questioned Liz.

"Not that I know of but..."

"Then I'll get my wedding dress." Liz hurried off to the attic.

"You know, Uncle Jack, marriage has been so good for her, being married to you she thinks that I need the same thing."

"I'll take that as a compliment, but she does get excited once in a while. Now, what's going on?"

Ply filled his uncle in on all the info about the robberies. "The guy who owns the farm equipment shop in town, what is he like?"

"Honest as the day is long." replied the gent. If you think he may have anything to do with this caper I surely hope you are mistaken."

"Good." affirmed Ply. "Maybe I could go over there and familiarize myself with what some of this stuff actually looks like. I need to know where serial numbers are on each model, so I don't have to waste time looking if I come across a clue."

"You had training in this?" quipped the gent.
"No, I've just seen you work."
"Why do you waste your time in a cave?"
"Providence, I guess."
"Okay, give me a hand with a few things around here and we can leave by mid-morning tomorrow."
"Let's do it."

At that moment Liz returned with her wedding dress, "I can hardly wait for this to happen Ply. When are you bringing her in for a fitting?"

Jack stood up and gently lifted the dress from her arms. "Honey, I know that you are beside yourself beyond measure about Ply and this young lady he has met but please..."

"Please, what?" she asked excitedly.

"Please don't scare her off by being too helpful."

"How is helping her with a dress being too helpful?"

"We are staying at house of a friend of hers and the friend says that Jane gave up the game due to a broken heart." interjected Ply. "I don't know if she has any money left from playing pro tennis, but she has told me she really isn't good enough to continue in the pro circuit so..."

"So, she will need the dress!" concluded Liz and took back the gown.

"Why don't we wait until she shows up?" said Jack.

"Well, okay." agreed Liz. "I'll try to behave, but that's not a promise, just a mere attempt."

"You ready to do some work?" queued Jack to Ply.

"The poor kid is starving why not let him eat?" quizzed Liz.

"He has had three helpings already!" stated Jack. "If you feed him anymore all he will be able to do is sleep!"

Ply downed the third glass of milk and kissed his aunt on the cheek, "That was delicious. If I lived here, I just might weigh three hundred pounds."

Jack strode, and Ply waddled, out the door.

* * *

Out in the barn Jack had a small vintage tractor apart repairing valves and gaskets. Ply followed instructions while Jack demonstrated how to clean and dress the valves.

"So," invited Jack, "What else can you tell me about this amazing entrance of a woman into your life?"

Ply filled his uncle in on the woman but not the weapon. As if she was not weapon enough without the ancient instrument. "I do think I am hooked."

"Your aunt and I are pleased. How did you meet her?"

"She works at a tennis club."

"You have taken up tennis?"

"Not exactly, or, not fully but it seems that I am learning a lot."

"So how does all this stolen lawn stuff fit into the story?"

"Wow," Ply mused out loud, "I don't think I can say much about that at this point in time."

"Where did you learn all this stuff? It takes a lot of training to be so secretive."

"When I came here in the summers and you were still working on cases you told me all kinds of stuff. I remember you saying, 'If stuff is really important and the less people who know about a case the better it is for all involved'."

The ex-cop glanced over at the youth growing up very quickly and smiled a thankful, contented grin. "Good for you kid!" Turning his head back to the chore at hand he thought to himself, *I guess you're not much of a kid anymore. Man, it happens fast.*

They puttered, cleaned, and assembled in silence for a good while, simply enjoying the presence of each other.

Friday morning they were both up early, did the morning chores together, and were on the road by nine-fifteen.

* * *

Brian Spoudice and Curtis, his younger brother of two years, started a small repair shop of lawn mowers and small electrical appliances while Curtis was in his junior year of high school. It was not long before people from a fair distance brought their needs to be fixed by the 'Spicy' brothers as they came to be referred to. They never got 'Spicy' unless someone had intentionally wronged them. The law was still upheld in that part of the country and there was no room for any of the rebellion outside of a few distant cities.

By the time Brian graduated the family barn was too small for the business and they had to rent a place outside of town. Shortly after Curtis graduated from college, they built a barn and had to add to it within the next twenty-four months. By the end of the eighth year they had purchased land and built a nice business of farm and lawn equipment of the higher end of the spectrum. The people were honest, the land had the blessing, and prosperity seemed to grow quickly.

Ply sat up in the passenger seat as they entered the front gates of the *Spoudice Equipment Complex*. Just inside the gate was a row of sparkling machines not unlike the ones that were missing from the 'land-of-the-richie's' as Mr. Johnson referred to them. He pulled out his phone and checked the pictures only to be soon convinced that these were newer models that were for sale.

Apparently, Ply thought to himself, *once a good design is in use it doesn't need much changing.* The vehicle came to a halt at the corner of the main building giving room for someone to use the roll-up door if the need arose. They both hopped out of the truck and walked over to the service area.

"Good morning, Mr. Morgan." grinned the young man behind the counter. "You're looking well".

"Thank you," stated Jack, "You guys busy?"

"We are busy enough but thankfully not going nuts."

"That is a rare thing. I thought it was usually feast or famine." piped Jack.

"It seems that often it is that way." agreed the attendant.

"Is Brian in?" inquired Morgan.

"Making another big purchase, sir?"

"Not this time, just a friendly visit."

"I'll let him know you are here. Have a seat in the waiting area or have a look around the yard if you like."

The two wandered over to the waiting area and Ply familiarized himself with some of the fliers that were available. *These are nice toys and they were not cheap,* he thought to himself. For a short second he wondered how anyone could ever afford such things but then realized that he was not really into high finance and this was just stuff that was needed for some to do their jobs.

"Hey Jack, wha-cha-up-ta?"

"Good to see you again man!" greeted Jack as he rose when his friend entered. "This is my nephew Ply. He is interested in some of the equipment that you sell."

"Some?" quizzed the owner as he quickly sized up Ply. It didn't usually take long for a man of his experience to recognize if someone was a paying customer. It appeared by the dazed look in the youth's eyes that he was not necessarily accustomed to the gadgets that were in his showroom.

"Can we talk in your office?" inquired Jack.

Glancing to Jack then again at Ply, a little confused, he said, "Sure." Ply gave a polite smile, confusing him even more.

Inside the office Jack got right to the point. "The reason for our visit is that there had been some maintenance material disappear from various ranches a few counties over. I don't think you are in any way involved but this young man needs to familiarize himself with various models and the location of the serial numbers for each machine so when time is of the essence, he won't have to try to find them."

Again, Brian glanced at Ply, *There is the confidence,* he silently concluded.

"I have a list of the missing material and the serial numbers of each item and who is the owner," stated Ply. "Would you like a copy just in case anything shows up?"

"That just might be handy." commented Brian.

"Some of this stuff has been gone for over three years and if it was sold by someone else and traded in on your lot it might present a clue as to where the rest of the stuff is being dealt from." explained Ply as he connected his phone to Brian's computer.

Brian studied the printout.

"They are listed from the most recent to the oldest as far as time missing."

"Good work." observed the businessman. "How long have you been doing P. I. work?"

"Ahh... This is my first case."

"And you're this well organized and come up with all this information? How long have you been on the case?" he queried printing off the list.

"A little over a week and a half." was the reply.

"Good grief! If I ever need a detective, I'll know who to call."

"Thank you but we haven't caught the thieves or retrieved any of the goods yet." Ply stated and then thought to himself, *Perhaps the praise is a little premature.*

Brian was about to set down the list when he snatched it back up again and said, "Hold on. One of these looks familiar. I'll be back in a second."

It was Ply's turn to be surprised at the knowledge of the businessman. In about three minutes he returned with a sales slip for a trade in from someone he had not done business with before.

"I think this might be one on the list. This fella came in about three weeks ago and we gave him a trade." he noted as he handed the invoice to Ply. The young man studied the invoice and did not see anything that concerned him.

"May I have a copy of this on my phone?" asked Ply. "I may have to pay this man a visit, or at least give him a call."

"He said he bought it about three years ago from someone online. It has worked well for him. He just wanted a little newer model, said it was good for business to have a nicer model for all to see."

"Maybe he will tell me who he bought it from. Let me call him now." suggested Ply.

"Let me call him." stated Brian. "I am the one he already knows."

The owner dialed the number and after a few minutes of polite conversation, he thanked the customer and hung up.

"He says he got it from a place called *Integrity Maintenance Machinery* online. It was a good machine and the price was really reasonable, so he went and picked it up himself. That's Alan Johnson's place! I sure hope he is not involved in all this mess. He and I have been on good terms for quite a while."

"Johnson," inquired Ply, "Has he got a cousin named Abe?"

Brian looked at him astonished, "They're brothers! How did you know that?"

"There is a worker named Abe Johnson who is a maintenance man for a few of the ranches in the area of the castle we are staying in. He seems okay but he got himself elected chair of the committee of all those who have lost equipment in the area. He says he has lost two machines from the two places he is working at. He can't find out who is doing all this. There are just no clues whatsoever."

"Is that so?" solicited Brian.

"Wow," commented Jack, "How much are you out?"

"According to this about six hundred dollars, but if it will help you find those rascals, I don't mind the contribution."

"How much would it cost me to rent a machine?" probed Ply.

"What is it you are after?"

"You see what these guys are playing with, what do you have that might be a temptation?"

A sly smile crept across the face of Mr. Spoudice, "Let's catch these rodents with some really nice bait. If I lose the toy the insurance may pay for some of the cost but now that they have incriminated me, I am just as ready to see these guys come to justice as anyone else. Are you pretty sure you can catch them?"

Ply gave a very quiet swallow.

"I have a year-old model that is still brand new. It has a few extras on it, so it has sat around for a while. What say we bait the hook with some tasty carnage?"

"I don't think I could pay for such a toy." informed the sleuth.

"What's this? Getting cold feet already? It is my expense not yours. If this is an honest mistake, fine, but if whoever is involved with this racket tried to get me into some trouble, there will be fireworks."

Ply looked at his uncle with a question in his eye.

Jack's look seemed to say, *This is your idea, are you man enough to go through with it?*

Ply resolved the interrogation with a positive, "Let's do it." That settled the matter but Ply still had one more question. "Excuse me sir, are you able to cross reference these serial numbers to a picture of the machines they represent? I haven't been able to get into the place where I can do that."

"One has to have a franchise to get to that information. You have twelve machines there and it may take a while. Why don't I get one of my girls to search them out, build a file, then I will send it to your phone."

"That, sir, would be most helpful. If I see one that may match, I can cross reference one to the other. Thank you."

"Hey man," agreed Brian. "It looks like we are all in this thing together." They packed the machine on a small trailer and hitched it to the truck.

On the way back to the Morgan farm Ply asked Jack, "Can I

borrow this truck for a few days I don't think I can attach the trailer to my car."

"I don't see why that would be a problem. How soon could you get it back?"

"Is early next week soon enough?"

"Sure. Let me know if anything else comes up?"

'Thank you, sir".

"My pleasure."

They arrived back at the farm about noon. Liz had a meal ready for the three of them. Ply and Jack dove in and Liz pecked at a small portion. By one PM Ply was back on the road headed for the castle. He made one small stop on the way back.

* * *

Ply arrived back at the castle a little before four. Glenn Olson had all of the grass cut and most of it bailed as Ply came up the driveway.

"How'd it go?" shouted Glenn from the top of the bailer.

"Got just what I needed!" exclaimed Ply.

"Wow, that's a beauty. How much did that thing set you back?"

"Let's just say it is on loan till I catch the rascal who has borrowed the other mowers without the owner's permission."

Glenn looked at him with a quizzical wonder.

"Sometimes the Lord provides in ways that actually blow our mind." replied Ply.

Glenn got the picture that no more information about this fancy gadget was coming forth, so he invited, "Can you drive a tractor?"

"I suppose if you give me a few quick lessons."

"Left foot, clutch, right foot, brake, throttle here on the steering wheel, try not to get yourself into too tight a corner seeing the tongue is short on the trailer. Load up the round bales on that wagon tied to the truck and Edith will instruct you on how to load the trailer."

"Sounds simple enough." swallowed Ply.

With all three working, Glen and Edith pulled out about ten minutes before Jane pulled in.

"Wow, the place looks lived in." she beamed.

"Hi. It sure is good to see you. In about ten minutes I'll have this mower put away then we can talk. Oh yeah, I may need a shower."

"Please." she grinned. She parked her car in the garage and took in her suitcase and the food she brought.

After cleaning up Ply opened the door to his room and was slammed in the face with the aroma from the kitchen. "Wow! What smells so good?" he asked, taking the stairs three at a time.

"Hot spaghetti, warm sauce, and steamed garlic bread, when did you have time to do all of this?"

"It only takes twenty minutes to cook spaghetti and I nuked the sauce and the bread, so it would be hot. It has been thirty-five minutes since I drove up and I thought it might work."

"What a delightful surprise," he grinned, "Now it is time for one for you, but first you need to sit down, hold out your hands, palms down. No, no, you have to close your eyes. It's heavy so spread out your fingers."

"Aaaahhhh!" she screamed.

"I'm sorry. I didn't mean to frighten you." he apologized backing off a little.

That just gave her more room to maneuver. She jumped up, threw her arms around his neck and started to squeeze, all the while trying to plant her lips on his.

"I'm sorry it's so small but if I win the reward money then I will get you a bigger one."

The ring was a small diamond with three rubies around it in a gentle twenty-four karat gold setting.

"I promise I'll never wear any other ring but this one."

"Well, that's fine for now." he agreed. She hugged him and stared at the rocks.

"Ahh, you're not making this any easier." he announced.

"Oh, sorry. I guess we better start making some plans, huh?"

"I really don't know what to do so clue me in."

"Okay," she smiled, "We need a great big wedding... with the whole world invited. Yeah, I think Barb will be thrilled so we can have it here."

"Heh...heh...here?", he stammered. "Won't that be expensive? Remember, I used to work in a cave."

"I don't expect Barb will charge us much, besides I made a little playing in the circuit, so I can help in a few things."

"Oh."

"Okay," she glowed, "That's settled, now what's your surprise?"

"My surprise? Do I have another surprise?"

"I sure hope so. I saw those expensive gadgets parked in the garage. There must be a story behind that. If there isn't, there sure will be!"

"Oh yea, ah... that!" he stammered. "It is a bit of a long story, so we better sit down and eat."

"How did you get all that grass cut and get the new mower cleaned up so quickly?"

"Monday, I did some whipping and thought I could use the sword to cut the grass. I could have had the entire yard done in about eight hours my time but only ten minutes real time, but what would I do with all the tall grass laying around? Then, what if someone came along while I was chopping the grass with the sword. It might look like the grass was falling down in waves at a very fast rate. The owner is going to have a hard enough time selling this place as it is. We don't want the rumor going around that the place is haunted!"

Ply twirled a fork-full of spaghetti on his plate.

"I met a gentleman named Glenn Olson at the Monday night meeting and helped him for a few days with some chores at this place and he jumped at the chance for some free feed for his animals. He left just before you pulled in."

"So that is what all that farm equipment was on the road for. Was all that big stuff here on the property?"

"It sure was." he replied. "He got it cut, baled, and loaded on the trailer in less than two days."

"So, if he is so willing to feed his animals with free food why do you have that new machine?"

"You noticed that the place looked lived in. I couldn't cut grass that tall no matter how big a mower I rented, but Mr. Olson had one he was willing to use for free." Ply stuffed another fork-full of dinner into the front hatch and swallowed just barely chewing. Jane held her gaze on him and tried not to register the shock of being engaged to a vacuum.

"He cut the grass at about five inches so all I need to do is trim it with the new mower and the place will look as good as new."

They sat, talked, and ate for about an hour.

She kept interrupting, but he was patient and finally he ended with, "Abe Johnson was not too happy with me taking all the serial numbers and model numbers and addresses of people who lost their toys."

"Oh yeah?"

"The man who came to see me about the missing stuff was Abe Johnson..."

"I remember." she said.

"The name on the receipt of the traded in machine was not Johnson but it was purchased from a place called *Integrity Maintenance Machinery.*

"Okay?"

"And a gentleman named Al Johnson owns the shop and the two are brothers."

She sat back on her chair for a second then asked, "So when do we go?"

"As soon as the new toy gets stolen."

"You're going to let him steal it?"

"That's what Mr. Spoudice said needs to happen."

That eyebrow...

"Since he is now incriminated with stolen goods, he is ready to catch the rats, so he offered a nicely baited trap."

"But what if he never gets it back?"

"He's ready to take that risk."

"Is he filthy rich?"

"Probably not any richer than a tennis star." he muttered glancing around the room. Again, the eyebrow but this time it was a little different.

I wonder how much he knows? she pondered.

* * *

"Have we got time for a little game?"

"A game of...?"

"Tennis, what else?" she responded.

"I thought you gave it up."

"I did, but only for a while."

"You said you were not good enough to play professionally."

"Let's just volley a little. You make me run a bit with your magic sword but be gentle. You know just enough to boost my game but not severe enough to crush my ego... totally." she exhorted looking away trying to hide a pained look.

"Is there more to this story that I haven't yet heard?" he interrogated.

"There is." she replied looking back to him with a widening grin.

"Do I ever get to hear it?"

"In time." she cooed.

"Do you need to warm up?"

"I could be ready in twenty minutes."

"That makes just about one hour after we have eaten." he observed.

"Very good," she encouraged, "Don't do any strenuous exercise until about an hour after a big meal."

"Spaghetti is a big meal?" he voiced.

"With as much as you ate, of course." she giggled kissing him just above the ear as she went up to change into her exercise clothes.

"That sounds like a challenge." he noted. "I'll take it"

"In about forty minutes of play she was soaked and said, "My turn for the 'magic'."

"How is you playing with the blade going to improve your game?"

"If I can speed myself up, I can see just how the ball moves. If I can hold the toy and a racket I can play and improve my shot and my return. My big problem is I have no one who is really good to play against."

He 'served' the ball to her and she gave him some pointers. It took some time, but he did learn, a little. "Can we do some of this in the morning? I have spent the day traveling and working on the yard and I'm pooped."

"Yeah," she agreed, "It might be time to cool off and get some sleep. What do you have planned for the morning?"

"Obviously a lot more tennis." he joked.

"Does it bore you?" she quizzed.

"Not in the least."

"Good." she beamed. "I'll see you here at nine sharp, complete with apparatus and we will do some more practice. I need to do some running first. It just may be time to get this thing going again."

"There is a lot more to this story." he muttered.

"There sure is." she said her eyes twinkling.

* * *

The practice the next morning went as before. Jane got hot and sweaty and Ply quietly danced around, until she got to playing with her racket and the sword. She did not cool down a lot, but he was running until he got to the place where he just let the balls go.

"Okay," she announced, "It's cool down time." He packed the instrument into its case, she wiped the racket and set it out to dry then the jogged around the property a few times.

"It seems to me that you are a lot better at this than you are willing to admit." accused Ply in a gentle tone. "Am I in enough to get a little more history?"

"Yes." she smiled. It certainly is time. I had to test myself to see if I still had the 'knack'." she quoted. "I think with a little more practice I may be able to get back into the circuit."

"You want to play again?"

"No." she stated flatly. "I want to play still. Here is the story. You remember the Maserati?"

* * *

Vroooom, the engine roared and the tires squeaked as they flew around the corner. The vehicle seemed glued to the pavement. She laughed and was falling marvelously in love. They both were playing the game and the stakes seemed to be high and exciting. Both were winning but the match against each other had not yet happened. Lots of money had been won by each and they were both riding the crest of the wave of life.

"At the end of the season it was me against him."

"What season?" questioned Ply.

"Well, it wasn't Wimbledon. That would have been a year down the road." she informed him. A quick look and she said, "You're getting an eyebrow!"

"One year away from Wimbledon deserves the eyebrow, or maybe even two." he proclaimed in astonishment.

"Every time I beat him, he would become a little more aloof." she continued.

"If he won, he was high and fun but if he lost, he would crawl into himself and hide. We had each won two games and the final of the tournament was upon us. At the end of the tournament I had won the four of six. He did not 'hop over the net', instead..."

Her speech slowed, and the pitch of her voice rose just a bit, "On camera and in front of thousands of spectators, he smashed his racket against the net post and destroyed a thousand-dollar tool as he shouted to me..."

It had been almost three years, so the hurt was not as severe, but she had never before confessed to anyone,

"He said to me..." she repeated as the tears of lost love and the reality of his idolatry showed itself to her once again, "He said, 'Listen Bitch... I win... all the time... every time'."

There, she had said it, and Ply gently held her in his arms as she sobbed over the loss but rejoiced in finding out before it was horribly too late.

"I gave up." she stated as she backed off a little from his embrace. "Not only on him but the game and almost on life itself. After the awards and the crowd had dispersed, I locked the trophy in my locker and went for a long walk. I wanted to cry it out, but it just did not seem to want to come. The hurt and the crash of the infatuation of the broken heart and the empty promise of winning hung around like a vulture waiting for breakfast. The down after winning the tournament and the down from losing a relationship just seemed like life was not worth living...

"There was no sidewalk. I was walking beside the road and a bus was coming. It would be so easy to just slide under the wheels. I think the driver knew how I was feeling because he had his foot off the gas and was gently pumping the break so if he needed to stop very suddenly, he might have a chance. I could see his face of concern but not of total fear, but I thought he looked worried. Then I thought, 'Maybe God has something for me'.

"When you showed up at the tennis courts, I felt my heart skip just like it had in the past and I said to myself, 'Whoa girl, don't let THIS happen again' but there was something mysterious about you that attracted me. When I found you cowering in the corner with the all those balls in the air..." she giggled a little as he wiped a tear from her eye, "I wanted to cuddle you like a hurt child but again I had to control myself. Last weekend you gave me a proposal but no ring and all this past week I have been thinking if it would be worth the risk. I hated the pain. I remembered the time you protected me and then did not want anything in return. I was so confused. Then you gave me the ring and I thought I just might get my game back also. Did you ever think that sometimes someone up there really loves us and wants the best for us?"

Gasp, beautiful smart girls really make things complicated, he thought.

"How about a nice warm shower and then some lunch?" he invited.

"A shower?" she inquired with eyes wide in astonishment.

"Separate showers." he corrected.

"Can we go somewhere for lunch." she coaxed as they headed for the stairs.

"I am just about out of money. When we find these crooks, we might have some reward money, but I really need to watch my pennies."

"Let's go to the cafe in town. I have a few bucks in my pocket. If it cuts into your pride, then you can pay." she coaxed and handed him a one hundred dollar note.

He looked at her somewhat bewildered. She reached up and kissed him on the cheek. "Don't get heady about it. We can talk money a little later. If I get my game back, money may not be a problem for a while."

"There is one other thing." announced Ply fondling the one-hundred-dollar bill.

"What is that?"

"Now that we are engaged and there is no one here but us it is going to look pretty suspicious to some about our romantic activity..."

"If you make one false move, I'll...", she started to say.

"Let's review." he interrupted. "Two people of the opposite sex, in a great big house, a million miles from nowhere, madly in love can only lead to mistakes that happen naturally. I need to find a place in town to sleep at night. Love is not just a desire to spent time with each other and when you kissed me, I figured it was time to do some preventive therapy, like not be so close to you at night."

"My door is locked, and I don't want to spend the night here in this great big place all alone." she stated.

"Let's go to lunch, we can talk about it there." he offered.

The ten-minute drive into town was quiet. The back booth was empty, and they slid in opposite each other, greeted the waitress politely, ordered sodas and water, then told the girl they needed some time to make choices from the menu.

Ply was starved as usual, but Jane had lost most of her appetite with the news of having to stay alone in the castle. Nice as it was, she did not like the creaks of the furnace and fridge and the groans of the building settling at night. With Ply there she felt safe and secure but with him gone... she did not want to stay alone.

Ply was ready to order but Jane just sat there staring at the menu until someone quietly slid in beside her.

"Barb?" staggered Jane. "What happened? Why are you back so soon?"

"Aren't you going to introduce me to your 'friend'?", she stated as she noticed the rocks on her finger.

The ring looked good on the slender finger of her friend.

What would it be like being engaged? thought Barb. *The right man, the right place.*

A glance at Ply and reality quickly settled in. *It would have to be the right guy!*

"Ah, Barb this is Ply Gallant. Ply this is Barb Cully, the owner of the castle."

"Barb? The owner?" was all that managed to stumble from his lips.

"Yes, the owner." replied Barb. "And it is not a castle, it is just a summer workhouse I got a little carried away with on the construction."

"Why are you back so soon and how did you know we were here?" asked Jane.

"When you called about wanting to use the court, I figured something drastic had happened. I wondered if you even wanted to get back into playing. I was so excited I lost my concentration and was eliminated so I get to hang around a bit. Judging by the rock on your finger you two just may need a chaperon so I thought I'd surprise you and show up just to make sure the two love-birds don't get into a compromising position before the wedding. At the top of the hill about a mile before the driveway I noticed a car pull out and followed you here. I'm free, you guys are madly in love, so I can help until the wedding."

Jane threw her arms around the pro and kissed her on the cheek. "Thank you! Thank you!" she cried complete with tears. "We were just discussing where Ply would stay because things are getting a little too comfortable between us and I did not want to stay in that great big place all by myself but if you are here then I won't have to."

Ply got the waitress's attention, "We need another menu and what would you like to drink, Barb? May I call you Barb?"

Jane's appetite returned with a vengeance, grabbing the menu she turned to the dinners.

Barb ordered a water and when the waitress returned to take orders Jane blurted, "I'll have the salmon with a baked potato, green beans, peas, and carrots, and a full buffet." Looking up she noticed the looks of the other two. "I'm sorry but all this practicing has made me hungry."

"And you sir?" invited the waitress.

"Is there something you would like?" he asked Barb.

Barb looked at the waitress in a knowing fashion, "Hi Sue, good to see you again, I'll have my regular for this hour."

Sue returned her gaze to Ply. "I'll have the double cheeseburger and large fries... and on the burger... mustard, relish, ketchup, onions, lettuce, and salt and pepper."

"There is ketchup and salt and pepper on the table." pointed Sue to the tray by the wall of the booth then left to fill the orders.

"That is half a pound of red meat!" exclaimed Jane.

"I've been working hard too." said Ply. "Cutting grass, learning to play tennis, falling in love. I got to keep up my energy for all this stuff." he excused as he set the menu on the table.

"Is he like this all the time?" asked Barb to Jane trying to defuse the situation. The two girls laughed, and Ply took a sip of his soda.

"So," Barb teased looking at Ply, "You must be getting pretty good if you are improving the game of this one." she nodded towards Jane.

The third sip stopped halfway to the mouth. "Didn't she tell you about the wrong bat I used at the courts?" he stated.

"Oh really? Then you have improved! See what happens when you have a good teacher?" Barb beamed and glanced at Jane who was a little wide-eyed herself. "Seeing I lost the last four sets I have played I may need some encouragement. But it is not all about me. The reason I am here is to find out about this lady beside me. Are you preparing to get back in the game?"

"I was thinking about it, but I really need about six months to get back into shape. Ply is a fast learner and has helped me in a lot of areas but with you here I suppose we can find out pretty quickly how long it will take me to get ready."

"How long have you been playing?" the pro asked Ply.

"I met Jane at the courts about six months ago." he replied trying to avoid the question.

"That's not what I asked!"

"I'm still working at the courts." interrupted Jane trying to rescue her beau from being trounced by her friend.

"When I first met him, he was playing with a racket ball bat! Can you imagine? Cowering in the corner from a tennis ball thrower."

"With the way I feel I may need someone of his ability to reboot mine. What say we have a little spar after lunch?"

Ply closed his mouth and set his drink back on the table.

"Come on, Barb," encouraged Jane, "You're a pro and he has been playing for six weeks. Are you really that distracted and down?"

"I'm just teasing the poor guy. It really is you I want to play. You were practically undefeated in the circuit and working your way to the top. I want to see how far you have fallen and what it will take to get you back. How much have you played in these last couple of years?"

"I've been running four or five times a week and had a chance to play with a few who are fairly good. I've thrown a lot of games to encourage some into the circuit." she glanced at Ply to see if he would remember her 'story'. "But until now I've not been ready to do too much." replied the younger woman.

Barb looked at Ply as if sizing him up for the task. "So," she coaxed Ply, "What is it you do for a living?"

"My last job I was doing tours in the largest cave in the continent." he proudly said trying to impress her.

"A cave tour guide?" Barb responded with a startled look in

Jane's direction.

"We all have our little secrets my dear." rebuked Jane with a saucy look.

"Secrets?" she returned.

"Let's see how I do at the game this afternoon." Jane teased, anxious to find out for herself the extent of her abilities.

"I can hardly wait." replied the owner.

The food was delivered, and Ply slowly pecked at his hamburger and nibbled on the fries. The waitress brought the salmon for Jane and French toast for Barb and the three ate in somewhat awkward but expected silence. Barb was the one who was excited. Almost too anxious to see how Jane would fare on the court.

* * *

Ply was finished first and quietly excused himself. "I need to wash my hands." and slipped out of the booth. When he returned the girls were finished and arguing over who was going to pay the bill.

"Don't fret ladies I already got it!"

Both their looks seemed to say, "You rascal!"

The ride back to the castle was again, rather quiet. The girls prepped for the match.

On the way downstairs Barb commented to Ply, "Jane tells me you are getting good." she teased looking at Ply.

"How often does surprise and excitement get in the way while you are playing the circuit?" he questioned trying to diffuse Barb's interrogation.

"Every time you get on board a plane," declared Jane, "You just might like it, but you never get used to it."

Barb nodded her head in agreement. "Now that I'm warmed up, I guess you are first to beat the road runner." she teased glancing at Ply.

"Not till an hour after a big meal." he informed her hoping to spare his life for a little longer.

"Great." she announced. "We can sit on the couch and discuss what has been happening around here. The place looks wonderful, but it appears that the guy I had hired finked out on the job."

"You hired someone to do the yard work and they did not do

it?" questioned Ply.

"Yeah." snorted the owner in a rather disgusted tone. "So, I guess I get to pay you two instead."

"Ply did all the work." stated Jane dismissing herself from the embarrassment that she figured might be on its way.

Barb pulled out a small purse from a hidden corner in her handbag and counted out ten one-hundred-dollar bills and dropped them into Ply's lap. Jane tried to hide the grin, but it came out a knowing smirk.

"I have been living here for two weeks. The rent must be at least this much." blurted Ply as he scooped up the money and set it gently back on her handbag.

"Jane is my friend and apparently, by the rock on her finger, you must be a friend of hers, and friends don't charge friends who are here to help." stated the owner and plopped the cash back in Ply's lap.

"Then if I'm a friend why do I have to get paid?" he retorted with the return of the payment.

The three looked at each other for a few long seconds wondering what was going to happen next.

"Okay," surrendered Barb. "You win this round." she gathered up the currency. Jane was fully enjoying the bantering and had little trouble hiding her mirth until Barb stated, "From now on you are my personal indentured grounds keeper until you can beat me in a tennis set."

Jane met his gaze and slowly and quietly shook her head.

"And this is your first payment." demanded his new boss and dumped the dough back into his lap.

Ply was beaten, and it appeared he also had a new job. It sure paid a lot better than the last one!

* * *

On the court Ply got to face the star. She was gentle, at first, then she started to return her serves cranked up a few notches. He was able to get some of them until she poured on the steam. Ply was getting tired and finally just let the balls whiz past him.

"Okay," rescued Jane, "My turn for the torture." Ply could have kissed her, but the public display of affection did not seem appropriate at the moment.

"Thank you." he whispered as she came on to the court. He blew her a kiss and she accepted the gesture with a thank you from her eyes.

"How long you been playing kid?" barked Barb as he left the court.

"Only a couple of months but I've had some opportunity to get to know some of the game." was his reply. The lead player watched the amateur leave the court wondering about the edge he might have.

Jane shouted, "Ready", and the star refocused and served the ball. It was returned very quickly to the far side of the court as Barb stared at the lost point as the ball bounced against the clay then against the wall and meandered across the court.

"I guess I'm not playing Ply anymore." she admitted, retrieved the spongy sphere and was back into competition mode.

It was a tight game, but Jane managed to squeak ahead and gain the match.

They switched ends, serves, and played another game. This time Barb took the honor of the game, but it was time to see what happened when Jane was pushed to the limit. They played for the rest of the afternoon and Jane won in the set four to two.

"Let's break for a drink and a walk." stated the winner.

Barb just stared at the two. She was not angry but very much pleased and surprised. They all paced around the property to cool down.

"So, what is this secret of yours that tones up a greenhorn in one month and beats a professional when she returns from a championship?"

"What do you mean?" led Ply not wanting to reveal any secrets.

"I've been playing for eight years and I'm pretty much at the 'top of my game' so to speak. I get home to someone who quits the game of tennis two and a half years ago, and almost quits life, and she beats me, not just in the first game but in an entire set. What's the catch?"

The two remained silent for a few long minutes then Barb broke in once more. She turned to Ply and demanded in a tone that was half rejoicing and the other half very threatening, "This girl was on her way to Wimbledon and some arrogant idiot broke her heart and almost killed her by being so self-centered, it made everyone else sick and very angry. It seems that she is in love again and has her game back. If you as much as even entertain the thought of dumping this precious lady for anyone that might appeal to your lower nature, I promise you, I will personally hunt you down and take that arrogant little head of yours off with this very racket!"

Jane had stopped, and Barb turned around and hugged her opponent and cried on her shoulder. The emotional outburst was not really necessary, but it exhausted the pro. All of the tension of the past months of games and the relief of a fellow player getting back to what she was made for reduced her to a pile of mush. She reached over and brought Ply into the embrace and kissed him on the cheek. "I have never been so happy to lose in all my life." she exulted. "Thank you, thank you, thank you!" she shouted to the sky. "Now let's get cleaned up. I have some papers for Jane to sign."

* * *

An hour and a half later, Barb glided down the stairs, whistling a nondescript tune that Jane had heard before but couldn't quite place. A large ancient butternut double-decked secretary with cupped doors stood to one side of the library. Barb dropped the leaf and plopped some papers on the piece of ancient furniture.

"Miss Janie!" she announced in a boisterous gleeful tone.

Ply and Jane walked into the room. Jane knew what was on the mind of her friend, but as usual Ply was clueless to the plans of the ladies.

"You, my dear," announced the champion, "Are going to France."

"Come on Barb isn't this a little early? It is only a month away. How will I ever get into shape? Besides, I have a job and plans of my own."

"Jane, my delightful friend, I know talent when I see it. We have an entire month to get you ready. If I knew the secret of what you two have been up to I could have you ready in a week but a month with the old horse will have to do."

"Are you calling my wife to be an old horse?" blurted Ply.

"No sir, I am the old horse. Did you see her out there? On her first volley she beat the pants off of me. Do you know how many people have been waiting for this girl to get her game back? And I am the first to know, and when everyone else in the circuit sees her back in the game, there will be standing ovations across the globe."

"Barb!" interjected the younger.

"I'm serious. You didn't hear the comments that came out after you trounced that monstrous scoundrel. Look here," Barb opened one of the folders she brought down from her room, "I figured this might happen someday, so I saved the clippings from all the papers and magazines I could find."

The Paris Gazette:
"Young upstart trounces beau and gets a racket too close for comfort."

Tennis Magazine:
"Princess beats her prince only to see his fury unleashed."

Sports Illustrated:
"Young beauty crushes her fiancé only to have her own heart crushed by the reality of his arrogance."

The New York Times:
"Lady Jane slays the Dragon only to have her own heart slain by his majesties distemper."

"Look," invited Barb to Ply, "There are dozens of articles here about the match and the disappearance of 'Jane of Ark'. She had such a signature swing that is what some of them called her."

"You never told me!" questioned Ply.

Jane walked over and gently rested her arms on his shoulders and clasped her hands behind his neck, "What would you have done if I told you of all the stardom that was there and all I needed was someone to love me and support me and we could take care of each other?" she revealed.

"I guess I would have run like the wind."

"So now that you know, are you ready to run?" she cajoled and locked her elbows around his neck a little tighter.

This time he did not just think it but muttered to himself so they both could hear, "Man," he breathed, "Beautiful, smart, rich, talented girls sure make things complicated."

"Okay." chimed Jane dropping the embrace. "One can't just go do the Roland Garros without all the preliminary games. How am I going to get in?"

"Already done." chirped the star.

"I called the organizers and they said it was highly unlikely that anyone could ever be placed in a running tournament like the Garros without going through the ranks. I told them I was very aware of the fact but when I mentioned your name, they paused then I told them that you just trounced me on the court they called the rest of the organizers and asked if they would play you on one of the off courts. They confirmed the schedule and told me to fax the papers to them tonight, so they can advertise in the morning, sign here."

She handed to papers to the astounded girl. "We also have to make reservations tonight at the 'Hotel Eurostars Angli' otherwise there will not be room in all of Paris..."

"Oh, come on Barb. It's not that big a deal!"

"These aren't my words, honey. The organizers are so excited about getting you back on the court they made the prophecy! So, when are you two tying the knot?"

"We haven't decided on a date."

"What? No date?" exclaimed Barb. "I suppose no date, no location, no dress, no plans, no list of attendees, no..."

"We were wondering if we could have it here?" informed Ply.

"What? Here?" flabbergasted the older. "In this dump? It's a million miles from nowhere. You can't get married here! I won't have it."

Ply was crestfallen. "I thought you'd be thrilled to have your friend get married at your castle."

"When do you want to do this?" asked Barb.

"I was thinking a couple of months but now it looks as if I am getting involved in other things." stated Jane.

"I was hoping tonight." disclosed the gentleman.

They both looked at him with mouths open then to each other and laughed right out loud.

"If you get back into the circuit, I don't want to lose you to some other Maserati."

This brought the girls more outbursts of mirth. "No such opportunity." laughed Barb. "If this girl plays like she did today in half the games in the circuit, there won't be any Maserati's coming around to get beaten."

"Why not tie the knot in Paris?" invited the older.

"P-Pa... Paris?" stammered the groom-to-be. "Paris, Missouri? I don't know of anyone who lives there, and I used to work in a cave. I'll have to get my folks a hotel and..."

The girls looked at him in astonishment again with mouths and eyes wide.

"My dad just retired, and he worked in a factory all his life. How is he going to pay for a wedding in Missouri? Isn't Paris, Missouri a little farther off the beaten path that his place?"

This was too much. The ladies couldn't handle the situation any longer. Their sides hurt. Their cheeks hurt. Their mascara was blotchy. Finally, Ply left the two to figure things out and said, "I'm going out to cut the grass."

Fifteen minutes later Jane came into the kitchen, eyes still red from the previous scene to find Ply on his cell phone talking to...

"Yes, sir it's gone... I think it was there yesterday, but I haven't cut the grass for a few days and when I went out to do a little mowing, the lock was cut, and it was not there."

"Somebody stole the new mower?" gasped the girl.

Ply nodded his head and Jane darted up the stairs to inform Barb.

The Stolen Mower

The two came quickly into the kitchen where Ply was making a sandwich while still on the phone.

"Who are you talking to?" demanded Jane.

"How much was it worth?" questioned Barb thinking she was responsible.

Ply waved them both off and told the phone, "Hang on a sec. Look, ladies, I have business that I have to do."

Looking at Barb he stated, "Jane knows what is going on. Let her inform you on what has happened with the lawn mowers. It's okay." encouraged Ply. "There is a homing device within the computer of the machine. It takes coordinates from the GPS every three minutes. Brian Spoudice can tell exactly where it is at this moment, and for the past moments, ever since we have had it. All we have to do is go to Spoudice's place, download the info onto my phone and we can follow wherever this toy is taken", and returned to the call.

The ladies retreated to the sofa and in about five minutes Ply returned. "Jane do you have anything that might consist of an all-black outfit?"

"I am NOT getting married in black!" she announced.

"You are absolutely right. You are going to have the most beautiful snow-white wedding dress with a fifteen-foot train and five flower girls throwing rose and tulip pedals so anyone with allergies within a thousand-foot radius will sneeze their heads off. You are right. You are not wearing black on our wedding day. Today we are going to see if we can catch those crooks."

"I'm going with you!" proclaimed Barb. "If I find out who those rats are, I'll... I'll..."

The other two looked at each other, then at the angry woman. Finally, Ply stated, "Do you have a couple of video cameras?"

"Yeah?" she responded.

"You'll need one to guard the front and one to guard the back and one for the maintenance shed." informed Ply. "Try to keep them hidden. If I were any better at this, I would have had them in place before, but it seems that once in a while I, or we..." he glanced at the girls, "get a little sidetracked."

"So, I'm going to sit here and miss all the fun?" gripped Barb.

"First of all, you're not going to get bored by being here. Secondly, we need someone here so when the place looks empty you might catch some action. But I would like the action to be on camera and not on your person. Can you stay low, so no one sees you?"

"I can do that." she grinned.

"Good. We need all the evidence we can get cause if we can put these guys away, I want it to be for a very long time."

"Any idea of who might be involved in all of this?" asked Barb.

"It appears that a man by the name of Abe Johnson just might promote himself to lead suspect."

"Oh really? That just happens to be the gentleman who I need to talk to about not getting my yard maintained."

"A little more incriminating evidence." stated Ply. "If you can get him to come over and fix the fence then you can have a discussion about what has happened in the last months and why the property was not kept up. But only after he has fixed the fence."

"Sounds like fun to me!" agreed the star.

"The black outfit is so you won't be so visible at night." Ply informed his love. "Pack up for a few days. We will leave in the morning."

"Why didn't I think of that?" she muttered.

"By the way," butted in Barb, "Just where are you two sleeping?"

Jane and Ply looked at each other somewhat confused at the accusation. "Across the hall from each other." responded Jane.

"Since I'm the chaperon, that's too close! Now that I'm here I can protect you. There are silent alarms I can set all over the house and nobody will get in or if they do get in, they will not be able to get out." With hands on hips she informed the two, "One sleep at one end of the hall and the other at the other. There will be no midnight dancing between rooms after eleven and no sneaking to the kitchen before six. There are microwaves and fridges in each room so if you are 'starving to death' take a snack to your room!"

"Why all the commotion?" sputtered Jane.

"With this rebellion going on I don't want any incrimination evidence that you two couldn't wait until you were married. Living alone here provides just such an accusation to be brought forth and I don't want your reputations to be tarnished."

"Isn't that a little extreme?" said Ply.

"It most certainly is. You two have behaved yourselves perfectly but by being here alone you allow others to accuse you of wrongdoing and make the temptation too easy to fulfill. Remember," said Barb, "He wanted to get married tonight!"

They all laughed and the two moved their things to the opposite end of the hallway.

"Jane needs to meet my uncle, so we will be leaving in the morning." announced Ply. "Have a bag ready for a few days on a farm."

"Ah," she stammered. "What kind of farm? Are there pigs?"

"No pigs, but a heard of cows and a few dogs... And lots of very productive land."

Ply was up again at six and got breakfast ready for the girls. He found the thirty-two-ounce plastic cup that he had been using for his early 'snack' of cereal and milk and filled them to the prescribed levels. He was reading a book when Barb showed up somewhat sweaty and her hair tussled. "What happened to you?"

"I've been practicing my serves out on the court." she responded. "It sure is nice to get back to a place where things are familiar. Part of the game is how one responds to different courts. It makes it so much easier when you get to one you are familiar with."

Ply heard movement upstairs. "I'm making breakfast for when you guys get out of bed, but I guess you are already up." he sheepishly admitted. "I'll have this ready in about twenty minutes." he said as he got stuff going on the stove-top.

"Great!" quipped Barb. "That will give me just enough time to get cleaned up."

The two came down the stairs together to the odor of toast, bacon, and eggs. "Wow," exclaimed the professional, "Where did you find this one?"

"I think I found him in the tall grass when he walked into the courts asking to use a thrower." she teased.

Breakfast was served, and they chatted about the things Barb saw while touring. Jane knew much of what the routine was, but Ply sat there, ears tingling and astonished at the common place attitude of the women over the opportunity to travel to so many historic and exotic locations.

Shortly after breakfast the two were on the road to 'Uncle Jacks place'.

* * *

"Wow." stated Jane as they drove through the front gate. "This sure is a nice place."

"You probably won't have to worry about my uncle, but my aunt is practically beside herself about the plans we are making." Ply informed her. "Do you want to have your ear talked off or do you want to see the info that we need about the mowers?"

"It seems easy to say 'mowers', but I should be polite."

"You two are about the same size. She might want you to try on her wedding dress." suggested Ply. "She is helpful to so many seeing that they obviously have some money, but you can tell her what you need too. I know you will handle the situation properly. She knows I am as poor as a church mouse and they do not know about the toy and I did not know about your professional tennis until a few days ago so they may think you will be unable to do much financially. They really are terrific people but sometimes they may need to understand that charity is not what we are here for."

"I think we will get along just fine." announced the young lady. "We can talk on the way to wherever, but you just get what you need. We have to catch up to those crooks."

Ply headed for the barn and Jane walked towards the house.

That must be Mrs. Morgan, she thought.

"Hi," greeted the slender lady, "I'm Mrs. Morgan but you can call me Liz."

"Good morning." replied the younger. "My name is Jane Blythwood."

"How are plans coming along?" asked the elder.

"Plans?"

"Ply says you are getting married."

"We haven't got a date yet, but I think we have a choice of two places."

"How can you have a place without a date?" asked the older.

"We might get married in a friend's castle or tie the knot in Paris, France."

Liz stopped in her tracks and a questioning look flashed across her face. "What does your dad do?"

"My dad? He was a carpenter. He has roughed in houses for almost forty years but has developed some arthritis, so he is retired." teased Jane.

"So where are you going to get the money to get married in Paris? quizzed Liz.

"Can we talk?" invited Jane.

The two women looked at each other for a moment. Liz was in a stylish navy-blue pant suit with two-inch heels and Jane in jeans, a high cut blouse, and sneakers. "Do you have any coffee?" asked the casually dressed one.

Liz snapped out of the daze and said, "Yeah, let's go to the kitchen."

The drink was percolating, and Jane informed the Mrs. of some of her past. "I am a professional tennis player. I have applied to play in France next month and the friend who owns the castle says I should have no problem winning."

"This castle is owned by your friend?" wondered the elder out loud.

"Well, yes. I think it is money not spent in the wisest fashion, but it is her money and it is all paid for, so it might be fun to get married there but Ply seems a little anxious to catch the thieves. The poor guy is penniless, but he does know I have some but not exactly how much. He seems to think that he needs to provide for me but unless something miraculous happens I don't think he need worry."

"Oh!" muttered Liz. "I was really hoping I could help. Is there nothing I could do?"

"Look," said Jane in a pleasant but not condescending tone, "I have enough money I could buy two farms not unlike this one and still have lots left over. If I win in France it would double my assets. Why not just come and enjoy all the festivities?"

"I never thought Ply would marry into money."

"He isn't marrying me for the money." laughed Jane. "He's marrying me because I'm just about as crazy as he is, and we are both crazy about each other. I don't expect you married Jack for his money so why should Ply do such a thing? Money comes, and money goes. Let's be thankful for the abilities we have and how Providence has treated us and go from there. If a time comes where we need your help in any manner, we will not hesitate to ask but at the moment we are fine and wonderfully in love, just like you and Jack."

This maturity took Liz back a bit.

"And besides", remarked Jane. "I think the guy is brilliant."

"Ply?" disputed his aunt. "Brilliant?" She questioned aloud and thought, *What have I missed?*

"How often have you seen him?"

"He was here just last week but it has been a while since then. Doesn't he work in a cave as a guide?"

"Not anymore." proclaimed the bride to be. "I'll need some help with my bookkeeping. And he is employed as a ground's keeper at the moment with the lady who owns the castle, so he really isn't hurting."

"Is he good enough for that?"

"He can cut grass and add and subtract and I expect when he finds out what I'll pay him he just may jump at the chance. Besides, he has a crime to solve. That is why he is talking to your husband."

They looked at each other for a minute then Liz said, "Wow."

"Fun, huh?" grinned the guest.

There was a pause for a moment and Jane sipped her coffee then invited, "Ply says that you still have your wedding dress. Can I see it? I may need some ideas on what to do with mine."

This brought the two of them into the excitement of the upcoming ceremony and Liz responded, "Oh yes, it's upstairs. I had it out the other day when I heard about the plans." and off she rushed to fetch it.

* * *

"Spoudice Equipment Complex. This is Brian speaking."

(Pause)

"Hey Jack, what's new?"

(Pause, not as long as the first)

"Stolen? Already? This is just great. I sure hope Ply got the grass cut."

(Pause)

"I'm looking right now to see if it got unloaded anywhere."

(Another pause)

"It looks like it got loaded into a covered truck about a quarter mile from the property where it was and taken somewhere. I won't know where it is until they unload it and give it three minutes to re-establish communication with the satellite."

(Pause)

"Ply is there with his fiancé?"

(Pause)

"Rather than just wait why not bring the herd over and we can have lunch at McGowan's. Things are a little quiet here, but everybody has work to do. I can escape for a few hours. Let me load the program on to my phone and I will keep my eyes open while we eat and yak?"

(Pause)

"A tennis star?"

(Pause)

"Great we'll see you at one."

Brian hung up the phone, loaded the program unto his phone, told his brother what was going on, and headed for the door.

"Lucky skunk!" gripped the younger Spoudice.

"I've been following tennis for ten years. I wonder who the star is that this kid's going to marry?"

He looked at his desk, sorted the immediate from the necessary, made three phone calls, and within twenty-five minutes after his brother walked out the door, he was headed for the restaurant.

Curtis arrived about one-thirty. The only one finished eating was Ply. Brian looked up and said, "Curtis, how did you manage to escape?"

"I heard there was going to be a tennis star here and I wanted to meet her. I have been following the game for about ten years and I could not imagine who this kid could have lured into his clutches."

Brian was about to make introductions when Curtis interrupted, "Hang on let me see if I can spot the famous one." Jane bowed her head but not soon enough for Curtis to catch her eye.

That face? thought Curtis. *What is so familiar about her?* Mentally he flashed through those in the game at the moment, but nothing was recognizable.

Ply nibbled from his aunt's plate.

Curtis tried going back into last year's games, but nothing was coming up. Finally, it hit him.

"Jane Blythwood!" he shouted with a gasp. "Where have you

been hiding for all these years?"

There was silence for a moment as the patrons in the entire restaurant turned to face the woman. "Ahh... Ply can fill you in."

"Are you going to play again?" he pleaded.

"I have applied for the games in France in September. I haven't been accepted yet."

"YAAAEEEEESS!" shouted Curtis and all the eyes of the clientele turned from Jane and stared at the large boisterous man dancing by the table.

"I wish I could invite all of you here to see this girl play. I'll bet once word gets out all of the networks will be clamoring for the rights for this one. WAAA-HOOOO!"

The owner of the establishment quickly showed up and tried to calm down the patron but once he found out who was there, he decided that the meal for the entire family was on the house.

Ply sat, unable to chew with his mouth half open and two-thirds full of his aunt's mashed potatoes. A few stood up to get a look at the young gal. Finally, Jane stood up and held up her hands to calm the applauding crowd.

"Thank you for the recognition." greeted the lady. "I have applied to play in France, but that is a month away, and I haven't played in the circuit for almost three years so please don't expect too much."

Someone in the back started to clap and shortly the racket was almost too loud to hear yourself think. Once again Jane held up her hands and the noise cooled a little.

"I'm in town to spend a quiet time with my friends but I will be out that door in about ten minutes to sign autographs if any would like one. Thank you for the encouragement from such a wonderful crowd." She sat down but the buzz refused to hush. In ten minutes, she stood up and walked over to the door and started to sign autographs. Just before she left the table she whispered to Brian, "Have Curtis pick me up in about fifteen minutes. If he doesn't Ply and I will never be able to get any of that stolen equipment to their rightful owners."

Fifteen minutes later Curtis pulled in front of the crowd in his Lincoln. Jane waved to the crowd and hopped into the car and the two of them drove off. Ten minutes down the road a TV camera truck passed them traveling more than the speed limit allowed!

"Those guys are twenty minutes behind us." informed Jane glancing at her watch.

"If they find us, there will be no peace until we are all dead. Can you call ahead and have our stuff ready to leave as soon as we get there?"

They drove back to the Morgan Farm in silence at a little quicker speed than the posted limit.

When the Morgan's arrived at the farm, they quickly helped Jane and Ply pack. Back at the farm Jane pleaded, "Ply, we must get back to the castle as soon as possible."

"Why?" Asked her beau. "They are out of range. How will they find us?"

"They will stop at nothing to get the scoop on the 'star'." she quoted with her fingers wagging her head and using a sarcastic voice. "Mr. Morgan, how many of those people are even vaguely familiar with you and how many at the Spoudice Complex know where you live?"

"Well," he thought for a second. "There were some at the restaurant but pretty well everybody at the complex knows where we live."

"Do you think they will go to the boss or will they ask the first one they see about the possibility of where we disappeared to?"

"They could possibly ask anyone and get the farm's location."

"Okay." proclaimed Jane. "The next stop for the media hounds is your front door. How long do you want them to be pounding on your door all day and all night to get information that you do not want to give them?"

"That isn't going to happen!" exclaimed Liz. "This is private property."

"Okay Ply," coaxed Jane. "You tell them."

"Aaaah," stammered the youth, "I am a little hit by the fame of this one also. When she quit the circuit, it was mainly due to a broken heart from a rather frightening relationship. She was in the finals with her fiancée, and she won, and he flew off the handle calling her names and insulting her right on the court in front of the audience and all the TV cameras. The heartbreak and the selfishness of her friend and the downer after winning the tournament was just about too much for her. Her friend who owns the castle told me if I ever even looked at another woman, she would personally take my head off with her tennis bat."

Jane rolled her eyes.

"The comments in the papers and magazines were furious at Jane disappearing from play." continued Curtis.

"When the owner of the castle returned from Toronto after just wining a set..." continued Ply. There was a pause for a few long seconds.

"Well?" coaxed Liz.

"Jane beat her in the first match." informed Ply.

"Just how long has this girl that Jane beat been playing?" asked Jack.

Jane responded with, "She got her first racket when she was four. At sixteen when she graduated from high school, she skipped the college scene and headed into the professional circuit. She has been playing pro for eight years and has lost at Wimbledon twice."

"Lost twice?" stammered Liz.

"That means she has been to the top twice and few ever get there." returned Jane.

"Three days ago, Jane beat her after not playing pro for two and a half years." commented Ply. "Now do you get the picture of what the media just might do to get the rights for this girl?"

"I'm so sorry this had to happen to you people." teared Jane as she hugged Liz goodbye. "I promise we will keep in touch and do make sure you make it to the wedding."

"I wouldn't miss it for the world!" balled Liz

"We'll see you two shortly." encouraged Ply's uncle. "Use my cell number for I expect those clowns will have the land line tapped."

The two men shook their hands and their heads. "I'm sorry all this had to happen." groaned Ply.

"What?" stated Jack. "Do you know how exciting farming is? You plant the seed and wait. You repair machinery and you wait. You harvest your crops and you wait. The only real excitement that shows up is if a tornado blows through and you really don't want that to happen."

"It looks like a different storm is blowing through." replied Ply.

"Please don't tell them where I am," pleaded the girl, "I need the time to prep for this match."

"Mum's the word!" proclaimed Brian. "Curtis, that means no

one. Not even one of your tennis buddies until she is accepted in France."

"Yes sir." gulped the younger. Although Curtis was over forty pounds heavier, he was still no match for Brian. He would check the tennis schedules daily and see what is happening with the networks. As soon as there was word out that 'Lady Jane' was back on the scene there would be five hundred plus e-mails go out to his tennis buddies bragging that he was the first to recognize her in the restaurant.

The two sped away into the afternoon while Brian and his brother hurried back to the shop. Each for their own reasons, Brian to get back to work and to check to see if anything showed up with the mower that was stolen from him and Curtis to check the tennis network to see if there is any word about the Blythwood re-entering the game.

Fifteen minutes after Ply and Jane left, Brian and Curtis departed. Ten minutes later a large van with the local TV logo showed up at the Morgan farm.

"Hi," greeted the driver who met Jack at about twenty yards from the front door, "We are looking for Curtis Spoudice. Is he here today?"

"He was until he met a friend from the past then he and his crew headed off to Patosi." That was forty miles the other way from the Morgan farm and the truck took off in the wrong direction.

"If they come back, I'll do some dealing with them and if they do not cooperate, I'll call the station in the next county. That'll cool their heels." he announced to Liz.

Jack turned and walked back to the house as the dust from the van settled around his feet.

Exactly one hour and twenty minutes later the same video van rolled up to the front of the Morgan house with cameras running. "Can I help you?" greeted Jack with a big country smile and a firm handshake.

"We heard that Jane Blythwood is here, and we need to interview her." growled a young reporter.

"Jane Blythwood? Who is she when she is not at home?"

"Don't play coy with us. We know she is here."

A large hand, but not as big as Jack's, spun the reporter around and said, "Get into the back of the truck son. You're not going to lose this one for us."

The suit, tie, and face that shook the hand of Jack introduced himself as the owner of the station and apologized to Mr. Morgan. "We understand that Jane Blythwood was last seen in your presence and would like to know if she is here and if she is, could we conduct and interview?" he stated.

"She was with us, but she has left, and I do not know where she is at this moment." which was not a lie.

"Is there anyone else in the house we can speak to?" asked the newsman.

"I make most of the decisions around here," informed the larger of the two, "And there shall be no interviews at this time."

"Have you never heard of 'freedom of the press'?"

"Well," smiled Jack, "Freedom of the press does not supersede the equality of freedom to protect private property. I am the owner of this farm and I do believe you are trespassing. Could you please remove yourself and your crew from my property or I will have to press trespassing charges?"

Someone hopped out of the back of the truck and headed for the door about twenty feet behind them.

"Call him back." informed Jack with a grip a little firmer still on the well-dressed man, but gentle tone.

"And just what are you going to do?" teased the reporter.

"LIZ!" he called with his eye still on the well-dressed man.

Suddenly the very elegant woman showing up with a twelve-gauge double barrel shotgun, passed through the front door, and stood on the porch with her finger just above to the trigger.

"She can shoot out the eyes of a snake at one hundred and fifty yards and we don't want to get impolite."

The kid stopped in his tracks and made a bee-line to the back of the truck. The metal door was heard slamming shut.

"I think we get the picture." stated the newsman as John loosened his grip and the engine of the van slowed as it was put into gear. He silently walked to the passenger door, got in, and the van left the property.

"Once they are out of sight," commented Jack to his wife, "I'd better go and lock the front gate."

* * *

Back at McGowan's, the owner was talking to his painter getting a sign made that stated, 'Jane Blythwood, Rediscovered Here' complete with date and time!

"And make it weatherproof cause, it is going out front."

He also called the company that had the account for his highway billboards on the highway five miles either side of town to get the information updated. For the next three years he had more customers than he knew what to do with.

* * *

The two were back on the highway headed for the castle. Jack's truck was traded for the old white horse and Jane was driving. Ply was having a little trouble adjusting to the past two hours. "Whoa!" he stammered. "What was all of that about?"

"All of what?" she nonchalantly replied.

"Please," he begged. "Tell me what exactly happened back there at lunch."

"That, my beloved, is called fame! Immediate recognition, in the most bizarre of places," she lifted her arm and continued waving her hand, "where you never thought would be possible, right out of the blue someone from a long time ago recognizes you and, wham, your cover is blown." she dryly announced dropping her hand back to the steering wheel.

There was about ten minutes of silence as the car glided across the pavement.

"Okay! Now what do we do?" interrogated the young man who was not a little shaken.

"We live." flatly drabbed the performer.

"Okay. Where?"

"At Barb's castle for the moment." she grinned.

"What about your job at the courts?"

Another silent few seconds.

"When you proposed, I filed my notice effective as soon as Barb returned. I figured I was getting my game back and Barb would have something pretty quickly but one month might be pushing the envelope a little." she stammered, eyes a little wider than normal but still on the road.

"I told my supervisor that I might be getting back into the circuit. I had to rush to the door, so she would not tell everyone at the courts. I made her promise, on a stack of bibles, that she would not tell a soul where I was and not say a word about what is happening until the media got wind of it. For your encouragement and information, that is exactly what happened at McGowan's Restaurant."

Ten to fifteen more seconds of quiet thinking.

"Did you tell your boss that we were engaged?"

"I did not have a ring then and when I did, I didn't wear it on my finger but around my neck."

A few more long suspenseful seconds.

"How'd you get it over your head?" he grinned.

"On a chain, silly." she was glad he was getting a little more comfortable about the stardom.

"So, I have a month to solve the case, or until the peppered-ratzies get wind of our engagement." he thought out loud.

"Peppered-ratzies?" she questioned. "Don't you mean the paparazzi?"

"They are rats, no?"

"I see." she muttered to him. "Is this a dyslexia thing?"

"Mark Twain said anyone who can only spell a word one way lacks creativity." he admonished. "Now that your beautiful face is going to be plastered all over the place, I suppose we have to keep you in hiding until Paris."

"If I want my game back, you may be right." she agreed.

"Did you get what we went for?"

"Oh, yeah!" Ply smiled. "Thank goodness Mr. Spoudice is all business. He transferred the program to my phone as soon as we had ordered lunch. No evidence yet as to where they have taken the mower. I set up my phone, so it vibrates when the GPS coordinates show up."

"On vibrate?"

"I don't want anyone else to be notified that something is happening on my phone. If I answer my phone and a sat GPS shows up and the wrong person sneaks behind me, just to have a peek, the cat might be out of the bag."

She looked at him with that curious eyebrow rising, "How long you been doing this?"

"Obviously, in one sense, not long enough, and in another, much too long!"

It was just getting dark when they pulled into 'Barb's Place' as they decided they would refer to it from now on. "I sure hope Barb doesn't want to play at this hour. I'm pretty tired from all the excitement of the day." said Jane.

Barb greeted them by opening the garage door and waited as they parked and climbed out of the car. "Busy day!" she welcomed. "It was all over the news that the missing 'Jane Blythwood' has resurfaced and is on her way to France."

"What? Already?" exclaimed Ply.

"I expected that!" snorted Jane.

"He'll get used to it." Jane encouraged Barb. "Why on the way home he was almost laughing about the matter."

"You up for a volley?" invited the owner.

"I was hoping not tonight. It has been a very long day and I did not expect to be back this early. We were thinking about coming home tomorrow until I got recognized. How about first thing in the morning?"

"You do look exhausted." she agreed. "How about a hot chocolate and a short voice on what happened at the restaurant?"

"That sounds pretty good to me!" replied the younger while pulling her bag from the trunk. "Can I have a few minutes to clean up?"

"Sure. That'll give me time to thaw some muffins from the freezer."

"Muffins? In the freezer?" piped Ply.

"I'll bet if he knew they were there they would have disappeared by this time." giggled Jane. "Better get out half a dozen, or maybe even ten. Are they the ones with peanut butter and pumpkin?"

"What else?" quipped Barb. "I like to keep a bunch there so if I get back and am hungry it doesn't take long to have a nourishing snack."

Barb descended to the freezer and Jane hit the shower. Ply decided to have a look around the place again to see if there were any clues he missed.

As he jogged around the perimeter, he noticed the fence was

repaired by the shed. "I'll have to ask Barb about the construction of the front wall." he recalled. Not noticing anything out of the ordinary he trotted back in through the side door and found Barb in the kitchen with the goodies in the microwave.

"I saw you got the fence fixed." greeted Ply.

"Yeah." she sighed. "Sometimes keeping up with a place like this is a little expensive."

"Who did you find to do it?"

"Johnson got it done, after all, he is supposed to be the one in charge of the place." she moaned.

"Oh yeah," remembered the young man, "Did he accept any money for doing the maintenance around here?"

"That was a little discussion we had!" growled Barb. "Thankfully we had the words after he fixed the fence. He said that he did maintain the property and that I owed him for the work. 'Why was the grass four feet deep when my friends showed up?' I asked, and he did not have an adequate answer but denied that the property was a mess. I did pay him for fixing the fence but not for the yard work. He said that he would see me in court, and I returned with, 'That just may be the case'. He demanded cash which I thought was surprising and stormed off."

"There is another meeting on Monday night. I think I will go with my nose to the air and do a little more sniffing."

"I don't expect you'll find him there. I went into town to get some supplies and bumped into Glenn Olson and he told me that Johnson skipped town."

"He skipped town?"

"As fast as his little feet would carry him." she stated. "Olson told me he has a new job halfway across the country. I think he said he left yesterday. Any noise from your phone?"

Ply flipped it open and sped to the program. "Not a word yet. I wonder if it's going with him?"

"This might be a case for the FBI." cautioned the woman.

"You could be right but I'm not ready to get them involved yet." he responded.

"Oh, really? Why not?"

"I really do not want to share the reward money as yet. If this gets to the place where there are numerous states involved then we give them a call but until that happens, I am feeling a little greedy, besides, I just might have to pay for a wedding and the pockets are pretty empty at this point. A man really likes to supply for his bride even if she is the one who is making all the money." he gently explained.

"Here's Jane. Let's indulge in some warm muffins." invited Barb.

"Break my heart!" stated the wolf with his mouth already full with more than half of one.

They sat in the front room and discussed the day's activities. The girls daintily ate one muffin each while Ply sucked back two more.

"Man!" bellowed the boy. "These are great!"

"Too bad I only make them in batches of twenty-four." stated the lady as she winked at Jane.

"What did you have in mind with the secret compartments in the front wall?" queried the young man.

"Secret compartments?" responded the owner in a surprised tone.

"Yeah. All along the wall there are little compartments every twenty-five feet, that face away from the house. There are three, two-inch pipes in each one, even the two on each end. Not to mention the sealed door in the basement where I expect the pipes come in."

The blank stares from the girls told him this was something new. "Let's go outside and have a look." he coached.

"Not me." piped Jane. "I'm done for today." She hoisted herself from the couch and headed for the stairs.

"I'm game." invited Barb.

"Let's go." was his reply.

There was enough light from the moon to see along the edge of the wall and notice the small indent from the first brick. Ply pulled out the brick and showed her the pipes with the light from his phone. "You have no idea that this was done?" he asked.

"And you say there is a door in the basement that is locked?"

Ply replaced the brick and walked her along the edge of the wall. At the far end he stated, "Here is the eleventh one, all the same distance apart and all with three pipes in each cavity." He pulled out the last brick and showed the entrance to Barb.

She looked inside then at him for a minute, "All facing the street." she observed and turned to look down the wall to see the protruding bricks. She looked back at Ply, "Now let's go find that door you are suspicious of."

They walked quickly to the basement and Ply took her to the metal door that he had found at the end of a closeted corner.

"Why, it's the same color as the inside of the closet and almost impossible to see." she exclaimed.

"Why would the builder do such a thing and not charge me?"

"Did you have any extras added on after you finished the first bid?"

"Well duh." the lady announced.

"So, he hid the charges in the other extras." explained Ply.

"That..."

"Welcome to the world of construction."

"Let me get my ring of keys."

"I'll wait here."

The light from the room did not show the door very well so Ply held his phone while Barb juggled with keys. It took a few minutes of trying one finally worked.

"Well, well, well," stated the star, "I suppose if I did not have a key then I might have been able to accuse him of me not ordering such a thing."

There was a light switch inside at the top of the stairs. Ply flipped it on. They descended six poured concrete steps and found an empty room that curved at forty-five degrees in three evenly measured sixteen by sixteen-foot spaces. "This must be under the front curved porch." claimed the owner.

There was a floor drain at one end of the room and receptacles every six feet along the outside wall about forty inches from floor. There was a dehumidifier plugged into one of the receptacles and drained to the opening in the floor. The ceiling was made of concrete and sloped from the house down about sixteen inches. The floor level was almost three feet lower than the rest of the basement. Two, two-inch PVC pipes stubbed out of the floor about three feet on the opposite side of the room from the floor drain. "I'll bet these are the plastic pipes from the front wall." noticed Ply.

"How come I never noticed this before?" wondered the woman out loud. "The front porch is wooden and there is no concrete that I have seen out there"

"This must be below ground level." observed Ply. "This is

lower than the outside foundation." he observed as he pointed to the ceiling close to the building. If it was built properly there would be gravel up to the ground level so water would quickly run off. There would be a sump pump to dispose of any excess water..."

"Or a drain to a nearby ditch so the noise of a sump would not be discovered. I don't have a sump here. The rainwater drains into a ditch at the far end of the property. Then why did he build this room?"

"Did he offer to buy the place once it was finished?"

"He did mention that if I ever decided to sell, I might contact him first."

"The soup thickens!"

Barb paced around the room twice then said, "Let's go up to the roof."

"What are you going to find up there?"

"I don't think we will find anything, but we will see a lot."

"You can get up on the roof?"

"The roof, my good man, is one of the reasons I built here."

She locked up the newly discovered chamber and led the way to a back entrance, unlocked and swung open the door. It revealed a large room with patio furniture stacked up in one corner and a large double sink in an island five feet away from the counter that ran the full length of two walls. Two large refrigerators were planted in the middle of each counter with an oven six feet to the right of each fridge. The circular staircase in the middle of the room rose through the ceiling and continued up to the roof. Off to one corner was a very expensive telescope.

"Good night! Where did all this come from?" exasperated the kid. "I thought I had searched the whole house through?"

"Stick around for a few more weeks and you will find a lot more interesting stuff than this!" she teased. They headed up the stairs, past the second floor, and up onto a rubber roofed portion of the castle that Ply had not seen before.

"Is all this hidden from the eye anywhere on the property? I looked around while cutting the grass but did not see any of this."

"There is a parapet that circles the entire patio," explained the owner, "Some of it is in the form of a wall at the edges of the building but some of it fences in the stepper parts of the roof. When you get up here and climb up this Plexiglass lookout a person can see a little more than three hundred degrees around the building and on a clear night, like tonight, you can see right down there." She half pointed to a lighted complex about twenty miles from where they stood.

"And what is that?" interrogated the inquisitive youth.

"If I tell you, you must promise never to speak a word about this to anyone!"

"About this?" he said with the inquisitive eyebrows raising.

"About the room, the lookout, and what is visible from here."

"Mum's the word."

"Have another look around." she encouraged. "Tell me what you see?"

Being careful to take in all he could, he stopped his rotation and looked but did not point. "What is that tower?"

Barb, not turning to look at it, responded, "I think it is a radio tower but if there are cameras there with updated technology, they can tell what color your hair is in this moonlight. I think the building in the opposite direction is some sort of government building, but it is new within the last six years, and I don't think it belongs to the Master. He doesn't usually build structures like that. We should go."

On the way down Barb locked and barred the exit to the roof from the inside.

"I had this area built for stargazing and I used to have that telescope up here. I got a little too nosy with the scope and started looking around at the houses in the area till I found someone close to the tower scoping me out; only theirs that was tied to a very high-power rifle. I packed up the telescope and removed the lawn furniture and have kept it locked ever since."

"Do you suppose it is part of the rebellion?" asked the youth.

"Could very well be, but I don't want anything to do with them." she coldly stated.

As Ply walked behind her, he thought to himself, *Well, 'Miss Famous Tennis Star' you just might be getting yourself involved a whole lot more than either of us think.*

* * *

The next morning Jane was up first and nosing around the kitchen reminding herself where utensils, towels, pots, and pans were kept. It was becoming obvious that Barb had left no stone unturned, or store not visited, in supplying for the needs and even wants of her kitchen. Pulling out a silverware drawer she found a revolver at the back. She stared at it for a long moment then slowly closed the drawer.

"Well, good morning, Miss Janie!" she mumbled to herself. *Finding that sure is an appetite squelcher!* she thought.

Just then Barb walked in. "Are you okay? It looks like you just saw a ghost!"

"I don't think it was a ghost." she replied as she opened the drawer and showed her friend the find.

"I'm sorry for leaving it out." apologized Barb. "I wanted them available if anything exciting showed up."

"Are we expecting that kind of excitement?" questioned the guest.

"Perhaps I overreacted, but I don't like being here alone with the possibility of problems arising. These 'gentlemen' we are investigating don't seem to be the most wholesome type and if anyone shows up with intent to harm, I want to be at least somewhat ready with those utensils."

"Those? Are there more in other places?"

The star sized up her next opponent. "If you are going to stay here then I guess you need to know about what is here to protect yourselves. I'll give you both a tour after lover boy crawls out of the sack."

"Someone mention my name?" announced Ply as he pounced through the door and rushed to Jane's side. "I don't smell breakfast. Am I too late?"

"I guess we have the tour after breakfast seeing that the cook is up."

"Great! Do we get another tour?" he quizzed. "What are we going to find this time?" he grinned. Jane slowly opened the drawer and the Cheshire Cat expression melted from his face.

"Where did that come from?"

Barb maneuvered between the two and lifted the drawer past the stop to reveal another hidden compartment behind the utensils. All eyebrows went up except hers. "I have a number of these placed around the complex so if intruders arrive, I may be ready for them." she coldly announced. "If you two are going to live here for the next number of months you should probably know about the distribution. What do you want for breakfast?"

"How about some muffins?" piped Ply. "They will do until something else gets cooked."

"That would get us into the tour a lot sooner." commented Barb. "This means I just may have to cook!"

"How about all of us helping with the cooking?" encouraged Jane. "The more the merrier."

Barb set four muffins in the microwave and started the appliance. "Since they were in the fridge, they will only need two minutes for the four of them."

Ply moved towards the drawer and opened it again past the stop. "How many people know about your private stashes?"

"This makes three. I purchased all the guns from different people and places so no one person has a realistic knowledge of what is here."

Barb was looking at Jane, but Jane noticed Ply shaking his head as if to answer about the revelation of the sword to Barb.

The muffins were warm. Paper plates were distributed, and the tour began. There was a least one firearm in every common area on the main floor. There were two in the library and two in the front sitting room. Each were hidden in a special little compartment that fit the device snugly. There were felt linings on all of the hidden compartments so in a time of stealth, noise would not be an issue. They all were well oiled and often a stain was imprinted on the felt.

Near the end of the show Jane asked, "Where did you learn to use all these... things? Is there a shooting range around here that lets civilians use the premises?"

She looked at the two for a few seconds then lead them to the back staircase. It was smaller than the front staircase and used for hired help to get to the back of the house sooner than having to go all the way around to the front.

As Barb approached the stairwell, she opened a small cabinet and pulled out an inexpensive glass pitcher.

"This is just here for show to ward off the suspicious." She reached in and pushed up the top of the cabinet and the stairwell opened up from the second step up and hinged at the top of the stairs. The staircase lifted revealing a narrower staircase going down.

"I had this put in after a few walls were changed in the

basement. If you have a few different contractors at different times of construction less people know all the secrets." The down stairwell descended into pitch blackness. Barb walked down to the second step and waited three seconds and lights came on automatically.

"If you don't wait until the lights come on," she exhorted, "You find yourself locked down here for two hours. It's a safety feature I had built into the system. There is an emergency escape and I will show it to you, but you have to make sure you are prepared for it."

At the foot of the stairs there was another small shelf with a painted glass insulator apparently just sitting there. She picked up the insulator and the bottom of the shelf came with it. Under the base of the shelf was a hidden LED flashlight.

"If you run past the sensor on the third step the door will automatically close and the lights will not come on leaving you in a very dark place. There are sensors on the top three steps. If no weight is on the steps three seconds after the third is stepped on, then the door closes, and it looks like you ran upstairs instead of down here. The timer for the lights is set for only eight seconds and will not reset until two hours have passed and no one can get down here unless they blast their way in. I had this flashlight cupboard installed so I would have a light if someone was chasing me. I could run down here and pass all the sensors and be left in the dark. This flashlight would give a little light when I would need it."

They walked through a few empty rooms to a large room with paneled walls and carpeted flooring. Along one short wall was storage of canned goods and preserves. Without a trained eye it would appear the long shelves were against the outside wall of the castle. Behind the apple juice there was a small switch that activated a solenoid and part of the shelving moved slightly. She pulled open the door and stepped inside and turned on the lights. The room was only ten feet wide but fifty feet long.

"The switch on the outside only works when there is electricity. The one on the inside is simply mechanical so the only power that is needed is the strength to move the door. All these preserves are a little heavy, but the wheels are good and silent on the carpeted concrete." she said.

Behind the bookcase against the short wall over there," she pointed behind her to the left, "There is another staircase that leads to an ancient cave. At the mouth of the cave is a garage and three cars. I use the cars once in a while just to keep them running well. They run on standard IT technology so they can pretty well sit for months before using them and they don't need much maintenance."

Inside the room behind the canned goods was Barb's private shooting range. At the far end there were bales of straw, Styrofoam, and then heavy cloth material before the poured concrete foundation. Just to the left was a very large gun-case. Barb opened the case to display the contents. On one side of the double doors were numerous types of explosive actuated weaponry and on the other enough ammunition to supply a small armada.

Jane was again wide-eyed at the things she saw. Ply was a little nervous but able to hide his apprehension. *If I knew this girl was this well-armed, I might not have stayed here but she seems trusting enough to show us all this.* He thought to himself.

"I see that both of you have questions about all this so let me try to answer a few of them." observed Barb. "While I was planning this place during my games in Australia, I heard about the fuss that was starting in Germany and Russia against the long-term Leader. I wondered how I could protect myself and maybe be a help to some others but until now no one had manifested any desire to squelch the rebellion. I wonder why I am showing you all of this, but I have a feeling that perhaps you also have a part in this great plan of His."

"It certainly does seem that mischief has increased in the last number of years but what in the world can any of us do about such a large uprising?" questioned Jane.

"It seems that powers greater than ourselves are at play here." commented Ply.

"Apparently there are many things that are coming to the surface that few of us know about."

"I had a bowling alley planned for this corner of the house." continued Barb. "At least, that is what I told the contractor. He might have developed a little suspicion seeing that I had twenty-four-inch concrete walls poured around this place, but it was shortly after these plans were shown to him, he invited me to sell the place to him if I ever wanted to get rid of it. Looking back, I see that timing is everything. I should have timed the bowling alley a little better, but the give-away is the bunker walls. Oh well! As someone important once said, 'Live and learn and die ignorant at last!'"

"How did you learn about using all of this kind of stuff?" asked Jane.

"I took a few 'Right to Carry' courses in various countries while on tour, but never applied for a license."

"It could be that we may need to know about how some of this stuff works seeing we are getting into some rather deep waters with this lawn mower case." proposed Ply. "Is there opportunity for you to teach us about some of this?"

"I was hoping you would ask." smiled Barb. "I really did not want you two here by yourselves without knowing how to protect yourselves."

Jane looked at the floor and Barb said, "What?"

Ply spoke, "You give us a one-hour lesson, here in the dungeon and we will give you a one-hour lesson on the court." Jane nodded in agreement.

Barb was the one somewhat taken back by this announcement, but she got the picture that their secret of Jane's game was part of the bargain. She walked over to the case, pulled out a drawer, lifted a handgun, and said, "This is a Glock, nine-millimeter..."

* * *

Eighty minutes later Barb was the first dressed and ready for the lesson that would improve her game. Jane was next to appear with Ply right behind her toting the tattered guitar case.

"Right!" smirked Barb. "You're going to sing Elvis songs so I can bat balls to the rhythm of antiquity."

"That is why I carry it in an old guitar case." Ply pulled out the old guitar and demonstrated that the strings were missing as to lead the curious astray. Replacing the guitar, he stood and explained to the uninitiated that she need not be fearful, but as he and Jane were a little surprised at the revelation of the sword, she would probably be also. He drew out the sword and Barb was immediately fascinated.

"Where-did-you-get-that?"

"That is a long story and I will tell you someday, but we don't have time for long explanations. This toy opens time according to the user's wishes. No matter how fast you bat the ball at me I can return it anywhere I wish at whatever speed I wish."

Barb was somewhat cynical until she glanced Jane's direction.

"So, this is what improved her game?"

"No, this is what helped improve her game." informed the young man. "As she trained her eyes what to look for, her game improved."

Ply demonstrated to Barb like he did to Jane some of the aspects of the sword. Shortly they were on the court and he had Barb running faster than she had ever anticipated with this boy. In twenty minutes, she was soaked.

Finally, Jane suggested, "Okay, it is time to switch places. Ply you serve and Barb and I will return." Jane gave Ply her racket and she took the sword to Barb. "We will hold hands for the first few volleys until you get the hang of this thing. It is truly unlike anything you have ever practiced with. I'll take the sword and you hold my hand as Ply serves. I will slow us both down so the ball crawls through the air, that way you can see where the ball is going, how it is spinning, and you can act accordingly."

Ply served the ball and the two at the other end of the court disappeared. Jane talked the maneuver through with Barb as she played the ball. Barb smashed at the ball and it skidded inches before line and hit the wall bursting with a loud pop and landed a mashed mass in the center of Ply's court.

"What did I do? What just happened?"

"One down and thirty-five to go!" laughed Jane as she timed back. "As we adjust our time frame the regular time frame stays as it is. If you hit the ball ten times faster that it is going. The result is what you just witnessed. Let's try it again."

Jane coached Barb to watch the ball and hit it back gently using the flat of the sword as she might do so in a game. It took about three tries and she got the hang of it.

"Okay, now you try it by yourself."

Jane dropped the timing difference and let go of Barb's hand. Ply served the ball and Barb tried to return but only batted the ball with the flat of the sword.

"How do you change the timing?" she asked.

Jane took hold of Barb's hand and Barb felt the change take place but was not able to do so herself. They tried four times, but the star could not adapt herself to adjust the time frame. Finally, Jane held on to Barb's hand as she prompted her to watch and react. It did finally improve her game but not the degree that it did for Jane.

They played for about thirty more minutes and Barb was thankful for the experience and her game was improved but the question still nagged her.

"I just can't get that thing to work." she announced.

Ply thought that it just might take some time getting used to it but after a few more tries she was unable to do the 'magic', as she called it.

"So, this thing is not going to work for everybody?" Ply finally announced.

"Apparently not." exasperated Barb.

"And it seems to work better with some than with others." observed Ply.

"You've had a lot more practice." said Jane.

"That may be true, but I don't think that's the only thing that's different. Right from the start it seems that this toy and I were almost made for each other."

"Where did you find it?" asked Barb.

"I found it in an old cave."

"Did someone leave it there?" inquired Jane.

"It appears so, but who and how long ago was it left there?"

"That thing looks almost brand new so how old can it be?"

"That is correct, but I've never seen metal like this before. Look how it glows and reflects the light. Have you ever seen anything like this before?" asked Ply.

"What are you driving at?" responded Jane.

"Whoever built this thing understood that time is adjustable and figured out how to do it." reported Ply.

"Within western cultures, some believe that space is bent and by that bending of space gravity is generated. If that is the case, then bending space generates gravity. If this was known in some of the ancient cultures, then the changing of gravity by the bending of space could give the scientists of those cultures the ability to do things that we know nothing about. For instance, the Incas built Machu Picchu without the apparent aid of the wheel. If they understood about the bending of space and found out how to do it, they would not need the wheel to move heavy objects, they could just float them to where they needed to go."

"That is impossible!" stated Barb. "They did not have that kind of smarts in those days."

"Why not?" corrected Ply. "We have been taught that we all evolved from goo from the Gulag but the only evidence they have is found in textbooks. As a result, we think that the older cultures were just cave men. Just because a teacher says something doesn't mean it's true. We are no longer taught to test but to swallow, 'Just believe it because I told you so.' This is exactly what they told us not to believe fifty years ago. 'Don't believe something just because it comes out of a person's mouth.' And now they do the same things and refuse the principles of testing veracity to be allowed. Just because it is not common knowledge that we understand how something works, does not mean that an earlier culture did not either. We think we are so smart because we have all these so-called modern appliances but every culture on earth thinks they are smarter than anyone else in all of history."

"So, you are saying that this thing could be years old or even from some ancient civilization?" asked Jane.

"I'm not saying that it is, but I am saying that the possibility is there."

"Alright." agreed Barb. "Now we have this thing what are we to do with it?"

"If the Leader really is in full control like He says He is, it has been given to us for a reason." observed Ply. "I never would have met Jane without it. And Jane may not have gotten her game back. Perhaps we have it simply to discover what can be done in realms that are not superstition but have real physics behind it. For example, Jane and I have no trouble in getting this thing to function, but Barb seems to be unable. Is it the case that only some can actually get this thing to work? Is there some triggering mechanism that some people do not have or is it that it just needs to be developed and is buried a little deeper in others? I don't know if we can answer that right at this moment cause I'm not really ready to announce to the world what we have here. If this thing gets into the wrong hands is it able to override the authority of the Leader?"

"Alright." stated Jane. "You said that you believed that the Master is fully in control then it is He who allowed you to find this and to test its abilities."

This hit Ply with a bit of a start. He thought of the presence in the cave while he was imagining fighting with the lions and dragons. Here Jane had the answer.

"What are you thinking about?" queried Jane.

It took a few seconds to respond. "Finally," he realized, "Now I understand".

"Understand what?" she reiterated.

"It is so farfetched, if I told you, you might think me crazy."

"I already do, so what difference does that make?"

"Okay, I'll tell you, but let me process this for a few more days just so I may be able to get it straight. Hey Barb, can we practice with this thing in the shooting gallery?"

"The shooting gallery? What on earth for?"

"Once I realized that this thing adjusts time, I needed a place to test it. I thought about baseballs but figured at one hundred miles per hour, if I got hit it just might hurt. That is how I ended up at the tennis courts. I had five machines at full speed and the balls just crawled through the air. Next, I tried a BB gun and caught the BB with my bare hand. I found a police practice range and managed to catch and deflect fifty-millimeter shells.

"I think Jane may need some practice in deflecting bullets if we are going to take on these clowns that have helped themselves to other people's property. So now, my dear," encouraged Ply, "It is your turn to learn to deflect bullets. Are you ready?"

"No!" stated Jane looking over at Barb. "I am not going to stand in front of a gun while someone starts shooting at me."

"I can understand how you feel but I think this is a good time to learn be able to defend yourself with the toy so when the need arises you know what to do. If you get good enough you can deflect the bullets away from harm."

"Let me think about it for a bit." she stalled.

The three went to the kitchen and started to get lunch ready. Ply showed Barb the supplies he had bought, and Barb showed what she had. Together they came up with a number of very good meals.

Barb asked Ply what he was thinking about down in the shooting gallery.

"While I was first playing with the sword, I would often get the impression that someone was watching what I was doing. Once in the cave where I found it and again in my apartment. As we talked in the basement, I realized that it was the Master telling me He knew I had the toy."

Jane looked over at the two and said, "I have felt that also, but

I realized that it was the Master right from the beginning."

"How did you know it was Him?" asked Ply.

"I spend time every day with Him, morning and evening. So, I recognized the sensation and His presence. It only happened once but I know He knows I have the sword and am responsible to act as he directs when I use it."

"Then how come I did not feel anything when I used it?" asked Barb.

"I was the one who timed it out and you got the benefit of my responsibility." answered Jane. "It doesn't make you any less of a person, just someone who has different gifts and abilities."

Barb thought about some of the other reasons she had left the tennis circuit, but she was not ready to share those yet. "Let's eat." said Barb putting on a happy face but still a little confused as to what the Lord was doing in her life at this moment in time.

"I'll tell you what." said Jane during lunch. "Let's go downstairs and Barb can shoot, and Ply and I will watch."

Barb hesitated then slowly agreed. After lunch and clean up, Ply went up to his room, grabbed a few things, then they descended to the range. Ply had the sword and Barb aimed at the target with a thirty-eight special. She started to squeeze the trigger and the two behind her disappeared. Jane watched in amazement as the bullet slowed to almost a standstill as it moved down the lane.

"Wow." she said as they entered back into normal time.

"Good." cheered Ply. "As Barb shoots again, we will catch the bullet."

Barb lowered the weapon. "You're going to what?"

"We will catch the bullet." repeated Ply.

"Shoot down the lane and we will travel faster than it and bring it back to you."

Ply rolled up his shirt sleeve and donned a heavy leather welding glove. Jane held on to his arm and the two chased the projectile and brought it back to the shooter. It was still hot as the two dropped the sizzling lead into a bucket of sand at Barb's feet immediately after Barb pulled the trigger.

Barb looked at the two with great suspicion. "Hey, Ply," she challenged, "Why don't you pull the trigger and Jane and I will chase the bullet. I really would like to see this thing actually happen."

"Ah... Sure." Prior to this, having never shot anything larger than a BB gun, he was a little unsteady but held the pistol with both hands, just like he had seen in the movies, pointed, and fired. Jane grabbed the projectile out of the air and she and her companion walked back to the bucket of sand as the smoke finished exiting the barrel.

"How fast can this thing go?" asked Barb.

"Ply says he has slowed a fifty-millimeter shell to a crawl, but he really does not know the full capabilities of the toy." repeated Jane as they came back to real time. Barb had to sit down for a few minutes just to take in the reality of what actually happened.

"Can I get you something to drink?" asked Jane.

"That might be nice." agreed the newly initiated.

Jane left and returned about five minutes later with a glass of dark soda and handed it to the woman. "I sure hope I don't need all of this." declared the lady. She took another sip. "But thanks anyway, and you chose the right additive!"

"It does take some getting used to." remarked her partner.

"It is always nice to be ready when trouble arises, but I do hope I never have to contend with something like that!"

"Next," announced Ply, "Is the ability to return the projectile to the location of your desire. I do think this will take some practice seeing that the lead is traveling at a speed or greater than when it left the barrel of the gun."

The girls looked at each other and remembered what had happened when Barb returned the tennis balls too fast.

"Alright." announced Barb. "I'll do the shooting but be careful not to hit me with the return fire."

"Let's try this," stated Ply, "You sit halfway down the lane and shoot back at the safe. Jane and I will bunt the bullet into this bucket of sand or back to the stops at the far end of the range. If we set a target and Jane can practice returning."

"And if you miss the bucket of sand or the backstops then the bullet just might ricochet all over the room?" questioned Barb.

"If that happens, we will grab it and dump it into the sand pail." stated Ply.

Barb just looked at him. "Oh yeah." she remembered but had a little trouble comprehending all that went into the action.

They got into position and Jane held Ply's hand while Ply held on to the handle of the sword and Barb fired.

"Watch the bullet just like you would a tennis ball." encouraged Ply as the projectile slowly approached them. "And bat the lead as you would a ball with a racket to the place where you want it to go." He tapped the lead and the bullet buried itself into the back stop at the back wall.

"I think I have it." encouraged Jane. She took the sword and held Ply's hand and Barb fired again. She deflected the lead to the target but not the center. "Let me have a few more tries." she coaxed. Three shots later she was hitting the target almost in the bullseye.

"Now, that was not so bad. Was it?"

Jane was delighted at the progress, but Barb said, "I think I need to sit down. Let's close up and have a little more of that refreshment."

The three cleaned up the room and the equipment and returned to the living room upstairs. "You say you do not know the full potential of this thing?" solicited Barb.

"How are you going to find that out?" returned Ply.

The three sat in silence mulling that one over for a while.

* * *

A full week had passed and no buzzing on Ply's phone. Not that he wasn't busy, keeping the grass cut with a rented mower that Barb insisted she pay for.

"I think it is time to call Mr. Bryan," mused the sleuth.

"Hello, Mr. Spoudice? I haven't heard a word about this missing toy of yours and I was wondering if I had erased something from my phone."

"Can you open the program?" asked the businessman.

"I think so." Ply started the program on his phone.

"It seems all right from this end," announced Brian. "Sometimes if the machine is in a shed or on a metal truck the satellite signal cannot get to it. If the thief disconnected the battery, then there would not be contact either. Even if they start it under a metal roof the machine will not register. It has to be out in the open. It appears that these guys are professionals and are doing all they can to keep this thing hidden. If they are familiar with the model and serial number, they can very easily find out what accessories are on the machine. Clearly these guys know their stuff and are taking all the necessary precautions."

"How long should I wait?" asked Ply.

"Do you mean how long am I willing to take to catch these rascals?" replied the voice on the other end of Ply's call. "If it takes five years and we catch them it will still be worth it. Hang in there, kid. If I find out where it is, or it even shows up here we may be able to go from there. Keep in mind criminals always do something stupid sooner or later. We'll catch em."

"Thank you, sir. I'm not used to handling so much expensive equipment."

"What's the grass look like out there? Do you need another machine?"

"The owner has rented a mower and is a little concerned herself about the fancy one that disappeared."

"Is she available and willing to talk to me?" asked Brian.

"She is here. Let me ask her. Hold on." Ply quickly found Barb and invited her to speak with Mr. Brian Spoudice.

"This is Barbara Cully."

Good morning Ms. Cully, my name is Brian Spoudice and I represent the business that loaned Ply the machine that disappeared..."

"Yes sir, we are doing our best to track the stolen equipment." she interrupted.

"These characters have incriminated me by selling me one of the stolen machines. This is my risk in the loaning of the machine to Ply and I would like to inform you that you are at no risk at all of losing anything, even if I never get the machine back." he kindly attempted to persuade the woman.

"Thank you, sir, but it was my property it was stolen from, so I do feel that I am somewhat responsible."

"Please," he pleaded, "Ply is a relative to one of my very best friends and my brother and I are great fans of yours. I just don't want you to feel obligated about the mower that it affects your game."

"Well thank you sir. I'll not let that happen."

"Very well then, may I talk to Ply again?" She handed the instrument over to the boy.

"Sir?"

"She will be all right. I'll keep my eyes open for anything that may turn up online also."

"Thank you, sir, have a good night."

"Don't worry about that machine. We have others that people are ready to purchase. Sometimes I look for a loss to write off at the end of the year."

"Thank you for being so encouraging about this. I do think it will show up eventually. I just want this to happen sooner than later."

I can understand your concern." stated the businessman. "We'll keep in touch."

"Will do." agreed the youth. "You will be the first to know if anything shows up."

"Any news on the date of your wedding?" inquired the businessman.

"The girls are working on that," informed Ply, "I think they want to see how France goes and go from there. If Jane gets too busy in the circuit, then it may have to wait for a bit."

"How do you feel about the wait?"

"I'm okay with it." grinned the youth. "As long as it doesn't take a year or two. I think there is too much going on with this sudden rebellion and I really do not want to miss marriage, especially to this one."

"All right my good man," encouraged the elder. "We will keep in touch."

"Yes sir, and, thank you for the encouragement!" Ply hung up and felt good about what was happening.

* * *

Two days later Jane woke up with a funny feeling having used the sword the night before. "I had a dream last night." she informed Ply the next morning. "I dreamed the sword came apart and a smaller blade was hidden in the shaft."

"How did it come apart?"

"It seems that there is a button that can be pressed. I noticed while I was playing with it that some of the jewels on the hilt move. What would happen if they were pushed in all at the same time?" Ply scampered up to his room and retrieved the instrument.

They looked at the hilt together. "It appears that there are six similar jewels near the blade end of the hilt." he observed. "They all seem to move a bit. Can they be pushed in all at once?"

With three fingers each they tried to push but it was just too awkward. "I have an idea." she noted and grabbed a rubber band from the kitchen junk drawer. She folded the band in half and passed the band around the hilt over the beads. "If we pull the band tight so all the jewels are covered it just might..."

Ply very gently grasped the sides. "It is a little loose, but it isn't coming out!"

"Try twisting it." informed Jane.

Slowly he wiggled the stock of metal, but it still only moved a little.

"Let's trade places?" asked Ply.

As Jane let go of the rubber band the blade snapped into place with a 'click'. The two looked at each other recognizing that the buttons were not quite pushed in far enough.

Ply twisted the band around the hilt almost to the place of breaking, but the blade only wiggled in the hilt. Jane noticed that the band was not evenly around each jewel. "Loosen the band and try with the twist of the band between two of the buttons."

"Well, well!" he exclaimed. This time Jane gently lifted off the blade to reveal a *Épée* blade about sixteen inches long.

"A bayonet mount?" blurted Ply letting the band loose.

"Apparently." she responded.

"Wow this is even lighter that the other." thought Ply as he adjusted the time frame. Quickly he returned to let Jane in on the adventure. "Where are we going to use this?"

"Let's have a look at the blade." she suggested. It was three sided from about five millimeters from the hilt till about two centimeters from the tip then it narrowed to an extremely fine point. The three sides were equally sharp as the principal blade.

"If this thing could talk," pronounced Jane, "What stories would it tell?"

"I would be afraid to ask." he replied.

"Look at the base of the blade." he noticed. "There are two flat surfaces opposite to each other, almost as if this blade is removable also."

Again, Jane walked to the kitchen drawer and returned with a small adjustable wrench, with pink plastic covering on the handle. She handed it to Ply. He looked at it for a second and wondered why they even made tools for women with pink plastic handles. *I suppose so men won't use them,* he thought to himself. Grasping the tool, he adjusted it, so the jaws were over the flat surfaces and tried to twist, but no response.

"We may have to loosen the jewels." concluded the lady. Ply tightened the rubber band the blade seemed free. Jane donned the leather welding gloves and unscrewed the long thin blade to reveal a six-inch stiletto. "I don't even want to think why this toy was created." she murmured. Then added, "Or even how it was made."

The utensil was reassembled and put back into the guitar case.

No word about the lost mowers from the Spoudices'. Ply kept himself busy with the grounds and letting Jane and Barb use the sword to spar improving the game of the two. They became very adept at watching the movement of their opponent's racket and judging what would happen to the ball when it landed. They had to get ready for France and both were getting in better shape. Ply helped with Barb as she was still unable to make it work.

Ply had been thinking about how this thing might actually work. He pulled the toy out from the guitar case and stood in front of the mirror. "I can make myself fully invisible just by bending space, but I cannot bend just part of space. What if I open really slow...?" He moved the sword into 'operational mode' for lack of a better terminology and watched himself disappear. He tried a few more times but all seemed impossible. He put the toy away and went to sleep.

The next day after practice, while putting lunch together, Ply mentioned, "I tried to do something with the sword last night, but I was unable to make it do what I wanted."

"Testing new theories?" surmised Barb.

"Somewhat." he returned. "Let me explain. The lower three dimensions demonstrate that the higher dimensions employ all the attributes of the lower in a more complex form."

"And..." she droned looking at Jane who was busy adding calories to be burned off building stamina for the upcoming contests.

"Since the higher dimensions employ all the attributes of the lower in a more complex form, then, space must be curled on all three axes."

Jane's forehead furrowed.

"What I tried to do was bend only one or two lines of space

instead of all three, making myself look like a ghost instead of becoming fully invisible."

The furrowed forehead added the single eyebrow. Her attention was captured, and the fork lay still, for a moment. She chewed silently and gears in her head whirled.

"I thought, if I fired up very slowly, I might ease into the zone one line at a time, but I couldn't do it."

The furrow disappeared but the eyebrow remained. "You really think it can be done?" she asked.

"It is just a theory, but I couldn't do it."

She got up from the table, leaving her hot breakfast and retrieved the instrument. She disappeared a few times then very slowly merged into the zone.

"That's what I did, and it didn't work for me either."

"Hush." she exhorted holding the sword in a vertical position between the other two. She closed her eyes and faded from full to one third to two thirds to fully gone. She appeared back immediately.

"That's it." encouraged Ply. "Now, if you can hold that pose while you are in transition..."

She tried it again but slipped through into bending all three. She set the sword down on the table, ate a little, and thought about it for a few minutes.

Trying it again, she kept slipping into full invisibility, but she was catching on and she was fading slower each time.

"You're really getting the hang of this thing girl." he observed. Barb sat there not being able to eat or comment with the science fiction happening right before her eyes.

Setting the instrument down again she announced, "I think I can do this, but it will take some practice. I'm going to take this upstairs to the mirror after I eat and see if I can do as you suggest. It looks like it can be done."

Ply thought about Barb not being able to get the toy to work at all and now him not being able to get it to work in this fashion. Maybe he just needed to hang onto her hand and feel Jane do it, so he could learn how. He wasn't fully convinced he could, but he would sure give it the 'college try'.

Almost an hour later she came down the stairs to find Ply writing at the butternut secretary.

"How's this?" she teased and glided into half visibility.

"Wow." he awed. "Can we try together?" He stood up, she timed out and took hold of his hand.

"We need a mirror." he blurted, and they ran to the front foyer.

They disappeared a few times and Jane admonished, "Are you trying to work this thing?"

"No. I'm just holding on."

She shook him free and brought herself into the new-found zone. She timed back, grabbed his hand and both of them disappeared in front of the mirror. "It looks like we can't do this thing together." she surmised.

"The individual factor." announced Ply.

"The what?"

"Barb can't get the thing to work at all and I seem unable to 'ghost' myself as you do. I'm not ready to give up yet, but if I can't feel you do this then I may not learn how to do it. Then again, maybe I don't have the chutzpah. It may have to do with capacitance." he observed.

"I beg your pardon?"

"Electronically, our bodies have a measure of capacitance."

"Hot diggity dog!"

"Try it again while holding hands and try to adjust a little differently."

She tried it and the half visibility showed itself, but it did not seem to hold. After a few tries she gave up.

"Wow." he reiterated. "I can feel it, but I have no clue how to do it."

"Time for the courts again." she promoted. "And I want to play with this thing when we are done there."

After the practice the two jogged around the castle a few times to cool down. "You go inside and play with the sword. I have some thinking to do." he declared. She kissed him on the cheek as she noticed an ooze of concern faintly cross his face.

"Good. We will talk when I come down." and off she scurried to get cleaned up.

Ply was a little bit hurt that he could not get the toy to do as he wanted, and she could. He paced a few more times around the castle. *Isn't that what marriage is all about?* he thought to himself. *You deny yourself so the other can develop the gifts the Lord has given.* He slowly walked around two more laps and then entered the house. Jane was at the top of the stairs with the sword in her hand.

"Watch this." she yelled and jumped from the railing.

"NOOOO!" he shouted and started to run to try to catch her. She one-third timed herself to appear like a ghost and floated across the top of the room using the sword for a sail and a propeller.

Ply stopped and watched as his horror turned from wonder and then to amusement.

"I don't know where I am going to use it, but I wish I could take it to the doctor's office next time I weigh in." she quipped with a smirk on her face.

"Why?"

"When I was trying to be half invisible, I felt a little lighter and with some playing I can make myself any weight I want to be." she smiled as she came to a perfect landing at his feet.

"Why would you want to get heavier?" he asked.

"If we ever go to Chicago, I will stay put a lot easier in the windy city with a few extra pounds." she articulated.

He just shook his head.

"What?" she returned. "Where are we going to leave this when we go to France?"

"Why can't we take it with us?" he asked.

"They have reintroduced X-ray machines on international flights. I did not think you wanted this discovered yet."

"That's for sure." he agreed. "How about the gun safe in the basement?"

"If the builder of the house ever shows up that might one of the first places, he looks for valuables." she observed. "Why not get that old guitar fixed, or at least strung and hide it under the bed in your room?"

"Why fix it up? Do you want to learn to play?"

"If I can at least do some easy chords on the thing," she pondered aloud, "It might give reason to prove that the toy is not hidden here in the case."

"If you like. When do you want to go? Where is there a music store around?"

"There is one about thirty minutes away. Let's go see what they can do for us?"

"Have you got anything in your purse other than hundreds?"

"Why? What else do I need?"

"If he sees all we have is hundreds he will want to sell us a new guitar and a different case. I haven't seen the need to carry mostly twenty's but if we have only big bills it may promote suspicion about getting this old clunker fixed."

"I see your point," she admitted, "We can stop and get some changed on the way. There is a bank on the way through town that may not know us seeing that I haven't really played yet."

"I can go in and you can wait in the car." he suggested.

"That may be the best."

* * *

The Music Palace appeared to be an old hamburger joint with a large room added to one side. There was heavy machinery on the other side laying foundations for another addition about twice the size of the first. Ply removed the guitar and left the case in the trunk of the car and they both walked in. They were greeted at the door by two people that asked what they were looking for.

"Hi." greeted Ply. "I need this to be restrung and tuned and some beginner books on how to play."

"Are you sure you want to spend the money on something in this bad shape?" asked the overly made up young lady.

"It is my first guitar and I would like to learn something about it. I got it for a song, and we'll see how much it costs to get it going." replied Ply as Jane rolled her eyes.

"When you get in, turn right and there is a service department. You might want to ask what it will cost to get it done and then make a decision."

"Thanks." said Ply as the two walked through the small cubicle. Inside there were more instruments than either of them had ever seen. Ply stopped about ten feet into the store and just starred for about fifteen seconds. A salesperson finally showed up with a recognizing smile on his face. "Can I help you find something?" he grinned.

Jane held her head low not wanting to be recognized and Ply held up the battered instrument.

The employee restrained himself by only thinking, *Do you need a trash dumpster?* but voiced, "Let me lead you to the service department." He slowly led the way as Ply was mesmerized by the racks of guitars, straps, chords, microphones and cables, T-shirts, violins, horns of all types, cellos, electric and acoustic instruments by the scores, hanging on the walls... Jane gave him a poke and he somewhat returned to reality.

"This your first visit?" asked the attendant.

"Wow. Do people actually buy all of this stuff?" was the feeble response.

"Not all at once but we do manage to keep an inventory that pleases most of those who come in."

The gentleman behind the service counter looked at the two and his shoulders fell about one full inch. "Can I help you?", he asked knowing that was what he was supposed to say but really wanted to laugh, or cry.

Jane butted in seeing that Ply was once again in some sort of daze that had appeared all too often in new situations. "We would like this guitar restrung, tuned and a book on how to play... a book for beginners."

"Are you sure you want to spend the money on that thing?"

"Why not, and what would it cost?" she asked.

"This is a really cheap guitar and not many of them were made very well. One of the tuning pegs is bent and may not be strong enough to take the stress of tuning. Often the pegs on this instrument don't hold the tension of the string and slip, making the instrument fall out of tune easily. New tuning pegs are forty dollars plus installation. The fretting on this model is notorious for being out just enough to sound only slightly out of tune with basic chords and horribly out when you get into bar chords. We don't waste our time replacing necks on these because the solid body is made of poplar instead of maple and really does not hold a longer neck because it is not strong enough. I can restring and tune it for thirty dollars, but I can't promise it will stay tuned until you get back to your car."

"Okay." she agreed. "How about some light Gage strings, a book for beginners, an inexpensive tuner and a set of new pegs. I'll get a friend to help with some of the other logistics."

"Whatever." He returned with a set of strings for ten bucks, a twenty-dollar tuner, and used book on the primary elements of guitar and basic music. "I would like to give you this used book on the basics. If you really want to learn to play, please come back and we can fix you up with something that is not expensive at all compared to a lot of what we have here, but I think you will be frustrated with what you have there. Would you like me to go and break the legs of the guy who sold it to you?"

"That won't be necessary." she smiled. "Thank you for your patience, expertise and the gift."

"Have I seen you someplace before?" he quietly whispered.

"I must look like somebody." she replied. "I get that all the time!" She pulled four twenties from her purse and paid for the equipment, grabbed the hand of her companion, pocked the change and the material, and escaped without further excitement.

France

It was the first time that Ply had ever flown and the ride across the pond seemed very long indeed. Ply downed his fifth soda after only being in the air for thirty minutes, Jane looked over and said, "Are you all right?"

"Just fine!" he replied looking more like he had downed a fifth of gin. "I'll try not to kiss the ground when we arrive."

She laughed and gave him a peck on the cheek. "Is there something you can do to keep you mind off flying for a while?"

"I was thinking I could memorize the numbers and the pictures of the stolen mowers just in case anything shows up."

"In Europe?" she asked.

"Why not?" he shrugged. "Brian says he sells these things all over the world."

She did not roll her eyes again, but it took considerable self-discipline.

"Okay." she turned to talk to Barb and was soon absorbed in conservation and plans for arrival.

Ply spent the next hours on his phone. To the stewardesses, it appeared he was playing a game. Mr. Spoudice had it set up so one could rotate the machine in any direction and as one zoomed in it broke down each machine and showed all the parts and assembly numbers of each machine part.

Wow! he thought. *No wonder it took so long to download the information. This might turn out to be very helpful.*

The landing was uneventful. True concerns for safety and better enforcement of fewer regulations had dropped the accident rating to almost zero. There were only two accidents and zero deaths during the last eight hundred years, nevertheless, the first flight for some is still a little nerve racking.

They took a cab to the hotel. Once registered, Ply was across the hall from the girls on the fifth floor.

During dinner Ply asked Jane if she was nervous.

"A little." she stated matter-of-factually. "I haven't played this court for a while, but I expect things will be familiar enough once I get on board."

"Wonderful!" mumbled Ply. "Then I will just be nervous for you."

"What on earth for?" she laughed.

"I've never been more than a hundred miles from home and here I am in a foreign country with no language under my belt and you're playing pro tennis!"

"Relax man." encouraged Barb. "Consider it a vacation. You get to see all the fascinating culture of other countries, experience all the sights, sounds and smells of other people and different places; there are many who would give their eye teeth just to hear of these things and you get to experience them simply by tagging along on the coattails of one of the best tennis players of all of history." Barb dropped her fork on the table, looked over at Ply and said, "And then you get to marry her!"

Jane just shook her head. "It'll be okay." she surmised. "All he really needs is something to eat."

"How do you know that?" he asked.

"Have you never heard, 'The way to a man's heart is through his stomach'? Let's go get a bite before he swoons from fear and starvation."

"Do they have hamburgers here?"

"Yes, but you may not like what's inside them. You will be better off sticking with chicken. Some of the cows here have a tendency to 'meow'!"

"Or neigh." added Barb.

"I've had Chinese before." he said.

"Not from this country you haven't!"

"Trust us Ply." exhorted Barb. "We will either help you or you can learn the hard way; and often it is via the food poisoning wing of the local hospital."

He gulped and mentally decided to go the easy route of listening to the ladies, in these matters anyway.

* * *

They talked for a while after lunch and Jane looked at her watch.

"I've got two hours to get ready for my first trials." she stated. "I really would like both of you to see me win or lose in this, but I must get ready. I need to run a bit and warm up so I'm not cold on the court."

"Where do you do that?" asked Ply.

"There is a gym that the pro tennis players get to use free of charge anytime they are in town." informed Barb. "All you have to do is present your ID and an authorized roster and you're in."

"How do you get an authorized roster?" asked Ply.

"Pick up a roster from the event organizers." stated Jane. "Then take it to the gym with your ID and have one of the officials autograph it and that's your ticket."

"It takes a few minutes if there is an 'official' at the gym but once your singed in you have not problems for the entire season, in France anyway." commented Barb.

"So, we better get over there." encouraged Jane.

"What about the one hour after lunch rule?" asked Ply.

"By the time she gets to be jogging around the upper deck it may well be longer than one hour and then she gets to play some pro." commented Barb.

"So, let's get over there." said Jane as she left a tip, rose from the table, and gathered her belongings.

"Who is going to pay for the meal?" asked Ply.

"Barb got this one and I will get the next." rambled Jane.

"Don't worry about money." encouraged Barb. "By the end of the games you'll have so much your head will spin."

Jane shook her head and responded, "I'm excited just to be playing again."

"Don't believe a word of it." whispered Barb to Ply as she gathered her stuff. "She is here to win and that is exactly what she'll do".

Jane managed to get in forty minutes of jogging and running prior to the match. Her first opponent was someone who had been eliminated three games back due to the fact that some of the newer judges had never heard of Jane Blythwood. Two were still skeptical even after all the info on her past had been presented to them. The enthusiasm of the older judges overjoyed just to hear of Miss Blythwood getting back into the games, never-mind that attempting to play at the Garros, didn't convince the new skeptics.

The judges agreed on one set just to see what would happen. Jane beat the poor girl Game, nothing in the four that she had to play. The die-hards tried not to rub it in, but the newcomers were duly impressed.

"Okay." they decided. "Let's bump her up to the next stage and try again tomorrow."

The judges split up into old and new friends and talked about the return of 'Jane of Arc' long into the night.

* * *

The next morning, the three had breakfast at the hotel.

"I think I'll go for a walk." stated Ply.

"What? Where are you going?" asked Jane.

"There's a park just across the freeway. I thought I would go for a walk and see some sights. Wanna come?"

"Come?" gripped the gal. "I've got a game to play. Don't you want to see me play?"

"I saw you beat the pants off that gal yesterday." rambled Ply. "And at the end of each game they said something about love! I did not expect tennis players to be so romantically involved with their opponents!"

Jane looked at him aghast.

"What if you do the same to this one? I don't want to be around when they announce from the stands that you are in love with this opponent also!"

"Good grief!" sighed Jane. "I'm sorry I never taught you how to score in the game." She moved over to his side and put an arm around his waist.

"If someone has no score at all that is called 'love'." she instructed.

"You mean that the word 'love' is actually a score in this game?"

"Well, yes and no." she grinned. "The word 'love' means that one of the players has not gained any points. They have no score."

"Really?"

Jane just looked at her beau and thought, *I don't think I have taught you anything.* Then she said, "The first point is numbered at fifteen; the second point is thirty; the third, forty and the fourth point is called game. You are my inspiration. If you are there I look over at your smiling face and I feel charged to do better than my best."

Ply just looked at her mulling over what she said. "Okay. If it is up to me then I'll make sure you win that game."

"I think to a good degree it really is." stated Barb.

"Wow. So, I have the gift of encouragement?" he beamed.

"When you attend my games for me you do." said Jane.

"Then I'll be there with bells on! Can we go for a walk in the park after the game? I really need to walk. It helps me think."

"What are you thinking about?" she coaxed.

"When you aren't around," he placed his hand on hers and dropped to one knee, "It is you that I think about. When you are around It is you, I think about." smiled the young man.

"Nice save." droned Barb.

During the game, every time things went in Jane's favor Ply hooted and hollered. When she got a point, he danced a little jig and sang a short song about 'Jane of Arc'. Jane loved it and so did the fans. It did not take very long for her to take all four games once again. This helped get them to the park a little earlier than if she had volleyed with her opponent very long, or so Ply was hoping.

Someone informed the media that this was the fiancé of the exemplary Jane Blythwood and after the game, even before she got to the locker rooms, the media hounded them.

"Congratulations." commended Barb who sat beside him throughout the entire show. "Not only did you encourage the pretty lady, but It appears that you also have the paparazzi on your trail."

"Excuse me." blurted a reporter. "Are you the one who is engaged to Miss Blythwood?"

Barb leaned over and whispered just above the din of the crowd into Ply's ear, "Just say 'no comment' until you get to talk to the princess."

Ply looked at her with a question on his face. Barb's eyes seemed to say, "Trust me in this one!" so they exited without speaking to anyone.

Back in the hotel room Ply asked, "Did I over-do this a little?"

"No, you over did it a lot, but I loved it, and so did the fans." encouraged Jane.

"I think the news people found out about us." Ply worried out loud.

"That just means we escape the hotel from a side door or an exit from a conference room. Here put these clothes on." she instructed.

"I've only worn these for half a day, and I didn't even get sweaty." gripped the newcomer.

"If we all change our clothes and exit some remote doorway, we may avoid the hounds long enough to get a quiet walk in the park. Get my drift?"

Ply was sent to his room and changed his pants and donned a T-shirt and a nice long-sleeved dress shirt over top then flipped on the TV to see what was happening while the girls got ready for the park. The only thing on was the match and not only was Jane the star but Ply even got some attention with the jig at each point. Then they announced that the rumor was that this is the fiancé of Miss Blythwood. Apparently, Ply missed it cause his back was turned to the big screen. He thought that all the handshakes were for his dance. "How on earth did they find that out?" he wondered.

A few minutes later there was a knock at the door. Ply opened it to see the girls dressed like tourists.

"One more hint," explained the latest attraction, "When someone knocks at your door look out the peep hole to see who it is. With some of these rascals they will barge in and not leave you alone until something controversial or dangerous comes out of your mouth. Then it is all over the papers and the media and the incident turns out really quite damaging."

"I'll try to remember that." mumbled the greenhorn.

Jane pulled out a colored dot from her purse.

"Are we planning a garage sale?" commented the novice.

"No." informed the star as she stuck the dot over the inside of the peep-hole. "This will help slow down any that are extra inquisitive about who is in this room. It will also help in deterring video coverage from the hallway."

"Video coverage from the hallway? What kind of perverts...?"

"All kinds of perverts and all kinds of people that want to see me lose so keep your guard up and try not to act too conspicuous."

Ply threw himself, back to the wall, and looked up and down the hall. "Do we need to hide our way to the elevator?" he whispered to the girls.

This action demanded a good shaking of the head. "Never a dull moment!" remarked the older of the three.

The park was pleasant and beautiful with the trees and flowers that were a little different than what Ply was used to. The two held hands as they walked and discussed plans about the upcoming games and the wedding. Barb walked behind them about ten paces as a good chaperon would. Jane had to encourage her to catch up a few times, so she could provide some input on the game schedule but when the subject turned to romance than she fell back, just enough to not interfere. They had almost an hour of enjoyment when Barb suddenly spoke.

"Rattzies at four o'clock!"

Jane did not look but scouted for an out.

"Out at nine o'clock." stage whispered Barb. "*Cafe Juan*. I think it has a back exit to a car park." Jane held a little tighter to Ply's hand as they increased their pace.

"Don't look back just walk as if you are in a hurry." she coached her beau. "If you don't want a repeat of what happened at the restaurant with the Spodice's."

That was all the encouragement he needed. In a few minutes they were at the front door. Barb was holding the door and glanced back to see if they had escaped. "It appears that the coast is clear at the moment but let's go someplace else for a drink." she murmured.

Barb greeted the attendant with a smile and walked out the back to the parking lot. She seemed to know her way around and the two followed her to the back entrance of another bistro then out to the street.

"There is a three-floor restaurant about two blocks from here if we can make it without being recognized." encouraged Barb.

"How did you do all this so easily?" wondered Ply.

"On your free time," explained Barb. "You scout out the area so when you have a need to escape from the 'hounds' or just want some quiet time to relax, you bribe the owners and the waiters and waitresses, so they let you through and then they steer the wolves from the media the other direction."

"You bribe them?" wide eyed Ply. "How much does it cost you?"

"One does not bribe them with money, silly. You bribe them with tennis trinkets like signed tennis balls. The winning point ball is good bait for a lot of them. Just gather up the balls at the end of the game, sign them in front of the one you wish to give it to and when you need to get through there is no problem."

"Is it really that easy?"

"It sure is!" stated Jane. "I forgot about that but thanks for the reminder. I promise I will get the balls from the next game."

"How are you going to do that while you are dancing around the court leaving your opponents lost in love?" bleated Ply.

"Do you remember those young kids that run around and chase the tennis balls that go foul?" voiced Jane.

"The ones that stand at the end of the net and fetch stray balls during the game?" guessed Ply.

"Exactly." inspired Jane. "They number the balls during play and at the end of the game we get them if we need them or else, they keep them for themselves. We usually get first pick, but they are happy with what they get. Tennis balls are not as collectible as baseballs..."

"Unless they are winnings from the great Jane Blythwood!" inserted Barb.

Jane ignored the comment and finished, "But it keeps some of the fans happy for a while."

"Like cafe owners and waiters in the heart of Paris?" guessed Ply.

"Precisely." added Barb. "That way if you plan your friends you can out-fox the wolves that dog you for stories that you don't want everyone in the world to know."

"Everybody has stories that they wish they could erase from their past." muttered Jane.

Ply looked at each of the girls and Barb was just slightly nodding her head. A look crossed her face remembering a few of the unreportable incidents. "I guess that is why He is not only the Maser but also the Savior."

"You are getting good at this sleuthing thing aren't you." smiled Jane.

At the top of the stairs in the restaurant they were greeted by the maître D'. A look of joy spread across his face as he recognized Barb then surprise as he recognized Jane. "What a delight to see you two," he flattered, "And Miss Jane what a magnificent game. A party of..." droned the Frenchman as he eyed Ply disapprovingly.

"Three." announced Jane showing her wonderful teeth. "Could we have that table in the corner by the window?"

"My pleasure." stated the waiter as he turned to lead the way.

I sure wish that smile was for me, thought the waiter to himself. *I would never have to worry about money ever again, and I could quit this stupid job.*

Barb sat with her back to the wall and clockwise Ply then Jane. All had good views out the window. The street below was a busy four lane with the north end of the park spreading out before them.

"Wow." exuded Ply. "What a great view. Can I take a picture?"

"Why not?" stated Barb. "It still is a free enough country."

"I just don't want to do anything that might cause some sort of stir." mumbled Ply. "I really am not used to this kind of lifestyle. You must remember that for the last three years I have subsisted on the occasional delightful meal from a relative or else pizza and soda and the interspersed feast of Dreary O's." he prattled as he focused his phone zooming in to the park.

"Are you not enjoying this?" asked Jane lightly.

"This, my dear, is a better vacation than I could ever imagine." Suddenly his phone started to vibrate. He lifted it back to focus on the park and in the far corner of the park was someone riding a mower that the phone recognized.

"You're kidding?" he interrogated his phone. He took the picture then the phone automatically brought one of the missing mowers from his list. At the bottom of his screen a message popped up giving instruction to check the serial numbers seeing as the device was too far away to do so.

"Are you okay?" asked Jane. "You look like you saw a ghost."

"Maybe I did." informed the sleuth. "I have to go and check something out. Order me a roast beef on rye and an ice-cream, and if I don't get back, eat the ice-cream and bring the sandwich back to the hotel in a doggie bag." With that he got up from the table, but Jane caught his arm.

"What did you see out there?" He showed her his phone and she said, "You have my number if you need me. If you don't get back here in forty-five minutes, we'll see you at the hotel. Don't go in the front entrance." she warned and with that he excused himself from the table.

Ply hurried down the stairway and out the front door. There

were not a lot of cars on the road, but they were going too fast to run out into the street. The traffic light was about three hundred feet from where he was, and the park was just on the other side. He sprinted to the light and just as it turned, he sped across all four lanes to the horror of the stunned drivers and disappeared over the hill into a grove of trees.

I sure hope the girls did not see that stunt, he thought. The sunlight was starting to fade so he had to get to the machine quickly. Two small hills later he spotted the device. The grass was freshly cut, and he slipped and skidded on his elbow staining his shirt. "Great!" he gripped. The mower turned towards the direction of the trailer to be mounted.

"I wonder if I can get a shot from here?"

He focused on the back of the machine as it was about to climb the trailer. The camera automatically zoomed in a snapped the shot confirming the numbers of one of the missing mowers. Ply refocused and took a shot of the plates on the truck. As it drove away, he noticed it was a park maintenance vehicle, so he snapped the side view also.

"Now what do I do?" he mused. Checking the time, he realized it was almost eight o'clock here and that meant about four in the morning Brian's time. "I'll wait a few hours then call Brian and send him the info. It just may be time to get the FBI involved."

He did not want to go back to the fancy restaurant with grass stains on his shirt and a tear in his pant leg, so he walked casually back to his room. He managed to get into the freight elevator and up to his floor without being discovered. He showered and changed his clothes and then there was a knock on his door. He lifted the sticky tab and looked through the hole. Seeing it was the girls, he opened.

"What happened to you?" asked Jane.

"Just a little sleuthing excitement." he showed them his bandaged elbow. "Oh, the mower is a match. I'll call Brian about five AM our time and one PM his, and let him know about the situation. I just might conference call my Uncle Jack at the same time. He might have a better idea as to what to do at this stage of the game. We know it was sold or traded to the park people here in Paris, so it won't be hard to find. I wonder if there are more?"

"Well duh." smirked Barb. "There are thirteen missing and now we have found one. That means twelve more to go!"

"Only eleven." corrected Ply. "One showed up at Brian's place. I was asking if more than one was sold to the park people here in Paris."

"Seeing that this is now an international caper it just might be out of our hands." commented Jane.

"I'm afraid that just may be so." slumped Ply. "Well, good-bye reward money."

"Don't get so discouraged." cooed Jane as she wrapped her arms around him. "There is much more than that measly reward money coming if you stay as my personal cheering section. The next game I play has a prize packet of almost eighty thousand. We can split it if you cheer me on."

"Eighty thousand dollars?" he gasped.

That is if I win all four straight. The higher I go the more competition I encounter but if I win the five out of seven in this next set, I get fifty, so will two and a half times the reward money keep you happy... For at least a few hours?" she teased.

"Good grief." he gasped. "Smart, beautiful, famous, rich women sure make life complicated!" he reiterated. The two ladies laughed.

"So how are we going to fool the media at the next game?" he invited.

"What do you mean?" asked Barb.

"It appears," concluded Ply, "That they will be knowing where you two are but how can I hide myself, so they will not find me?"

"How about a hooded sweatshirt and a large bill cap?" suggested one.

"How about a blanket in Spain and a turban on his head!" They all grinned.

"How about you sit the same place as you did for the other two games and then we will hide on them in Barcelona?" suggested Jane. "I will know where to look but I'll try not to goggle for the guy. If we can beat them by hiding on them, it just might make the match a little more interesting. I will need a little bit of a distraction for my opponent once I get up to the better players."

The plan started to take shape. Who knew where it would lead to. "Hey," announced Ply, "This is fun!"

* * *

The two flipped open their phones to the message, "Conference call from Ply Gallant". Both said "hello" at the same time.

"Greetings from Parly-Vox-Francis." teased Ply. "It is six in the evening here and I expect it is about seven in the morning there."

"Yes." both of them replied.

"We are fine, and Jane won both her matches straight and the media is going nuts, but we have managed to keep them off our heels for the moment. How are you two?" questioned the sleuth.

"You go first Brian." stated Jack.

"First of all, I did some advertising just after you left the first time we met. I said I was looking for some good trade-ins just to see if I could get any nibbles about the stolen toys. I got two from Johnson's place and three more from around the country that trace back to Johnson's place. That makes six of the twelve without finding the bait we sent to the crooks." informed Brian.

Before Ply could get a word in, being a little stunned at the effort the men had done on the other end, Jack spoke up, "You were correct about the police being paid off by the Johnson brothers. It turns out that they each got a hundred bucks, every time a mower went missing. When I called the captain, he was somewhat surprised but not totally seeing that they had been acting a little strangely. The only thing they were involved in so far has been the mowers."

"Now all we have to do is find the other six and the case is wrapped up." entered Brian.

Ply broke in with, "Then there are only five missing cause I just found one here in the park in Paris. You should find all the info on your computer when you get to the office."

"Whoa." chimed in Jack. "That makes the case international."

"I was wondering, so I waited to call you before trying to notify anybody else." mentioned Ply. "Who do I call now?"

"Why don't you talk to the police there in France and Brian and I will notify the FBI from this side."

"I was wondering but I needed to check first. I'll do that first thing in the morning."

"Perfect." agreed Jack. "That will give us time to get with the FBI and submit what has been lost and found up to this point."

"Hey, kid," joked Brian, "How did you find it? Isn't Paris a pretty big place?"

"I was in a restaurant taking a picture of a park scene and the phone zoomed in on the mower and stated that I needed to confirm the serial number. I ran across a crowded four lane highway, over two hills, slipped on the fresh cut grass, totally wrecked a good pair of pants and a nice shirt, but while I was down, I zoomed in and got the serial number and the phone said it was a match. It was driving up on the back of a Paris Parks truck, so I got the license number and a photo of the truck and driver. It should all be on Brian's office mail."

"You are amazing, kid." barked the impressed owner of the complex.

"Not me." replied the kid. "There is only one who is amazing."

"And on that we all agree." stated Jack.

* * *

Jane giggled at Ply, lost her concentration at one of the matches but won the other four straight. The five out of seven win won her fifty thousand dollars. The media went nuts and the French declared national parade days for the next three days. The three sat in a convertible during the parades. Jane sat in the middle up on the deck while Ply and Barb sat beside her on the seat. That put Jane sitting about shoulder level between the other two.

The parade stretched for six miles. By the end of the ride Jane needed help holding up her arms as she waved at the fans.

"The next step is Barcelona, Spain." yelled Barb to Ply over the roar of the crowd. "The organizers would not let her off the court until she had signed the papers."

"Does that mean that I don't get married?" yelled Ply.

"No." returned Barb. "It just means you get married a month later and half a million dollars richer!"

Ply sat back in his seat and his mind started to swim. He lay his head down on the side of the door and closed his eyes. The next thing he knew Jane was at this side comforting him with a cold wet face cloth.

"Man," he said, "You do all the work and I faint from exhaustion. Now that is teamwork."

Jane kissed him on the lips and the crowd went nuts. Where

else than Paris could that happen? The picture hit every newspaper in France and all of the tabloids worldwide.

JANE OF ARC SAYS YES TO SMALL TOWN BOY

was plastered on billboards throughout Europe and newspapers worldwide.

* * *

The plane for Spain was boarded and maneuvering into position for take-off when the aircraft was circled by seventeen military vehicles and three media trucks. Four of the military trucks had fifty-millimeter machine guns tied to a swivel platform on the bed. The passengers were told by the pilot to please remain seated and stay calm for the president of France was going to speak to the passengers. A motorized staircase pulled up to the side of the plane. The cameramen and the president of France came aboard flanked by six of the largest men Ply had ever seen. The size of the men made the RA two thousand weaponry carried by each soldier seem like toys, but Ply was suspicious they were the real thing.

The stewardesses and the pilot stood at attention as the leader of the country made his entrance. "Dr. Charles DeGaulle the seventh! The president of France." announced one of his militia. Everyone on the plane stood on their feet.

"Ladies and gentlemen," he announced in flawless English, "I apologize for making such a fuss over this incident, but it appears that I had to do something this drastic to save the reputation of the most romantic country in all of history. The marvelous country of France is the place for lovers. Granted, there have been a few other romances that have developed over the course of history but I have convinced myself, and these men here with me," moving his hands to bring the attention of the crowd to his armed servants, "That all other romances have been previously influenced, not only by the flair and beauty of our country but by the power of love that emanates from the center of Paris to every other corner of the world."

It was very easy to see that this man was first of all a wordsmith and secondly a politician but how he actually became president was escaping the minds of Jane and Barb at that instant.

"My cabinet and I have almost let the greatest romance of all of athletic history slip from our fingers." he said.

At this point Barb and Jane looked at each other and then over to Ply who was not shaking in his boots but if there was anything close to 'shaking in your boots' it was there dancing on his lap.

"It has been made evident," he continued, "During the recent parade that a proposition has been made without the consent of France. Therefore, I have decided that the marriage between the two most famous lovers on board this plane must not only happen within the borders of the most romantic and romance-oriented country of the universe, but within the gates of Paris itself."

The palms of Jane's hands were now wet with perspiration and Barb's collar started to glow from the audacity of this man. Neither said a word and wondered how much this was going to cost them, either to deny the president his wish or get themselves out of jail for the next game.

"I have placed a one thousand franc offering from my personal assets into an account for the wedding and to prove the boasted attribute of the country of love, have opened it to the public to make donations to the account." he continued.

"The account was opened two days ago and then opened to the public yesterday and at this moment there is a little more than five thousand francs an hour pouring in for this wedding. My cabinet has decided to personally invite the parents and immediate relatives of one generation each direction of the bride and groom, to live at the palace and be our personal guests of this generous country for a week prior to and one week following the wedding."

At this, the people of the entire plane, started to cheer; all except the three that just stood there dumbfounded.

"So," continued the gentleman dressed in the military uniform as the commander in chief, "We await the response and acceptance of the bride and groom."

Jane looked over at Ply. He had glued his teeth together and sealed his lips appearing to be frozen in fear and awe at the demonstration. As far as she was concerned it appeared that he had already been shot. At the hesitation to reply, the gentleman continued, "The other option we will present is accommodations at 'The Bastille' until they decide to..."

"We accept." yelled Jane.

"I am ecstatic that you see things as we present them in an easy to understand manner." grinned the president. "We will need three months to get things ready and will escort Miss Jane back here after Spain for fittings of appropriate apparel for the occasion." At this the leader signaled his men and they started to file out of the plane. As he stepped into the doorway he turned and said, "Of course the whole world is invited so we shall see you all there." He smiled and exited the plane.

The door was closed and once the tarmac was empty of military vehicles the plane was cleared for take-off.

"What did you volunteer yourself, slash us, for this time?" interrogated the clueless Ply.

"Remember, I prophesied that the whole world will be invited to our wedding?" said Jane. He returned a dazed look in her direction. "Well, it looks as if the president of France has done exactly that for us."

"The whole world?" he asked.

"It appears so." commented Jane. "Think of the commerce it will bring into Paris? If ten percent of tennis fans show up at the wedding, then the hotels will have to rent out houses to house the people. People will offer rooms in their homes for exorbitant amounts and the country will make a killing once again. It was a brilliant move on the part of the president."

"Aren't there elections scheduled here in six months?" reminded Barb.

"Oh, yes!" laughed Jane throwing her head back into the seat. "What a brilliant political move. It just might get him another six years."

"I'm sure glad you didn't get six years for turning him down." noted Barb sarcastically.

"Not just me, but we," reminded Jane. "We would not really have spent time in jail. It was just a form of political maneuvering."

"Well, just between you and me and Barb, I'm glad you maneuvered the situation saving our necks and a lot of explaining to have to be done in Spain." asserted the groom to be.

"She probably saved war from happening in Europe." noted Barb. "The Spaniards are almost as excitable as the French but seeing that it is just a game of tennis..."

"If it were soccer," bemoaned Jane, "Then the sparks would really have flown. I am so glad I get to play the cool, calm, game of tennis."

Will I ever get used to all of this? contemplated Ply. *I'll just enjoy the friendship of these two and take in what I can. This sure beats giving tours in a dark cave. I might even get a tan!* Looking over at his wife to be he voiced, "Are there beaches in Barcelona?"

"There certainly are, and you will NOT be showing up at any of them!"

"Why not?"

"Most of the beaches in this part of the world are nude."

"Why would you want to dress a beach?" he asked.

She looked at him, "Of course the beaches are not dressed. They don't need to be, but the people that attend them are not either and they certainly should be."

"What? Why? Don't they have bathing suits?"

"No, they don't! My only guess is that it is an outcome of the rebellion. The newspapers state they think they are progressive."

"This is much worse than I thought!" he mumbled.

"You're absolutely right." she whispered. "Cause you're not going to the beach without me and I am not going to a nude beach!"

"Thank you." he nodded. "I'll sleep better knowing that."

* * *

"Oh, you better call your parents." she coached. "I'm calling mine and will fly them out to Spain. If you call yours then they can meet you and me and each other. You did say they were retired?" He looked at her with eyes wide and her winning smile spread across her face. "I'll pay for the expense of them coming and going because the president is going to pay for the wedding and accommodations."

"I don't think they have passports."

"They don't need them if they are over fifty." she reminded him. "The rebellion just seems to surround the young people so those over fifty get off for a few years."

Ply dialed for his parents.

"Gallant residence."

"Hello Mom."

"Ply? Where are you?"

"I'm somewhere in the air over France on my way to Spain. Can you get Dad on the extension?"

"Hey kid, how are the caves?"

"Hi Dad, I'm not employed at the caves anymore, something else has come up. I am the professional grounds keeper of a star tennis player and I get to live in a castle and ride an expensive lawn mower."

"Then what are you doing in a plane on your way to Spain?" asked his mother.

"You're where?" quipped his Dad.

"You remember the girl Jane I told you about?"

"Yes." they answered.

"She has started to play tennis again and..."

"Is she this Blythwood girl the TV is going nuts about?" Q'ed his Dad.

"Yes and..."

"So, it was you that made such a fool of himself in the stands." concluded his father. "Where did you learn all that tom foolery?"

"She hired me as her own personal cheering coach. I get to encourage her, so she will win the games."

"Couldn't she have hired someone with a little more sense?" disputed the old buzzard.

"Dad, I would like to invite you and Mom to Spain to watch her play and get to know her."

"Now I'm sure you have lost not only your own marbles 'cause you are talking like you've lost everybody else's."

"Now George..." interjected his wife then he hung up.

"Mom? You still there?"

"Yes dear, you know we can't afford to go to Spain."

"I know but Jane has promised to pay for the trip, and you need to meet her because we are engaged." Silence on the other end for four long seconds. "Mom?"

"I'm here." It took a bit of time for his mom to get the idea that her son might be getting mixed up with a professional athletic woman. Trying to gain time and be polite she asked, "How did you meet her dear?"

"I told you already I met her at the tennis club. She is the girl who worked in the kiosk, remember?"

"Oh yes, how did she get into playing tennis so well if she

worked at the information booth?"

"Mom, I don't have much time here, but things have happened very quickly, and I had decided to get married and she said yes, and we would like you and Dad to come to Spain to meet her and get to enjoy her and her family. She says not to worry about the money cause all you need is already paid for. Get the neighbor to watch the house and collect the mail and come and have a good time. Besides we have a number of surprises for both of you."

"Surprises?"

"Mom, they are all good and you will be amazed how things are working out."

"I don't know about your father agreeing to just running off to some exotic place..."

"Okay," coached Ply, "You tell Dad that all expenses are paid and that you really don't need to worry about anything because Jane and I are going to handle all of your needs. We would like you to come to Spain and meet her, and her family. Talk to Dad about it tonight and let him sleep on it. Then bring it up again in the morning after giving him his favorite breakfast."

"You know that just might work." she agreed.

"Good." thanked Ply. "I'll call you about ten in the morning your time, so you don't have to call me. They have some beautiful clothing here in Europe."

"You are whetting my appetite. I haven't bought a new dress in almost ten years."

"Great Mom. I love you and will call you in the morning with all the information you need."

"I'm excited already." she giggled.

"Talk to you tomorrow, bye." Ply flipped his phone closed and started to tear up just a little.

"Aren't they coming?" asked Jane.

"I think they will." he comforted her.

"Mom loved to see the sights and sounds and smells of places, but they haven't been able to travel at all since Dad retired. We would drive to cities and visit places of important people of the last thousand years when we were kids. Mom loved it and we scraped and scrimped all year so we could drive fifteen hundred miles just to visit. We slept in tents and made sandwiches and had lunch at a fast food place, just so it would seem like vacation. Then we would talk about it for three months, and for the next nine, we would plan our next excursion. I think they will come."

Jane held him close, as close as one can get tied to a seat belt on a plane that was landing. She was tempted to cash in all her chips and send the family on an all-expense paid trip around the world till the money ran out but that was just a quick rash thought. "Someday..." she thought. "Someday it won't cost to travel, and we will visit unimaginable places..."

In less than forty minutes from take off the plane taxied onto the Barcelona tarmac.

Thirteen hours later Ply woke up in the middle of the night to phone home.

"Mom."

"Well, your plan worked. Your dad has been up since five making plans. I did not even have to make him his favorite breakfast, but I did just to ice the cake."

"You had cake for breakfast?"

"That's my boy, still the card."

"Okay. Bring a big suitcase each but don't put much in it so you have room for mementos."

"Is that something you eat?" she teased.

"Tickets will be ready for you at the airport. Jane and I will let you know as soon as we get things together from this end."

"Thank you, son." teared his mother. "I thought that our traveling days were over."

"If Jane has her way they might just get started again."

Spain

The next morning Jane greeted Ply with, "I sure am thankful we called our parents last night and they decided to come. Have you seen the news?"

"More excitement with the rebellion?" droned Ply.

"Lots of excitement but not about the rebellion." she commented as they walked into the cafe. Ply was struck by seeing pictures of each other plastered all over the screens and the announcement of the president of France. Those that had already arrived for breakfast started to applaud as the trio entered.

"This will be the biggest wedding in all of history and the whole world is invited." bawled the president.

"There are private residences available for accommodation and we have scheduled a parade so everyone that arrives gets to see the bride and groom up close. To reserve a room at a hotel or a private residence log on to..."

"I wonder how much of this is spreading over the continent?" Ply asked.

Barb had her tablet out and was checking just that. "It appears that most of Eastern Europe has received the news and the rest of the world plans to announce the adventure by this afternoon our time."

"Will I ever get used to this?" whispered Ply to himself.

"Don't worry." encouraged Jane. "Once I left the circuit all the noise died down in a matter of weeks. Don't answer your phone, don't answer your e-mail; things will get very quiet in a hurry."

"Sometimes, I wonder, when do we start?"

"First of all, we get married!" commanded Jane. "Then, once I'm pregnant, we can call it quits... for a while."

"For a while?"

"I might want to get back into playing." she stated. "And no matter if we have girls or boys, they will learn to play tennis!"

"And cut grass and splunk in caves." added the male of the

party. "So, I get some more time 'enjoying' this fame thing?"

"Might as well enjoy it while you can." spurred Barb. "There is always the castle when you need some down time."

"I'm almost ready now!" he gripped. "But I am enjoying the tennis games and the hoopla I get to generate while in the stands. Still, I'm nothing without you guys."

"That's usually the way it works." divulged Barb. "We don't get anywhere without the help of someone else."

"*Tres, por favor, por la eskina.*" Jane announced to the waiter and they were seated at a table in the corner. The bus boy had already set place mats, silverware wrapped in gold colored cloth napkins, long stemmed glasses sitting upside down on the dark red tablecloth. The waiter handed out menus then asked about drinks. They ordered dinner and sodas, returned the lists to the gentleman, and he left.

"So," inquired Ply, "What's the schedule?"

"I play four opponents this week unless I'm eliminated." remarked Jane.

"And you?" he addressed Barb.

There was a short pause then she admitted, "I'm the second opponent."

Ply glanced over at Jane with the question of how this might affect the relationship. Jane resolved the look.

"We have played each other before and a lot of times she has beat me. Friendship goes on beyond work and success. I expect we will both do our best and if we let the Lord be glorified the relationship will change, but only a little as the other goes forward with the rejoicing of both of us." she sat with a drab look on her face. "An example for old what's-his-face." she sputtered referring to her past relationship.

Ply cast his eyes in Barb's direction. "I did not throw the game at the castle and I will not throw it here. We are here to win but we are not always in full control of every aspect. If the clay is improperly compacted in one small area an ankle could be turned costing the game, a tournament or even a season. There are a dozen other things that could go wrong, but these are things you try not to worry about. The bottom line is do your best, Trust the Lord and practice, practice, practice."

"That's why we planned to have the parents arrive on Thursday. We play each other Wednesday. The eliminated gets to go to the airport and greet the folks."

The waiter brought the drinks and all three sipped in silence.

After a few moments of awkward quiet, Ply recognized, "I guess even the best friendships have their tests in love."

Jane looked at Barb and they both thought of it at the same time, but Barb got it out first.

"We haven't trounced each other that badly yet!" as the two girls laughed. Ply eased somewhat and the waiter brought the hot food. The awkwardness of playing each other was behind them for the moment, or, so to speak, a few days in front. They talked about lighter things and enjoyed their meal and friendship not letting future tournaments get in the way.

* * *

Thursday arrived and so did the parents at about two in the afternoon. Barb met them at the airport having been free from playing at the moment. Pictures from cell phones were swapped and Barb had no problem picking out the retirees from the crowd.

"Mr. and Mrs. Gallant?" she questioned as they were pulling of their luggage from the carousel.

The two retirees looked at each other.

"I am Barb Cully, and this is Jane's Mom and Dad, Greg and Carol Blythwood. You may remember Jane and I playing against each other."

The two pairs looked at each other without recognition.

"There has been a small adjustment to the schedules and Jane is at the courts as we speak, winning her next game I presume. We want to get you to the game as soon as possible so we decided to take you and your luggage to the hotel, get you to see the end of the game and some dinner then get you checked in. We have across the hall suites for each family and..."

'Where is Ply?" asked his Mom.

"You remember he is Jane's personal cheering section so in order for her to win the game he needs to be there. I can explain on the way to the hotel and here is a note from Ply seeing he could not get you on your phones."

"We didn't bring them. We didn't think thought they'd work here."

"We will get you some temporary ones just in case we get separated, could you please let us help? The game could be half over."

"Okay." They sheepishly agreed not knowing if it were the right thing to do but being in somewhat of a quandary.

Once settled into the taxi, Carol asked Barb about the games and how Jane was doing.

"She seems to win every game she plays. She did lose one when Ply was not causing enough of a raucous and she got a little distracted, but a good pep talk to the boy has managed to keep him in rare form."

"He does all this screaming and yelling every game?" asked George Gallant.

"Oh, yeah!" exclaimed Barb. "He is what brings us all together. He roots for her and writes songs and sings them from the stands... His voice is awful, but the fans and the media love it."

"And my boy is going to marry this tennis star?" puzzled his mom.

"Yes." admitted Barb cautiously. "We plan to fill you in on all the details during dinner after we check in. It is a bit of a roller coaster ride but there are times when there are opportunities to escape."

"Do you get to play at all?" asked Greg.

"Yes." responded the pro. "Jane beat me five out of seven yesterday."

There was silence for the rest of the six blocks to the hotel. A porter immediately jumped to their side as the auto arrived at the front entrance.

"I need all of these bags taken to room seventeen forty-six please." as she pressed a bill into his hand. "Driver could you please wait here, we will only be a few minutes."

In the elevator Barb explained to the porter that they will check in after the game and they would be back within three hours and to have the rooms ready that were reserved. The game had precedent over other things right at this time. The bags were left in Barb and Jane's room. Greg and Carol were pleased at the comforts of the room, but George and Ethyl thought they were absolutely marvelous. Bags were set to the side and the taxi rushed them off to the game.

On the way to the court Barb asked George and Ethyl, "So how much do you know about the game of tennis?"

"They bat a ball across a net a few times and someone gets a lot of money." droned George.

"That seems to be the common understanding of a lot of people but there are rules that need to be followed. All the lines on the court do have specific meaning and there is the scoring and changes of serves but I can explain all that to you as the game goes on." She gave them a quick rundown of the point system but then it was time to move to the field. They had arrived.

Barb walked over to the VIP gate, presented her card and the tickets for the folks then led them down to the six seats beside Ply. He was busy slaughtering an oratorio he concocted generating almost as much fuss as was on the court. Jane saw them arrive and waved her racket but did not get distracted, but her opponent sure did. Trying to take advantage of the moment she overcompensated, and the ball landed just the other side of the line.

"Point for Blythwood." came the announcement. A grin of pleasure jumped across Jane's folks as they looked at the score.

"You were right about a short game." commented Greg. "And Jane is really in rare form. How did all this happen so quickly?"

"I'll let Jane do most of the explaining but you can see that romance has a lot to do with it." nodded Barb in the direction of Ply. "They both seem too have very level heads, but I haven't seen Jane like this for years. I really do not like losing but losing to her... it seems to be a fact of life at the moment; and everyone with a tennis record seems to want a chance at it."

As the levels of the games progressed the volleys got a little longer. At this point ninety-minute sets were standard fare. She had been running for over an hour, four times a week just to keep her strength up prior to the introduction of the young man into her life. At the castle she managed to get into a routine of one hour twice a day, not to mention the chasing of the balls from the sword. Now it would be necessary to do more. Stamina was what she needed and the opportunities to improve with her parents here were limited.

As the game progressed, Barb explained to George and Ethyl, during the quiet moments, how the game functioned. It took a few serves for Ethyl to start to get the hang of it. George caught on pretty quickly and in a few moments was right up there with Ply rooting and hollering for Jane.

"Now I see where he gets it from!" expounded Barb in a somewhat flabbergasted voice. Ethyl giggled, and Barb returned the smile. Twenty more minutes and it was all over for the day. Jane was exhausted, sweaty, and smelly but she still left her opponent in wonder.

At the net she asked Jane, "It is great to see you back and even an honor to play against you but what is the mystery that gives you such an edge?"

Jane smiled, "Can you keep a secret?"

"Of course!" she stated wide eyed and listening.

Jane leaned over to get closer to her ear and without moving her lips whispered, "So can I!" and gave her a hug. "Thanks for the great game. You surprised me too with some of those returns." Then the awards were given.

While the two were at the net, Barb instructed the parents, "Please, all four of you wait here, Ply and I will be back in about twenty minutes. We need to get some stuff for Jane as she needs to be in the circle in a few minutes. With that they took off up the stairs and headed for the dressing rooms. They each grabbed a clean towel and a fresh, cool, but not too cold, water bottle and hurried out to where Jane was. Having done this a number of times before Ply was getting used to the routine.

The cameras were rolling, and the announcement was heralded.

"The winner of the two sets played out of a possible three is once again Miss Jane Blythwood."

The crowd roared so loud that she could not hear the questions of the reporter. After a least a full minute she received the microphone from the house announcer, stood up and addressed the thousands of fans.

"Thank you for such amazing support..." The noise became deafening and she had to wait. She knew well enough that the smile and tears of appreciation carried her well but that was not exactly what she wanted. "Who knew there were such wonderful fans in all of the world?" She encouraged and repeated her wait for the cheers to dim just a little. "I am very thankful to be playing once more..."

"This is going to take forever!" yelled Ply into Barb's ear but she only partially heard but fully understood. She nodded her head at him.

"I am looking forward to playing for a while..." As before, the noise from the stand drowned out her voice even with the microphone held right up to her lips. She dropped the mike and smiled. "Thank you for your marvelous encouragement." she ended, accepted the trophy and started to walk towards the change room.

* * *

The networks were furious! The broadcasters panned to the two announcers as they waited to get an interview with Jane.

One male reporter and cameraman crew started into the change room after the two girls. "Sorry boys," blocked Ply, "This is the girls change-room and there will be no cameras inside."

"You never heard of freedom of the press?" groused the ex-athlete reporter and pushed Ply out of the way.

From out of nowhere came two very large security guards and gently escorted the two in the opposite direction, away from their destination. "Sorry kids," they insulted, "This is Spain and most of us still have respect for people who need a little privacy."

The two in the broadcast booth kept up the conservation of the progress and points during the game waiting for time with the top performer of the moment, but, were somewhat disappointed when they saw on the monitor behind the camera in front of them as their shower-room scout was turned away. They both were professionals but to the trained eye something that they just saw brought disappointment to them. The network never let on, neither did they forget.

Twenty minutes later Jane and Barb exited from the woman's rooms and were hounded again. Jane smiled for the camera and Barb let her have her moment.

"That was an amazing match Miss Blythwood." trumpeted the reporter into the microphone, "How does one get into such good shape so soon from sitting around for two and a half years?"

"Wow!" Jane responded with her best smile. She wasn't really gorgeous, but she was extremely photogenic from certain angles, and these guys just happened to approach on the correct side. "That is the easiest answer I have had to answer all day." She paused just to get their response.

"Well?" primed the announcer.

"You never let yourself get out of shape."

"And exactly how did you do that? Were you not suffering from a broken heart?"

"You run six to eight miles a week, try not to leave it all for the same day, and trust Providence to work."

"Just how does this 'Providence' work?"

"You don't get real sick, suffer the common cold and flu each season, but that is normal. Try not to get hit by a car, don't go jumping off tall buildings, and just live knowing that things will eventually work out."

"We understand that you recently became engaged to be married. How soon and where is the wedding?"

"We are planning to be married in France in about three months. When we are done here in Spain we get to go back to France and make final arrangements."

"Will you win the rest of the matches here in Spain?"

"Are you a prophet?" she interrogated with a beautiful grin.

"A what?"

"Can you tell the future?"

"We certainly try."

"Then why should you expect me to be able to? But I will do my best. Why should I disappoint the fans by being half-hearted?"

"You did that once already." he condemned.

"That is why there is such a thing as forgiveness." she beamed.

"Thank you for the interview." hastened the surprised announcer and disappeared rather quickly.

Jane glanced at Barb and was quite surprised to see her livid. "Are you all right?"

"Those scoundrels!" she spat. "I sure hope I was out of camera range when he brought up that character. "Those TV clowns are like a package of rotten beets!"

"Beets?"

"When you squish 'em they go real red and bloody, but they have the heart of a rattlesnake."

"Ha, ha, ha." laughed Jane. "Let's meet the folks and go get something to eat. I'm starved."

Barb calmed down a bit, just enough to put a grin on her face, and accept the arm of her friend. "I see them in the stand where we left them." and she waved Ply to bring them over. Ply was familiar with the concourse, so they met halfway and headed for a quiet restaurant.

* * *

"*Siete, Por favor, cerca de la ventana.*" requested Jane slipping a note into the waiter's hand.

"*Si, como no?*" returned the waiter. He quickly walked away and, in a few minutes, ushered the party to a four-seat booth by the window with a table against the end and three extra chairs. On the ninth floor the view was pretty good with visibility at almost two miles in one direction. The waiter had loaded the table with menus before the group had arrived. As they were seated, he asked in a heavily accented English, "How was the game?"

"Terrific." replied Jane. "Would you like a souvenir?"

"It would be impolite to ask." bartered the gentleman although he already had.

"Oh nonsense!" exclaimed the champion. "I just happen to have the winning ball right here." She dug around the bottom of her bag and dug out a tennis ball with a small number 9 written on it. Let me sign and date it for you."

"*Muchimas Gracias Reigna.*"

Jane smiled at him and handed him the ball as Barb slowly shook her head. "Please give us a few minutes then we will be ready to order."

"*Vino?*"

Jane pointed to the menu and he returned with a bottle then quickly moved away from the table.

"It looks as if she's celebrating." whispered Barb to the folks. She waited until the waiter was out of earshot and dryly commented, "Just in case any of you missed that he referred to our star as the Queen of Tennis."

Jane blushed, and the rest of the table produced wide grins, except Ply who had his nose in the menu.

"I may need some help with this one." he mumbled to himself just above a whisper. He sat at the 'head' of the table with the parents beside their spouses in the booth with Jane to his right and Barb to his left.

177

"Hang on a sec, hollow leg, and I'll get my folks first." said Jane as she turned to her parents. Barb was already explaining the menu to George and Edith on her side of the table.

"What is *Salsa Picante*?" asked Ply to whoever was willing to reply.

"Hot sauce." returned Barb. "But you probably don't want any."

Why not? I like my sauce warmed up."

"That would be *'salsa caliente'*, sauce warmed, but *salsa picante* is peppers that burn all the way through."

"And if you don't flush the toilet fast enough it burns the porcelain." droned George.

Ethyl rolled her eyes, but all the rest of the jaws dropped. "How do you know about *'salsa picante'*?" asked Ply.

"When I was in college someone told us the story of an East Indian student who complained about the food being so bland." He took a sip of his drink. "The chefs of the cafeteria got together a decided to prepare a lunch they thought he would never forget. The day they had meatballs they placed two aside and cooked them specially for him. Part of the cooking process was to pour a little Tabasco® sauce onto each meatball until the entire bottle was split between the two pieces of carnage."

"Did they kill the poor boy?" asked Carol as a look of horror crept across her face.

George ignored her and continued with his story. "As the kid approached through the line the students working the line pulled out the doctored meat and said, 'These are for you'."

All glasses were left on the table as they waited to hear what happened.

"The three cooks came out of the kitchen and watched as the young man started to eat what they feared might be his last meal. He took a small bite and sloshed it around in his mouth. He didn't seem to mind but sometimes it takes a second or two for the spices to hit. He took another small bite and his eyes opened wide. The cooks watched wondering how long it would take them to get to jail and how long they would be in for when the student lifted his eyes to the cooks and raised two thumbs and said, 'this is quite good'."

"An entire bottle of that hot sauce?" proclaimed Greg.

George finished the story, "The cooks just returned to the

kitchen very thankful and shaking their heads in wonder. Someone from South America said it was like *salsa picante,* so you probably don't want it."

Ply sat there thinking about the differences in culture and how many more surprises lay ahead. "How about I just get some chicken?"

Once things were decided, Jane looked up in the direction of the waiter and he returned in a flash. She gave the desires of the group to the gentleman, asked if he would be so kind and open the bottle, he obliged, bowed then left.

"So," started Greg, "What is the plan and why all the rush to get us here to Spain?"

"Spain really is not the issue." said Jane. "It's France."

"France?" questioned Ethyl.

"Yeah, Mom." interjected Ply. "Jane and I are getting married in France. Paris to be exact"

Mrs. Gallant set down her glass and sat back as a look of worry and wonder came across her face. "How are we ever going to afford that?"

"That," returned Jane, "Is exactly why we rushed you here, so you could get yourselves prepared mentally, emotionally, and dressed appropriately. We have been 'invited' by the president of France to be married in Paris."

Jane stopped her conversation and took a small sip of her wine as the four glasses of the parents settled back down on the booth. "They have set up a fund and invited the people of Paris, and I think the rest of the world, to contribute. When he talked to us about it, he stated that there was already five thousand francs an hour going into the account. That was four or five days ago. We talked about it on the plane to Spain and decided it was just a political move seeing that there are elections in France next year."

There was a pause for a few seconds as Jane took another sip.

"The president wants us all to stay at the Presidential Palace." she continued and settled her glass on the table. "Which is nothing short of an ancient castle, for the one week before and after the wedding. I don't expect we will be bored but I do think we will be a little overweight once we get out of there if we don't watch ourselves. There will be lots of time to shop and sight see before the wedding, but once we get to the castle, I expect there will be preparations made for the wedding."

"Have you decided where it will be?" asked Jane's mom.

"At this point I don't know if we get much of a choice." admitted Jane. "It seems that the president has the power to make some of those decisions and we get to go along. It could be in any of the big old churches or even in the *Louvre*. I guess he gets to decide that since he is paying for it all. But I do get a lot of input into the dress. I'm going to have a fifteen-foot train with five flower girls just to keep the end of the train from dragging on the floor."

"And there will be twelve flower girls throwing rose pedals helter-skelter all along the aisle wherever we have it." added Ply.

"With all this money flowing in, how will he justify the expense?" asked Greg.

"These guys are professional politicians." exhorted Barb. "They won't have any trouble spending all that comes in. After all, they get to come to the wedding also."

"I was hoping I could buy a *Peugeot*." suggested Greg.

"It really is not our money, Dad." coached Jane. "If there is any left who knows what will happen with it, but it will take a lot to pay for the cooks and the pomp and circumstance and who knows what else? Look at the bright side. How many girls get to have a wedding fully paid for, in the heart of Paris, France; and stay in some of the most luxurious locations on the face of the earth?"

"And Mom," Ply encouraged, "That fund will pay for all the clothes you will need for the month while you are in France. That is why we told you to pack an almost empty suitcase. Anything any of you purchase in France, or here in Spain for that matter, save your receipt and make sure you give it to me, cause at the moment, part of my job description is balancing the books. I have a small metal file box with folders and envelopes, and I will keep track of all we spend and where, so we know where the money is going. If it appears that we are spending too much we will look where we can cut down but at the moment, it appears we can purchase what we need, and in some cases what we want."

He cast a cautious eye at Jane's dad and the two of them grinned.

"Do we get to explore the castle?" asked George. "I've never really been in one and would love to go snooping around to see if there are secret passageways, hidden staircases to the turrets... You know, all that mythical middle ages stuff."

"That may be the case, but we will have to make sure we have permission. You would not like someone snooping around your house without your permission." reminded his son.

"Your right about that." he agreed.

"How about dessert?" piped Ply.

"First course hasn't even arrived yet." exhorted his mom. "But this might be him now."

The food arrived, and thanks was given, for the game, the family and the meal.

"Man," declared Jane, "These portions are enormous."

"You gave him the ball." announced Barb. "All the rest of us got normal sized meals."

"Oh, well. There is probably someone here who can help me along if I get stuck." she admitted glancing at Ply.

"Well that's good to hear!" announced Ply's mom. "I'm sure glad that much hasn't changed."

* * *

After dinner Ply excused himself. "I really need a walk. Does anyone want to come?"

They all looked around the table at each other. "How will you not get lost? Do you know your way around well enough?" asked his Mom.

"I've got GPS on my phone, Mom. I'll be okay."

"There are some not-very-good parts of town not very far from here." revealed Barb. "Where are you planning to go?"

"There is a park about a half mile from here. You can see it from here. If I hike around there for a while will I be okay?"

"Two blocks the other side of that park is called, *Mundo Mafia Maldito* or, 'the cursed Mafia world'. If you stay in the park you may be okay, but it may not be a good idea at this time of night."

"Is there any other place that might be a little safer?"

"Not that I am aware of, but it would be better if you waited until morning." warned the older pro.

"How long before you head back to the hotel?" asked Ply.

"I thought we would just sit here and talk for a while." mentioned Ethyl. "I'd like to get to know these people a little more and the restaurant has lots of empty tables. What time does it close?"

"Not till eleven, Spain time." said Jane. "You must be tired."

"I think I am too excited to be tired. I wouldn't be able to sleep so why not stay here, at least for a while."

George was in the corner and leaned against the windowsill and shut his eyes. All the other eyes looked over at Greg. "I'm okay for an hour or so," he nodded, "But him?"

"He'll be fine." announced Ethyl. "He can sleep anywhere and almost in any position. In high school some of his buddies hung him up by his ankles for a prank. They came back about twenty minutes later and found him asleep!"

"Hanging upside down?" gasped Carol.

"He barfed out what was in his stomach and his buddies thought he was dead. They were all worried about spending the best part of their lives in prison when someone cut him down and when he hit the floor he woke up. Scared the liver right out all three of them but they never tried anything so stupid again. He still hears from them once in a while. Apparently, it did make an impression."

"I should think so." said Greg's wife as she glanced over to George to see him breathing gently and evenly.

"He'll be okay." informed Ethyl. "He'll probably sleep in the cab and then right through till seven in the morning. So how did you and Greg meet?"

"We were in high school together and were friends, but I was going with someone at the time." commented Carol. "He got a little too fresh and I broke off the relationship. I really liked him, but it seems he had some trouble with his lower nature. Never heard from or about him since. Every once in a while, I think about what may have happened, but my vows say forsaking all others, so I just forget and enjoy the life Greg and I have together. Don't get me wrong, I'm not trading in Greg for anything or anybody. It was just a high school romance that lasted for a few years then ended before disaster hit. Greg was there to pick up the pieces and it has been wonderful ever since, well almost."

"Almost?" asked Barb with a look of anticipation.

"We were trying to have kids but maybe we were trying too hard, anyway, nothing was happening, so we planned a vacation. We went to the beach in Costa Rica for one lovely month. It was in the off season, so we got a really good price. We were relaxed and comfortable and I got pregnant with Jane. The second last day I also got the flu. The next day we had to travel on the bus cause the hotel would not let us stay seeing I was sick, so we had to travel five hours in a bus through the mountains to San Jose. I puked my guts out the window and Greg was a perfect gentleman cleaning me up all the time, but I was furious and overjoyed at the same time. Angry because I was sick, but delighted I was with child."

"It looks like the flu didn't harm Jane any." quipped Barb.

"There were six people behind us on the bus," continued Carol, "Three in seats behind us and three on the other side of the bus behind us. Once I started throwing my lunch out the window Greg looked back as if to apologize for the mess and all six were on the far side of the vehicle with the windows wide open. I didn't think it was funny then, but we have laughed about it more than a dozen times since." The five laughed, George stirred, then settled back into a rhythmic slumber. "How did you and George meet?"

"We were just high school sweethearts and didn't want to wait till after college. George got a job in construction and had to move too far away to date but he did save his money. It was too far to travel each weekend and we just fell out of love, well I did. Someone new and exciting came into my life and I married him instead. Shortly after we were married, he was in a car accident and we could not have kids. He died about fifteen years later and one year to the day after my first husband died, I got a call from George. Not just a phone call but he showed up at my door complete with flowers and chocolates. I often wondered if he ever wanted to see me again but apparently, he did not want anybody else and just waited. When he thought I was available he just jumped in, re-stole my heart and he has been wonderful ever since. I sometimes wonder why I deserve such a great guy but, I guess that is what grace is all about."

All agreed.

"Ply showed up eleven months later but that was all that has been given."

"Isn't one of him enough?" nudged Jane.

"How many kids would you like to have?" she invited.

Jane lowered her head and thought for a moment. "I guess I'll be happy with what we receive."

Barb noticed the tension and broke in, "I have a friend who wanted twelve kids..."

"Twelve?" stammered Greg laying down his fork and sitting back trying to imagine such a tribe in one house.

"Until they had their first." continued Barb. "Then it got dropped to six."

"Six kids doesn't sound so bad." commented Ethyl.

"When number two showed up they decided they had one of each and there were no more choices, so he got himself 'fixed' so to speak and the four of them lived happily ever after."

They talked and laughed till almost ten thirty.

* * *

Ply had slipped out while the gang was talking and headed for the park. The group of six arrived at the hotel to find that everything was exactly as planned. Jane tapped on Ply's door but there was no answer. "Now what has he got himself into?" she pondered.

Just then a policeman walked around the corner. "*Senorita* Blythwood?"

"*Si.*"

"It appears that your friend had an accident in the park and is in the hospital." he said in Spanish. "If you follow me, I can lead you to him through town."

Barb was settling Ply's parents when Jane rushed in with the news.

"Can I go?" asked Ethyl.

"What about him?" sounded Barb. "He looks like he is already asleep."

"He'll be fine." buzzed his wife. "If he tags along all he will do is sleep. Might as well leave him here where he will be comfortable and somewhat out of trouble."

"Out of trouble?" queried Barb.

"Ply has to get it from somewhere." glibbed his mom not admitting that she might have anything at all to do with mischief.

"I'll ride with the policeman and you two follow in the rental." called Jane. "If we get separated call me and we can go from there." and she followed the cop into the elevator.

When the three arrived, they found Ply in traction with his left ankle bound in a cast. "What on earth happened to you this time?" interrogated his mother.

"Hi," greeted the injured, "I was wondering when you would show up. I had a little disagreement with someone in the park. You should see the other guy."

"What did you do to him?"

"Well, he got away before I could get a good hold of him."

"Good." piped up Jane. "Then you will not spend the next ten years in some Spanish prison. They are almost as comfortable as the ones in France!"

Barb glanced over at her friend and her look seemed to say, "Let's not go there."

Just then a female doctor arrived at the door. "May I come in?" she asked in perfect English.

"Please." pleaded Jane and Barb in unison.

"I think he will need to stay overnight and then keep off it for a few weeks." announced the doctor. "It is a nasty break but thankfully it was repairable. Some come in here with bones crushed so badly we have to amputate. This one got off fairly easily."

Ply did not think having your foot bound, elevated, and plastered was getting off easy, but he supposed that 'easy' in this case was a relative term. After all, he still had it and it might work again, some day.

"I guess I play without my cheering section tomorrow." slumped Jane.

"Who do you play against?" asked Ethyl.

Jane and Barb looked at each other with very suspicious frowns.

"Merodach." stated Jane.

"Win at all costs, Merodach?" echoed Barb.

"I'm going to need some sleep to be ready for this dragon in the morning." stated Jane. She leaned over and kissed her beau and said, "I'll probably not see you until tomorrow evening, but I will show up when I can."

"Can I stay?" asked Ethyl.

"They really do not allow visitors to stay overnight like they do in some hospitals, but I can bring you here first thing in the morning." announced Barb.

"That would be fine." confirmed the doctor as the three left the room.

When the four reached the desk, they were far enough away

from the room, so Ply was out of earshot. "How well does this guy obey orders?" questioned Jane to Ethyl while holding on to the doctor's elbow to include her in the conversation.

"What do you mean?" replied his mom.

"Is this guy going to stay off his foot for three weeks of do we need to leave him here. I want him healed for the wedding and I will need a cheering section for the next season."

"The next season?" staggered Barb.

"I will do everything I can to beat the dragon, but I don't think I can muster up what I need without Ply. I will not throw any games but if I can't do it then... You know how distractions affect your game."

"I do." responded Barb.

"That's Ply's line." smirked the young champion.

"That could be expensive." replied the doctor.

"That is okay." returned Jane. "I'm not making all this money just to spend on myself."

* * *

The next day as the two approached the net to shake hands, "Too bad about your boyfriend." leered Jane's opponent.

"How did you know?" asked Jane.

"Oh, a little birdie told me."

"This isn't badminton." replied Jane as she turned off the record feature on her phone. "Have a good game." She walked back to the edge of the court, tossed her phone to Barb, and turned to receive the serve.

The Merodach brat was good and Jane was a little distracted about Ply not being there to root her on, and then being injured and in the hospital, but she wasn't going to let a bad manners player win due to intimidation. The games were close, but Jane won the necessary four of the six games that were played.

It took two weeks before the doctor allowed Ply to put pressure on his foot. She made him stay in the hospital because his mother told him to. So did his fiancé. Jane wrote out a check and all were really happy except Ply, but he got over it, eventually.

Jane managed to play for another week and a half but without her cheering section her game faltered. She spent a lot of time at the hospital while Ethyl and Carol, hosted with Barb, enjoyed the shops and the amazing variety of restaurants.

After the tournament Jane turned in the evidence to the police. She did not want to lose but the pressure of Ply being in the hospital instead of by her side screaming on the court eliminated her, but it took a number of opponents to do so. She went on to win the next two but lost out in the third.

Jane was eliminated with six weeks left before the wedding. Ply was almost back on his feet but with one in a foot cast. Jane and his mom finally let him loose from the hospital but only after Merodach had received her sentence.

The police found three witnesses that had come forward to testify against Isabelle Merodach as she stood just behind the scene as Ply got his leg crunched by a back-alley brute. The three all had the cameras running on their phones.

When the evidence of the videos showed up one of the recordings showed Isabelle laughing as Ply got his leg crunched. She announced loud enough for the phone to pick up, "I get the championship for just one hundred bucks."

The judge looked over at the accused and it was apparent that his mind was then forever made up. The judge sentenced her for attempting to 'fix' a professional game and for assault and battery. She was assigned to stay in a 'Government Hotel' for ten years.

Isabelle stood up and yelled, "That is cruel and unusual punishment." with her lawyer still sitting but aghast at her audacity. He was so surprised he just sat there.

"You were not in the Northern Continent when you planned and executed this crime." stated the judge.

"If you continue to find fault with the justice system of Spain, I will accuse you of all of the other unsettled cases of 'broken bones' that have happened in that park for the last five years and you will receive life without parole."

Spanish government housing was limited to those who decided it might be profitable to ignore the laws of the present regime. It was not a holiday in any way shape or form and before long Isabelle was wondering if there was any way she could appeal. The Spanish refused and seeing she had not committed an international offense she got to stay where she was.

The Wedding

The return flight to France was uneventful save the apprehension of meeting with the president. As soon as the plane landed and taxied towards the gate the pilot came over the air and invited all to remain seated except row seven of first class. The three people that were not with the 'Tennis Crowd' were able to get off the plane first without the hassle of other passengers pushing and crowding. They wondered why all the special treatment from the airlines until they were met by a number of very large uniformed men with unpleasantly intimidating weaponry slung over their shoulders. Jane let the three go first and then explained to the officers that they were simply in the same aisle as they were. There are only seven of us at the moment but there will be more arriving for the wedding. The three were dismissed and the seven were cleared customs from a separate gate and ushered into a very comfortable twenty passenger bus.

"I've been thinking." stated Greg. "There are a number of reactions a person could have in this situation. First: one could think that the French government is honored by your presence and by some illusion of entitlement we deserve this kind of treatment.

"Second, which is the other extreme and equally ludicrous, one could imagine that they are abducted as prisoners of war and are being hauled off the castle to undergo months of interrogation under extremely harsh conditions; "Third, you could allow yourself to be blown away by the wonder of being invited to a place just because of the abilities and gifts of another person. What have I done to get myself here? Married a beautiful lady, had a daughter and recognized her gift at tennis and helped her develop that gift, but all of these opportunities are also gifts that I have just acted on.

"So, I'll chose to enjoy the ride and be thankful and helpful in that which I can be helpful with."

George thought about this for a moment and then decided that having an enjoyable time is better that growling and a smile actually cracked his wrinkled face. Ethyl saw the change and felt good that George was able to travel again even if it was not on his own dime. *It is often hard to accept charity, especially if you have been the main supplier all of your life,* she thought. *Sometimes you have to let the kids do what they are able when you cannot.*

George looked out the window at the sights of a somewhat different culture. Once he decided to appreciate the moment he settled back into the seat and closed his eyes enjoying the ride of a lifetime and fell asleep.

* * *

Preparations for the ceremony of the year, although the year was by no means over, were under way. Tuxedos and dresses were being made to order.

"None of this rental stuff for this wedding." demanded DeGaulle. "How many maids of honor are you planning? I am hoping at least five."

Five? gulped Jane. *I was only planning two,* she thought.

"And how many bridesmaids do I need?" she solicited.

The leader thought for a moment, "Do you think fifteen will be enough?"

"I should certainly hope so." Then she said to herself, *I just may have to get out not only my college but my high school yearbooks to find that many.*

"And how long will it take you to get them here?" demanded the over-anxious gentleman.

"I'll make some phone calls first thing in the morning."

That evening Jane, Barb, and Ply got their heads together and filled the roster of needed attendants. Friends and friends of friends were invited and hurried off to Paris for the vacation they never thought of and the opportunities that were hard to imagine being involved in the wedding of the century, as one newspaper called it. As if there would be no more weddings for the next seventy-five years or even any more important!

Wow, thought Jane. *Sometimes we really have a narrow focus.*

Money poured into the fund with the promise of seats for those who donated, and dresses and tuxedos were ordered and made. Seeing as the clothing was made for each individual, part of the package was giving the wedding clothing to those who wore them. Some had already decided to auction it off immediately after the event, but others figured it would be more valuable later and planned to keep the apparel for themselves.

All of the dresses were of a similar style, color, and material but each bridesmaid had the opportunity to add some special individual touch to the design. This made the line-up pleasing to the eye but not hypnotic. The five maids of honor wore a light mauve and the fifteen bridesmaids wore a light blue. All the material was satin that had to be made in advance but not quite that which was used for royalty which was reserved for the president and his officers. So much for not upstaging the bride and groom.

The men had tuxedos made of black satin and cotton. Their shoes were all black leather, but they were allowed to choose which type and style from a specialty shoe shop in town. A few of the guys chose dressy cowboy boots seeing as they were from ranch country in the western part of the continent.

The main ceremony was to be held in the *Eglise Americaine,* a Paris Protestant Sixty-Five Quay D'Orsay, Paris, France.

Overflow Crowds at:

Notre Dame,

American Chapel on Twenty Third Avenue George V,

Sacred Heart Catholic Church. Thirty-five Rue Du Chevalier de la Barre, Eglise Saint Sulpice Two Rue Palatine.

The Friday night rehearsal went off without a hitch. All of the lines had been rehearsed with a few minor changes seeing as the two wanted more traditional vows. They were planning their marriage to last longer than the honeymoon. They had received excellent counseling from some of the more conservative among them as well as some interesting observations from some that thought that marriage was just a waste of time.

"We are to enjoy ourselves and not let the 'restrictions of the past' interfere with out pursuit of happiness." spouted one.

Little did the counselor know that the 'pursuit of happiness' historically meant seeking the reality of the higher heavenly dimensions and not just catering to our lower natures.

There is always conflicting advice available. It is our job to test and sort out reality, Jane reminded herself. *Someone once said, 'If you reject reality, it is bound to soon hit you on the nose', or something like that.*

Saturday arrived and preparations for the two o'clock wedding started at eight in the morning for Jane. The maids and flower girls were invited to arrive to dress at ten giving them a little more time to eat a later breakfast and bath prior to arriving.

Jane was a little frustrated about missing her morning and evening runs, but she didn't let it bother her, too much.

"I'll just have to make up after all this is over and start again next season." she said to herself. *I probably have enough money to last at least till spring.*

It was brought to her mind all the starving children in the world that had arisen due to the rebellion and was smitten by the riches she had stored away. "Forgive me for being so selfish." she stated in half a breath but just loud enough to be heard by one of her attendants.

"Selfish?" questioned one of her ladies in waiting that had been hired for the wedding preparations. "With a ceremony like this you ask forgiveness for being selfish?" she asked with astonishment.

"I am truly sorry for any trouble that this has caused any of you ladies, but all this pomp and circumstance is the president's idea." announced Jane to her helper. "He actually threatened to throw me, my fiancé, and a friend of mine into the *Bastille* unless we agreed to his plan."

"Really?" questioned her maid in a somewhat unbelieving manner.

"I get all of this attention just because I can play the game of tennis fairly well." stated the star. "We were on the plane to Spain for the next round of games and the president boarded the plane with a slew of armed guards and 'invited' us to have the wedding here in Paris."

"Some people have all the luck." stated her assistant.

"This is just a temporary reward that I do not get to celebrate in heaven." reminded Jane to the young lady. "There is no peace from the paparazzi, or as Ply refers to them as, 'the improper Ratzies', and you are forever wondering if your quiet dinner will be interrupted by someone who thinks you are terrific but all we are doing is using the gifts God has given us to honor His name."

"That is easy for you to say." quipped the maiden.

Jane rehearsed the 'discovery' by Curtis to the young girl and told her that it is not all beauty and glory.

"If there is a job that needs to be prepared for and the media will not let you practice nor sleep then the job will not get done to the degree that practice and rest will provide for. Fame and fortune are terribly overrated. People think you belong to them, abuse you, and when you don't come through, they blame you for messing up and toss you out the window into the dumpster below."

Jane smiled down at the girl who was working on one of the hems of her dress.

"So, money and recognition rob us of quiet simple things in life?" questioned the girl.

"Pretty much if you let them." stated Jane. "You always have to be on your toes, or the press will find something that they think is horrible and blab it all over the place ruining your life and the lives of others that you care about."

"I never really looked at it that way, but I guess your right?"

"Look at the movie stars." commented Jane. "Every time one gets bored with their present 'spousal unit' the press gets hold of it and blabs it to the world. My dad likes to read about it and then he goes over and kisses Mom and thanks her that they are not filthy rich."

"Is it your mom's fault that they have no money?"

"Not at all." replied Jane. "My dad was a carpenter and made good enough money, but he put it into other things rather than things for himself."

"Like what?"

"He paid a lot of money to put me through tennis when I was a kid. The least I can do is pay his way to follow me around when I play. Often, he refuses and stays at home and just watches me on TV, but he suffered much for my sake."

"Sounds like a familiar story." said the maiden looking up to the star. "It is usually someone else's effort that got us to where we are. As my friend says, 'That is why He is the Savior and not just the Master.'"

The two continued the fitting and the finishing touches on the dress basking in the glory that is not their own but that was given to them by a greater.

The men did not show up until noon seeing they were not the stars of the show.

The invited started showing up three days before the wedding and parked themselves 'in line' until they blocked not only the sidewalk but the roadway also. They were given coded numerical numbers with the promise they could not be copied and dismissed to clear the path. They were instructed not to show up prior to two hours before the ceremony. Those who did had their tickets confiscated and told to go to the back of the line. Those that refused to leave got to spend the night in the nearest 'Government Hotel'.

At noon the guests started pouring into the sanctuary. The preparations for the event had just been completed but the candles on the candelabras were not lit until just before the ceremony started.

Prior to the entrance of the bride, six young flower girls flung rose petals as far as they could. Each of the girls had a dress the same color as the petals they were casting, red, yellow, white, blue, and two with multicolored dresses and petals to match. Antihistamines had previously been provided for those with allergies. Indeed, all the president's men had thought of everything.

The bridal gown was a shimmering white silk imported from India. Final stitches were being made just before her entrance. The train was fifteen feet long with five young bridesmaids holding the ends floating to the full width of the aisle.

Jane arrived at the back of the church and looked up the aisle towards Ply.

"Yikes." she mumbled under her breath. "It looks a hundred miles long."

During the night the sanctuary had been decorated for the festivities. The ends of every other pew had an arch with flowers woven across the span of the aisle hanging from the curved structure. The pews without arches had tall candelabras with seven candles on each. They were not in a straight line like a menorah but six in a circle and one in the center.

In spite of all the candles and the heat generated by the hundreds of adoring fans and family the building was still cool. The stone structure kept the place cold in winter and cool in the summer.

"I'm not supposed to run into his arms but step slowly up the aisle towards the groom." she reminded herself quietly under her breath.

The music changed, and the procession started.

"Don't get dizzy. Don't fall over. Don't trip over your dress." she reminded herself as she made her way down "death row" as someone referred to it. Ply thought that they were just jealous because they did not get to marry the beauty.

"With an attitude like that," commented Barb a few days earlier when she heard the comment, "It just may be the case that he is the beast!"

"We think of the strangest things at a time like this." thought Jane as she kept her eyes on the one, she was headed to spend the rest of her life with.

Fifteen minutes down the aisle, just ten feet from the stairs to the platform her dad stepped out from the aisle and took her arm. She looked into his face for a short second and saw his cheeks were spotted with glistening moisture.

"Who gives this woman away?" asked the priest.

"Her mother and I do." answered Greg very proudly.

Jane stepped up to the platform where the priest and Ply were waiting. The girls dropped the train onto the floor and took a seat on the end of the first pew.

A charge was given explaining the responsibilities and opportunities of marriage in the Lord. Jane was so excited about just getting married she was glad the charge was recorded because then she could consider the words of the preacher at her leisure. The high of getting married was enough to sail her off to 'Never, Never Land', never-mind the pomp and circumstance the president demanded. It took all of her self-control to stay calm in the midst of the madness of preparations and ceremonies and special dinners. She was glad the honeymoon was for an entire week, because she would need the rest.

"Let us pray." invited the priest and the two in front of him got down on their knees on the steps to the platform. Cameras flashed and the face of the president flushed red with embarrassment and mild rage. Many in the audience were snickering at the joke that had been played. The political leader closely scrutinized with his eyes each man and woman in the wedding party. There appeared to be two males that needed to spend a few nights in special accommodation. The rest of those on the platform seemed oblivious to the writing on the bottom of Ply's shoes. Someone had written the letters 'LP' on the bottom of Ply's right shoe in the arch just under the heel. On the left shoe was written the other two letters that spelled 'HELP'.

The video cameras zoomed in on the bottom of Ply's shoes

and the overflow crowd got to see the plea in large lettering flashed across the screen. The action brought most of the crowd to their feet in a standing ovation to the rascals who had the felt tipped pens.

Back at the ceremony, the preacher heard the commotion and peeked at the crowd and quickly said, "Amen."

The bride and groom rose to their feet and the snickering ceased when he stated, "Do you, Explicitus Davidson Gallant take Jane Gwendolyn Blythwood to be your lawfully wedded wife to have and to hold for richer, for poorer, in sickness and in health, as long as you both shall live?"

"Explica-what?" she stammered just above a whisper and looked in horror to her right.

"That's me. Say yes." he stage whispered.

"How am I supposed to marry someone who's name I don't even know?" she asked.

"It is my birth name. I had it changed on my driver's license, so I wouldn't have to go through the third degree every time I got stopped by a cop."

"What else don't I know about you?" she quietly steamed as her eyebrows scrunched into gorgeous angles.

"Can we get on with this I have a tennis star I need to marry."

He looked over to the priest who had beads of sweat forming on his brow and dripping down into his glasses, with the look of amazement and a little perturbed at the embarrassment of the moment. He quickly glanced at Jane and back to the priest.

"I do." announced Ply.

The pause and the stutter caused a rustle and whisper among the audience.

"Yes. I surely do." he quickly blurted again causing the hush to fall again on the crowd behind them.

The priest gave her a cautious glance and wondered if this girl with almost all the talent and half the money in the world really knew what she was getting herself into.

Ply looked over to his soon to be wife and whispered just loud enough so the three of them can hear, "Gwendolyn?"

"I thought we practiced this." whispered the robed gentleman between clenched teeth and smiling lips. This confirmed to the official that these two did really not know who on earth they were getting involved with and he mentally put a three week to six-month expiration date on the union. Another pause and the audience started to get restless bringing him back to the job at hand.

"Do you, Jane Gwendolyn Blythwood take Expliticus Davidson Gallant to be your lawfully wedded husband to have and to hold for richer, for poorer, in sickness and in health, till death do you part?"

"I certainly do." she grinned which was not the rehearsed phrase, but it brought a giggle from the seven hundred people behind them and more applause from those in the three overflow churches.

"If for any reason there is anyone who thinks that this union should not be completed speak now or forever hold your peace." stated the minister and had to bite his own tongue. Thankfully he chose discretion as the better part of valor and kept himself out of prison for the rest of his life by keeping silent instead of questioning the service this late in the game.

"Since there is no objection," he paused then said to himself, *That has been verbalized*, then continued in a loud voice, "Before the assembly of this body, the high governing body of this land and the Lord of all creation I now pronounce you man and wife," then to the two of them he stage whispered, "You may kiss the bride."

He certainly did!

* * *

They had heard about the tower that overlooks the river. All things had been prepared for the consummation.

Jane tugged at his sleeve as she hurried up the stone staircase. He thought he was excited, but her anticipation was never so evident, until now.

She kissed him on the stairs, and she dropped the keys on the steps. He was not about to enjoy her unless it was fully private. He laughed and grabbed her hand; he noticed a small round object jutting out of the stone in the lip of the ceiling and the wall of the stairwell. *How many are there?* he asked himself.

He held her close and put his finger to his lips. She blinked in puzzlement. He hugged her and nibbled on her ear.

She giggled in excited anticipation.

"This stairwell is full of cameras." he whispered in her ear.

She looked around and noticed the small balls in the corners at the top of the wall.

Grabbing her hand and her keys they ran up the remaining twenty steps. Every thirty degrees up the round stone staircase there was a small round object almost unnoticeable in the poorly lit corridor.

They entered the large round chamber more than twenty feet in diameter. A canopied ceiling that started at the top of the twelve-foot high wall arched over their heads to a height of over twenty-four feet to the peak. Round decorations every eight inches on three levels decorated the dome.

An almost floor to ceiling curved uncovered window four feet wide was opposite the door from the stairwell. A carved mantel above the glass boasted in royal lettering of the romance of France. Cupped plate glass filled the opening without any opportunity to let fresh air into the room. The sealed opening also prevented anyone from falling, or diving, into the river one-hundred and sixty feet below. The floor was carpeted until thirty inches from the wall. This left the furniture against the wall resting on the stone floor, but bare feet could find the comfort of the thick carpet.

There was a curious rosewood topped table beside the window. It appeared that the legs of the table were African antelope antlers. A multicolored doily centered the table with a single lamp on the doily.

Just to the left of the horned table was a large chest of drawers. The chest was made of redwood and stood almost six feet tall. There were two large drawers on each of the five levels.

"There is enough storage space here to house an entire family of six." commented Jane. "Why would they put such a great dresser in a room this far away from everything?"

Ply glanced at the piece. "Would they hole up a family of six in a room like this unless they wanted something out of them?"

A long French settee lined the wall halfway between the window and the stairwell. Various pieces of Louis XIV furniture filled in the spaces along the outside wall. Beside the stair well door was a sink and towel rack with fresh facecloths and towels, one set bright red and one royal blue. Next to this was a drawn curtain. Behind the curtain was a bidet, a toilet, and a shower stall.

Right in the center of the room was a king sized four poster bed, without any coverings for the posters. The top blanket was an enormous eiderdown ranging from three to four inches thick.

Jane dropped her shawl with invitation in her eyes. Ply grabbed the thick blanket from the top of the bed and threw one end over top of the girl. He spun her around once and tackled her gently to the floor, her muted screams of protest coming from under the blanket.

On the chest of drawers was a CD player with AM and FM radio.

"What are you doing?" came the muffled voice from inside the tent.

He ran over, switched it on to FM radio, found the first station available as he rotated the dial and cranked up the volume to almost full blast. Diving into the rolled eiderdown he maneuvered to his wife and held his finger to his lips. He held an air vent aloft with his foot so the two would not smother under the thick insulated blanket. By the time Ply got there the air was getting a little stale.

As the radio blasted something in French, Ply whispered, "This place is full of cameras."

"What?"

"Just like the stairwell." he said. "There has to be a hundred in the ceiling."

"How come I didn't see any?" she asked back just audible enough to be heard under the cover above the noise of the instrument on the dresser.

"I think that each one of those little balls has a camera in it."

"Why would they do such a thing?"

"Use your unsanctified imagination, gorgeous."

She thought about this for a moment then with eyes wide responded, "What are we going to do?"

"What we are NOT going to do is give these guys the live video of our romance from ninety different angles, so they can broadcast it all around the world!"

"They wouldn't dare." she fumed.

"Then why would they give us a honeymoon suite in it with a million cameras in it?" he challenged.

Another few minutes passed with blinking every two seconds as a new revelation of what the cameras could have caught hit her bright little mind.

"What are we going to do?" she repeated.

"You pretend you're unconscious, I'll lift you to the bed and we can each get a good night's sleep."

"What about..." she started.

"I've waited a year for this." he reminded her. "A few more days of torment isn't going to kill me and if it kills you..."

She wrapped her arms and legs around him and planted her lips on his.

"Please don't make this any more difficult than it already is." he mumbled with his mouth full.

She laughed and feigned a faint in his arms.

"You crazy woman." he said, "How am I going to untangle from this?"

"Do you want to sleep here on the floor?" he invited.

"No." she snored.

"Then please cooperate."

"Spoiled sport!" she teased.

"I am indeed spoiled rotten baby; I'm married to you."

She unwrapped enough for him to move, crawled out and lifted her to the bed. She was wrapped in the great blanket and had to use two pillows to get her head comfortable. In one of the drawers he found another blanket and after killing the radio crawled in beside her, snuggled his back into hers and fell into the most delightful asleep of his life, up to that moment anyway.

The next morning, she hauled herself out and washed her face. He lay there waiting to see what would happen next. She picked up her shawl and waltzed over to the window.

"I just love it here." she said and did a little twirl right in front of the window. "Don't you?"

Ply stumbled out from the enormous bed and walked over to the window. "What a beautiful view." he stated following her lead in an attempt to keep the goons happy. "What say we get dressed for breakfast?"

With a short inspection it was discovered that the curtained rest area was hidden from the cameras so they each separately shower and changed out of sight.

"Thank you for a marvelous night." she teased and threw her arms around his neck. "I can hardly wait to do that again."

To keep from laughing he bit his lip trying not to bit hers also.

Hand in hand they trotted down the stairs to the dining area where some of the family had gathered already.

"What's for breakfast?" quizzed Ply.

"There are five types of cold cereal, three different flavors of oatmeal, five types of bread, eight different spreads for the bread, two different toasters, three microwaves, four blends of coffee, six types of tea..." recited his dad.

"I sure hope we get enough." interrupted Ply.

"How was your night?" asked Jane's mom to Ply.

"Mother!" glared Jane.

"Well," began Ply, "We are married."

"Now that that's over with..." mumbled George. "How about breakfast!"

Ethyl shrugged her shoulders and grabbed a plate. "The way to a man's heart..." she reminded everybody.

"I suppose that depends on what he is hungry for." whispered Ply to Jane.

"That sounds healthy." encouraged Carol as she dropped some bread into the toaster.

The six of them talked of what they might get to do today, and Ethyl silently wondered where she might find a place that sells baby clothes.

It just may not be long before it is grandma time, she thought.

Saint George and the Dungeon

During breakfast George lightly touched one of the servers on the arm, "Is there any opportunity for a tour of the castle?" he asked.

"Certainly." informed the young man. "Just out that door," he pointed with his head to a large archway behind him, "There is an information rack with tour schedules. There is a vending machine that can give you as many tickets as you wish. If you use the promo code 'Guest Three Forty-Seven' then the tickets are free."

"The tickets are free?"

"The code changes daily but the tickets are good for one entire week as a guest of the prime minister It will probably take more than one or even two days to see what you want to in this big a palace."

George moved in a little closer, "Are there any secret passages?"

"This, sir, is an ancient military compound built in the seventeenth century. It was in aged disrepair for some time, but the past prime ministers have been able to secure a number of stonemasons to get the building back into its original shape. The question you need to ask is not if, but how many, and where, do they lead to?" grinned the attendant then returned to his duties leaving George dizzy with excitement.

"Anybody want to go on a tour of the castle?" asked George to those at the tables around him.

Carol and Ethyl had already decided that shopping was going to be their main duty of the day. They would spend some time in a few of the exclusive shops of Paris for ideas then head to the tourist traps and load up on some nice clothing for themselves. Next their plan was to head to the newborn department in a number of large department stores to grab a suitcase or two of clothes that would be fitting for either girls or boys.

"We're busy." said the two older ladies.

"I would like to just wonder around and show Ply some of the sights." said Jane rubbing her leg against Ply's under the table.

"I guess that just leaves you and me." agreed Greg.

"When do you want to go?" invited George excitedly.

"Let's finish breakfast first then we can go from here."

George let out a sigh showing his impatience and Greg chuckled.

Twenty minutes later the two moms bid their farewells till the evening meal and headed for the street.

Jane stirred her coffee and chatted quietly with Ply as the two dads got ready to tour. George already had four tickets, two for today, and two tomorrow.

"Are you two okay alone for a while?" asked George a little concerned about leaving his kid in a strange city, in a new country for the first time. He found it a little intimidating himself.

"They'll be fine." encouraged Greg as he nudged George towards the door to start the tour. "She has been here six or seven times before and is very well aware of all that is here and knows how to protect herself."

"Oh really?" was all that George could manage to say before they were out in the corridor.

They decided on the self-tour seeing that they were guests of the castle and that was one of the more trusting options. They were admonished to obey all signs on closed and locked doors but hallways and rooms that had doors open or no doors at all they were welcome to explore. The guidebooks for the self-tour were almost an inch thick with pictures of rooms and histories of each corner of the castle complete with who lived there since its completion in sixteen forty-three. There were stairways to dungeons, turret lookouts and towers that were temptingly available.

The two talked for five minutes deciding where to go first. Agreeing to start with the towers and end up in the dungeons they scampered off like a couple of teenagers just having received their first motorcycles.

They took their time climbing to the highest lookout post in the tallest tower. Greg, being twelve years younger, managed to do the stairs a little quicker than George but was patient. George hadn't been so active for a long time and wished he had spent more time on his bicycle instead of the couch in front of the TV. Chopping and stacking wood helped but it was nothing like running, riding and lifting weights. Things would surely change once he got home.

The turret had square notches for shooting from but being so high they wondered how could they possibly hit a target?

Consulting the guidebook, they found that shooting a message from one part of the castle to another on this side of the building made it easier and quicker to communicate. Sign language was used once line of sight was established so the enemy would not hear that the castle was preparing for battle. Large bales of hay were kept at various points on platforms that jutted from the structure giving a quick method of notice to all who needed to prepare. Visibility from the lookout was almost five miles in some locations and two miles at the least. Getting the castle prepared for battle only took about fifteen minutes leaving the invading armies in a poorly defended area while the castle being closed up tighter than a drum. If an army circled the castle, then most of the invaders could be quickly eliminated by the well-stocked military in the building.

Once cannons came on the scene the building suffered some damage but shooting from an elevation always had the advantage.

The two made their way down the stairs checking out each room admiring the architecture and art of the times it was made up for.

The republic was established in eighteen seventy-two, but Charles de Gaul, who ruled from nineteen fifty-eight to nineteen sixty-nine, made many forward advances in the customs and culture of the nation of France. There were three rooms dedicated to his leadership.

An entire wing of the sixth floor was dedicated to Louis XIV with costumes on wax figurines of beautiful maidens.

The room that got the two into trouble was one of Napoleon's. There were five rooms on the fifth floor that boasted of his reign and romance. Wax soldiers stood guard almost everywhere dressed in the style of the times.

There were two large metal swords crossed over the mantle of the six-foot high by ten-foot wide fireplace in what appeared to be a good-sized ballroom. Wax figures circled the perimeter with flintlock rifles held by both hands in the front of each warrior.

"Do you fence?" invited George to Greg.

"Fence?" he replied. "As in sword fight?"

"Yeah."

Greg wondered what he was up to as he glanced up at the

metal weapons. "I did a little in high school and played with it some in college but never went very far with it. Nothing like Jane and her tennis."

George hauled over a luxuriant Louis XIV padded high back chair and set it just under the mantle.

I'm sure glad there is not a fire in that chimney, thought Greg. *It would prove to be a very expensive tour. It still might be if that give way under his weight.*

George placed one foot on the edge of the chair and nimbly lifted his other to the opposite side as not to disturb the ancient material. He stood up to his full height and reached up and removed the two swords from their rests.

Greg was so wide eyed he did not notice twelve of the soldier's eyes following their every move.

George tossed one of the instruments to Greg as an invitation to play. "Nothing around but wax to watch us." he encouraged his sparing buddy as he hopped from the ancient furniture.

Two other guards dressed in ancient looking war apparel slowly moved their fingers to the triggers of the old flintlock rifles that were held in ready at their shoulders but not aim position.

George held the weapon in position and moved to the center of the room with his left arm behind his back.

Greg glanced at the soldiers around the room and did not notice the movement of the eyes that swiftly moved back to the staring straight ahead position. He walked into the ring and lifted the metal thinking, *What does this guy know?* They bowed to each other and brought their arms into position and touched steels.

Faster than anything Greg had ever witnessed George lunged and almost threw the sword from Greg's grasp. Greg tightened his grip as he barely managed to keep the instrument from flying but did not stop the whirl that the force of the advance twisted him into. He quickly regained his composure and brought up the tool for a battle he did not expect.

A dozen eyebrows raised on six of the 'wax' figures.

"Where on earth did you learn to do that?"

"By the end of high school, I had it pretty well perfected." replied George. "College gave me the advantage of gaining many trophies, but I did not qualify for the Olympics seeing they only had the safe sport of 'Fencing' and nothing more dangerous than the decathlon."

A bead of sweat developed on Greg's brow as six other figures looked at each other in preparation for what might happen next.

"Do you wish to play?" invited George.

"As long as no one and nothing in this room gets hurt."

The metal met again and the two danced around in rather exciting sword play for a few minutes then the guns of the six dropped into firing position, three at each of the swordsmen.

Thankfully they both noticed the movement at the same time.

The six quickly moved from their frozen state into a menacing circle around the two would be ancient heroes.

"Please replace the swords to their original position." instructed one of the guards.

George gently received the other instrument from Greg and moved slowly to the chair he used as a stool.

Three of the men with flintlocks followed every step. George hoisted himself back on to the ancient furniture and replaced the weapons. He hopped down but did not look at any of the guards. Inspecting the chair, he was thankful that nothing was out of order other than a little dust from his shoes. He gently brushed it off with the palm of his hand and slowly picked up the expensive furniture and returned it to its original setting.

"Stand next to each other with your hands up and face the west exit." commanded one of the figures that was not displaying any tendency of being wax.

"Which way is west?" whispered Greg to George.

"How should I know."

"Just behind the old guy who seems to think he is some distant relative of Zorro." blurted one of the costumed men.

Greg bit his lip but couldn't help the slight smirk from crawling across his face.

"Please surrender your tickets." stated the soldier closest to the two.

Greg slowly dropped one arm and reached into his shirt pocket and pulled out two tickets that were dated for today. He handed them to the guard who reached out to take them.

"So," greeted one of the soldiers to the two offenders, "You want to live like they did in the old days? Perhaps you need some cool down time as guests of the king." The soldier drew his own sword and gave George a slight poke in the rump, not enough to draw blood but enough to get the picture that the toy was sharp, menacing and able to do as the wielder liked.

They moved into the hall and the soldier whispered, "Left." They walked towards what looked like a blank stone wall and one of the other solders in front touched something in the wall and it opened to a long spiral staircase.

"Going down." voiced the one with the sword.

All eight started down the dark stairwell. Within less than a minute the wall behind them closed and the slight lighting that resembled candles in old holders was all that lite the descent. Thankfully they were spaced just a few feet apart so there was sufficient light to see once your eyes got used to the light.

Down, down, down they went. It seemed like half an hour before they reached what might have been the basement. The approached a 'T" and the guard said, "Left."

The hallway continued about fifty feet with the sparse lighting to another stairwell that descended farther.

"If we go much farther things will start getting warm." joked Greg.

"No talking!" commanded the official with the sword. "And keep your hands high."

They dropped another thirty feet and there were cells in a circle blocked by a floor to ceiling iron gate.

They were granted separate cells. The doors clanked shut and the guards left trying to be quiet, but one said, "I wonder what the president will say about these two."

* * *

They sat in silence on the iron bunks for long enough to spook George.

"I'm sorry, man." apologized George in the almost total darkness. There was one candle like fixture in the center of the hall between the four cells.

"How were you to know the wax would come to life." said Greg.

George laughed a few a short bursts.

"You were mighty good with that sword up there. I was

regional champ and I thought you were just going to let the thing fall once I had you in touch. Then you flung my sword almost right out of my hand. It took all I was worth to keep it. Why did you give up on playing?"

George was silent for a while.

"I got too cocky." George admitted almost in tears.

Greg was real quiet now and waited to hear what his new friend had to say. After fifteen seconds George sniffed and said, "I was in my first year of college... We were in the final match of the school tournament... I never thought that 'pride comes before a fall' could work itself out so literally."

Greg could hear George wipe his eyes and blow his nose. Greg quietly got up and walked to the bars, so he could hear better. A few more moments passed as the confessor gathered strength to continue.

"I was going to win the tournament no matter what... I flicked his rapier away and stabbed him in the chest. I guess in the duel my tip cover had come off, but I didn't seem to notice or care. My point struck him in the chest but thankfully his sternum prevented any entry."

George was in full sobs now and Greg had to sit down just to try to imagine the scene on a university campus.

"I got expelled from school and I was very thankful I missed any of his organs. It didn't take long to patch him up, but I had never picked up a sword or rapier since. Today when I saw those two swords hanging on the wall and the thrill and excitement of living in the age of knights got the better of me. Thankfully age and lack of practice has me considerably rusty."

Good grief, thought Greg as he leaned against the back of his bunk. *Considerably rusty?*

Another few minutes passed.

"Did you ever tell Ethyl?"

"Who would ever marry an almost murderer?"

Greg thought about it for a moment then said, "I suppose lots of girls but none as nice as Ethyl."

"So, I kept quiet." replied George.

The two men sat in silence for a while. George managed to get a grip on his emotions but reliving a scene so traumatic was difficult to say the least.

After almost half an hour of quiet Greg asked, "I wonder how long they are going to keep us down here?"

No response from the neighboring cell.

"George?" he called but not very loudly.

Greg listened carefully and heard smooth even breathing. He sat down on his bunk and snickered quietly to himself.

Ethyl said he could fall asleep anywhere, he thought. *Wait until she hears about this one.*

He checked the time on his smart phone. Almost four o'clock. Supper was from four-thirty to six. "This just may be the first meal I've missed on a non-voluntary basis in a very long time." he mumbled to himself. "I'm not surprised there is no cell phone reception down here." He shut down the instrument and put it back into his pocket.

George stirred, "Where are we?"

"Dungeon," smirked Greg, "Guests of the king of France."

"Oh yeah, how could I forget."

Things were quiet for the next half hour then they heard noises in the stairwell and saw lights coming down the stairs.

"Hey George, you hear that?"

"I wonder if they decided that we weren't deep enough."

"If we go any deeper, we just might get wet. The water table can't be much lower than this." replied Greg.

The lights approached and shone in their faces.

"Now what did you two do to get yourself in such a mess?" asked Carol.

"Oh no." cited Greg. "They brought the women!"

"Someone had to bail you out."

"Jane?"

"Sword fighting in the Napoleon war room of all things. Now the president wants a demonstration."

"He what?" exclaimed George.

"You two have been chosen for his evening entertainment."

"Do we still get to eat?" asked George.

"I suppose if you survive the tournament."

"The tournament?" queried Greg.

"Apparently you guys put on quite a show on the fifth floor and now the president wants to enjoy the action." explained Jane. "Why did I ever ask the Lord never to be bored!"

210

"Can we appeal?" asked George.

"He said if you want to appeal you can sit here for the night and ask yourself the same question in the morning." cautioned one of the guards.

"We'll go see the king." surrendered Greg.

"We are expecting him also." informed the guard. "Once word got out about the excitement you caused on the fifth, they could fill three bull-rings if they held the contest off till Saturday."

"I think we're in trouble mate." teased Greg in a down under accent.

They tromped up the stairs to the first landing from the dungeon then took the elevator that appeared once a rock was pushed.

"How come we didn't take the elevator on the way down?" asked George.

"You wanted the original castle experience, so we walked." replied the guard. "They didn't have elevators in the seventeenth century!"

* * *

"Well!" shouted the president as they entered the fifth floor Napoleon War Room. "What's this I hear of you using the furniture for a step stool?"

"You what?" exclaimed Ethyl.

"I thought..." whispered George.

"Speak up son." yelled DeGaulle.

"Sir!" shouted George in a military style. "I would like to ask the conditions of the duel."

"Conditions of the duel?" repeated DeGaulle. "What are the normal conditions of a duel?"

"In Olympic tournaments the duel is considered over when the point of the rapier touches the target of the opponent." recited George.

Jane's one eyebrow went up and Ply's mouth dropped. Ethyl looked around to see if anyone else was talking not believing that George could be so bold in front of royalty never mind know all about sword fights in the Olympics.

"We are in the thirty first century sir and have enjoyed peace for over a thousand years!" exclaimed George.

At this Ethyl fainted and was seated in the Louis XIV chair George used as a stool. George did not notice seeing as she was behind him in the crowd.

"True." said the president. "We have the king here wishing to be entertained and seeing that this castle was built in the seventeenth century, we shall compromise and deal the duel with eighteenth century rules."

George just stood there for a few seconds. When the president stood George said in his loud military voice, "As you wish sir."

Swords were doled out to George and Greg not unlike the ones that were on the wall above the mantle. George gently dragged his finger across the business end of the blade. Realizing they had just been polished and sharpened he quickly made a decision.

"The king of France will start the competition." announced the PM.

"On your mark!" shouted the king.

BOOM. A musket fired from one side of the room and a wax statue fell on its face on the opposite side.

Greg drew his sword and approached George.

George dropped his sword, fell to one knee and bowed his head to receive his eighteenth-century reward.

"Halt!" shouted the president. He left his box and climbed down to the floor and walked over to George. "What is the problem here?" he quietly asked George. "I asked you to give us some entertainment..."

George interrupted the PM, "I will not fight to the death with a friend."

"Very well." stated the PM. "I will find you a more worthy opponent."

He walked over to Greg and removed the instrument from his hand.

"Will this do?"

"It certainly will." agreed George.

Ethyl fainted for a second time and they had to remove her from the competition.

"On your mark!" shouted the king.

BOOM, and another wax figure dropped.

The two approached each other and raised their weapons till

the blades touched. They backed away and proceeded with the match.

George dropped his weapon to the floor and to his knee and bowed his head once again.

DeGaulle threw his sword onto the stone floor and it clattered across the masonry. He walked over to George got down of one knee and asked. "What is troubling you my brother?"

George kept his head low for a moment and the president lifted his chin to see a tear in the eye of this great warrior. George, in almost a whisper told the gentleman of the college incident.

He stood up and adjusted his microphone.

"Ladies and gentlemen. I have decided to update the standards of the competition. It appears my friend is not wanting to face death as yet, so we shall run with the standards of the Olympics of the present."

DeGaulle swiftly approached George and whispered, "Are you sure you want to do this?"

"I almost killed a man once and I swore I would never put myself in that position again. With the rules of the Olympics, I can play."

DeGaulle turned and walked from his opponent, lifted his sword from the floor and said, "Let the games begin."

They both approached each other with one hand behind the back. George felt the rush of his college years return.

Careful old boy, he thought to himself. *You're not as young as you used to be.*

The swords touched and George dove in, dug in, and swiped the blade of the minister. He had to swing around just as his men had told him they had seen earlier.

Surprised, the president took a step back to catch his balance.

"Fun, huh?" teased George.

"I have never lost yet, and I will not lose today." whispered the president between clenched teeth.

I don't think I can allow you to do that, George said to himself.

Charles charged, and George was ready, remembering to anticipate every move. With sword outstretched he charged and George quickly side stepped and let him pass.

George was beginning to wonder if every one of the previous opponents of this leader threw the match just because of who he was.

DeGaulle turned and charged again.

George thought, "I better end this in the easiest manner so neither of us lose face."

Degaulle's sword smashed into George's and it appeared that Charles threw George to the ground.

On the way down George kicked the sword from the hand of Charles, landed on his shoulder blades, and immediately nipped up to his feet, and caught the sword of his rival, tripped Charles, and he landed with a gentle thud on the rug. There was a thick wooden beam twenty-five feet from the duel. George flipped the sword and caught it by the blade. Before Charles could get back to his feet George threw it towards the beam. It hit the wood, dug into the beam, and held fast. George jumped over Charles and threw the other sword at the far wall more than fifty feet away. The crowd hushed in anticipation of another ancient weapon possibly being destroyed at the hand of this one who had just humiliated their president. Time seemed to slow as the instrument flipped end over end on its way to the far side of the room. DeGualle, in horror and almost in tears at the thought of losing a tool of ancient warfare to this foolish alien.

The tip of the projectile grabbed unto the wood, buried itself about three inches and stuck fast. Charles let his head drop onto the floor relieved at the sparing of the instrument. The crowd jumped to their feet and gave the competition a standing ovation. It had been a long time since George had heard and enjoyed such a hubbub.

George reached down and took the hand of Charles and helped him to his feet. Not knowing exactly what to do Charles shook the hand that spared his life and the two walked through the ring to stand before the king.

"The judgment shall be decided within the hour." stated the king. "We shall recess for thirty minutes then return with the verdict."

The king signaled to the president and the two of them left the room to a large closed conference room. No one else was admitted.

All the excitement was not very good for poor old George. He wasn't used to so much exercise never mind the excitement of an international duel with professional war time arms. As the king and the PM spoke, he wondered what would happen to him. Running was not an option as every eye from the crowd was on him.

I could faint and play dead but that would only postpone the torture, he thought. *Lord, it seems I have let the sins of my flesh override judgment and discretion again.* He hung his head a stared at the carpet. *Perhaps even to the extent of the demise of myself and my family.* He looked up and searched for his kin. He found Jane and Ply on the outskirts of the room with Greg, Carol and Barb. "Where is Ethyl?"

Ply made his way over to his dad. "Mom fainted and they took her to the hospital. She is expected to be okay, but we decided that she should not see the duel."

"I suppose it is best that she isn't around to hear of my execution."

"Dad," exclaimed the boy, "You never told me."

"What was there to tell?" he said with sad eyes. "I can fill you in a little later, at dinner, if we all live to enjoy another one."

At the appointed time the king and the PM exited from the chamber.

The entire crowd stood and waited for the king to be seated. The monarch motioned for the crowd to do the same.

"I would like all of you to please remain seated." stated the king as he rose to his feet. Most of the crowd stood but the king ordered then to sit. They obeyed like confused puppies.

"Today," started the king, "We have seen a very different competition."

The audience burst into applause and started chanting the name of the president. The king held up his hand and slowly the spectators calmed to silence. Just as the noise was about to be fully eliminated the king spoke again causing the hush to fall deeper.

"The prime minister and I have had a lengthy discussion on what should be done to this man who has publicly embarrassed not only his host but also the entire country."

This brought the crowd into an almost gang warfare attitude. George thought that he might get lynched. Ply was wondering if any of the wedding party would possibly get out of the country alive. Jane just waited, looking for an out.

The king realized that he was stirring up the crowd and that was not his intention. "This man has not humiliated us but has shown us tactics that up to this point in history have never been demonstrated."

The mood of the crowd started to change.

"We should not treat this man as a criminal but as our beloved president has stated he should be treated as a hero for showing us such amazing skill in the study of sword-play."

Every time the king paused the spectators grew a little more positive on the outcome of the battle.

"Therefore, it has been decided that this expert at warfare shall become the official instructor of all of France and for his victory today we shall grant him honorary citizenship."

By this time the fickle crowd had completely turned and was hooting and hollering rejoicing in the judgment of the king.

The president who had settled standing by George's side, lifted the arm of his foe and the crowd chanted, "Long live DeGaulle. Long live DeGaulle."

George looked to the skies and said a very quiet thank you. Then he looked at his kid who was somewhat dazed in wonder and amazement.

* * *

The next morning newspaper read as the front-page headlines:

BOOGIE WOOGIE BUZZARD BOY
DANCES CIRCLES AROUND NATIONAL CHAMP

Humble pie is never easy to accept especially if you think you are the most important person of the most important country of the world. Never-the-less the king had convinced the PM that no matter how good you are in whatever discipline you are good in, there is always somebody who eventually comes along and is better than you are. The record you make is simply the goal of whomever comes next.

Charles DeGaulle VII had finally accepted the fact that he was no longer the greatest swordsman of the world, even if it meant surrendering the title to someone older that he was. What the PM was not willing to sacrifice was the nationality of the winner. France must still be first in all things, so he would arrange the granted citizenship of his opponent retroactive to the past five years. This would eliminate the possibility of someone in the near future reneging on the citizenship. Someone a number of centuries ago had formulated a law that if you were born in a country you were a citizen for life of that country. Granted citizenship from another country did not negate the citizenship of the country of one's birth. If one held onto a citizenship for longer than five years, then that citizenship became irrevocable.

One of the deterrents of becoming a citizen of multiple countries was if you committed an international crime then you had to serve your sentence in each country that you were a citizen of. If you committed an international offense that had a punishment of twenty years in prison than you got to spend that twenty years in prison in each country of your citizenship. If you were a citizen of three countries, then you got to spend sixty years in the common goal! Some were a little more common than others!

Thankfully, thinking had not been eliminated with modernity and justice.

"How many others had had a similar experience in their lives and had buried their talent out of fear and frustration?" asked the king to the DeGaulle in the conference room. Waking up the next morning the question was still on the president's mind, so he decided to try to do something about it. Apparently, the king had a lot of good ideas that the PM had neglected to invite into the conversation making the king not only a friend but also an adviser seemed to have great potential for advancement at the moment. He would try to convince the rest of his colleagues into accepting some more input into some of the affairs that needed to be addressed.

* * *

The promised ceremonies went as planned. George gained an exclusive passport and more trophies that he knew what to would do with. He remembered the trophy barn of Mohammad Ali. A barn full of so many trophies that he could not keep the animals out of, and all his treasures were desecrated with feces.

Store up your treasures in heaven where neither rust corrupts, nor thieves break in and steal, he reminded himself. He enjoyed the recognition but pitied those who were jealous of his abilities.

"Someday I will get old and all of my abilities will be gone." he told the people as they cheered him at the ceremony.

By the way I feel today after the strain of yesterday, he thought to himself, *Old may have already crept in.*

* * *

The two weeks of ceremonies was over. The king had given Greg and George a personal tour of the castle that took two more days. They walked all the secret tunnels that led to dungeons where bones were found in some that had been long forgotten even after the clean-up. They descended stairwells of hidden escape routes that led to docks that were only accessible at low tide. Hidden rooms and stashed treasures were viewed and then the two were led around by the king so the memory of finding the exact location would be almost impossible.

The trip home was uneventful save the overcrowded airports with well-wishers and congratulations not to mention the people who just wanted to be able to say hello so they could tell their friends, "I saw Jane Blythwood and her husband Ply at the airport, she nodded to me as if we were old friends."

Jane was wondering what to tell her mother about the 'honeymoon suite' but decided against it if she ever wanted to play tennis again in France.

She grinned as she remembered the excitement of the rendezvous with Ply at the 'four hour stay' hotel the day her father-in-law got all the attention. *No cameras, no nosy microphones, just the two of us. I never thought it would be so wonderful. It really is the commitment that makes it all worthwhile. Thank you, Lord, for all the amazing wonders we still get to discover,* she silently prayed.

Some mothers just want to know too much about their kids, she told herself as she walked past a mirror at Barb's castle.

Suddenly she stopped and looked in the mirror. Not only was Jane there but too much of her mother came back in her own reflection.

"Oh, Lord," she pleaded as she moved away from her reflection, "The ball doesn't bounce too far from the court."

Johnson's Place

Breakfast was again eggs, toast, jam, and a few muffins dug out of the freezer since they were back at the castle. Now that the stash had been revealed it was going to take some work to keep it up to the quantity that Barb had stipulated. They worked together making six double batches and that made one hundred and forty-four, so they were well stocked for a while. Barb wanted a minimum of fifty in the basement. They had some time, but it took time to make them. She kept the freezer at minus forty degrees which kept things fresh for a much longer time.

"What time is practice this morning?" asked Ply.

"I don't think there will be a practice this morning." she volleyed.

"Have you given up the game... again?"

"Not very likely. It just seems that there might be something more important to do at this moment. If we get back by the end of the month or so, then we can continue practice..."

"So, you need a vacation?" he interrupted.

"No. I need a diversion. Look here." She held up her tablet and showed Ply the view. "This is Johnson's place. There is a pond here at the back and a pathway cut around the pond through the tall grass." She zoomed out a little. "There is a wooded area that circles the property where the road travels through the woods. The property line may be the road. There is a small side road just off the driveway opposite the Johnson estate. There are a few picnic tables there for travelers. If we parked the car there, we could approach under cover of the sword if we needed to come back to do any clandestine operations."

"Clandestine operations?"

"Yeah. We go looking for a mower, are blown away by the prices he is asking for them, ask if he has any used mowers and snoop around and talk to some of the employees."

"So, when do you want to go?"

"After breakfast we could pack and be out of here by eight or eight-thirty. We could arrange for accommodations in the motel about fifteen miles from Johnson's place and show up first thing in the morning."

"That makes us back by Wednesday or Thursday." he added.

"Anything else you want to see while we are in the area?" she queried excitedly.

He looked at her a little wondering. "What is the weather supposed to be like?"

She swiped her tablet and said, "Rain Tuesday and nice on Wednesday right through to the next week."

"How far to that town where they have all the shows and attractions?"

She swiped back and zoomed out, "Forty miles from the motel."

"Have you ever been there?" he asked.

"Once when I was a kid." she replied. "Dad worked a lot of overtime one summer and took a week and a half one year and we saw a bunch of stuff but that was almost fifteen years ago. I expect a lot has changed."

"So, going again would be a fun adventure?"

"Well," she declared, "I hope it won't be too much of an adventure. We are going to need our adventure energy at Johnson's if we are allowed to see what he may have."

"So, we make a week or two vacation out of it?"

"I thought you'd never ask." she said as she jumped up and threw her arms around him.

"Do we take the 'card' or cash?"

"Why not both? We can always get a little cash if we need to but take some and hide it in the guitar case, leave a few hundred in our pockets for food and gas, and we are set to go." she announced handing him five one hundred-dollar bills. He handed back two and she put some in the guitar case. They left the castle at eight-forty-five after having cleaned up from breakfast and set the alarms. A number of hours later they signed into the motel and took in a show at the "Visual Verbiage Venue" in one of the most favorite tourist spots within a five-hundred-mile radius.

* * *

The next morning the two drove to *Integrity Maintenance Machinery*.

"Man," whispered Ply to his wife, "This place is a far cry from the Spoudice establishment."

"And look at all the cameras." commented Jane in astonishment. "What do you suppose they are hiding here?"

There were a few machines in the front showroom but other than that all they found was information of ordering different makes and models.

"Can I help you find anything?" intruded a doughnut filled salesman in both looks and in speech.

"We are looking for a good mower that will cut about a dozen acres without totally wearing out the operator." chirped Ply to the amazement of the lady beside him. "We are newly married and inherited a nice house but there is a lot of grass to cut."

"We have a few examples right here in the showroom."

"They are really nice. How much are they?" When he found out, Ply asked if there were any fairly good used machines around. "I'm sorry. I really did not expect to pay that much for a lawn mower."

"We have some used machines up the hill in the maintenance shed." informed the salesman in a lifeless tone. "Somebody up there can help you." He turned back and headed towards his desk, his doughnuts and his redesigning of his body mass. Ply and Jane left holding hands by the door they came in.

"Friendly bunch." he quietly consoled her halfway up the hill to the shed.

"It appears they are spending their money on things other than keeping the place looking professional." announced Jane as they approached the opened roll up door.

"Hi." greeted a much thinner worker in his mid-thirties. "Anything I can help ya'll with?"

"Hi. My name is Ply, and this is my wife Jane. We are looking for a nice mower but not quite as expensive as a new one. What have you got that still may have some life to it?"

"We got a couple that have just come in but haven't had time to clean 'em up yet." said the worker and turned signaling them to follow. "Sure is a pretty day for cuttin' grass." he announced.

"They are calling for rain this afternoon." smiled Ply enjoying the simplicity of the man and the pleasant conversation. "What is it you do here?"

"I just help around where I can." he rejoiced. "I ain't smart enough to work on them machines, I tried 'em a couple a-times but got some of the parts put backwards." his eyes laughed at his own inability. "But I can remember every machine that has ever come through these doors and I been workin' here for near fifteen years."

"Is that a fact." responded Ply. "Sometimes being able to remember things is better than all the machines that have been put together."

"The first year I started we sold a whole bunch of machines and I can remember everyone."

"If I showed you some pictures could you tell me if you have ever seen them before?"

"If you got the serial numbers." stated Dolph.

"Let's sit down here at this table." invited Ply. "What's your name?"

"Hutte" he stated. "Adolph Hutte, but you can call me Dolph."

"A pleasure to meet you Mr. Hutte." beamed Ply. I'm Ply Gallant." Ply pulled out his phone and brought up the list of missing mowers. The very first one was recognized by Dolph.

"We got that one right here in the shop. That is the one I was gonna show you."

"Really." offered Ply. "How about this one?" Ply zipped down to the bottom of the list and spread his fingers to bring up the font size.

"That one came through here about three years ago. The twenty-eighth of August I believe." Ply taped in the new information just below the serial number.

"Do you remember who you sold it to?" asked the sleuth.

"I do believe it was a man named Almendras. I think he had recently moved from Spain. His accent was really thick."

"How about this one?"

"Yes siree." dimpled the delighted helper thrilled with the prospect that he could be of help to a new friend. "That one we shipped all the way to Germany. Mr. Johnson really likes to sell these used mowers overseas."

"Do you remember what company it was sold to?"

"Oh yeah." smiled Dolph. "It was Kline Pharmaceuticals."

Ply added the date and place of sale to the list.

"I'm going out for a walk." said Jane. "It is a little stuffy in here with the smell of all these machines and the gas and oil on the floor."

Ply glanced over at the star and smiled releasing her from her prison of boredom. "How about this one?" he addressed Dolph.

"Wait a minute." Dolph addressed in Jane's direction. "Ain't you that tennis player we heard so much about?"

The two looked at each other. Before she could respond he said, "Yes you are." and proceeded to list off all of her accomplishments from the very first game she had played professionally.

Never before had she met someone who had all the facts so straight. Her mouth stayed open but had considerable trouble making coherent pronouncements. Ply was equally amazed and for a minute forgot what he was there for. Jane had a few 'trophies' from the latest tournament.

"You deserve a special acknowledgment." she congratulated the gentleman. "I just happen to have here a remnant from my last contest." she pulled out a yellow ball from her bag with a 7/5/F written on it in very fine ink. Jane signed the ball and handed it to Dolph. "Do you know what this code means?" she asked.

"Is this the ball from the seven to five set you played?"

"Yes." she encouraged smiling. "And the 'F' means it was the final winning ball I scored the winning point with."

Dolph picked the ball from her hand and looked at it in astonishment then dropped it back into her bag. "I can't afford such a trophy."

"I'm not selling it to you it is a gift for being such a loyal fan." she said as she dug the sphere back out.

"A gift?" He asked as tears formed in the corners of his eyes. The prize was placed into his hand. "Nobody ever..." Jane wrapped her hands around his and the ball, "Well then let this just be the first of many."

"Of many?" he opened his hand to see the trophy he knew would be coveted by thousands, "I promise I will take perfect care of it."

Jane gave him a gentle hug and kissed the ball leaving a perfect imprint of her lipstick. "There." she proclaimed. "That makes this the only one in existence with that on it."

Dolph walked over to the parts department area and pulled out a zip lock bag just the right size for the award. "There, now it won't get messed up."

Jane walked back to the car cheeks moistened by the emotion of the last few minutes.

"Wow Lord." she whispered. "How many more fans do I have that are that loyal?"

She realized she would never find out but was thankful for meeting just one.

How humbling, she thought. *Lord, help me to play the best I can in all fairness no matter what happens,* she thought knowing mental activity was not invisible to the Creator.

When she arrived at the car, she sat there for about twenty minutes pondering about what had happened and enjoying a time of worship. Finally, she slipped back to the present and wondered what to do next.

Perhaps we have seen enough, and I will ask Ply if we can't get the rest of the information tomorrow. I'm getting hungry, she thought.

As she reached for the door handle, she saw Abe Johnson walk briskly out of the back door towards the maintenance shed.

That's interesting, mused the new bride. When the boss arrived at the scene there was some yelling then a loud crash.

Looks like it is time for the toy, thought the young lady.

What shall I do with the car?

Quickly she slid over to the driver's side started the engine and moved the vehicle out to the roadway. She turned left and slowly sped up to just over the limit. She cornered hard, only slowing down a little as she fish tailed unto the gravel that led to the picnic tables.

"Good. Nobody here." She steered the old white horse out to behind the last table, jumped out and grabbed the sword.

"I may need a disguise. Why did all this have to happen so fast?" she gripped. Quickly she hauled out her makeup kit.

"How about somewhat of a scary face? Deepen the eyeshadow with sharp edges down the cheeks, brighter than red lipstick and lots of talcum powder in the hair, fluff it up... a lot. That should do it!"

Ramping up she made it back to the site to find the warehouse where she left Ply. The room was empty.

"If I can find Dolf then it should be easy to get Ply out of here." she thought. Speeding up her own time frame she raced around the complex but could see no one on site either from the windows or through the glass doorways.

"I guess it's time to set off a few alarms." She ramped down to just above normal and pulled open a door. The security camera caught the door opening but did not register anyone coming in or going out. The alarm on the door sounded but the watchman found the room empty.

"Must have been the wind." said the guard to himself.

Not wanting to attract any more attention, Jane ramped back up and adjusted her weight, so she was almost weightless. She jumped from the first floor and landed quietly on the second floor and listened. Not a sound. There was a kitchen off to her left and she grabbed a glass twelve-ounce tumbler and moved down the hall. At each doorway she quietly placed the bottom of the glass against the door and put her ear inside the cup. Every room was quiet. There was a window at the end of the hall that looked toward the warehouse.

"I can't waste much time gawking." she peered out the glass and saw a side door not quite closed. Slowing down, the door closed and then she noticed that there was no hardware on the outside of the door except the hinges with special non-removable pins.

"Then someone must have let them in." She jumped down the stairs and landed at the door and pushed it open just enough to get out.

"That was not just the wind." stated the guard in the security room but by then Jane was already inside the warehouse and had scouted most of the building. She found the lone hallway that led to the back and the special conference room that Johnson constructed for lock down purposes. All the doors were locked, and she could not get in.

"I do remember Ply telling me that this could cut anything." She ramped up and sliced the metal double doors about two inches from the hinges and frame and watched them crash to the concrete in the hall. Four of the twelve men inside had guns and started shooting as soon as the door hit the concrete. Jane sped up till the bullets crawled and she batted the bullets into the wall at the end of the hallway.

This might just call for a little ghosting, she smiled to herself and passed to two thirds out. Adjusting her weight, she leaped into the air and floated towards the direction of the guns batting the projectiles into the rug as she glided through the air. Two guns fell to the floor and eight men turned and fled. The superstitious workers scattered like insects fleeing an anteater. The other two with guns continued shooting while the two who were more curious than superstitious hid and watched. Johnson started to back away but continued firing. Jane realized that he was not going to quit without a little persuasion, so she batted a bullet into his left calf muscle. The back of his leg exploded with muscle and blood flying.

The lessons from Barb taught her that only hollow point bullets did that kind of damage.

The pain almost knocked him unconscious and the force of the bullet, tripled by the extra energy from the sword, spun him around and he dropped to the floor. His gun slid across the rug to about ten feet from where he landed.

She put on a horrifying face, went up and cut his pistol into pieces. She kicked the shattered weapon across the floor scattering the parts across the room. She destroyed another visible weapon in a similar manner.

"Maybe you will think twice about using them again." she said in a high-pitched witch-like falsetto. She landed on her feet, stuck the business end of the sword very close to his neck, and asked the fat man in charge, "Where's the boy?"

Johnson barely glanced towards the locker room, but Jane caught the gesture. She brought the blade to the top of his head thinking she might give him a close-shave-haircut but put it out of her mind. She ran into the shower room allowing the door to close behind her. Looking around, she did not find the kid. She scouted the showers by the lockers. No sign of having been cleaned for months.

"Man." she said in a half whisper. "Some people live like filthy pigs." Not finding him she dropped the timing to normal and said, "Ply?" in a quiet half volume voice. She listened but heard nothing.

"Okay Lord, where is he?"

She noticed that only one locker had a padlock on it. She cut the lock, caught it before it fell to the floor, and slid the pieces into her pocket. She pulled open the door and found her unconscious husband as he slumped to the tiled floor. She untied his gag and stuffed it into her pocket and grabbed the hand of her beau.

"Is that sirens I hear?" she voiced right out loud. *I wonder who called them?* she thought.

Ramping back up she slung him over her shoulder as she brought the two of them to be almost weightless.

One uninjured employee had picked up a weapon that had been dropped by one of the frightened men and ran to the locker room.

Jane noticed the light start to change in the room and looked towards the door. As it slowly opened, she gently laid her burden on the floor and waited.

The intruder moved his weapon into position as Jane ramped up to projectile velocity. The bullet exited the gun at such a slow rate she slowed down just a touch to bring the metal to tennis ball speed.

Being in no mood for horsing around, her anger had roused, and she batted the metal as if she was playing the final smashing stroke on the winning set. This sped up the missile exponentially and it smashed right through the intended target. His knee shattered from the front to the back tearing his leg in two. The bullet skipped once across the carpeted concrete, passed through two block walls, and ended up in the double brickwork of the main building as her opponent dropped into unconsciousness. Adjusting the weight of herself and her burden, Jane had no trouble carrying Ply. She rushed out of the building and with the sword in motion and got him to the car and to the picnic tables in less than two seconds Earth Standard Time.

The ambulance and police arrived and started gathering people to question. They found the cut double doors into the conference room and immediately attended to Johnson and the man who lost part of his leg. They were both unconscious and needed medical attention badly. The man with the lost leg was taken first and another ambulance was called after they had Johnson's leg bandaged, applied a tourniquet and got an I. V. in place. In a few minutes he woke up and was furious.

Ply had a bump on his head but other than that he seemed all right. His breathing and pulse were still in range of not being serious.

Ply opened his eyes and shook in fright at the sight of what was holding on to him.

"It's okay hon. It's just little old me made up to scare the goons." she comforted.

He took a deep sigh and relaxed into her arms and rested a moment. "What's all that noise in the distance?"

"I think it's the police."

"Police? Where is the sword?"

"In the case, where it belongs."

"So now what?" he said.

"I don't know. I hate to flee the scene of a crime especially since we have been involved but I'm not ready to reveal the sword to the police. They might confiscate it as needed evidence and then it is gone forever."

"Where are we?" petitioned Ply.

"At the picnic tables across from the Johnson property."

"Can we hide it in the trees and come back for it later?"

"That may be our only option at the moment." She was not pleased, and her face demonstrated a minor look of disgust at leaving the toy where it could possibly be found.

"What if we bury it and come back for it tomorrow?"

"Then we better do it quickly. Can you move?"

"I think so. My head hurts and I'm a little stiff but otherwise..."

They looked for a place to stash the case and contents then Jane had an idea. "What if we bury the case, leave the car here, and fly back to the scene. We can find a place to hide the sword there and come back for it later. We may need to dump it into the pond or there may be a better place to stash it. The grass is pretty long by the tree line. We can crawl out of there and say we hid until it was safe to come out."

Looking for a location to hide the evidence they dug a hole and buried the case under a bunch of leaves and needles. Ply took a good look around at the foliage and the trees. He tried to memorize shapes and logs as not to lose the case. He glanced over at Jane and blurted, "You better wash your face."

"Oh yeah, thank you." and she hurried back to the car with the sword in motion. Ply had hardly turned around to resurvey the situation and she was back clean and polished complete with wet hair.

"Won't your wet hair cause questions?"

"What shall I do?"

"Take the sword and your brush and run down the highway till it dries. If you arrive with wet hair..."

"Brilliant." she agreed and then disappeared only to return again in less than ten seconds Ply's time. She had tied her hair back into a ponytail with a piece of string she found in the back of the old white horse.

"While we are here, can I try something?" she asked Ply.

"I suppose, what do you want to do?"

"While Johnson was down, I wanted to give him a very embarrassing haircut. He really has nice hair, but I wanted to cut a stripe out of it right down the middle, kind of like a reverse Iroquois."

"And?"

"Well, I didn't want him in the same time frame as I was for two reasons. First, he is a lot stronger than I am and second he might recognize me and what the sword can do."

"That makes three."

"Okay. I wanted to see if hair insulates the time change."

"So, you want to do what with me to test that theory?"

"If I grab onto your hair and I adjust my time frame will you do the same?"

"Why not?"

"That's what I want to test."

"Okay." he replied.

She held onto Ply's hair and timed out and then back to normal again.

"Feel anything?" she asked.

"No. You just disappeared."

"Well that is good to hear."

"I should warn you," interjected Ply, "When I tried to cut the hairs on my arm I bled profusely until I re-energized the sword and I healed almost instantly."

"It healed almost instantly?"

"No scars, no scab, or nothing. I was amazed." he said as he rolled up his sleeve and showed her his arm. "If you want to cut hair, don't cut it too close to the skin or you will take the scalp off also."

"So how do I test it?"

"Very carefully!" was his response.

"Let's get over there." and the two held hands and hurried to the middle of the woods.

"A fence?" She stopped and dropped the hand of her companion. The fence was chain link with a carefully trimmed two inches from the bottom of the fence to the ground. There was a fence post about five feet away and she noticed there were plastic insulators between the post and the chain links. "Wait a minute, I think it is electrified." She approached very slowly, and the ends of her hair stood on end. "I wonder if it is tied to the alarm system?"

"Where do you get these ideas?" he questioned.

"You're the electrical geek! Didn't you feel it when you got close?"

"No, but alarms are a slightly different field. I hope you did not stir up too much curiosity by getting so close. If the system is sophisticated enough to measure capacitance then they already know something is here."

"We'll just jump the fence. Hold my hand, I will lighten our weights and we can be invisible at the same time."

They hopped over the fence, arrived at the edge of the trees and invisibly moved through the tall grass to the edge of the pond. Jane emptied her pocket of the cut lock gently into the pond then pushed the sword under the water into the dirt about two feet from the shore. She buried the handle right into the mud so the only thing that would discover it was a pressure washer or a metal detector. She dug up a rock that was in the mud and set it on the bank in the tall grass. She pulled out a small clump of grass and laid it across the rock.

They developed an alibi, so the two stories would match, and headed toward the emergency vehicles that had arrived. Jane counted off the paces from the tall grass to the area where it had been mowed. Now she could more easily retrieve the blade when there was an opportunity.

* * *

"We gotta get out-a here." Dolph told his family. "I think Johnson is coming over to kill us all."

"What kind'a foolish talk is this?" shouted his mother.

"Mr. Johnson fired me. Then he sent me home and told me to stay there. I was loading my stuff into the truck when I heard a crash.

A few minutes later I heard some gunshots in the back of the warehouse where the secret meeting room is, so I got out of there really fast. He might be in some sort of trouble and Mr. Johnson don't take trouble real well. I think he means to come here and get rid of all of us."

"Don't be so foolish." squawked the woman. "You've been workin' for him for more than ten years now. Why would he do such a thing?"

"I don't really know but I never seen him so mad in all my life."

"Why don't you just get on to your room a cool off little. I'll get you something to eat. In fact, I'll just make lunch a little early."

Dolph went to his room and lay down on his bed but he couldn't get the mischief of his employer off his mind. He hopped off the bed and threw back the covers and looked for a minute then went out to the kitchen.

He came back into his room, fixed up his bed, and climbed out the window and headed towards the barn with an old video camera and a tripod. He set up the camera and pulled his truck behind the old barn.

An hour later he drove off and was never seen again. At least, that's what the police report said.

* * *

Abe Johnson's phone rang the special tone he had for his brother calling. He picked it out of his pocket and without looking said, "Yeah."

"Hutte gave a bunch of information to that brat kid from the farms..."

"How did he get there?"

"Never mind that." stated Abe. "Get yourself over to the Hutte residence and finish what we had planned."

"I'll have to get the stuff first."

"How long will that take you?"

"An hour at least. What if the family decides to run?" asked Al.

"I think they are too stupid." recited Abe. "I sent Hutte home and told him to stay there. I expect you'll find him just where I sent him."

"I agree. I'll get there as fast as I can."

"And finish the job." admonished his brother.

"No trouble at all."

* * *

"There they are!" shouted Johnson. "That's the two that shot my leg and tried to rob me!" A policeman approached them.

"We came to look at a mower and the next thing I knew I was in the tall grass with a very sore head." stated Ply. He showed the officer the bump on his head.

"That is a nasty one. How did you get it?"

"I was in the maintenance building talking with an employee named Adolph Hutte when Johnson came in and started yelling and throwing furniture. He broke a wooden chair over my head and knocked me unconscious. The next thing I know I am lying out here in the field by the pond. I am thankful they didn't throw me in."

"And you?" interrogated the officer.

"We came together looking for a mower. The prices were much more than we wanted to pay for a new one, so we went to the warehouse to see a trade-in. I got tired of the odor and went for a walk. I heard a crash and then saw some men run over to the warehouse with guns, so I hid here in the tall grass until two big guys brought out Ply gagged and unconscious. They threw him into the tall grass not far from where I was hiding. I was scared to death that they were going to find me, but they turned and ran back towards the buildings. We did not want to get out until we were sure it was safe. There was a lot of gunfire and I did not want to get hurt. What happened in there?"

"A few of the employees are talking about a ghost with a sword." laughed the constable. "They are practically in hysterics, beside themselves with fear."

"A ghost?" stated Ply as the two followed behind the cop.

"Can you imagine? Ghosts of all things!" voiced the officer. "With swords!"

"Did you find my cell phone?" asked Ply.

"Your cell phone?"

"Yes sir, I was showing some photos to an employee and Mr. Johnson came running in and hit me over the head and the next thing I remember was waking up in the tall grass missing my cell phone."

"Where did you lose it?"

"I was in the warehouse talking to Dolph. If you can find him, he can verify my story. He is an employee here."

They approached the main office and found all but Mr. Hutte there. A few of them had very conflicting stories but no one mentioned the room in the back of the warehouse.

"Which one of you is Dolph Hutte?" asked the officer that had retrieved the two from the field.

"Nobody that goes by that name has ever worked here." announced Johnson.

Jane glanced at him with a look of disbelief but said nothing. The chief of police looked around at the people that had gathered. "Okay, it appears it is time for all of us to take little ride to the station."

At that moment the FBI arrived. The lead agent looked around at the scene and enrolled the officers by stating, "This is a federal case with international complications. Tell us what you have found. We will need your assistance in the further interrogation of these people." and started the entire process again.

Each one was interrogated individually by the two agents, Jenkins and Robertson, while the two police officers stood over the rest of the employees and refused conversation between any of them. The hours dragged by and the only thing that kept Johnson quiet was the search warrant that was already in the hands of the FBI.

As Ply was interrogated, he was asked, "Where were you when you were struck over the head?"

"In the back maintenance building." he responded. "That was the last place I remember having my cell phone."

"Why don't we go have a look?"

The two walked over to the warehouse.

"I was sitting here talking to Dolph when Abe Johnson came in and he seemed very angry." stated Ply. "Dolph and I were discussing all the missing mowers I was investigating, and he could remember every model number and serial number since his employment. He was telling me where the missing mowers had been sold and I was recording them in my phone," Ply explained, "Johnson came in screaming and cursing. Then he hit me over the head with the wooden chair. The next thing I remember is waking up in the field in my wife's arms."

"So, your phone was left in this room?"

"This is the last place I remember it. If Johnson has it, or had it, who knows where it is now?"

"Let's have a look around." encouraged the agent.

They walked around looking in garbage cans and in closets for a few minutes.

"What is your phone number?" asked the agent.

Ply gave it to him, and the man called Ply's phone.

"I'm sorry but that number is not within receiving area. Please leave a voice message. At the end of your message you can press '1' for more options or hang up." recited the machine as the agent was on speaker phone so both could hear.

"That means that he has removed the battery or destroyed the phone." stated Ply.

"You wait here, and I'll go back and ask him."

"Can I snoop around to see if there are any more mowers here while looking for my phone?"

"Yeah." allowed the Agent. "Just don't leave the building."

Ply scouted around continuing to look for his phone.

"Lots of cameras here too." observed the sleuth as he walked around.

"I wonder where the main observation room is?" he thought. "Finding that just might give us the clues we need in a lot of areas."

Fifteen minutes later the FBI agent showed back up.

"Johnson refuses to admit any knowledge of you owning a cell phone." grumbled the gentleman.

"Where is the control room for all these cameras?" asked Ply. "There might be footage of what happened here if we can get to them before anyone else does."

"How long you been at this PI stuff kid?" asked Jenkins. "We can always use good agents. It seems that finding honesty is becoming a rarity."

Ply rubbed the back of his head. "A little longer than I wish at the moment."

The two grinned at each other.

"Find anything while I was away?"

"The only thing that seems a little suspicious is something in this tank that is bubbling away."

The two walked over to an acid tank the was giving off a foul odor. At the bottom of the tank was something dissolving in the acid.

"I wonder what this is used for?" asked the agent.

"Don't ask Johnson." stated Ply. "He may not know that he even has it."

"You gotta join our team." laughed Jenkins as he walked out to find an employee to question about the tank.

He was back in two minutes.

"A worker says it is needed to etch metal, so it can be painted." stated Jenkins as he walked in the door. "He says there are tongs hanging on the wall to retrieve what is in the tank."

Hanging of the wall just beside the acid tank there was a large pair of stainless-steel tongs. Ply grabbed them and fished around at the bubbling object only to retrieve his almost fully dissolved phone.

"I guess that ends that." droned Jenkins.

"Not if the phone had time to send the information to the Spoudice computer." mentioned Ply.

"If the phone was closed for thirty or forty seconds then all the new info that I had put into the phone regarding the mowers would have been transferred to Brian Spoudice's computer."

"Can you remember his number?"

"Can I play with your phone a bit? I might remember."

"Sorry. Is there someone we can call that will have the number?"

"Look up *Spoudice Maintenance Equipment* on the net and it will be there." said Ply. "When you get through ask for Brian, tell him who you are and ask if any new info came in from my phone."

Jenkins walked across the room and talked quietly for a few minutes.

"How many mowers had you found?"

"All thirteen if the last one was recorded."

"He says he got new info on twelve mowers."

"Then all we need to do is find Adolph Hutte and you have all the information you need." stated Ply.

"Johnson says he has never worked here." commented Jenkins.

"Check his IRS records and see where he has worked in the last fifteen years." admonished Ply. "I'll bet that will bring some reality to light."

The agent looked at Ply and wondered. "Where does this kid get all these ideas?"

"Seeing that Johnson has stated that Dolph never worked here it might be prudent to find him before Al Johnson, his brother, finds him." admonished Ply.

"How do you suggest we do that?" tested the agent.

"Talk to the police in the interrogation room and get his address." said Ply. "Then get over to his place as soon as you are done here and see if anything suspicious has happened."

Ply and Jane were eventually released seeing that they were the ones with the most credible story and that Ply had previously been introduced as the one who found the mower in France. It eventually came out that there were some in the warehouse, two in Germany, one in Australia, one in Canada and two still in this country.

Abe Johnson was patched up in the hospital and then held in custody without bond and charged with federal theft and international racketeering. They still needed to find his brother Al.

* * *

That evening at seven o' clock Robertson and Jenkins knocked on the door of a small house that belonged to Mr. and Mrs. Sigmund Hutte and their two children. They had searched the IRS and found that Adolph indeed did work for Johnson and the fact that Johnson lied about it meant greater trouble for the business owner.

With the evidence they mustered from the IRS records it was discovered that Dolph still lived with his parents and sister. They lived out in the country between a couple of large farms. It was a little difficult to get to and not really worth planting. The corner was too far away from either farmhouse to graze cattle or raise chickens so an acre each were donated by the two farmers. There were lights on inside and a radio but no answer, even to the pounding of the door. Robertson stayed at the door while Jenkins took a look around back of the small structure. There was a breaking of glass from the back of the house and Robertson hid behind a tree and pulled his gun. Jenkins showed up opening the door with a grim look. "Better call an ambulance." he said. "But I think it is already too late. We better have a look around."

Scouting the house, they found in one of the bedrooms what

first appeared to be a lot of blood dripping from the bed. Throwing back the covers revealed some plastic bags filled with water and ketchup. A few of them had holes in them and had bled out the liquid. They found the spent bullets and four shells, dropped the evidence into a plastic bag, and stuffed the bag into a pocket. Robertson noticed the window open and footprints headed towards the barn.

"What do you suppose happened out there?" he nudged his buddy. Out in the barn they found an old frayed extension cord plugged in and a lot of footprints.

Jenkins took a bunch of pictures. "It looks like a vehicle came and left a number of times here recently. I wonder what all this is about?"

An ambulance arrived and loaded the three corpses into the back. Fifteen minutes later the confirmation of their death was announced. Apparently, they had been murdered within two hours after the arrival of the police to the business of Abe and Al Johnson.

* * *

The next forty-eight hours were spent by Ply and Jane enjoying the attractions of Budson and adjusting their body clocks to a little later for evening work.

Two days after the episode at Johnson's place Jane and Ply returned late at night for the sword. The weather was a little cooler and a fog had settled over the area.

"Drop me off at the gate and you take the car to the picnic area." Jane told Ply. "I'll meet you there once I get the toy."

"How come you have so much clothing on?"

"It makes me look about thirty pounds heavier for the cameras and with the hood up," she flipped it over her head, "I'm almost impossible to recognize facially. When I pull the strings tight all you can see is my eyes and my nose."

"How long you been doin' this?"

"Like you say," she reminded him she opened the car door, "In some cases not long enough and in others much too long." She maneuvered out of the car and went up to the gate. She turned and waved Ply off and once he was onto the highway, she started to climb the gate. Immediately lights came on and she jumped back to the ground and turned around pulling the strings on the hoodie. She ran off into the trees for a little more protection.

"I'll wait a few minutes to see how long the lights stay on."

A quarter of an hour later she decided another route might be better. Looking over the property from her vantage point she noticed that the trees went all around the estate.

"I'll tromp through the woods to the other side of the pond."

It took another twelve minutes to get to a place she thought she might make a better entrance. She moved up to the fence but did not touch it.

Suddenly she realized, "They cut the blasted grass!" she announced to herself in exasperation.

The grass had been cut so now all she had to gauge the whereabouts of the sword was the shoreline and the rock she set up.

She looked across the field to the place where they had jumped the fence a few days earlier. Studying the situation, a little more closely, she noticed that the grass had not been cut with a mulching mower but with a regular blade. The thrown grass from each pass made it easier to see where the tall grass might have started.

"The grass on the bank of the pond has not been whipped so I need a place to hide, that might be it." she told herself.

Mentally she paced off the ten steps hoping she had it nearly right. "There are only a few differences in the edge of the pond, so I hope I can get close to the actual burial site." she softly mumbled.

As she touched the fence the lights in that area came on. She scaled the chain link and dropped into the grass about twelve inches from the fence.

"Now to get to the edge of the pond."

The grass was not cut at the rocky shoreline of the pond giving her somewhat of a place to hide. She ran to the edge of the pond all the time looking for her markers. She got to the edge and nothing looked familiar.

The lights were still on and she crawled across the rocks through the tall grass to the assumed sight. She gently slid her hand into the pool not wanting to raise ripples and dug into the soft bed.

"Nothing."

She withdrew her hand from the water and thought about what could have happened.

"Okay Lord where is this thing?" she asked.

She looked at the shoreline a little closer and decided that the rock she turned up was about five feet from where she was. There was a breeze that gave the pond small waves that reflected in the lights that announced her entrance but not quite fast enough to push all the clouds and fog away.

This fog just might protect me from visibility of the cameras on the roof of the main building. she thought to herself looking at the full scene around her. *If I can't see them perhaps, they can't see me.* She slid through the tall grass and dropped her hand back into the pool. Digging about six inches into the mud she realized it was not there. It wasn't quite cool enough to need all of the clothing she had on and the extra nervousness of not finding the toy brought great beads of sweat all over.

She heard the gate swing open down on the driveway.

Lord, please help me find this thing.

Taking a quick glance, she noticed someone getting into a car and making a bee-line for the fence where she crawled over. She rolled over into the pond hoping she didn't make too big a splash.

Part of her training was running and holding her breath, so the lungs would use up as much oxygen and possible. Then as she cooled down, she practiced holding her breath just to see if she could break the record, she had heard of twenty minutes. All she ever got to was fourteen and then almost fainted.

She furiously started digging in the area where she thought the sword might be. *It doesn't matter how much mud I stir up now, I have to find it.*

She noticed a glow on the surface of the water and stopped digging. The lights from the car passed and she waited ten more seconds before returning to work. She had made a trench about three feet long and six inches deep and realized she needed to surface and check her bearings. Lifting her head so her eyes were level with the surface she noticed the car was on the other side of the pond. She stood high enough to get her bearings and saw the turned rock.

"I'm a little far out from the shore."

She moved in with a fresh breath and started trenching almost a foot closer to the shore. Twenty long seconds later she cut her finger on the metal hilt. Gently she wrapped her hand around the tool, swished it off under water to clean the mud from the toy, and wrapped her hand around the handle.

Come on thing, warm up, she almost screamed under water.

Waiting another fifteen seconds she realized that the water kept the tool cool. The reflection on the surface returned and stopped just above her.

"I still have about three minutes of air left." she reminded herself.

She let the weight of the tool carry her to the bottom. With her hand on the hilt she raised it out of the water and held on as tight as she could, hoping it would warm up so she could transition. She saw something skip across the top of the water about one inch from her hand. She almost willed the transition and hopped to the surface of the pond. Having made herself almost zero weight she flew to the surface. A small projectile headed her direction. She batted it into the water, jumped to the shore and then to the fence line where she and Ply entered previously.

She turned back to see what had happened. There was a great cloud of water descending on the ground from the route she took jumping out of the pond.

So, the vacuum I leave behind drags the water from the pond to wherever I jump to, she thought. "What if..."

Jane hopped to the back of the car and sliced both back tires. The car was pointed in such a way that the driver could shoot towards the pond from his side of the car.

She cut out the top of the car just above the back seat, jumped back into the water, timed back to Earth Standard Time (EST) and sank to the bottom. With the sword just out of the water she super timed out, pushed with all her might from the floor of the pond, and brought up almost two thousand gallons of water following her toward the disabled auto. She touched down with her feet on either side of the cut open car, timed almost to EST then jumped from the car. Timing out again it took a few strides to get to the fence line as the water crashed into the car.

Jane hopped over the fence and back into the woods, so she would be less likely to be seen and brought herself to EST.

The water flooded the front and back seat right up and over the windows. The driver tried to escape but the water was much too fast and pushed him against the door of the vehicle.

The gun was still in his hand and a shot was fired into the air. Jane immediately timed out as she saw the explosion from the barrel of the handgun and jumped towards the projectile. She used the blade like an aileron guiding herself to the flying bullet. She grabbed the bullet and let it carry her to about eight hundred feet above the ground. She batted the metal back to the pond. Adjusting her weight and her time, she coasted back across the fence and into the woods to watch the end of the show. The driver opened the car door and was swept into the pond with the water losing the gun in the mud on the bottom.

"Let's see if this guy gets out of the pond." thought Jane.

As she watched, a head bobbed up over the water sputtering and cursing. He started walking and swimming back to the car.

Good. He is alive but not necessarily in his right mind, she said to herself, timed out, and in three strides she left the wooded area and made her way to Ply's car.

"Let's get out of here". she encouraged her husband. "And turn the heat on full blast, I'm freezing."

"How about you holding onto the metal of the car while the sword is in gear?"

"What do you want to do that for?"

"It just might render the car invisible and we can get away without being seen."

"I'll freeze to death!"

"I'll keep the heater on, and I will boil over!"

She grabbed onto the metal. Ply could feel the car enter into the timed zone.

"Wow." he said right out loud.

"Hang on baby it just might get a little exciting."

Ply left the lights off until they were about five miles from the turn off to the picnic tables as Jane held on to the tool with all her might. She dared not let go of either the car or the sword. Her hand was getting tired.

Ply had to employ all of his driving skills passing exits that were unreadable and barely recognizing cars that he passed due to the speed of the car in the new time frame. All the while the speedometer did not register over fifteen miles per hour.

"Perhaps we can stop so I can change clothes seeing we are three exits past the picnic tables." pleaded Jane a few moments later.

Ply slowed down until the speedometer practically registered zero, but it still seemed that they were flying past the roadside.

"Hey Jane," he shouted, "Slowly come back to normal and we may be able to get off somewhere."

She timed down slowly, and the car almost stopped in the middle of the highway. Ply snapped on the headlights and pushed his foot to the floor. This just happened to be the old white horse that they were riding so acceleration was not the main feature of the car even for the original owner. Twenty seconds later they were doing seventy and Jane had the sword in the case and was removing cold wet clothing.

"Thanks for thinking about a change of clothes hon." she said. "This will warm me up pretty quickly." She dumped the wet clothing on the floor in the back on top of the old guitar case and settled back into the front passenger seat snapping on her seat belt. Just as they were about to make a 'U' turn at the next exit, flashing red and blue lights appeared in the rear-view mirror and ricocheted around the inside of the car.

* * *

"May I see your driver's license and proof of insurance please." stated the police officer.

"Sure." said Ply as he slowly dropped his arms from the top of the steering wheel. He handed over the documents to officer and he returned to his cruiser.

Jane looked over to Ply and in a few minutes the officer returned.

"What exactly happened back there at mile marker two hundred thirty-eight point six?"

"Was there an accident?" asked Ply. "We didn't see one when we drove past."

"It appears that you stopped in the middle of the right-hand lane, turned on your headlights, and then accelerated up to the speed limit."

"Are you sure it was this car?" asked Ply.

"I'm pretty sure it was this car." stated he officer. "Why were you stopped in the highway?"

"We got on at one hundred eighty-seven point eight, about four exits back and have kept to the limit ever since."

"How many miles you got on this car?"

Ply turned up the dash lights and read to the patrolman. "Two hundred and seventy-six thousand eight hundred and forty-four." the officer adjusted himself so he could see the odometer.

"Could you give me the key and pop the hood please?"

"Sure." Ply handed the keys to the cop and popped the hood. He walked to the front of the front of the car and lifted the hood and looked inside checking things out with his flashlight. He let the hood drop allowing it to latch.

"You don't have anything that might make this car go a lot faster like a spare motor in the trunk?"

"No sir."

Ply unlatched the trunk so the officer could have a look. He walked around to the back and lifted the trunk lid only to find a pair of wet smelly running shoes and a lot of fast food garbage. He gently closed the back of the car.

"How fast can this car go?" asked the cop when he returned to Ply's window.

"I don't really know." responded the driver. "I may have had it up to eighty a few times, but I don't like to run too much faster than the limit as it makes my insurance go up."

"Do you think it will go over one hundred and forty miles per hour?"

"This old rattle trap?" replied Ply. "If it did, it just might shake apart."

Looking at the condition of the heap the officer tended to agree with the youth by a nod of the head.

"Okay," he yielded over the papers and the keys and encouraged the two, "Drive safely."

Ply started the old white horse and pulled out into traffic, not that there was much at that time of night.

"That was too close for comfort." stated Jane when she figured they were out of earshot.

"Did you see the name on the badge of that copper?" stated Ply.

"I kept my head down and looked out the front of the car so he might not have recognized me." stated the star.

"E. Merodach."

"I sure hope he is not related to the tennis player." stated Jane. "That would be too much of a coincidence!"

Back in the cruiser Merodach checked the speed trap screen again.

"Three hundred and forty-eight miles per hour." he mumbled to himself. "How am I going to explain this one?"

* * *

The Area of Cedars was a very large area that spanned just south of the North West Territories of what used to be Canada to the Mason Dixon Line in the center of what used to be the United States of America. The east-west boundaries were the Rockies and the Appalachians. Within the first half century of the reign of the Master many areas were relegated to agricultural use. The Area of Cedars was divided for use in four ways. The first was the entire area was divided into forty-acre sections. With each one hundred and sixty acres one section was wooded and three were planted crops. Annual crop rotation was encouraged and enforced for the best productivity of the land. Most of the treed sections were to remain treed for fifty years so a ready amount of lumber could be used for various purposes. The Area of Cedars was divided up, so a number of places used fifty-year cycles, some used twenty-five-year cycles, and others used ten-year cycles. When a fifty-year cycle was complete the forty acres was switched to crop growth, so soil nutrient conservation was preserved. With this system the Sahara Desert was pushed back to almost nothing by the end of the first three hundred years. Propagators of global overpopulation were debunked and there was always enough food for everyone on the entire planet with plenty left over.

The Anothen ran everything from city planning to law enforcement but within the last hundred years earth-bound civilians had been granted rights into certain areas of government. Police forces had sprung up in the individual areas and as were allowed by the Anothen. All that area was governed by one police force and expansion was allowed gradually.

"You got a minute chief?"

Ronald Webb, chief of the Area of Cedars Police Department had two hundred and fifty-seven officers with twelve in various stages of the apprenticeship training program. The chief was on the phone and normally did not like to be interrupted but knew when something important was up exceptions were made. His men were also familiar with his policy. When it was abused the offenders heard about it quickly.

At six feet two inches and two hundred thirty-five pounds he was finding it a little more work to keep his body fat less than six percent. He was managing with three visits per week at the local gym. Most of his life he found just working and not eating too much sweets kept things in check. The transition started at forty. Now at fifty-two he had settled somewhat into the routine of running and swimming to keep his tone.

He was on the phone with the mayor when he turned to see one of his officers almost ashen.

"Can I call you back?" he politely asked the mayor. Setting the receiver down, he invited the recent grad to have a seat.

"I wanted you to see this before the dispatcher got wind of it and it went viral." Merodach dropped the printout of the speed trap unto the desk.

The chief glanced at the readings and the posted limits in the areas of offenses but stopped at the last entry and sat up with a start. "Is this some sort of joke?"

"Not unless there is a problem with the equipment." answered Merodach.

"Any other discrepancies since this one?" asked the chief.

"I thought I'd better bring it in to get checked before another error turned up and we missed a fine." responded Merodach.

"That might have been the best thing to do. Sign out of that cruiser and sign into number thirty-six." commanded the chief.

"Thank you, sir."

"You're dismissed."

Merodach walked out of the office and registered into the other car. His job that night was to catch speeders, so he stationed himself back under the bridge. He thought about what exactly had happened and decided to check out the info from the car he stopped just after the jet went through.

"Ply Gallant." he typed into the cruiser's computer. "Maybe I should have done this earlier." he mumbled to himself. He read what came up on Gallant.

"No previous convictions in the last five years. Married that famous tennis player and it seems that he is somewhat involved with the Johnson thievery ring. He pulled up the case and read through what had been entered.

"There was some discrepancy in the testimonies of those that are involved in the case," he observed, "A ghost with a sword that bats bullets back to the shooters?"

Suddenly he remembered the shooting gallery and the projectiles he slipped into his pocket.

"A sword that bats bullets? How could that happen? Is it magic?" He mulled the thoughts over in his mind for a while. "And that car going so fast then seeming to stop on the highway then accelerate to cruising speed. It is also pretty mysterious."

All that night he watched the traffic for minor offenders, but it was pretty quiet till about two AM when a car flew past him at one hundred twenty-seven MPH.

He could see the taillights flying over the next hill and identified the year make and model but could not get the color. He radioed to the next cruiser four exits ahead to watch for the low flying vehicle and gave him the description.

A few minutes later he heard back that the vehicle was approaching the exit very rapidly. The second cruiser entered the highway doing about seventy and waited for the speeder to catch up. It didn't take long. As the expensive import flew past, he flicked on his lights and took up the chase. The Porsche sped up to one hundred and sixty-five, but the cruiser got the plates on the one hundred and twenty frames per second infra-red camera attached to the chase cruiser. He slowed and called it in only to find out that it had been stolen. The owner of the vehicle said he could stop the car and the officers agreed. The owner of the import stalled the car and applied the brakes remotely and the car stopped but not before the driver ran it into the ditch and tried to escape on foot. By this time Merodach and a few others were on the trail. One of the officers fired a net over the running suspect and he was captured like a wild animal. He pretty well behaved like one, spitting a cursing blaming the cops for all the wrong things that had happened in his life. The import escaped with minimal damage and was returned to the proper owner once all the paperwork cleared.

The suspect was apprehended, charged and sentenced for a felony seeing that the car was worth more than ten thousand dollars.

"That proves that this speed trap is working properly." said

Merodach to himself. "I still wonder about the other."

The Drone

"There has to be a better way to control this car when we are in the time zone." Ply announced to Jane once he was sure they were out of earshot from the cop.

"What do you mean?" she asked.

"It seemed that we were going much too fast, but it handled like we were too light for the roadway."

Ply noticed the police cars headlights in the mirror and set the cruise a little slower than the limit.

The cop followed them till their turn off. Ply slowed down until the officer passed then he took a longer route around the area just to make sure he wasn't tailed.

Back at the castle Ply parked in the garage and they talked as they got ready for bed.

"Can you dump down to zero gravity without changing the timing too much?" Ply asked.

"Why?"

"If we can get the car down to almost zero gravity, we might be able to maneuver it pretty easily in the air with little stubby wings rather than great long things that are on regular airplanes."

"You want me to zero gravity the car?"

"Sounds crazy, huh?"

"I don't know if I can do it myself let alone the car. It was really weird riding the car this evening."

"It was really weird driving this evening."

* * *

The next morning Ply continued thinking. "How can I test this without killing us or the car or all three?" he thought right out loud. He played around a few scenes in his head for a few hours then something fresh came to mind.

"Hey Jane." he called. She looked up from the tennis magazine she was reading.

"If you sat in the car and gravity out, I could watch and see what happens with the car. Are you willing to try this?"

"Sure."

Ply brought the car out to a spot in the middle of the lawn where there were no trees for about sixty feet each direction.

"You hop in the car and try to anti-grav but not very quickly. I'll stand back and see what happens."

"What do you expect to happen." she asked.

"I don't exactly know but I am real curious about finding out."

Jane climbed in the passenger side, closed the door and rolled down the window. Ply stood back about ten feet and watched as she anti-graved very slowly. Nothing disappeared out of view.

"Okay." he said. "Now come back quickly."

She timed out and the car immediately dropped to the ground as if being let down from a jack too quickly.

"You better put your seat belt on." admonished Ply.

"Why don't you try this stupidity." she said as she dropped the sword by the seat and started to climb out.

"Cause I can't do it, remember?"

She stopped with one foot on the ground and looked at him with a disgusted glare of impatience. It had been some time since she was at a loss for words.

"I'll teach you how!"

"We already tried that, and I can't seem to get it to work as well as you. How about we try something else."

"Like what?"

"If you anti-grav up a down a little I want to see if the car will rock like a cradle."

She crawled back in and fastened her seat belt. Picking up the sword and grabbing on to the metal of the door she timed up and down just a little and the car rocked like a toddler in a jumping swing.

"Perfect." he shouted. "I'll take the car over to the machine shed and make some minor body changes."

Jane got out of the vehicle and slammed the door a little too forcefully.

"You okay babe?"

"I'm this close to making a few minor body changes on you

after that back jostling exercise."

"I'm sorry hon. I think we can get this thing to actually fly."

"How are you going to do that alone?"

"Ah, I can't"

"Then make it a lot softer landing than what just happened there." she steamed.

Ply walked her back to the house leaving the car in the middle of the yard.

"Can I help you back to the house?"

"What are you going to do with the car?" she asked.

"Nothing unless you feel comfortable in riding in it." he replied.

"Can we get softer seats or even some thick foam cushions?"

"Sure." he agreed cautiously. "How is your back?"

"My back is fine." she replied. "It is just that I have not had a spanking like that in years."

Ply muffled a laugh and bit his tongue, but the smirk spread across his face. She still had the sword in her hand, so he only thought, *Did it do any good?*

* * *

Back in the maintenance shed Ply was puttering and cleaning. "Well that isn't going to work." he gripped to himself. "What am I going to do now?" He parked the old white horse back of the maintenance shed and took a long walk around the building.

"It is going to take a lot of money to get the car fixed up, so it is flyable." he voiced as he walked. "What about a drone?" There were lots of possibilities and different styles and sizes that were available.

He finished the lap around the yard and went into the house. Jane was preparing for her daily run around the property. She had increased to six miles a day greatly increasing her stamina.

"If we bought a small drone then we could have the problem solved in a few short days." he informed her.

"What problem is that?" she asked as she stopped at the door on her way out.

"The problem of the flying car."

"I didn't think the car was a problem, but I do think flying it is!"

"You are exactly right. You go for your run and I will search the net for a drone that might suit our purposes."

"It seems to be your purpose at the moment!" she cajoled as she jogged out the door the screen door banging behind her.

"I love you!" he shouted. "I'll see you when you get back." She left him at the door with her ponytail swinging as it did the first day he got hooked. He enjoyed the moment of her posture and the love they enjoyed, slowly closed the inside door and got on the tablet to look for used or new drones.

* * *

Forty minutes later she walked in all sweaty and smelly. "Why on earth do we need a drone?"

"We don't NEED a drone." he replied. "But we could fly around anywhere we wanted once we became invisible and zeroed out our weight without anyone knowing we were up there."

"It sounds too dangerous." she decided and thought the conversation was over and headed for the stairs to the shower.

"Isn't it dangerous for you to ghost out and jump off the railing?" reminded Ply. It took a few seconds for this to sink in, but she slowed her ascent.

"But I was in control then."

"Why won't you be in control when we are both up there?" he replied. "It just means we have to trust each other."

"Let me think about this." she headed for the clean-up but with a considerably different attitude than she had a few minutes ago.

Forty minutes later Jane descended with an idea of the own. "What if I time out like you say and you make a harness that will fit both of us. We would need a drone that would be big enough to carry both of us, but won't that be expensive?"

"Not if you drop both of our weights to almost zero."

"And what if someone starts shooting at us?"

"We have the sword already in somewhat time change mode just to make us invisible. We can time out more and either catch the bullet, bat it back to where it came from or dodge it. Bating it back might get us into more trouble. If we catch it and put it in our pocket or drop it into a pond, then we can get out of Dodge pretty quickly.

If we get a drone with a forty-pound payload we can even time out the drone for a few seconds till we get out of sight, then scamper back to where the car is or head for home if need be."

"Won't we drop like a rock if we time the drone with us?" she asked.

"That may be true depending on how much it is timed out but if we only do it for a short time then we can be invisible until we are out of sight and the drone will be invisible also."

"Just how do you plan to do that?"

If I put a switch on a wire and attach one end to the drone and the other end to an anti-static wrist strap, then we can time the drone as we need to. Opening the switch will break the time change circuit to the drone and it will be visible again, but we will be back to zero weight and the drone will pick up pretty quickly."

"This is something we are going to have to practice either over water or on a bunch of old mattresses before we try it over the ground." she cautioned.

"If we get a forty-pound payload drone we can put a couple extra battery packs on board for longer flights."

"You are whetting my curiosity." she responded her curiosity winning over her caution.

"We can have one here by the end of the week." he said.

"We must be absolutely crazy!"

"I knew that before I married you. As a matter of fact, that was one of the criteria that had to be part of the package." he reminded her.

She gave him a light fisted smack on the shoulder.

"Having a little extra money to do all this experimentation with is just an added bonus." he said. "But like you say money comes and money goes so let's just enjoy what the Lord has supplied but not be too foolish about it."

"Buying a drone and going skyward with the sword is not foolish?"

"I suppose." he replied. "But that depends on who you ask."

* * *

The drone showed up and Ply was ready to do some testing.

"I sewed together one set of two repelling harnesses and two boson's chairs for another set." he explained. "I suppose we should use the harnesses first seeing we can land on out feet. If we get used to landing on our feet, we can try the boson's chairs."

"What about the free-fall system you thought about?" she inquired.

"I don't think we will need to try that quite yet. When we get comfortable in the air, we can set it up and give it a try from a considerable height. I don't want to crash land in a free fall before we are ready..."

"I'm never ready for a crash landing from a free fall." she interrupted.

"Good point, so we will just get used to this thing one step at a time."

"Where do you want to try it out?" she asked excitedly.

"Let me get used to flying this contraption first. I think it will be safer to crash the drone without us tied to it. When I feel confident enough, I can land us safely then we can find somewhere to try it."

"Can't you control it from your phone?"

It says there are lots of devices you can control it from. I was thinking of doing it from a tablet. Some of them have a hook for a lanyard. With the lanyard wrapped around my wrist there is less likely that the controller would end up in free fall."

She thought about this for a minute. "Things can go wrong pretty quickly up there can't they."

"That is why I need to fly this thing without us attached to it, just so I may think of most of the problems that could arise."

* * *

Ply spent the next four days testing flight patterns and learning the battery life in hours and minutes on each specific battery. Just before the battery died, he brought the thing back to the yard and switched batteries. He hovered the thing six inches above ground just to get an accurate reading on the battery life with no load on the drone except the camera that came with the unit.

Next, he tested the unit with three milk jugs with ten pounds of sand in each tied to the harness, so he could see the differences under load. He recorded all the parameters in the tablet and programmed them so loaded there would be ample time to do what was needed if an emergency arrived.

"I don't want this thing getting blown out to sea with the beautiful one and I riding at three thousand feet." he decided. "If the wind gets too strong then we will just have to either land or bring the thing home if we can."

After a few more days and multiple tests, he entered graphs into the tablet and paralleled the battery cells to the on board computer. With all the batteries connected and the three milk jugs tied on he had just over eight hours of flight time.

"I sure hope that is long enough to get us where we need to go. I wonder if some solar cells would make this thing more efficient?" He thought about it for a while then decided, "I don't need so much stuff tied to this thing it looks like a flying yard sale."

* * *

The two of them were strapped in for the first test flight.

"Let's just try a little up and down." suggested Ply. "I'll set the lift to thirty pounds and you time out, so we lift off then hold the time and I will try to bring us down softly from about three feet."

She nervously nodded her head. Ply had good control of the craft and they floated up to three feet then he set them both down gently.

"How was that?"

Jane waited a second or two before replying, "Let's go to five feet." She brought them up to five or six feet and set them both down gently once again.

"How high do you want to go?" she asked with an inquisitive grin.

"We are invisible." stated Ply. "The camera is not picking us up, but I don't want to go higher than the treetops until it's dark out."

"You mean like after sunset?"

"Like about two hours after sunset so it is really dark. I don't know if this will make us invisible to radar so staying low might be a good idea."

"How are you going to navigate at night?" she asked.

"First of all, you stay close to home until you recognize the landscape. At night you guide yourself by the treetops and not the roadways, unless they are lit up".

"Where on earth did you learn that?"

"Uncle Jack had a small cottage he inherited on a lake and he taught me how to navigate a boat by day and by night. Two very different operations but if you can do it you accomplish the same goal of getting home safely."

"You're kidding."

"Let's go for a short ride." Ply flew them down the drive a few feet above ground. Jane ducked as they scooted under the arch in the wall. Ply glanced over and shook his head. She grinned sheepishly. They glided down the roadway to just before the highway and Ply brought them back the same route.

"As you can see it is easy to follow the roadway in the daytime. I'll show you what it is like later tonight but let's first get these batteries recharged so we may have some time if we get lost. I don't expect we will, but I want things fully charged so we have time to float and find. Ever seen the stars from six hundred feet?"

"Not yet." she grinned. "But I can hardly wait."

* * *

By ten o' clock the batteries were fully charged and both were almost too excited to get this thing happening. They went outside but the temperature had dropped considerably.

"We better get some more clothes one." said Ply. "With the wind from the blades it just may get chilly up there."

"How about a wide brimmed hat to keep some of the breeze out of our hair?"

"Do you have two?" asked Ply.

"I have a few of straw and one is not colored if you want to wear that?"

"Do they have chin straps?" he asked. "What if we caught in a down draft?"

"Are you trying to talk me out of this?"

"No. I just want to be ready and I don't want to have to chase a hat halfway around the world."

"How long are you planning to stay up there and where do you plan on going?"

"Not real far tonight but I do want to see how it works."

They each donned a harness and Ply clipped the two harnesses to the hook on the bottom of the drone. He devised two anti-static straps tied to each other, so they would not have to hold hands giving them freedom of each of their limbs. Ply adjusted the drone to lift itself and the straps with a slight tension on the harnesses and Jane zeroed out.

The three shot up into the air and Ply made some minor adjustments on the tablet. They leveled out at the tops of the trees.

"Let's go a little higher." she said and timed a bit more, so they floated up to twenty feet above.

"So, you can control up and down by adjusting weight." admired Ply.

"That is pretty easy." she agreed.

"Let's fly around and familiarize ourselves with the yard and the house from different angles and heights." encouraged Ply. "That way we can recognize the place if we need to get back in a hurry."

Ply had the camera on record, so all the exercises were visible for later, but things looked a little different with two eyes than just one camera lens.

"Wow." stated Jane. "This is beautiful up here".

"Are you okay with going a little higher?" asked Ply.

"How high did you want to go?"

"I thought if we got some shots from a thousand feet we could learn to recognize where the house is from a lot of places that are close."

"Hold that tablet so I can see it and I will run us up there." Jane timed out and the two of them climbed twenty feet a second to a thousand feet.

"Okay, that may be high enough for the moment." said Ply. He slowly rotated the aircraft, so they could get a picture on camera of every angle.

"I wonder what the wind speed is up here? We seem to be drifting."

"Maybe we better call it a night and see if we can get back home." agreed Ply.

They dropped slowly and headed for the castle. Between the two of them they glided up and down over treetops and houses and got back home safely. Ply leveled off just above the back door and

Jane let them drop slowly to the ground.

"I never thought about wind speed and having to figure that into the equation." spouted Ply. "From what I understand the higher you go the faster the wind speed depending on the atmospheric conditions."

"So, if we went up to two thousand feet the wind might be a whole lot faster?"

"That would depend on wind direction, fronts, barometric pressure changes, and a bunch of things."

"I'll bet there is an app for that on the net." she suggested.

"I'll try to find one in the morning. It is probably for aircraft use but perhaps there is one for drones also. I wonder if you have to register?"

"There may be a site for student use to figure out wind speeds and aircraft speeds at specific angles to the wind."

Ply looked at Jane.

"I did take some math in high school." she exhorted him.

"What would I find such a thing under?"

"I'd start with 'atmospheric wind speed in directional flight'."

"Alright." he answered. "It is almost midnight and I am tired after the excitement of the ride, so I may want to sleep in, in the morning. I'll look it up then."

"Can we go up again after my run?"

Ply looked at her in surprise. "I thought you would be nervous about going up again so soon?"

"Sometimes I get used to stuff pretty quickly." she responded.

"It appears that way. We should stick to the area here and go up from between the trees, so we can duck out of sight if we need to. Maybe I'll rig up a white dot we can see from above the trees to pinpoint our landing spot. Do we have an old white towel you don't mind setting on the grass?"

"I've got lots of bath towels from hotels how about one or two of those?"

"You stole towels from the hotels you stayed at?"

"No." she responded a little disappointed at the accusation. "I bartered a few from managers and owners with a winning ball."

"The old winning tennis ball trick." he mumbled. "How can we use a few to get a discount on a newer car?"

"What's the matter with the old white horse?"

"It has a quarter million miles on it. It's bound to fall apart sooner or later."

"The mechanic says we can probably get that again if we take care of it." she responded.

"I think it looks awful and I would like a little nicer looking car."

"I tell you what. If you clean it up, inside and out, we'll see how much it costs to get it painted."

"That might help. I feel a little like a cheapskate driving around in the old heap with the number one tennis star beside me."

"Are you letting all this money go to your head? It helps me travel incognito. Remember what happened at the restaurant with the Spoudice's?"

"Oh yeah... okay."

"We just got a new toy and what we are doing with it is probably as illegal as shooting bald eagles, and you want to spend more money on a new car?"

"I'm sorry." he said dropping his chin. "Sometimes my wants outrun what we really need."

"We can look and see what is available." she encouraged. "I don't know if I want Merodach knowing where we live. He did catch us in the horse. I wonder what he clocked us at?"

"Have you changed your address on your license yet?" he asked.

"We don't really have a permanent address yet. Are we supposed to change our cards before we have one?"

"I don't remember what the time frame is, but I don't think it is longer than three or six months."

"There is another reason to try to keep out of trouble. It has been almost a year since you moved out of the apartment and I haven't been home to my folk's place since we moved here at the castle."

"I don't think Barb is willing to put us up forever. Don't you think we should find a place of our own?"

"What about using your apartment as a permanent address until we have someplace else?" suggested Jane. "I don't think my parents are going to be really happy with us living with them."

"I don't know if I still have it." stammered Ply. "I haven't paid the rent in months and..."

"I've taken care of it up till now." said Jane. "If we needed some place to go in a hurry that was all that was available, so we had better get our addresses changed first thing in the morning. I have talked to Barb about it numerous times and she is more than willing to have us here. She says it keeps the place lived in and there is someone here when she gets home from her games. Besides, she really seems to enjoy our company."

"Even if we are married and she isn't?"

"It seems so." replied Jane. "I don't really understand it all either, but it is what she wants at the moment."

"We should spend some time on the net looking for a house. We really need to start living on our own." stated Ply.

"Don't you like it here?"

"I love it here, but it isn't ours, besides, can you imagine what a place like this would cost to purchase?"

"I don't even want to think about it! Barb will be back in a week." said Jane. "We should talk to her first, but we can look but let's not make any offers until we talk to her. She has been acting strangely lately and she hasn't told us what is happening."

"Strangely?" he asked. "How?"

"She doesn't seem to have the stamina she used to. She is not running as far nor nearly as long as we did last year. I wonder if she is sick?"

"Sick? Why would she not say something?"

"We'll have to talk to her when she gets back."

"Okay." agreed Ply.

* * *

The next morning, they were up in the air by a little after ten. Just after getting all the paperwork done for their new address at Ply's old apartment.

"What is that approaching?" asked Jane.

"It looks like a flock of birds headed our way."

They got close enough to recognize. "Do you want goose for dinner?" invited Jane. "I could get one or two without them even knowing."

"How would you do that?"

"I could just lop off a few heads and we could catch them on the way down."

"What about the shower of blood that would fall on the houses below? Not to mention the goose head landing on someone's roof or windshield!"

"Oops." she thought for a few seconds. "That would create a lot more excitement than we expected."

"If you want goose I know of a good restaurant, and we just might stay out of jail."

"That sounds a whole lot more relaxing." she responded. "But goose does sound like a welcome change".

"Ever had it before?"

"Sure." she said. "I think the best place to get it is on the street corners of Spain, but I haven't been to every city in the world yet."

"You planning to go?"

"It does sound like fun but with the rebellion picking up speed and Merodach on our trail it would be better just to stick around home for a while."

"What do you want to see next?"

"How about Johnson's place?"

"I don't know if we have enough battery time left."

"Okay." she said. "Let's go home and get closer to ground. There are a few things I want to try with this toy."

"I do think you are having too much fun".

"Or maybe not quite enough." she smiled.

* * *

Back in the yard of the castle Jane explained what she thought she could do. "I think I can time us and the drone in two separate zones."

"You can separate the timing of the drone from us?" asked Ply.

"That is why I wanted to come home and try it from a few feet and not find us in free fall at four thousand."

"Thanks for thinking."

"Actually, I just about tried it up there but thought the better of it. We will see if waiting was the better idea."

Ply just looked at her and was thankful she was a little more disciplined than some of the other friends he had.

"Do you want to try this by yourself or can I come along and enjoy the ride?"

"How can I do this myself?"

"The tablet has a lanyard on it. You strap the tablet to your belt and set the lift for whatever you want, twenty or thirty pounds, and you control the lift by timing with the sword. If you don't go too high or if we find a place where there is a lot of room I can watch to see when both you and the drone disappear."

"How about the boson's chair. I can sit with the tablet on my lap and the sword in my left hand. I can control lift when I need it in a hurry. I'll put the switch so I can reach it with my right hand and not cut anything with the blade in timing mode."

"That sounds like you are thinking."

"Hey," she teased, "I'm not just a pretty face."

He gave her a quick up and down look. "You're telling me!"

She gave him the appropriate smack on the shoulder.

* * *

They unhooked the harnesses and clipped on the single boson's chair. She lifted off as normal then everything disappeared from Ply's view. She reappeared almost instantly but was at the tops of the trees.

"How on earth are you doing that?"

"Hush and let me concentrate." she yelled back. Both she and the drone disappeared again, and she was gone for a full thirty minutes. Suddenly she was between the tops of the trees and the towel on the ground. She glided down to a perfect landing of the middle of the towel and said, "I think I drained the batteries".

"What?"

"I think I drained the batteries. I'll have a look."

Ply glanced at the tablet and sure enough the battery time left was ten minutes with a thirty-pound load. "How did you manage that?"

"I flew up to a thousand feet and dropped the timing. That gave me enough time to set the tablet on GPS to know where the house was. Once that was entered, I could go where I wanted and with the drone at a different time, I could keep afloat with both of us invisible."

"So how long have you been gone in your time frame?"

She showed him a watch she had placed on her wrist just to see if this were something, she could double time. The clock was six hours different from the time on the tablet that readjusted as soon as it was back in real time.

"You've been up there for six hours?" he asked. "Where did you go?"

"Yeah and I'm starved. How about that goose you promised me?" she responded avoiding her question. "I'll tell you where I went after I catch my breath."

He looked at her a little puzzled. "We better take this stuff inside and take the old white horse. The batteries can recharge while you have a good meal. It is only been an hour since I ate last."

"That never seemed to hold you back before." she teased.

* * *

Jane ordered a full side of goose while Ply just had a grilled cheese sandwich thinking he would need some room to help the poor starved lady across from him devour parts of the bird that were unwanted by the big-eyed beauty. He was not disappointed.

"There is an old app here that was developed by Garmin a long time ago and most of the stuff is now considered public domain." Ply opened the conversation about an application for the tablet.

"It was developed for small personal aircraft in the early two-thousands. They adapted it for underwater use and for cave use in analyzing atmospheric components like contaminants and poisonous gasses. With the purchase of a few masks we can splunk in any cave we want to and be safe as long as the battery doesn't die on our tablet."

"Sounds too dangerous." she said.

"If we get the entire kit, we can deep sea dive without going down."

"What are you going to find there?"

"All the gold doubloons that the Spanish lost in storms in the Bermuda triangle."

"And just what are you going to do with them?" she interrogated dropping her fork.

263

"Sell some of them to the highest bidder and give some of them to various museums in the world." he sheepishly replied.

"And when are you going to be free to help me with my game?" she asked lifting her glass for a drink.

"I thought you gave that up?"

"You don't get it do you?" she set he glass down a little too quickly on the top of the wooden table but thankfully it did not chip.

"Get what?" he asked considerably alarmed at her rising anger and disappointment.

"Why do I eat with a knife and a fork?" she asked.

Oh boy, he thought. *Lessons on etiquette at this stage in life might mean...*

"I don't have to eat with a knife and fork." she interrupted. "I can eat like the barbarians of the rebellion with just my fingers or just grab this silly bird and bit off a piece and toss the rest back on the tabletop."

Man, thought Ply. *I've never seen her like this before. What on earth have I done now? Worse, how do I fix it?* he thought staring at her wide eyed.

"I don't have to play tennis." she again interrupted his thoughts. "But if you want to live peaceably with this old girl, she needs an outlet with some pretty stiff competition. She also needs a cheering section that proves his undying love for her." She sat back on the bench of the booth almost in tears but trying to control herself.

"When do you play next?"

"There are schedules in the kitchen, library, and I even put one on the bulletin board in the back maintenance building, and you ask me when my next game is?"

Ply sat and thought for a few seconds but not too long for her to get up and leave. He wondered if that would be her next move. "I have been pretty selfish lately." he admitted. "I'm sorry".

She sat back up and reached for her drink.

"I did notice the schedules, but I haven't taken the time to study them. I have been having too much fun with the new toys and really enjoyed your excitement also, but I need to ask you what you want to do rather than just do what I want hoping I can talk, or drag, you into participating."

"My next game is in town here to start the season. Seeing I was eliminated I will have to start from fairly close to the bottom again. But that is no big deal. The money I win will cover expenses." she paused and then bit the inside of her lip a little. "It is not that we don't have enough but I just don't like to blow it."

"I really have enjoyed having a little money but perhaps I am getting carried away with all the fun of new toys." he apologized.

Slowly Jane went back to devouring the bird.

"Does this mean we get to go home, kiss and make out, er, make up?" he asked sheepishly.

This finally brought a smile and her appetite returned. "Not until I've finished pecking at this bird." she teased back.

"Where did you go that took up six hours of battery life and only thirty minutes of real time?"

"I went out to the coast." was her simple reply.

"And what took your breath away out there?"

"The storm." she gently said while stuffing some more dead bird parts into her mouth.

"The storm?" he asked eyebrows plastered to the top of his forehead. "What storm?"

"Maybe I better start from the beginning." she took a sip of her drink to wash down the greasy goose. "I was thinking I could use the wind to take me where I wanted to go instead of using all that battery power, so I zipped up to three thousand feet and timed out to almost nothing." She swirled her mashed potatoes with her fork and took a small bite, swallowed, and continued.

"I managed to time the drone in a little different rate than I was, so we wouldn't fall like a rock but all it did was make us like a half sheet of paper and the wind blew us wherever it wanted."

Ply sat patiently and listened, but it wasn't real easy seeing he was a little nervous not being in control.

"I had to get some sort of control back seeing I was blown around like dust, so I timed me back to a little weight and the drone leveled out in a few minutes. We hadn't fallen at all. As a matter of fact, we were another two thousand feet higher and I was wondering if I was going to run out of air. By the time I had what I thought was control I was at six thousand feet and still in the middle of some pretty high winds. I was in the clouds but that Garmin program you installed gave me enough sight to level according to the earth and get a GPS reading. I laid my GPS position across the earth program and found I was about three hundred miles north of Vancouver. Suddenly six thousand feet above sea level did not seem like quite enough. I was still in the middle of the clouds, but the surface of the earth was only five hundred feet below me according to that Garmin thing."

"You got lost in the Rockies?"

"I didn't say I was lost." she refused to admit. "Just a little tossed by the wind."

More than a little, Ply thought.

"I needed to get out of the clouds, so I took a deep breath and went up. At fifteen thousand feet..."

"Fifteen thousand feet?"

"I came out of the clouds and the storm into the brightest sun you could ever imagine but it was still a little cold. I brought up the weather map to see where I could get a cloudless area and found one over the center of Alberta. I landed in a wheat field and just lay there for a few minutes soaking up the sun,

I checked the battery levels and they were okay so I decided that the west coast, away from the storms, would be pretty to see so I buckled back up and hopped over to the clear area by the ocean. There were no storms forecast but that should not always be your only leading."

She stabbed another piece of bird and ate giving her a short respite. Ply was again polite with the expenditure of much discipline. She thought it was cute.

"I was flying practically at zero grav along the coast enjoying the beauty when I was suddenly pulled up and out by a very quick wind. It seemed to be coming out of nowhere. I tried to elevate but if I was upside down, I would have plunged right into the ocean. Saltwater baths I didn't think were good for the apparatus so with the tablet in hand I tried to get enough stabilization to do something safely." she took time to have another bite and a drink.

"Well?" Ply announced a little too loudly for the quiet restaurant.

People from other tables looked at what appeared to be a tense situation getting worse and Jane had to stop her explanation expecting too many curious ears tuned into the conversation.

"We can talk in the car." she ended the conversation in a voice that was a little louder, so the neighbors could get the point that it was over for their ears. He was somewhat disappointed for causing such a stir. She cut off a small piece from the foul and pushed the plate an inch in Ply's direction. That usually was the sign of whatever he wanted was his, so he picked at it with his fork until the bones were clean.

* * *

Back in the car Jane was encouraged to continue.

"So, what happened next?"

"I think I better drive and talk seeing that you are the one that is having a bit of trouble with all that happened."

He surrendered the driver's side. Once he was strapped in, she continued, "I was blown about a hundred miles out to sea."

"What?"

"I got back safely, okay." she reminded him. "So just sit tight and I will finish the story. A similar kind of thing happened as I was over the Rockies but being over the water made things a little more problematic." She glanced over to his to see if he was still okay. He seemed to be controlling himself but stretching the definition to the limit.

"I had learned a lot in the last storm so this one was not as difficult in the sense of being lost. I did have the GPS, so I could find my way home. I timed a little to add some stabilization to the craft and get reoriented. I looked up and there was this tremendous wave about to crash over top of me, so I zipped up to five thousand feet and found myself just about out of the storm. I could still breathe at five-K, so I took a deep breath and elevated to seven. At that elevation the sun was out once again and I recalibrated to GPS but found myself one hundred miles offshore from San Jose, California. When you time out it takes a minute for the tablet to reconfigure. I needed some free fall space to get my bearings correct. Ten thousand feet gave me space to do so and I ran up and free fell three thousand feet and the tablet re-calibrated."

"So, you went South and West." confirmed Ply in a tone that surprised the star.

"Yes," she confirmed, "But the battery life was starting to show only half life left so I thought I'd better get back home."

"Thank you." he spoke softly.

"Once I knew where I was, the shortest distance between two points is a straight line, so I bee-lined back to the general vicinity of home, recognized the landscape and dropped in."

"Why did you not kiss the ground once you were home?"

"What makes you think I didn't?"

"I didn't see you do it."

"That doesn't mean I was not on my face rolling in the grass delighted to be safe. At least in my head. I didn't want you to destroy the toy knowing you might have lost me to your foolish whims, but I am ready to go back up with you if you would like a little excitement."

"Man!" he exclaimed. "This super-hero stuff is not all it has been built up to be."

"Well." she somewhat agreed. "Maybe not all."

He just looked over in her direction, returned his gaze to the front windshield and slowly shook his head.

"What?"

"My dad used to say, 'Women, you can't live with 'em and you can't live without 'em'." he repeated still shaking his head. "I think it is better to live with them but sometimes the contest is almost a draw."

"One more thing." she added.

"Yeah." he said after a moment of quiet, trying to encourage her to finish what she started without getting distracted.

"While I was upside down over the ocean it seemed as if someone was watching. I tried to keep control and not let the sensation bother me but..."

"You too?" he asked.

"What do you mean me too?"

"When I was in the cave just after discovering the sword, I felt as if someone was watching. The same thing happened in the old apartment but just once. I think it is the Master letting us know He knows what we are up to."

"You're kidding?"

"He is supposed to know everything and be involved in every situation. Who else could it be?"

"Let me think about this for a while." she replied.

"I wondered if you would think me nuts for suggestion such a thing."

She glanced in his direction remembering the previous conversation.

"Watch the road would ya." he encouraged her.

Barb's Illness

Barb came in about one thirty AM. The two were fast asleep just as she had planned. She quietly slipped into her room got ready for bed but didn't sleep very well.

It was time to tell them, she thought to herself. In the morning, she got out of bed, threw on her housecoat and crept downstairs to greet the two as they ate breakfast.

Jane saw her first as she came through the door. "Hi." she greeted earnestly. "How goes the game?"

"I expect the games are going very well." she quietly announced.

"Would you like some breakfast?" invited Ply. "We cooked enough for an entire army."

"I can see that." agreed the older. "Who do you plan on feeding all this to?"

"We were going to dump it into the freezer and have stuff ready for quick meals when needed. It is wonderful to live off your muffins, but Ply likes variety." blamed Jane.

Ply looked up at the accusation and Barb smiled and slowly shook her head.

"How come you're back so early?" asked Jane. "Aren't you supposed to be playing in Australia?"

"I'm not hungry right at the moment." said Barb avoiding the question. "But we do need to talk once you have the kitchen cleaned up."

Now Jane was concerned. "Are you okay?"

"That's what we need to talk about." she repeated and lifted herself off her chair. "I'll be in the library. Come talk when you are ready, but clean up first, it will take a while".

Jane watched Barb maneuver out of the kitchen. Suddenly her appetite crashed. She scraped what was left from her plate onto Ply's and set her dishes on the table.

"What's going on?" asked Ply.

"I don't know, but I don't think I like it." stated Jane as she hurried out to the library. She reached the door just as Barb slid rather in-glamorously onto the couch.

"Are you sick?"

"Is the kitchen cleaned up?"

"Ply can do that, what is wrong? How can I help?"

"Please," invited Barb, "Clean up with Ply. This is going to take some explaining."

Barb looked considerably paler than Jane had ever seen her. She rushed back to Ply who had finished his second plateful and about to reach for another even after Jane dumped her remnants in front of him. Jane grabbed his spoon and plate and said, "Barb's sick, I'm scared, and you're finished eating."

"Barb's sick?"

"I've never seen her like this. I think it may be serious."

Ply sat there in somewhat of a stupor.

"C'mon Ply." encouraged Jane. "Get the batteries in! We have to get all this cleaned up and the dishwasher going before Barb will even talk to us."

Ply got up and started putting things away. He and Jane finished cleaning up the kitchen and within five minutes they were back in the library. Barb was half lying down on the couch. Jane brought over a wing back chair close to Barb's face.

"Now!" cried Jane almost in tears. "What is happening? Why...?"

"I haven't been to the games in eight months." proclaimed Barb.

Jane sat up totally surprised. "What? Where...?"

"I've been getting my house in order."

Jane leaned into Barb and the tears flowed a lot freer.

"Two years ago, I was having chest pains by the sixth game." announced Barb. "I didn't let it bother me too much, after all, your heart gets a good workout during a couple of sets." she laughed but Jane just held on to her hand. "At the end of the season I saw the team doctor. He suggested some tests. I did some cardio tests, but nothing ever showed up." She placed her right arm over Jane's shoulder. "I don't think they wanted to take the time to make me run the equivalent of two full sets, so they dismissed it as just an anomaly."

Ply was catching on to something very serious going on with the two girls, but he did a good job of keeping his mouth closed and his eyes and ears open.

"By this time, you guys had shown up here and I thought I better keep what was happening to myself. I tried to comfort myself that my illness was what prevented me from winning when you skunked me right on my own turf." she grinned. "But then you went to France and slaughtered anybody that had the nerve to show up on the other side of the court...."

Jane noticed it was getting a little harder for Barb to catch her breath. She released her hold on her friend a little and sat her up with some pillows while Ply scouted for a few more boxes of tissues. He also brought the trash basket a little closer to Jane.

"I don't know how you didn't notice what was happening while we were across the pond. I managed to keep up but slept a little longer than I normally did. I am glad you never noticed the medications."

"What did the doctor tell you?" pleaded Jane as Ply got up and went slowly out of the room. Barb noticed but Jane did not.

"She said it was my heart. They did a number of tests that showed nothing but as things went on, degeneration happened faster."

"Degeneration?"

"She says it is a new discovery. It happens to some people with heart problems in their history but apparently it has something to do with generational degeneration." said Barb. "My dad had it and I lost my older brother three years ago, and it appears that now it is my turn."

"Your turn?" She questioned as tears flowed through the hoses of the eye ducts again.

"The doctor said I had only a year left."

"Had?" whimpered Jane.

"That was eight months ago."

Just then Ply showed up with the sword. "Hold on to Barb and I will hold on to you, and please, let me explain." stated Ply in a tone that commanded attention. He timed out and the three disappeared from view but not from each other. "When I was testing out this thing, I was going to shave my face with it..."

Jane and Barb exchanged glances and a, "Now what is he up to?" betrayed their looks.

"I couldn't see myself in the mirror so shaving my face was

pretty well out of the question."

Their looks said to each other; Where is this going?

"I shaved a bit of my arm and within minutes I was bleeding profusely."

"Ply, what..." interrupted Barb but he kept on.

"I had used the sword later the next day and found that my arm had healed with no scars or any evidence that I had even scratched myself."

The look on the girls' faces told Ply that they might be catching on to where this might be headed.

"If this thing has healing powers that work in time change mode, we just might grow old with you." he lovingly said to Barb.

"I do feel a whole lot better just as you were talking but what will happen if we all let go." asked Barb trying to shake loose.

Ply quickly jumped back to normal and the three were in normal time when Barb finally shook lose.

"Please don't try that again." exhorted Ply. "We don't know what will happen if you suddenly let go in time change mode. It could be nothing, but I don't want to be the first to try to find out and I don't think you do either".

"What's gonna happen?" asked Barb. "Am I suddenly going to melt?"

"Since you are feeling better, I'll take you outside and show you."

Jane looked at him with the most curious face Ply had ever seen. Barb jumped up from the couch then fell back down again.

"Let me catch my breath." said Barb as she sat up a little.

"Your color seems much better." remarked Jane as she stared in wonder as the girl seemed to heal right in front of her.

"How many lives are you planning to save with that thing?" asked Barb in wonder of how she was feeling herself.

"Just one at a time and we are going to start with you." said Jane.

"Can I tell my doc..."

"Not yet." interrupted Ply. "Let's just see what happens with you and that heart of yours first."

Barb sat up for a few more minutes then stood and said, "Let's go."

"I'll show you out in the back maintenance shed with a piece of wood." All three made their way to the back and into the shed. "I first tried it with a rock and all it did was get warm." said Ply as he opened the door. "Rocks are a lower dimension than plant life, so I thought I would try it with a piece of wood. Jane, you hold the sword, Barb and I will hold unto Jane and I'll drop the wood. Stay timed out until the wood hits the floor then come back as quick as possible." Ply grabbed a scrap piece of wood from the pile and the three held hands.

"Ready?"

Jane timed out and Ply dropped the piece of wood. All three jumped back as the wood burst into flames.

"What happened?" shouted Barb.

"The friction from space reshaping so quickly only got the rocks hot but I expect the farther out one times the hotter the rock gets. The wood, on the other hand is a dimension higher than the rock due to the life properties of the wood and the reaction was much more extreme. I expect the degree of time change is proportional to the reaction that happens as it snaps back to normal time. I haven't tried it with a live animal because I don't want to be cruel just for curiosity sake but we as humans are two dimensions higher than that piece of wood and we just might dissolve if we time out too quickly. Yes, Barb you just might melt if you shake loose from a deep time change."

Barb flopped down on the chair by the workbench, ashen once again. Jane grabbed on to her arm and timed out, so her friend could catch her breath. Once they were back Barb asked, "What other little tricks can happen with that toy?"

"I think I'm afraid to ask." stated Ply.

"I haven't been able to breath so easily for months." said Barb as she looked at Jane. "How about a little volley?"

"What?" exclaimed the younger. "You were about to expire in my arms and now you want to tear around on the court?"

"Why not?" she glanced at Ply and then the sword.

"Cause I don't want to be the blame of sending you home early!"

"I'm not going home early." she shot back. "Remember 'it is appointed...'" she stopped for a second refusing to finish the quote. "And I don't think the appointment has arrived yet."

"Let's see how you feel tomorrow." encouraged Jane to the

two.

"Can we at least go for a walk if only around the yard a few times?"

"Okay." said Jane. "Ply, you keep your phone handy and if we need you, I will call, and you bring the sword."

"Okay."

The walk was refreshing to Jane and Barb was chipper as her normal self. They circled the yard twice, but Jane did not want to overdo it, so they went in.

"What did you do with all that breakfast?" asked Barb.

"We stuck some in the fridge and the rest in the upstairs freezer."

"Would it be too much to ask..."

"Now I suppose you are starving to death." teased Jane.

"Not nearly." she rebuked Jane with a look. "But I sure would like something to eat."

Jane felt severely reprimanded by her casual attitude at such a time as this. "I'm sorry for being so crass."

"I guess I'm just a little touchy about the subject of 'passing away' at the moment." apologized Barb.

They returned to the kitchen and Jane was still nervous about the difficulties of her friend. "You just sit down there, and I will get you what you need." she commanded and moved towards the fridge.

Barb jumped up and beat Jane to the cooler and blocked the door before Jane had a chance to open it. "Hey kid." she teased her friend. "I'm not dead yet and I don't know what happened back there in the library, but I haven't felt this good in months."

"How then can I help?"

"Don't pamper me and treat me as an equal." she said. "I am sick but it's not contagious. We have been friends and helpers to each other for a long time now and I don't expect that to change." she reprimanded. "Well, not too much but under the circumstances..."

"You have been such a help to me in all my dreams," Jane reminded Barb, "How can I help you achieve your dreams now?"

"I guess I need to decide what my dreams are." she stated somewhat confused. "What is it I want to do or accomplish 'for the rest of my life'?" she asked as she grabbed a few containers from the appliance. "I have retired from the circuit but not without some questions from a few of the organizers. I told them my games have been failing and they did notice that but wanted to keep me going. I finally told them my doctor commanded me to take a rest for a while. They wanted to know for how long. I said just for the next season. They somewhat balked but with my scores dropping they let it go."

The loss was hard for Barb. Her food was in the microwave and a look of sadness crawled across her face. Jane came over and gave her a hug and both held in a tight embrace until the buzzer sounded. Barb let go and reached for the warm food. "Sometimes I wonder why some things have to happen so fast."

"Tell me about it." said Jane.

Barb looked up a little confused.

"I had to be back on the professional courts in a month instead of taking it slow and easy. Wham, back in the circuit again." Barb sat at the table, bowed her head for a few seconds than started shoveling, as much as a polite respectful person shovels when she is suddenly so hungry.

"Thank you for all of your help in getting me playing again."

"All I did was tell a few people what they needed to know, and the Lord took it from there."

"He sure did!"

"Playing the circuit is pretty hectic." said Barb. "Maybe now I need to rest a bit and enjoy the life I have left. The doctor sent me home to die." She set the fork down and looked at Jane who had made herself a cup of hot chocolate and was sitting right beside her.

"To die?"

"It has been a complicated last year." remembered Barb. "There was only one of the organizers who wanted to know all about what was happening. I swore her to secrecy and the rest all fell into the excitement of the upcoming games." she forked another mouthful of eggs down the hatch, "I told her I would let her know about what was happening. You know, keep her informed, but maybe I just need to slow down a little and smell some roses." She piled a mound of eggs on a piece of toast and took a bite. "I've developed a file of all the things I need to do or have done after I'm gone but with this new treatment things just may get postponed for a while."

"What would you really like to do?"

"I have been doing it for the last ten years, but it seems I need to develop other interests."

"What would you like to do that you haven't had the time or opportunity?" asked Jane.

"Interesting way of putting it."

"Do you need anything I can help with?"

"You already did with that magic toy of yours."

"How much time did the doctor give you?" Jane asked again not really believing nor even wanting to believe the previous announcement.

There was a pause for a few minutes as Barb chomped on a few more mouthfuls.

"Well?"

"She says I may have a much as four months."

Jane sat back in her chair and thought about all that needed to be done in that short of time. "I'm not going anywhere till I have seen you through no matter how long it takes nor how much it costs me." Jane encouraged her friend through a face of dripping tears.

"Now that was before old lover boy showed up with the enchanted pig sticker." stated Barb. "And I feel like I have new lease on life but who can I tell?"

Jane just shook her head.

"What?" asked her friend.

"You really are feeling much better and acting much worse."

"I suppose I deserve that."

"How can I help in getting your house in order?"

"It is all pretty much done." commented Barb. "I've seen the lawyers and the doctors so not much left to do except get rid of all the stuff nobody wants."

"What have you got that nobody wants? Or better yet, who is the nobody that doesn't want it?"

"What do you mean?" asked Barb a little cautiously.

"Who are you leaving the house to? What do Ply and I have to do to get it in shape to hand over to your next of kin?"

"I really want you two to take care of the place until all of the paperwork goes through..."

"So, I guess Ply and I really need to think seriously about renting a place once you are finished."

"I don't want you to leave while I'm sick." she coaxed.

Jane wrapped her arms around her friend, "We aren't going anywhere until you ask us to." she whispered in a controlled sob. "We just want to help where we can."

"It's going to be okay." whispered Barb. "Trust the Lord and He will work all things out in better ways than you ever expected." she comforted her friend. "I already talked to the lawyer and he says all things are ready for transfer when I am gone. There won't be any taxes to worry about nor fees, all that is taken care of. I just want you and Ply to be happy so what can we do together to make that so?"

"What do you want to do?" asked Jane.

"I've spent most of my life working and making money so now that I have a few months left, and that toy of yours seems to make things a little easier to handle, I want to play a bit, but I don't have anyone around to play with except you two so what do you want to play?"

"What about all the friends you have had over for stays and parties and vacations?"

"Most of them were just fair-weather friends." sighed Barb. "There really isn't much time to develop real friends, but you and Ply have been great and true friends."

"What made the difference?"

"When you called and asked if you could use the court."

"That's it?"

"You've allowed me to hang around with you two as things developed and I have really appreciated seeing real love in action."

"What about your family?"

"Look hon," Barb explained, "If anything real drastic happens just call my lawyer..."

'What do you mean by drastic?"

"If I suddenly skip town in my sleep." was the sarcastic reply.

"Who is your lawyer?"

"He's Japanese. I met him and helped him get over here to practice universal law. He was from the northern part of Japan and wanted to come over here to practice law before the rebellion fully took over his country. We got him out just in time."

"What's his name?" asked the younger with her phone ready to enter his number.

Barb paused for a few seconds and Jane lifted her eyes to meet hers. Her eyes sparkled in mischief and mirth. "Songbird Sing."

"You're joking!"

"I think it's a pen name. He adopted it for his American friends, so the goons would not be able to catch him so quickly."

"What's his number?"

"It is in the folder upstairs. Come and I will show you how to get to it." Barb rinsed off the dishes, left them for the next dishwasher load, and headed for the stairs. Barb's room was the one on the end marked 'Venus'. Barb swiped her card and the door opened. The room was eight sided like all the rest on the floor, but each wall had a picture of Venus Williams sweating it out on the court.

"Where did you get all of these amazing photos?"

"They were public domain on the net and I just had them blown up and made into wallpaper. All except that one." Barb pointed to a small twenty by thirty-six shot of Venus laughing. "That one cost me twenty thousand dollars and I think I am the only other one who knows about it save a few of her close relatives. They wanted the money to do something for the black kids in their neighborhood. I asked them what they wanted to do. They told me, and I wrote out a check for twenty grand. I should have given three times that amount, but I was feeling stingy that day and I really wanted that photo. They are one of the groups I have helped out for the last six years and they are forever grateful. I think that is the only evidence outside of her dental records and I am obnoxiously proud to have it." Barb stood and looked at the star on the wall for a moment. "See," she proclaimed. "Just how much of a sinner I really am? If I had just bought a small house and sent this money to the *Kids in Crisis* program, I could have supported almost half a million kids from birth to eighteen with enough left over to send most of them to trade school or get them started in business..."

"Welcome to the club!" responded Jane.

"Sing can lead you through all the steps that need to be taken. All my estate has been dealt with and there is really nothing to do but enjoy ourselves and spend some of this silly money I have left." Barb opened a closet door and the two of them walked in. The small room was octagonal like all the rest of the rooms but considerably smaller. On one side of the closet were tennis outfits from her earliest days to the present. There was a layer of dust on most of the clothing. The other side of the closet was full of trophies from all over the world.

"Sorry for the dust in the place." apologized Barb. "The maid doesn't get this deep very often." She looked around and the history of her life that was in this closet, never again to be experienced in this life, dropped her mood to just above depression.

Jane put an arm on her shoulder. "The Lord knows, sis." she comforted. "All this stuff will feed another thousand kids from birth to eighteen."

Barb looked at her as if to say you haven't seen the whole story yet. She slid back a rack full of clothing along the rod and leaned her left hand on the wall beside the rod and swiped her card over what appeared to be nothing. The wall bumped open just like it did in the basement. "If I die before I get you coded into all of this you can use the sword to get in here. I hear it can cut through anything." Barb walked into the small room. It appeared to be leftover corners from all the octagonal rooms in that part of the house. Barb let the door they came through close up again. They would have been locked in total darkness save for a faint glow that Jane couldn't even guess where it was coming from. Barb swiped her card once more and the wall in front of Barb started to lift. It rolled itself right up into the ceiling exposing shelves and drawers twenty-four inches wide and about sixteen inches deep. The shelves contained some of the most coveted awards Barb had won.

"Notice Wimbledon is not here." said Barb a little caustically. "As if I don't have enough that I have to answer for." She lifted a zippered file folder, opened it, and read a number for Jane.

"Hang on a sec... okay, once more." Jane loaded the number into her phone and Barb returned the folder to the shelf.

Barb pulled out one of the drawers halfway to reveal stacks of hundred-dollar bills. "I have had a miserly habit of keeping some spare change around." she smirked. "Now what am I going to do with all of this?"

"Ply can probably help you with a lot of that!" said Jane.

"I also want to do some good in this world before the rebellion fully takes over."

"In what ways?" asked Jane.

"There are a lot of people in the world that don't have near enough to live on." replied Barb with her eyes wide with excitement, "I have been helping about a hundred kids with schooling and clothing for the last number of years." explained Barb. "I just took on another thousand in the last eight months and I would like to go and see them before I die."

"Just how do you plan to do that in your condition?"

"I didn't until Ply brought the stick. If we can travel with the stick, we can see what we want to and when I feel bad, we can time out for an hour and be ready to go again."

"When do you want to start?" asked Jane.

Barb grabbed a half a dozen stacks from the drawer and handed them to Jane. "I'll bet Ply can build us another drone that can get us to where we need to go." she elated thinking she just may have solved that part of the problem. She picked up another eight bundles, pushed the drawer closed with her elbow and kicked the baseboard. The roll up wall dropped, and the exit door popped opened. "Let's go." said Barb. "We've only got fifteen seconds to be out of here. If we don't, we are stuck for two hours."

Back in the bedroom Barb headed for the doorway.

"Wait." shouted Jane.

"What?"

"Where are we going with all this cash?"

"I was going to give it to Ply so he could build a drone and we could fly around."

"That may not be such a good idea." said Jane. "He isn't used to having that much cash just to spend on whatever."

"Hasn't the kid ever seen money before?" asked Barb.

"No." stated Jane dumping her stash on the bed.

"What?"

"I think he is going to go nuts if he sees all this money and the damage just might be irreparable."

Barb was little dumbfounded, "Why?"

"This kid was bought up pretty much penniless. He is having a little trouble dealing with the money I won in France, not to mention Spain, that he knows nothing about yet. If he sees all this cash it just might go to his head thinking he can spend all he wants on whatever he wants whenever he wants without thinking of the accountability to the Lord for all this stuff. You just admitted that you have had struggles with the same kind of thing, but I don't expect it could be controlled if it hits this poor guy this hard. Look at what has happened to all of those poor people that have won millions by the lottery and are penniless in a few short years. Let's go a little slower on this and see how you do with the new treatments. We'll ask Ply about what he can do after we clue him in on the plans to visit the orphans."

"Do you really think he will have that much trouble?"

"Remember what happened when you told him I'd be half a million dollars richer after Spain?"

"He fainted right there in the parade car."

"Exactly. What's he gonna do when he sees this bank job wad if it gets dropped in his lap?"

"You may have a point." agreed Barb as she pulled out an empty drawer from under her bed. "We'll dump it in here, so we don't have to go to the closet for a while."

* * *

"Is there any way you can hook up a third harness on this thing?" suggested Jane as she pointed to the drone that she had risked her life on a few days earlier.

"Why not two chairs and a harness or two harnesses and a chair?"

"Why not get a third chair for long journeys?"

"I can do that." he replied.

"Do it!" commanded Jane.

"Ya-Vol!" exclaimed the brat husband throwing his open right hand into the air and snapping his heels together.

"You know that saying your dad had about women..."

"Yeah." he said casually dropping the salute but remaining at attention.

"Well I just bet there are times it applies to men!"

* * *

Ply worked quietly in the back maintenance shed for a few days finishing up the changes on the support for the drone. He built a rather large six-sided frame of aluminum and tented it with four mill clear colorless plastic. The floor was one-quarter inch acrylic so the weight of anyone of them could be placed in specific spots, so they could rest their feet during long flights. The boson's chairs could easily be removed, and the tent folded into quarters for storage. Ply made a large canvas zippered bag to store the apparatus in when it was to be left somewhere. Even the drone slipped into the bag and all was hidden from view.

"This will take a good supply of leaves to cover if we need to leave it in a wooded area." he said to himself. He packed a small hatchet and a folding leaf rake into a corner for hiding the bag when it may be needed.

"If we fly this into a foreign country it may mean getting passports stamped. How are we going to manage that?" He thought about it for a while. "Maybe the girls will have some ideas."

* * *

"Where do we need to go to test this thing out?" asked Ply as the three discussed testing the new apparatus.

"How about into town to get some groceries?" suggested Barb still feeling a bit hungry from the treatments from the past eight months.

"Where and how are we going to hide it while we are shopping?"

"Why not behind the store with the employee parking?"

"Is it out of sight from all traffic and pedestrians?" asked Ply.

"That could be a problem." commented Jane. "If we just leave it somewhere what if someone discovers it by accident and gets curious?"

"How about a picnic lunch or dinner?" suggested Jane.

"Where can we do that?" questioned Barb in a rather sarcastic tone. "How long is it going to take us to find a secluded picnic area without people around?"

Jane dug out the tablet and turned on the *Real Time Earth* app. In fifteen seconds, she had found the least populated areas on the continent. "At the top of *Mount Saint Jacob* on the west coast there is nobody there and no one in sight for ninety-five miles. If we landed on the plateau close to the top of the mountain, we could watch the ocean from five thousand feet and enjoy the fresh air."

"What is the weather like for the next few hours?" asked Ply.

"There is a storm out in the Pacific, but it is not supposed to land till tomorrow afternoon." she replied.

"The west coast?" asked Barb. "Isn't that a long way away?"

"It sure is if you are walking." agreed Jane. "But if we time out then we can probably get there in about ten minutes real time and be back here before midnight our time."

"That is if we stay to watch the sun set on the coast." corrected Ply.

"I don't think I have enough time left to get used to this timing out thing." stated Barb.

"You don't have to get used to it." smiled Ply. "You just get to come along for the ride."

"So now it's my turn?"

"We have been riding the crest of your wave for such a long time." reminded Jane to the star. "We didn't think we ever could return the favor but now we get a chance. Fun, huh?"

Barb had to squelch the rising pride within her. It finally hit her that in this case she really could do nothing. Jane put a gentle arm around the shoulder of her friend. "They used to call it giving back." she said reading the struggle on her face. "When we seem to be in control for such a long time it hurts to realize all of our gifts are different. Winning is not always the most important goal but to us winners, it just seems to be way ahead of whatever comes in second place."

Barb lifted her arms to Jane's shoulders and gave her a gentle hug realizing her learning days were not yet over. "Thank you." she sniffled.

"Let's go to the kitchen and get some lunch packed." suggested Ply.

* * *

Two medium sized coolers were filled with drinks, sandwiches, and muffins. The coolers sat between the three on the deck of the new craft. Within an hour real time they were ready and packed in.

"We are going to have to watch a lot closer for airplanes as we approach the coast." exhorted Jane. "Last time I was out there I had a few close calls."

"Close calls?" questioned Ply in a worried tone.

"It wasn't really that bad." replied Jane trying to diffuse the tension. "You just jump or drop." she stated matter-of-factually. "Unless you are caught in a gaggle of aircraft." She looked over at the two wide eyed passengers. "Then you just got to keep your wits about you and your eyes open. When they circle, they are traveling about three hundred miles an hour. In open flight they are doing anywhere from five to eight."

"Is this little sermon supposed to be instructive or cautionary?" asked Ply.

"It just may fit in both categories." corrected Jane as she snapped her seat belt.

With both Jane and Ply at the controls Barb hung on and more often than not closed her eyes. It took a few minutes but finally she was able to look around without being too frightened. "You can see everything from up here." wowed Barb to the other two.

"Not quite." corrected Ply. "With all this stuff in the cabin and the framework we have a number of blind spots."

"That is why we installed the Garmin program on the tablet." said Jane as she turned the toy for Barb to see.

"You guys really thought of everything." stated Barb.

"Not without a little trial and error." said Jane with a quick glance towards her husband.

Ply's look seemed to say, *Let's not go there.* Then he voiced, "I think the third passenger is having enough culture shock in what she is experiencing at the moment."

Jane looked over to see her friend somewhat white knuckled. "You could be right."

The timing in the craft helped Barb once again and got the three to their destination pretty quickly. "That looks like the place there." announced Ply. "Let's drop to about a hundred feet and see if we can find any picnic tables or at least a good place to land."

They circled the lake once to find out what was there and chose a spot on the north side.

"Hey, look!" shouted Barb. "Isn't that a cabin down there and smoke coming out of the chimney?"

"Why did we miss it earlier?" asked Ply.

"Maybe because the smoke is white, and we just weren't looking for somebody to be up here." said Jane.

"I don't want us to be noticed." said Ply. "Maybe we better find someplace else to picnic."

"Let's land on the other side of the lake and see if they are registered and how many there are of them."

"You can do that?" asked Barb.

"There are some satellites that are armed with infrared and can scan any place at any time." stated Ply. "It just takes a little searching to find out which ones and if they are overhead."

Both girls looked at him with questions and suspicion on their faces. "And how do you know that?" asked his wife.

"You can find out just about anything if you ask the right questions." was his reply.

"And just who is it you ask?" interrogated Jane.

"Well," stammered Ply, "That also is part of the answering questions equation." avoided the boy.

They landed in a quiet clearing amid a cluster of trees and let the drone hover over the framed tent. They needed full reception, so Ply exited the craft and sat cross legged on the moss. Twenty seconds later he signaled to the girls that they needed to get back in and escape while they had the chance.

"Just touch part of the inside metal frame." commanded Ply.

Jane picked up the sword and timed out as fast as she could. The craft shot upwards just in time to see a bullet from a rifle pass underneath them.

"Let's go to four hundred feet above ground level and scout for another location." instructed Ply.

"What was all that about?" asked Barb being the first one seated as Jane held on to her arm. Once she was strapped in and anti-static strapped to the craft Ply was next to be seated. Finally, Jane got to strap herself in as Ply held on to her arm to keep continuity.

Ply did some maneuvering on the tablet then showed the girls what he had discovered while seated on the ground.

"I don't know who this guy is but apparently he doesn't like visitors."

On the tablet there was an infrared image of a man in the woods about sixty yards from where they landed, and he had his gun pointed at Ply. "Rather than ask questions or be found out I thought it better to get out of the way."

"It seems we did that just in time." shivered Barb a bit dazed by the quick thinking of Ply and Jane and in great wonder at the properties of the sword used in avoiding a problematic situation. "How come we didn't hear the gun go off?"

"Sound travels a little faster than a thousand feet per second.'" said Ply. "The bullet from that gun travels about three thousand feet per second so we will see the bullet before we hear any sound."

"Or be hit by it." shuddered Barb.

"That is why we got out of there as fast as we could." explained Jane. "Once we timed out, we could outmaneuver the bullet, but we had to get on board first and bring the craft to the same time as we were. This way we all could move faster than the bullet."

"Good grief." exclaimed Barb. "How did you ever learn to do this stuff?"

"We had some good practice and a lot of learning opportunities at Johnson's place." snarled Jane.

Suddenly the Garmin beeped. Jane handed the tablet back to Ply and he brought up the program. "It appears that our friend below has spotted the drone and is attempting to take it out. There is another bullet headed our way."

Jane unbuckled her seat belt but not her anti-static strap, so all would be in the same time frame. "Bring us around so I can bat the bullet into the lake." she suggested. "Then I'll time out the drone, so he doesn't see it."

Shortly the projectile was in view and Ply adjusted the drone. Jane opened the door and tapped the metal back towards the lake. Barb sat there her jaw dropped in horror and wonder at the antics of the two.

"Let's get out of here!" encouraged Jane as she brought the drone into invisible mode and returned to her seat. "Are you okay Barb?"

"Perhaps." she replied.

"So much for a fun evening at the park." growled Ply sarcastically. "Anything else you want to see while we are out here?"

"How about a run up the coast just to show Barb?" suggested Jane. "If we start about three hundred miles north of Vancouver, we can tour the coast almost to the cape. What does the battery look like?"

"We are at eighty-five percent." stated Ply. "There is a storm over the northern part of Peru, but we can jump over that if we want to go farther south."

"Will we have enough gas to do all of that and still get us

home?" asked Barb.

"I don't see why not." said Ply. "I put eight hours of batteries on this thing but seeing the drone is timed out also we can probably go longer. We'll keep our eyes on the meter, so we don't have to recharge."

They dropped to about two hundred feet above water level and kept to more than fifty feet from the shoreline and cruised the coast.

"Keep your eyes peeled for seagulls." reminded Ply. "We don't need any more dazed creatures crashing into the basket." he said with a smirk like glance at Barb.

"What is that supposed to mean?" she teased back.

They zipped up over the Rockies and settled down along the coast.

"If we go too much farther north, we just might get cold if we have to make a quick escape back home." stated Ply. "Not that we would be cold very long, but we can play it safe this way."

Barb looked over and said, "When have we been playing safe in this contraption?"

Jane grinned, and Ply nodded his head and shrugged his shoulders in agreement.

* * *

Much of the coast Barb had seen but not from this angle. They finally had to settle on three hundred feet above sea level to avoid masts of the many sailboats that were encountered in the harbors and out in the bays and on the ocean. In their time frame it took almost eight hours, but the drone only used up two hours of battery from leaving home. A few stops were made for eating and the like, but these areas were found where nothing was around but trees. The contrast of differences along the water's edge delighted all three as they took in the tour that no one had ever been on before.

"How about heading home for some rest?" stated Ply as they rounded the tip of what used to be referred to a Baha, California.

"Sounds good to me." yawned Barb tired from the day but not of the tour.

Jane and Ply worked together and in a few short minutes they were lowering to the back of the castle.

"I'll get dinner going." called Barb as she hopped out with a basket and headed towards the house. Ply and Jane loaded the collapsible aircraft and had it in the bag and into the shed within five minutes. The drone was flown into the house and up to a spare room to charge up for the night.

Dinner was canned salmon. They had grilled salmon and grilled cheese sandwiches just to top off the day.

"So," began Barb, "Just how many miles did we log on to that thing today tooling around the country?"

Ply had the tablet on the table beside him and started the calculation. "It looks like we traveled about sixty-five hundred miles since this morning."

Barb set her sandwich down on her plate, "Just how far can that thing go on one charge?"

"I don't know." answered Ply. "I suppose it depends on a lot of things."

"Like what?" asked Barb.

"Like how much you time out as you travel. How much you time out the drone, so it doesn't use all that much energy."

"So, we could go to Europe or Africa without having to recharge?" asked Barb.

"I suppose that could be done." returned Ply. "What are you going to do about passports?"

"It could take months to get them." agreed Barb. "I don't think I have time for that."

"Then what's your plan? Just float in, say hi to the kids, and then float back out?"

"Probably not the right thing to do is it?"

"If we are going to break the law why not kidnap the dictator while we are there?" suggested Ply.

"That will just get a whole lot of innocents killed." stated Jane. "Any more wonderful suggestions?"

The three sat in silence for a few moments.

"What about the organizer that you confided in?" suggested Jane. "Does she not have some authority in getting visas?"

"Well duh!" said Barb as she looked over at her friend. "Apparently my mind is going also."

"Not very likely with the plans you have." interrupted Ply. "With all the extra visas the Lord has floating around I just bet He has at least three or four for each country we need to see." The other two heads turned and looked at him. "Make a list of the countries you need to see with the dates you wish to be there and send them off to your friend and see what happens."

"Why don't we start with just one and see how things go?" said Jane.

"Okay." said Ply. "Where do you want to go first?"

"Madagascar." said Barb without needing to think.

"How are we going to get you in and out without an airplane ride? Your passport has to get stamped to make it legal."

"Isn't there some sort of visa you can get that lets you in under your own steam?" remembered Jane. "We didn't need new passports to get into Spain from France."

"That is because they are all part of the European Union." returned Barb.

"Isn't Africa part of a Union with Madagascar?" stated Ply. "What if we all get African and European Union permissions then we can show up where and when we want?"

"I knew there were some brains under all that brawn!" stated Jane.

Barb looked over at Ply, eyes wide and eyebrows up. *The kid can't be more than a hundred and thirty pounds soaking wet after a long shower and a soak in the hot tub,* she thought. *Brains maybe, brawn... not a chance!*

* * *

"This is Barb Cully. May I speak to Mrs. Bridgit Kiehl please." spoke Barb into her phone. A few moments passed and then, "Hi Bridge, this is Barb, how are you?

"Well, I'm okay. How about you?"

"Not quite ready to head back to the courts but feeling much better."

"What happened?"

"I have a friend who is working on a secret treatment for my disease and it seems to be doing wonders."

"Will they be publishing results soon?"

"It really is early in the process, so I don't expect news for a while, but it does make me feel a lot better." stated Barb. "We need to make a visit, so we can get open visiting rights to both European and African Unions if that would be possible."

"How soon can you get here?" asked Mrs. Kiehl.

"How about tomorrow morning your time, say, nine o'clock?" There was silence on the other end of the line. "Are you still there, Bridge?"

"Yes." she stammered. "Where are you calling from this appears to be a North American connection".

"Time seems to be of the essence seeing I may not have much of it left for this life, so we are able to make it there tomorrow, but we need to meet you someplace private."

"How about the forest north of Gothenburg. I could be there by nine if you wish."

"Can you find a place private?" asked Barb.

"By nine most people will be at work and not strolling through the woods. I can find a place."

"You will need to wear a large wide brimmed hat and carry a mirrored compact open in your hand so we can see the reflection from over your head." suggested Barb.

"Won't the trees be in the way?"

"They could be, but I think we can find you. Can you be somewhere in the middle of the forest?"

I don't see why not but isn't that a lot of trouble?" asked Mrs. Kiehl.

"You know how some of us are about the paparazzi."

"Are you sure you're not paranoid?"

"I'm not really sure of much but I am concerned that there is still so much to be done with so little time left to do it in." commented Barb.

"Are you sure you are up for the trip?"

"Oh yeah. I haven't felt this good in almost two years."

"Are you getting back into the games?"

"There are a few things I would like to do first. If I heal then you can bet I'll be playing again but if this is only a temporary cure then I may need to pursue other priorities for a short time."

"You seem to be talking in circles Miss Cully."

"Shall you be there in the morning?"

"How many passports do you have for this trip you are planning?"

"There are three; Ply and Jane Gallant and Barb Cully."

"We will have the expense money with us in dollars. Will that be alright?"

"I expect that will work."

"Great." finalized Barb. "We will see you at nine in the woods." she tapped the conversation closed and looked up the astonished glares of her house guests. "What?"

"Where is Gothenburg?" asked Ply.

"The south-western portion of Sweden." replied Barb.

"And you expect to be there at nine tomorrow in the morning?"

"Her time yes, but they are six or seven hours different from us, so we better get some sleep, or we just might be up for a few days."

"That means we leave at one in the morning." said Ply in a mousy voice with his eyes wide.

"That will give you four hours sleep." grilled Barb. "Aren't you glad you didn't join the army?"

"We should be back here by breakfast tomorrow." said Jane. "That should give us time for something to eat and then get a good nap in."

"Well I plan to get a head start real soon." grumbled Ply as he headed for the stairs.

"We'll see you in four and a half hours at the take-off site." announced Jane as she made her way upstairs. "We should be landing about half an hour after take-off. Wear some really warm clothes." Ply and Jane sorted out some long pants and insulated clothing and set them aside for the trip.

* * *

"That is Gothenburg about fifteen miles south of us." stated Barb. "We just need to move north a few miles and we should find a reflection of a compact sitting beside a lady with a large brimmed hat about the middle of the forest."

Ply received the tablet and tuned to the infrared satellite. "There she is." he smiled. "A hat and a mirror in the middle of the trees."

"How about Barb and I going to meet Bridge and you stay here with the drone?" suggested Jane. "That way she won't get to see what we arrived in and we won't have to make any difficult statements."

"Fine with me." agreed Ply. "I didn't see anyone else around for about a thousand yards, so you have some time. If I need to disappear I can time and jump just as Jane told me to. You have small mirrors to get my attention?" the girls checked their purses and showed Ply their reflectors. "Good. I'll see you in about half an hour EST."

The two followed the path for almost three hundred feet and came across a slender blonde sitting on a bench with a compact open next to her. She appeared to be reading a book, but she was carefully scanning the area around her every few seconds. She closed the compact and the book and placed them in her bag as the girls approached. She glanced at her watch as she stood to great them. "Two minutes early. I hope you didn't lose your luggage. Something has to go wrong no matter what flight you take."

"There is always a first for everything." smiled Jane delighted to see her friend again. Jane and Bridgit hugged and Jane dropped a fat bubble envelope in her bag.

"If that is not sufficient funds let us know and we can get here fairly quickly to supply what is needed." whispered Jane into her ear.

"If it is anything, we agreed on it is more than enough." responded Bridge.

"Barb is feeling a little generous at the moment so just be thankful." encouraged Jane. "We will be at the number we called you from unless anything exciting happens. Just give us a call and we will set up a place where we can pick them up."

"With this incentive it should only take a few days, a week at the most, but you never know what happens with these things. Are you playing at all this year Jane?"

"I was going to start next month but with Barb to take care of there may be other responsibilities that need to be addressed."

"You're not missing any games on my part." blurted Barb.

"You're absolutely right." replied Jane, leaving her sparring partner in somewhat confusion.

"So, what has gotten you three all fired up and running around the world this time?"

Barb looked at Jane and said, "We have some plans to see some of the more impoverished people of the world, so I can place some of my money in some sort of investment that may have benefits beyond space and time."

"Surprising how a little thing can change our focus so severely." smiled Bridge.

"Give us a call when you have things ready and thank you for all of your hard work on such short notice." said Barb with a forced smile extending her hand as a signal that the conversation was over. Jane looked back at the organizer and said, "We'll keep in touch," and turned to catch up with Barb.

"What was all that about?" asked Jane as she caught up with her friend.

"Did she imply that my illness was just a little thing?!" stormed Barb once they were out of earshot.

"Perhaps," said Jane trying to think of something to calm her friend, "But in light of fifty thousand years in eternity will it matter if you live to twenty-five or to eight hundred and twenty-five?" she allowed Barb to think about this for a few dozen paces. "Lots of Antediluvian people lived to be more than nine-hundred years old and what does it matter now? What do we know of them? What did they accomplish of lasting effect? In light of eternity we get only what the Lord gives us. Sometimes He gives us a few extra years like He did Hezekiah, but lots of times it's game over in a flash with no opportunities to make amends or plan as well as you have."

Barb looked back, but the passport lady had headed towards the city and was long out of sight. "I'm sorry. I felt like she was speaking flippantly but in the context of later on, it doesn't really matter what happens here and now as long as we continue to trust..."

"It may not be that simple but having that attitude may help in difficult times. Jesus tells us in John seventeen that He wants to have us with Him. I think the wording is, 'that they may be where I am'. We can't be both places, either here or there. Here we are with each other for a very short time; there we shall be with Him and each other for ever and ever and ever... Now tell me, which is better?" They walked on for a few more minutes in silence. "Isn't this where we were supposed to meet Ply?"

"I thought it was around the next turn."

Ply sat on a bench with the bag packed behind a bush playing with the tablet.

"I think we need to escape while we can get out." said Jane. Ply got up and headed back to the bag. They were out of sight as they quietly set up the drone and were in the air in less than three minutes.

"Want to see anything special while we are here?" invited Ply.

"My bed." growled Barb.

"Sounds good to me." agreed Jane.

"Then home it is." stated the pilot. Within an hour real time they were all quietly sleeping off the jet lag they acquired jumping back and forth over the pond.

* * *

Three days later there was a call on Barb's phone from a familiar number.

"Bridgit?" asked Jane.

"The incentive payed off." bragged the woman from Europe. "When and where for the drop?"

"Already?" said Barb.

"Ready to use as of today."

"Hang on a sec..." Barb placed her finger over the microphone on her phone. "How soon can Ply be ready to go get the passports?" she asked Jane.

"I'll have to ask him, hold on." and she ran off to find the boy.

"Hey, Bridge, can I call you back in about half an hour?"

"Sure, I'll see you then or just hear from you?"

"Probably just hear from us but don't be surprised."

"I have to get to know your friends better." said Bridgit. "The forest is full of soldiers. Apparently, something happened a few days ago and the whole country is biting their nails."

"Oh really? I'll call you back as soon as we get info on arriving. Bye." and Barb hung up.

Ply was just coming in when Barb closed the phone conversation. "Here it is three o'clock in the afternoon and we get another midnight run to where?"

"Well it won't be the forest north of Gothenburg." announced Barb. "The woods are crawling with soldiers."

"I wondered if we stirred up some excitement coming so close to the city." mumbled Ply. "Remember I asked if radar could pick us up or a blip of us. Apparently, they found something that scared them royally."

"What if we come in low over Norway just the other side of the border?"

"Isn't that north of where she is?" asked Jane.

"We can talk to her and see what she thinks." said Barb pushing the buttons to get Brigit back on the line.

"You guys really have trouble telling time!" stated Bridgit as she answered the call.

"We'll take that as a compliment. How about in the woods just the other side of the border west of Oslo or do you have another idea that will work better for you?"

"I have a friend with a cottage north of Lillehammer." stated Bridgit enjoying the clandestine nature of the conversation. "Why don't I give her a call and we can go from there?"

"If you call us once you are situated, we can be there in half an hour." Silence on the other end. "Bridge are you there?"

"I won't ask you to repeat that, but I'll take your word for it. I'll get in touch as soon as I can." Bridge clicked off.

* * *

At two PM the next day Barb's phone startled her. "Hello?"

"All ready." announced Bridgit. "How soon can you be here?"

"We can be there in half an hour."

"Can you find me using GPS?"

"I expect so."

"Okay then, just follow the St. Lawrence River. Don't look me up until you are almost here. I'll see you shortly." Barb's phone went dead.

"Let's get out of here!" shouted Barb. "Warm clothes on and over the clouds we go."

Twenty minutes later they were over central Norway. Jane looked up Bridgit's number and GPS-ed it. "It looks like she is over on the northwest tip of Denmark?"

"I thought she said Norway." exclaimed Ply.

"Just follow the phone." said Barb.

They timed out a little farther and jumped over to Hirtshals.

"Sure enough." said Ply. "Right there in the middle of the woods." They dropped and quickly packed the cabin and the drone into the bag.

"I'll stay here and be ready when we need to go." stated Ply. The two girls walked quickly over to Bridgit.

"What are you doing all the way over here?" asked Barb.

"It's a long story but it appears that the military of Sweden thinks we are being invaded by aliens..."

"Are my antenna showing?" teased Jane checking under her hair.

"I don't think it's funny and neither do they apparently. They have been all over the short wave but have managed to keep the TV and the radio people out of the loop. Either they have threatened or actually taken some of them out for a few days, but things are quiet everywhere except the military frequencies."

"What's all the fuss?" asked Barb.

"I have a good friend in the military who is a colonel. She and I were grade school and high school friends. She had been telling me that the 'Service' has been keeping their eyes on me for a few days since the UFO landed close to where I was. I told them I knew nothing of a UFO but when I turned in the passports to be filled in for the two unions, they were a little suspicious. I managed to escape over to Denmark, but I do think you need to get out as soon as you can." Bridge looked a little concerned. "What on earth are you guy's playing with anyway?"

"I think the last people we want to know about it is the military." stated Jane.

"Was what we gave you enough?" asked Barb.

"More than, and here are the leftovers."

"Keep it for all your trouble and if you need more there is nothing, I can do with it after I'm gone so take this bundle also." said Barb as she handed her friend another stack of bills.

"You guys better run I think I hear a helicopter." encouraged Bridge. "I know of several families that would love to have some extra groceries, new bedding..."

Barb and Jane took off toward Ply. They got the cabin assembled and the drone in the air when the helicopter appeared overhead. They timed out and took off straight up to six thousand feet and then out to the ocean towards Canada. In four minutes they were hovering over the castle and dropped to the white towel on the back yard.

"We better get this thing put away ASAP." said Ply and started folding things up even before the girls got out of the cabin.

"Maybe we better lay low for a few days." said Jane. Barb was quiet but a little nervous having been discovered by the 'Service' of Sweden. Ply packed away the toys but said nothing. Jane could see he was thinking but not quite ready to expose his thoughts. "Are you okay?" she asked her husband.

He nodded and pointed to the house with a nod of the head.

Once inside Barb grumbled, "Well, we got the passports, but now can we use them?"

"I think so if we do it quickly." stated Ply.

"What do you mean?" asked Barb.

"If we stick around that only gives the army more time to figure out where the sword is..."

"Do they even know it is a sword?" asked Jane.

"They do know there is something but who knows what they will do to try to figure out what we are up to." thought Ply out loud so the girls could follow his line of thinking. "Perhaps they will start to configure satellites to look for the interruption the sword generates but that may take a few days. I think we can get in one trip and one trip only. I say we strike now while we may have a window, but we might want to keep out of Europe."

"Well that was a lot of money wasted!" grumbled Barb.

Ply ignored the comment and continued. "You said you wanted to go to Madagascar? Where exactly do you wish to go?"

"There is a globe in the library." said Barb. "Come, I'll show you."

Barb spun the globe around so the island off the East coast of Africa was most comfortably before them. "Here is Vohimarina. Just to the north of here is a large old castle that used to belong to one of the kings of the ancient tribes of Madagascar. I bought that old castle and had it fixed up, so the kids could use it, but not fixed up enough so those of the rebellion would want it. It is livable and somewhat comfortable but by no means elegant. With a little more fixing up it could very well be, but that would attract the wrong kind of person. I want the funds to go to help people, not assist the rebellion."

"How soon can you be ready to fly?" asked the lead pilot.

Jane counted off the time zones. "Ten hours backwards so if we leave here at six in the evening, we can get there shortly after eight in the morning there."

'When is the last time you were up for twenty-four hours?" said Barb somewhat fatigued at the sound of the marathon.

"So, would you like a three-hour nap till then and we can eat on the way?"

"Sounds good to me." agreed Barb.

* * *

By ten after six they were headed south-west crossing the Atlantic not much slower than the radar blips trying to catch them. Jane slowed down once they were over Zaire, Zambia and Mozambique. They followed the coast of Madagascar up to cape Amber then south to Vohimarina. They hugged the west coast a little more than a hundred feet above sea level and came landward just north of the city.

"There it is." said Barb. "I recognize it from the pictures they sent me."

What a dump, thought Ply. *I guess Barb was right about not making it too tempting for the rebels.*

"It looks terribly in disrepair, but my architect and engineer friends agree that it is still sound but not very beautiful. We added a few special touches to keep the mold and mildew out thanks to the induction technology that is so prevalent worldwide. There are small units that keep the humidity down in each room. I don't exactly know how they work but..."

"The technology was kept locked and hidden under patents until the Ruler arrived." stated Ply. "Within a hundred years the 'IT' buttons, as they were referred to, were so commonplace only a few plants were left open to keep the world supplied with replacements."

They landed in a wooded area about one hundred yards back of the mansion.

Ply continued, "They have to recycle the old worn out induction units but they usually last for about one hundred years. They could build them so they lasted longer but the cost efficiency was too small, so they passed a law that all 'IT' units had to last a hundred years. That kept the balance of production and replacement to a little more than two fairly large plants. One was in South America and the other in what used to be Russia. It didn't take very long for everybody to get on board with the programs of the Master. If they refused, He just refused rain to fall in their area. Some thought they outsmarted Him by building in an area where there was no rain and then He sent floods. For the first forty of fifty years some scoffed at His powers but once the evidence came in pretty much everybody towed the line."

The cabin bag was stowed under a pile of leaves in a small wadi and the trio made their way to the orphanage.

"Barb Cully!" shouted a maintenance worker. "What a pleasant surprise."

"Charles Coney!" shouted Barb and held her arms out wide for her friends greeting. They embraced and Barb held on a little too long for cultural acceptance. Jane and Ply glanced over at each other wondering about what past opportunities might have been here. Charles backed off a little and questioned, "Are you okay, sis?"

"It's been a very long time..." she admitted with moist eyes.

"What's goin' on?" he asked.

"We just thought we would hop in for a short visit." stated Barb as she hooked her arm in his and walked him toward the main house. "I don't know how long we can stay so let's see the kids and everybody else."

"They're about to sit down for breakfast. How did you all get here?"

"How isn't important just yet. The fun part is that we are here for a very short time and I would like to see the kids before I travel again."

"Are you going to introduce me to your friends?"

"I'm sorry." apologized the woman. "This is Jane and Ply from America."

"I'm Charles from Great Britain." he smiled at the introductions. They shook hands and Barb hurried them off to the old castle.

Breakfast was maize boiled into some sort of soup with bread and local fruit from the trees of the plantation. Plates, bowls, and cups were all made of tin with a sparse sprinkling of stainless flatware. Knives were only used by the staff but pulling off a hunk of bread was not something new for the people of Madagascar.

The crowd in the dining hall was rather boisterous until Charles walked in with the guest on his arm. As soon and they were noticed a hush fell on the crowd of children and they all stood to welcome the new arrival.

The director, William Fanshaw, stood to his full slender six-foot two inches height and was delighted to see the star tennis player arrive for a visit.

"Ladies and gentlemen," he addressed the crowd, "This is the professional tennis player Barbara Cully."

The children immediately burst into applause. Barb walked up to the front with Charles and slipped her other arm into William's. After a few seconds of recognition, she held up her hand to silence the children.

"Thank you for a marvelous welcome." stated the star. "Please sit and enjoy your meal while it is hot," but the kids just stood there.

"You need to sit for the kids cannot sit if there is an important guest standing." William informed Barb. She immediately sat in Will's chair, but the kids still stood. Someone brought in a stool from the kitchen and Will seated himself and the rest of those in the house sat freely.

The buzz of regular breakfast soon took over and William asked Barb, "What brings you here in such a hurry so there is no announcement or planning?"

"I have to take a very long trip and wanted to see you one more time before I left." said Barb. "And I have never met any of this batch of kids."

"Jennifer is still here." said William. "She is now the head cook."

"She is no longer a kid?" asked Barb.

"What makes you think she ever grew up?" asked the director. "Even though she never grew out of some of her childish laughing ways."

Barb got up and went into the kitchen. She was out of sight before many of the kids could see her rise so only a few stood up. By the time the others had noticed the first few jump to their feet, glance over to where Barb was, the double doors into the kitchen were swinging to a close.

* * *

Jenny was stirring something on the stove when Barb came in.

Jenny turned as she heard the doors squeak as they opened. She dropped the spoon into the pot as Barb approached her. Barb's eyes looked so sad. They ran to each other and crashed into a deep embrace. Barb shook with tears and Jenny held her close for an entire minute.

"I have to stir this stuff, or it will burn." she said, and half dragged Barb over to the hot stove. "Now, Momma, tell me, what is the problem?"

"You can't tell anyone else for a full year." Barb managed to stumble out.

"Are you getting married?" asked Jenny then thought of a more horrifying scene. "Are you pregnant?"

Barb laughed and cried at the same time. "If only it were that simple."

Jenny removed the pot from the heat and set the spoon down on a plate, "Let's make you a nice pot of my special coffee and you can tell me all about it."

Barb managed to take a deep breath, more like a refreshing sigh, and sat at the old table in the kitchen. The coffee being mixed was the special top of the plant beans that was reserved for very special occasions. The beans were never longer than a few weeks old, so it was usually the best coffee in the entire African union. Barb was humbled at the honor of being able to receive such a treat and insisted that Jenny celebrate the reunion with her by serving herself a cup of the special brew. As Jenny prepared the drink, Barb thought about the best way to tell her friend. Jenny set a large mug in front of Barb and a small fancy cup and saucer at her place beside the guest.

"Now," announced Jenny as if she was the oldest and wisest dorm mother of all time, "Tell me what is eating you."

"I believe Jesus died in my stead, so I am going to heaven." said the older.

"Isn't that what this place is all about?" stumbled Jenny. "Isn't that why we choose to live as we do knowing it is safer and more secure in Jesus that all the riches of all the presidents and kings of all the world?"

"I'm going in four months and I came to tell you..."

Jenny jumped up, almost spilling her coffee, "What?"

"My older brother died a few years ago and now it is my turn." Jenny dropped to her knees and hugged what she could of Barb as she sat at the table. This time the tears were from the African.

"There won't be a problem with the orphanage." stated Barb. "I have some very capable friends that are willing to take over all the arrangements and finances, so life here will not be a problem as far as that end of the situation is concerned. How is the political situation here?"

"As yesterday and as tomorrow." replied Jenny shrugging her shoulders. "In all things we have to trust the Lord".

"Tell me about it!" stated Barb but Jenny did not understand the phrase or the sarcasm.

"We have to trust God and plan in such a way that we may live for another forty years but be ready to die tomorrow." said Jenny.

Barb took a small sip of the delicious coffee then bent into a hug with Jenny. "My friends in the dining hall will be taking over all the aspects of offshore operations. As long as the Lord is still in control, we should have no trouble in completing our task." She paused for a moment. "Apparently mine is almost complete."

They enjoyed the gentle embrace for a few moments longer.

"Anyone you want me to look up?" invited Barb.

"There must be billions of people up there from all of history and you think you will be able to find my sister? Isn't that the Lord's job to sort all that out?"

"I suppose." returned Barb. "I never really thought about it that way. I guess if you take Hebrews twelve literally then they see all we do and there are few surprises for those who are watching."

Jane came in and found the two in a teary embrace.

Barb turned to Jane, "This is Jane Gallant. She and her husband will be taking over my part of the support needs you people receive from me."

"Do you play tennis also?" asked Jenny.

"Yes, I do, but not for as long as Barb."

"That is true." said Barb not speaking about the victories Jane had in the recent past.

"Did you play across from each other?" asked Jenny wide eyed. The two stars looked at each other not wanting to go into all the hoopla of the recent season.

"I'm sorry to pry..." sputtered Jenny.

"Yes." responded Jane. "We have played across from each other and sometimes she wins and sometimes I do. So that probably makes us pretty even."

Barb held her tongue for the moment but just before they left, she would tell Jenny about the amazing ability this lady has on the court.

* * *

Ply sat with Charles and William asking questions about the operation of the ancient place. "How long have you two been here?"

"I have been here twelve years and William ten." responded Charles. "It was an old mission school in town that turned into an orphanage in the heart of the city then problems started with the recent rebellion. Miss Cully bought this place and moved us out here and the problems have been a whole lot simpler."

"She had the well dug and all the appliances have IT technology in them so pretty much everything here is good for a hundred years." added William.

"All except us." chuckled Charles.

"Why not?" said Ply. "People are living for seven and eight hundred years since the Leader took over."

"He has been in control for over a thousand years and His own word tells us that it is only to be for a thousand years. This must mean that the end is going to happen pretty soon."

"The end?" said Ply.

"Are you staying the night?" asked William.

"You'll have to talk to Barb. I don't know exactly how long she wants to stay."

The two looked at Ply. "Let's see what is on her agenda." said Charles. "We have extra rooms and beds at the moment, but they might not be exactly what you are used to."

The three chatted until the two visitors came out of the kitchen. All of the kids immediately stood on their feet. William stood and said, "Let's thank the Lord for what we have received," bowed his head while the kids seemed visibly relieved, "Lord, thank You for all that You have provided and thank You for the guests You have sent here today. Give us safety as we go to our various activities this day. Amen."

The final consonant of the last word was drowned out in the consuming noise of the kids evacuating the building.

"Kids," smiled William, "It doesn't matter where you are, they are pretty much the same wanting to get to the fun things of life. It will be stone quiet here in about five minutes, then you can tell us what is happening."

Just then Jenny came out with a tray and some nice cups for the guests. "Coffee anyone?"

Ply had heard about third world foodstuffs and refused the offer. Jane, being more polite, said, "Yes please." Barb just watched for the reaction of Jane. The hot liquid hit her taste-buds and it only took a second for her eyes to pop open and say, "This is delicious!"

"Maybe I could try a little." stated Ply cautiously. By the fourth cup he needed to find the restroom, either that, or a tree, and by now it was needed pretty quickly.

"We have thousands of bathrooms here." teased Charles. "There is one marked 'boys', but I don't expect you could read it, so choose one of the millions of trees that are in the vicinity. Don't go to deep into the woods, there are some pretty exciting animals out there."

Ply got up and ran to the perimeter of the compound and stepped behind the nearest tree listening and watching for the dangers of the forest.

"You rascal." exhorted Barb. "You know better than I that most of the animals that are dangerous don't come out till night."

"He does seem like the curious type and I didn't want him going too deep into the forest. There are spiders and snakes that can take out a leopard, and they stay up all day."

"The spiders or the leopards?" trembled Jane.

"They won't come near the compound." said William. "Jenny here has taken out three about two years ago and we haven't seen any since".

"Jenny?" asked Barb.

"When there is trouble all the kids yell 'Annie get your gun' and she shows up and the threat is eliminated pretty quickly."

"You have guns here?" asked Jane.

"Sometimes the monkeys get a little greedy about the food we have here. They will show up in packs of thirty or forty and raid the camp. When we first moved out here, we lost three kids in a monkey raid."

Jane looked at Barb who was almost in tears over the situation.

"Did you know about this?"

"Of course she knew," interrupted William, "She was the one who talked us into the arms supply. When the monkeys came back six months later, we were ready for them. We knew there would be a raid, so every kid learned to shoot. Jenny just happened to be the best of the lot. Once the monkeys realized their friends were dying, they have stayed away. We haven't heard from them since."

"What about the rebellion?" asked Jane.

"They know we have nothing here to steal here except our firearms and they are locked up in a deep basement. Once the word got out about the monkey invasion, we haven't been bothered."

"One of the kids overheard a conversation in a bar in town." started Charles. "It appears that they are afraid to take on the monkeys because they are so strong and when word got to them about us defeating an entire colony nobody has had the nerve to even come close."

"It really is a blessing in disguise." said Barb. "All we have here is old single shot weaponry, but Charles here has made some rather unique improvements and they don't have to reload as often as a single shot demands."

"Do all the kids here learn the art of weaponry?" asked Ply.

"Only those in the upper grades and only those with high enough grades." responded William. "There has to be a certain amount of trust built before one passes a loaded gun into the hands of a minor."

"Any evidence of joining the rebellion is frowned upon and internal rebellion to rules and schoolwork get immediate disqualification from the training program." added Charles. "But there have been a few that have fled to the left. All we can do is trust the Lord and make sure those that have fled don't get into the stores of ammunition prior to running away."

"Why do the rebels not want your weapons?" asked Ply.

"They think we do a great job of teaching the kids to shoot but our weaponry is very old, so nobody wants anything to do with it."

"We pack our own shells and mold our own lead, so ammunition is not too much of a problem." added Charles. "If they ever decide that all we have is theirs, then they can come and take it, but that would mean a change in a lot of things."

"A change?"

"The rebellion would have to be pretty desperate to want the antiques we play with here; not to mention all the trouble of having to make your own ammunition. In the west it is available but here on the island pretty much everything has to be imported. The more modern machinery is a lot more accessible, lighter, and automatic. Why would they want to steal the junk we have?"

"If they have nothing?" asked Jane.

"If they have nothing and they know we are armed how soon are they going to make a raid on our locked storehouses?" commented Charles. "We post guards every night for purposes of wild animals that tend to want our food but every person who shows up at night gets fed and watered and asked if they want to stay the night in a comfortable bed."

"There are comfortable beds here?" asked Ply.

"Comfortable is a relative term," said Charles, "The beds here are a lot more comfortable than the forest floor. And there are no army ants to carry you off in the night."

"I'll try not to wander off in my sleep." shuddered Jane once again.

Barb just shook her head at the scare tactics of the two running the school. Ply asked, "What's the plan for tonight?"

"Tonight?" asked William. "What's the hurry?"

"I don't think we can stay very long." responded Ply.

"It is Thursday and not much happens here on weeknights."

"How about a surprise bonfire?" suggested Barb. "Let the kids toss sticks into the fire and tell how they met the Lord."

"Most of the wood has already been burned from around the compound." replied Charles. "There are lots of dead trees in the forest but hauling one back is going to be a big job."

"What if Ply gets it ready and all the kids bring back a piece, then in a few trips we will have enough for a good fire." stated Barb.

"What kind of magic do you have up your sleeve?" asked Charles.

"I don't do magic," returned Ply, "Don't believe it exists. What if Jane and I go out to the woods and see what we can find and then come back and report?"

"You will need a guide." said Charles and he sat forward a lot more interested in their plan.

"We've got GPS." said Ply as he stood and signaled to Jane to follow. "Barb, if you stay here, we can trace your phone right back to camp." Jane got up and walked with Ply out the direction they came into camp. Charles jumped and followed close behind. "Could you please get us some water for our little trip into the woods? We will meet you at the edge of the trees."

"Sure." answered Charles and he turned back to the main kitchen. When Charles returned with the water, about ten minutes later, the two were holding hands and already at the edge of the forest and headed in. Charles broke into a run as they disappeared behind a tree. *What are those greenhorns doing?* he thought to himself. *Do they know anything about how to act in the jungle or even what to look for?*

Ply and Jane, still holding hands, reached the bag covered with leaves and brush and Ply grabbed the sword. Immediately the two disappeared from view if anything or anyone was actually watching. Once Charles was out of earshot, Ply explained to Jane his plan and how the two were to work together.

A few moments later Charles showed up and Ply said to him, "Let's go have a look and see what we can find."

Ply led the way still holding onto the hand of the beauty and Charles followed a few feet behind. Ply seemed to know his way through the trees which seemed odd to Charles. In fifteen minutes, they came across a very large tree that had been recently felled with all the branches skinned off and chopped into twelve-inch pieces.

"What happened here?" asked Ply. "Here is a tree already to go back to camp. When did you do this Charles?"

"I didn't cut this down!" exclaimed Charles. "How did you know this was here?"

"How could I have known it was here?" questioned Ply. "You were with us in the woods all the time."

Charles picked up a piece that had been split. "Who on earth cut this? No saw marks at all, just perfect straight cuts."

"Does it belong to somebody?" asked Ply.

"There isn't anyone around here for almost eight miles and we would have seen and heard them come down the road."

"Then this is ours for the taking?" said Ply.

The tree had been long since dead and Charles would have heard a chainsaw this close to the camp, but the clean cuts on the wood were not cut with a chainsaw. *Coming unannounced and now this tree down in this manner. What is this new technology that is so secret that they have to even hide it from me?* "Let's get the kids and haul it back to the bonfire site." he said, picking up a few of the larger pieces. Ply and Jane followed suit and made their way back to camp.

The kids loved the night off. The fire and visitors made things all the more special. Many of the children told again of their experiences with the Lord and Barb was left in tears as she heard of the fruits of her spending. By ten o'clock William had sent the kids to bed and the fire was almost out. Barb was exhausted, but Jenny came through with some of her special brew that perked her up considerably.

At eleven forty-five the three met quietly in front of the kitchen and walked towards the forest. Charles watched them from an upper window.

I'll do some investigating in the morning, he thought.

* * *

Ply looked back to see if anyone was following them. He really didn't think they could get away, but it looked as if they had.

Jane grabbed the sword and they were in the air in microseconds.

"Let's fly just above the treetops and then about fifty feet above the ocean till we get to the horn of Africa." suggested Ply.

"Isn't this a shipping lane?" asked Barb. "Aren't there a lot of big boats that we might bang into?"

"Good grief, you are right." said Jane.

Ply stopped the craft in the middle of the discussion. "What is the best way to get to the horn without getting too much attention?"

"What is at the horn of Africa?" asked Jane.

"I thought we could hover there and make it look like we are taking off or landing to throw the scent away from the school."

"We are a hundred miles out from shore is that not far enough?" said Jane.

"With the piracy returning from the horn the lanes have gotten really wide again." said Ply, "I forgot all about that".

"There is a lot of desert just a little north of here why not scoot up the desert?" suggested Barb. Ply turned the ship towards land. The going had to be slow but they were still below the radar. Three hours later they were in the middle of the Sahara Desert and

Ply popped up to nine thousand feet and flew directly to Mexico City. He dumped down to below radar and took the gang home.

"Noon and I'm going to bed!" announced Barb.

"Who are you going to tell?" teased Jane.

"I already told her; good night... or good afternoon..." she said while she was climbing the stairs, "Or good grief."

* * *

The trio slept right through until four the next morning. Ply stumbled out of the suite he and Jane were occupying and headed for the stairs.

"Where are you off to?" whispered Barb as he passed her door.

"The trough! I don't do too well not eating."

"Whatcha cooking?"

"I was going to start with a bowl of cereal cause it is fast and once you two got up I could have something ready."

"What are you two whispering about?" yelled Jane from the suite.

"We are discussing what to vacuum up for breakfast." yelled back Ply.

"There is stuff in the fridge." yelled Jane a little confused at Ply's terminology. "You don't have to vacuum stuff off the floor for breakfast."

"If one eats breakfast as fast as I plan to it might be referred to as vacuuming."

Jane appeared in a warm thick housecoat. "I could be ready pretty quickly for something also. It appears that Jenny's coffee has worn off already. Man, that stuff was good."

"I suppose if we were any more awake, we might have brought home a bag but showing up at market with European dollars might have caused a stir with the government." commented Barb.

"We don't need to attract any more attention than we already have." added Jane. Ply had his nose in the fridge, seeing he was first down the stairs and into the kitchen.

"Eggs are on the middle shelf." said Barb as she got out the toaster. "Sausage is just below the eggs."

Jane opened the microwave and Ply set in the food to be warmed up while Barb set the table for three.

"I guess today is house tour day." said Barb as she placed the flatware around the place settings.

"How much more is there to see?" asked Ply.

"It's not just a matter of how much but a matter of remembering codes and programming computers for your access." said Barb. "I figure if you're quick we may have the job done in...," she thought for a moment, "three days."

"Three days?" exclaimed Jane. "What have you got hidden here?"

"Well," returned Barb, "I figure you have seen about one fifth to one quarter of all the hiding places and secret compartments and escape routes that are here. You have heard about the vehicles in the cave, but you haven't been to them and if you try it without the codes you just might find yourself in a lot of hot water."

"Hot water?" asked Ply.

"Well, not very hot, but surely a lot of water."

"Are there any blueprints for all of this stuff?" asked Ply.

"There may be, but they would be scattered around with all the different contractors I have used for each individual addition."

"So, nothing is written down?" asked Jane.

"If you write it down, someone might find it but now that I am about to escape in a few months, I suppose selling the house might need a guide on how to safely get around."

"You could hide it in the library in the basement." added Jane. "That way we could reference it when we need to brush up. We could do a test run every once in a while, just to keep us on top of it all. Why do we need to know about all the secret passages in the castle?"

"Because you two are the heirs." whispered Barb to Jane. "If old lover-boy is going to have trouble with a lot of cash, how will he able to handle all this property before I die?"

"Why do we need a place this big?" whispered Jane pulling Barb out of the room.

"How many kids are you planning to have?"

"As many as the Lord gives, but I don't think I am capable of bearing enough children to fill all the beds you have in this place." replied Jane a little sarcastically.

"I do believe the record is sixty-nine kids from one womb but then again you may not be involved in that competition." joked Barb.

"In order for me to have even close to that many kids I would have to have triplets each year for the next twenty years. And if that happens, I will stop at nine and get both Ply, and myself, fixed!"

"Nine kids all under the age of five," suggested Barb, "That does sound like a hand-full".

"If I get nine kids under the age of five, I will petition for a resurrection and make you head nurse!"

"I suppose I deserve that."

"What happens if we refuse the castle?" asked Jane.

"It will probably go to probate and all the lawyers will argue and come up with excuses to drag things on till all of my money goes to their pockets and the kids I'm supporting starve." suggested Barb.

"I don't suppose it will take very long for us to decide since I do believe you are right about probate".

"Welcome to the fallen world." groaned Barb.

"Thankfully there is a better one promised!" responded Jane.

"COME AND GET IT BEFORE I EAT IT ALL!" yelled Ply from the kitchen.

"Now that is a promise, he's probably able to keep." stated Barb as she headed back to the food. Jane followed close at her heels.

* * *

Ply dug out a legal pad from the old butternut secretary and a pen to take notes on the tour. All morning long they spent practicing, writing, and making sure they understood all the implications of the basement escape route. The hidden staircase was introduced with the shooting gallery and they had that well deciphered. The tunnel took a few more minutes to catch on to.

"There are twelve, four by eight panels in this wall." stated Barb. "Number six is the door into the cave. If you walk straight from the foot of the stairwell and go left one panel, you have the door. You have to kick the baseboard at the seam of the fifth and sixth panels and then tap four times in the middle of the seam to get the door to open. I'll do it first and then you two can try it a little later." she kicked the baseboard with her toe just hard enough to get Jane a little worried and Ply a slight grin on his face.

"Aren't you afraid you are going to break something?" asked

Jane.

"There is a concrete pillar right behind the switch and if it is a little corroded you need to kick some of the oxidation off, so contact is made. There is a five second window to start tapping the wall and another five seconds to get all four knocks in. If you miss the timing you have to start over." She kicked the baseboard again and rapped four times at her shoulder height. The door popped open and then swung slowly inwards to the cave.

"I had it swing in so if there were kids needing to escape, they would not get crushed by the door."

"Good plan." stammered Jane.

"If someone is chasing you and the door closes it is pretty easy to figure out the code but if it takes more than three tries to get the door open," explained Barb as she entered the cave, "The lighting comes on and leads you to a dead end about a mile and a half away."

"Can they ever get out?" asked Ply.

"Of course, but this just gives you more time to escape." About twenty paces into the cave Barb pointed to a rock that looked a little different from all the rest on the floor. "If you roll this rock, then in ten seconds the lighting will change, leading whoever is following you into the blind alley." she kicked the stone and it moved just a little. "It doesn't have to move much but it does have to move." Ten seconds later the lights flicked just for a part of a second.

"Did we lose power?" asked Ply.

"Good for you." stated Barb. "That is the reaction that is supposed to happen. No, we did not lose power. All the lighting down here is on special IT buttons so if the outside power is lost you can still get out. The lights flicked over to 'dead end' mode. Let me show you." She led them to a slight turn to the left and part way through the turn she pointed her flashlight behind a large rock.

"Here is the hall to the cars." The turn was acute and double. It was somewhat of a challenge to the newcomers to find the path in the dark. The flashlight helped but with the black on the walls it would be almost impossible to find the opening without prior knowledge. Once around the turns, Barb touched the wall and the lights came on inside that part of the cave.

"Let me take you back so you can see the difference." she pointed the flashlight to the dark path behind them and they walked through. "As you can see, the tunnel to the cars is practically invisible from this side of the cave even with the lights on in the other route. The reason I designed it like this is the pursuer would not want to go into a part that is not lit unless he knew of the secrets. Once you've been through, there a few times you are comfortable enough to go to the cars even without the lights."

They walked another fifteen feet into the tunnel. "There is a small switch here that turns off the lights if you need to. I'll leave them on at the moment until you feel safe enough to go back into the recess in the dark. If you touch the switch, which is just a static plate, the lights will not come on for two hours. It also shuts all of the lights out for the entire cave. So, if someone is in the dead end, part they are stuck if they do not have a flashlight."

"Just how long did it take you to figure out all this and how did you describe it to the contractor?" asked Ply.

"I took a course on computer control. I have a maintenance person come by every quarter and test the IT buttons and replace all that are getting bad. The buttons are off to the side of the house in one of the maintenance sheds. I can program the computer to do as I like. I guess I have to teach you how to do that also." she stated. "Hmm, is there enough time?"

"There never is enough time to do all that we want to." said Jane.

"I did take control in my electrical training, but I haven't used it much as of late." said Ply. "It seems I have been chasing around a few very famous tennis stars and one of them really has me distracted."

"I'll take that as a compliment." laughed Barb knowing full well that it was Jane that was the distraction. The three vehicles were another four hundred feet and around a three rather sharp bends. "We should take these out for a bit of a spin just to keep things functional." coaxed Barb. "Then you will be somewhat familiar with the way out and the way in. The keys are under the passenger side back seat floor mats." They were a little dusty having sat for a few months this close to the mouth of the cave. There were eight fifty-gallon rain barrels piped together so the machinery could be rinsed off rather quickly if the dust was too bad. If the barrels were not full when the lights came on in the second tunnel, they were filled to a float switch from the house supply. If the rain had filled up the barrels since the last visit there was no water wasted. The three worked together cleaning off the cars. The water ran out the front of the cave and down the hill to the river below. The vehicles were less than ten years old and ran on common IT technology so getting them going was not a problem. They toured for about fifty minutes, then returned the cave.

"How about putting a big plastic tarp over the cars to keep the dust off them?" suggested Ply. "Then, in a hurry all you have to do is pull off the tarps and get under way."

"See," said Barb, "Two heads are always better than just one."

"Is there another way back to the house or do we need to go through the caves again?" asked Jane.

"I cut a path through the forest that is not very visible from the air, but I'm getting tired and don't know if I can make it all the way back to the house without a bit of a rest." stated Barb.

"Why don't I run back and get the sword and in a few minutes real time you will be as good as new." said Jane.

"When the last set of lights comes on in the caves all the doors in the house are closed and locked. You probably can't get in unless I use my card and palm to open the doors."

"I'll put that on the list to reprogram all of us to be able to get into the house." announced Ply scribbling as he talked.

"Will a rest help?" asked Jane.

"What if you ride piggy-back and I will take you home?" offered Ply.

"Cause I weigh a hundred and forty pounds and I don't think you can carry all this weight all the way home."

"Well if I can't then just push me off the side of the cliff and Jane can drag you back to your bed." insulted the male chauvinist.

Barb stopped in her tracks. "You can't weigh much more than a hundred and thirty!"

"In my apprenticeship I slugged a lot more weight than that." corrected Ply. "And if I faint you will have a soft landing." Ply took a step down and Barb crawled on his back, locked her legs around his waist, and draped her arms around his throat.

"That might shorten the trip a little." gasped Ply and she loosened her grip and dropped her arms to just above his shoulders. "Thank you". They trudged up the hill to the castle with Jane behind the two in case any fatigue set in and the poor boy collapsed.

After a good forty-five-minute hike, mostly uphill, Barb teased, "Home is in sight, horsie."

Thank you, Lord, confessed Ply silently.

Once inside the house Jane ran up to get the sword and Ply gently set Barb on the couch in the library. Within ten minutes EST Barb was roarin' to go again. "I don't think I'll ever get used to that thing." confessed Barb.

"I don't think we are supposed to." stated Jane.

* * *

It took two weeks of training to get the two to the place where they were comfortable with all that Barb could remember of the secrets of the castle.

"I didn't think Old Timers would set in so early." confessed Barb.

"I think it is called Alzheimer's." corrected Ply and Jane gave him a rebuking look.

"Aren't you supposed to get Old Timers when you are old?" grumbled Barb. Ply figured it was another good time to sound like a giraffe.

"Okay," announced Jane, "We are done with the house for the moment. How about a little entertainment?"

"Do you want to watch a movie?" suggested Ply.

"I was thinking of Budson for a final vacation. We can take the sword and recharge Barb whenever she needs it. There is lots of stuff to see and do there, and..."

"And what?" coaxed Barb.

"There is a guy there named Callaway who had a wonderful routine that runs for three weeks straight. That way you can laugh yourself to sleep every night. There are lots of other shows but his has an eternal perspective with a lot of good clean humor. I haven't heard you laugh real hard for a long time." stated Jane with a loving tear in her eye.

"Won't that be expensive?" asked the older.

"If you are asking what it will take to get you laughing again, if I don't have enough money, I might be inheriting some that could go to the good cause." stated the girl.

"I don't want you spending all of your money on me!"

"Why?" returned Jane. "Aren't you spending, and haven't you spent, all your money on me?"

Barb pouted for a few minutes then announced, "I'm sure glad it was Ply I bartered with about doing the grass and not you. When do we leave?"

"Why not first thing in the morning?" suggested Ply.

"Cause we have laundry to do, bedding to wash, and dishes to clean, not to mention the house had not been vacuumed for three weeks and it is a little dusty in here."

"How about the day after tomorrow?" whimpered the boy. "We can all pitch in and get the place ship shape tomorrow then leave if you are pleased with the job we have done."

"I could call the maid." announced Barb.

"I will help clean the house but I'm not wearing a tu-tu." said Ply. That got the three of them laughing and settled on a plan for the vacation.

* * *

They took the van from the mouth of the cave. It was set up with curtains on the windows, so Jane could treat Barb with the sword while they drove around the small town. Having the public notice two of the passengers disappear and then reappear was not on the schedule. Usually it only took enough time for Ply to make a stop and get a few supplies and/or snacks for the three of them and Barb was ready to go again for a good while. By the end of three weeks Barb needed a treatment every day and coaxed the other two it was time to head home.

Back at the castle the owner demanded one more round of familiarization of all the special endowments of the castle. This time they took the sword with them everywhere they went. Finally, Barb was satisfied that they had all they needed to know to keep the place running and relaxed, a little.

Sing was kept on board with the degeneration of the star. Nine days after the return from Budson, Barb refused to come down for breakfast or even answer her door. The 'Venus' room had been reprogrammed for Jane to get into all the nooks and crannies. She carded herself in and found her friend appearing to be comfortably asleep, but she was stone cold.

Jane called Sing and said, "The party was over or just beginning." and hung up and wept by the side of her friend.

Having been previously briefed, Sing made some calls canceling the appointments of the day and headed for the Cully Castle. Halfway there he called the ambulance and told them of the need to get to the Cully residence.

Twenty minutes later Ply heard sirens and Sing was at the door. "What happened?" he asked.

"Jane said the party was over..." replied Sing. Ply didn't wait for the rest of the quotation. He ran up the stairs and knocked on the door that was slightly ajar.

"Come in." whimpered Jane.

Ply entered slowly and found his wife with her arms wrapped around her closest friend and the pillow practically soaked through. "They're here." he said quietly.

"Why do things have to happen so fast?" repeated Jane as she crawled from the bed into her husband's arms. At least the goon was smart enough to do the giraffe.

* * *

The funeral was quiet with a few close friends from the circuit. Jane called Bridgit and she arrived just in time for the service. Barb's doctor was there, complaining that she might have been able to do something else for her patient. The two were silent on the aspect of the sword and thanked her for all she had done. Barb had written a note to her and Jane handed it to her as she entered the funeral parlor. Jane was thankful no mention of the sword was made but assured her doctor that she was receiving the best care possible. Ply and Jane's folks showed up; Pastor did the honors of laying Barb to rest.

Two days after all the business of letting Barb go, Sing knocked at the door with the announcement of all the paperwork finished. He handed a copy to Jane and she left them on the secretary in the library. Numbness had set in and the loss of a loved one was becoming difficult to overcome.

"Why does the hole of love lost have to be so deep?" she whispered into Ply's ear.

"You've lost before," stated Ply, "And you healed but it took some time. No one will ever replace Barb, but you have all of eternity to laugh and love and even spar on the courts." The encouragement was wonderful, but the hole was still there for the time being.

"I guess the deeper you fall in love with someone the longer it takes to fill the hole." realized the star as she leaned into her comfort for the moment.

Jane just lay in bed and lounged around the house for days. Ply was getting a little concerned, so he called her mother.

Jane's Announcement

"Is there any way you could come and maybe cheer her up a little?" asked Ply. "She doesn't want to go the doctor and she has been throwing up. I don't think she is sick but maybe just sick by losing her best friend."

"How is she in the afternoon?"

"She doesn't seem to be sick in the afternoon just listless not wanting to do anything." he replied.

"We'll be there first thing in the morning." announced Carol with a conviction Ply had not heard from her.

"Your parents will be here tomorrow in the morning." said Ply to Jane later that day. She just nodded her head and went and lay down on the couch in the library.

The doorbell rang at eight thirty the next morning. Ply answered to find Carol and Greg with three large suitcases in tow.

"Where is she?" demanded her mom.

"She's on the couch in the library." he said. "I think she was there all night." Carol left the bags for Ply and Greg to attend to and went straight to her daughter. "I need a picture full of cool water and a nice glass please." she yelled from the room.

Ply dropped the suitcase on the floor and hurried to the kitchen and filled a pitcher of water and ice. He grabbed a nice glass from the cupboard and rushed to side of his mother-in-law. "Will this do?"

"Yes, thank you," said Carol, "Now we need to be left alone for a while. Will you be close enough to hear or shall I call?"

"I was going to take Dad outside and show him around a little, so you can call us on the phone. We may not hear you if you just shout."

"That will be fine but don't leave the property." she commanded.

Three hours later Greg got the call. "Okay boys, get yourselves in here."

"We are on our way." responded her husband. Ply had the cage dismantled on the second floor of the shed, so no questions were asked about the drone. Greg was interested in riding the fancy mower and was cutting by the arch at the entrance when Carol's call came. He lifted the blades, put the tractor in road gear, and rushed back to the shed.

"Carol needs us inside now." he called out to Ply as he parked the toy. Ply dropped what he was doing and the two jogged back into the house.

"Your wife has an announcement." stated Carol in a tone that left the boys confused.

Jane was on her feet, her eyes still red from the sorrow of the loss of her friend but seemed to be getting around with a new-found excitement.

"We're having hamburgers for dinner and put the buns in the oven." she stated a little flushed at the excitement of it all.

Ply rushed out to fill the order of his wife and Carol just shook her head.

"You're going to have twins?" stated Greg.

"I don't know how many she is having but it seems that the new husband is still a little unclear on what is happening here." flapped Mrs. Blythwood.

"HOW MANY BUNS DO I NEED TO PUT IN THE OVEN?" yelled Ply from the bottom of the stairs.

"Just one!" yelled back his mother-in-law from the library.

Oh, yeah, thought Ply. *They are down here.* He ran over to the doorway. "Just one?" he asked.

"Just one." repeated Carol.

The look on Ply's face seemed to say Carol and Greg had finally lost it. "Okay," and he went back to the kitchen. *I will have two and Greg will have two, but the girls will probably have only one each. If I cook an extra, then that would make seven.* He put seven pre-cooked patties on a large plate and placed them in the microwave, fired it up, and headed back to the crowd.

"There are seven patties in the microwave."

"How many buns in the oven?" asked Carol.

"Just as you said," replied the greenhorn, "Just one."

"Now tell me in a full sentence how many buns are in the oven." commanded Carol.

Ply was getting a little frustrated at all this playing around. "There is one bun in the oven." he stated firmly and rather loudly.

"Thank you," she stated, "You may return to the kitchen and study the situation."

Ply returned to the cooking and sat on a chair and stared into the stove. It took another full five minutes before he realized what was going on. He jumped from the chair and rushed to the library. "Is Jane pregnant?!" he shouted.

"Well, duh!" said Carol. "I was beginning to wonder if I needed to present a picture of an ultrasound!"

Two days later Jane was up and running around getting things ready for the new addition to the family.

"It looks like the Lord has provided a shovel to help fill in the hole." said Ply as he leaned into Jane while she was cleaning their room. Jane gently slipped her arms around the guy that was also helping fill the hole and whispered, "Thank you." into his ear.

"Do you have designs at this hour?" Ply asked with a look of anticipation.

"With Mother here?" she admonished. "Not very likely!"

Carol refused to leave Jane's side so Ply and Greg had a lot of getting-to-know-each-other time. They cut grass and cleaned up the vines from some of the trees. Ply's phone rang, and he was invited into the house. *Nice to know I'm still welcome,* he thought.

Jane was sitting at the secretary in the library, "How long have these papers been sitting here?" she asked Ply.

"I think Sing left them there almost three weeks ago."

"Oh yeah, I remember. They are all the papers from the transfer of the house and all Barb's accounts. There is stuff here about the school in Madagascar and all the info about the kids she is supporting. I went through it all and it looks like all has been completed."

"Sing said there wasn't anything we needed to do about the transfers." said Ply.

"I remember Barb saying the same thing. But there are a few things we need to do."

"Here I am." agreed Ply.

"I think we can let your apartment go. We don't need the room nor the expense so if there is anything you want from there go get it and we will close out the account at the end of the month. We need to update our driving papers and passport info at the office, but I think we can just call that in. I'll file these papers at the bank in the safety deposit box. Anything else we need to do to get ready?"

"Why not make up a baby room out of one of these extra rooms? You and your mom can decorate while I clean out the old apartment." suggested Ply. "Why don't I get some cleaning supplies gathered and I will leave in the morning. It may take a few days to get the place cleaned up but..."

"That's fine." agreed Jane. "Mom will be here, so I won't have any trouble and if there is, she can help in a lot of ways. Does Dad need to go with you?"

"I don't think so. I don't really want him to know how much of a pig I really am. What do you want me to do with my dishes and furniture?"

"What are they like?" she asked.

"It's a cross between early church basement and unwanted garage sale castoffs. If I sell it, I could probably double our assets." She just looked at him as if he were talking to a wall. "The stuff in my apartment is probably pretty much junk but perhaps some of the resale shops would like to try to sell the stuff. I don't expect it will get us much of a reward in Heaven, but we will be rid of it."

Jane glanced up to the ceiling and looked at her husband wondering if some kind of dementia had set in since the ceremony. "So, you are leaving in the morning?"

"That's the plan. I'll call you every night and let you know how things are going."

"Are you sure you don't need Dad?"

"Positive."

Carol and Greg stayed on while Jane and Carol planned a few changes around the house. The two rooms at the top of the stairs were changed from the guest rooms as Barb had left the to a large nursery and the other room for Jane's specific desires. A few large glass cases were purchased for her tennis trophies. Greg was mandated to assemble the stuff that came in and retrieve the stuff from home that Jane wanted. Jane did not have the heart, nerve, or crassness to do anything with the room 'Venus' for a good long while.

The Proposal of the Anothen

The meeting had been called in great secrecy. Only the Master and the three were on the docket.

"First of all, I would like to thank you for all you have done for the kingdom." stated the Master. "Progress has gone as planned and many are thankful for that. Time is running out. The garment is wearing thin." With these words he had to open their understanding. "There is an old artifact employed from warfare that has not been used for a long time."

The three looked at each other in surprise. The term warfare had not been referenced for hundreds of years.

"My word will manifest itself again even as it has to this day. I have risen up one who has a tool from the ancient past. He does not consider it magic and it is not. He has not yet fully understood the power of the tool, but he is learning at the rate I have chosen to teach him."

"Excuse me, sir." interrupted one of the three. "Have you been personally leading the anointed for this task?"

"You know me well enough to know that I do not have to manifest myself to teach."

The three nodded in recognition.

"If you remember the mad dogs of a number of years ago that seemed to disappear, it was this man who took them out. The rain that night washed away all the evidence and the next he burned down the barn destroying the rabid contamination of that area."

The three looked at each other in amazement as once again the Master proved himself.

"You will remember when Dagon was destroyed before me, did the builders repent or choose to build another idol?"

"They chose to build another idol." stated one.

"The same is happening again. The cancer has returned, and my administration shall be challenged once more. As a result, I have a special assignment for the three of you."

With anticipation and wonder the three leaned forward and listened closely.

"Your mission, should you choose to accept it..."

After the briefing the Master stood, and the trio followed suit. With a slight smirk he said, "This tape will self-destruct in seven seconds..."

The agents looked at him, recognized the phrase and the smirk. The quartet left the room laughing.

* * *

Ply was at the apartment getting things hauled away and packed up, so he could leave the building to be rented to someone else. Most of the furniture was gone, some to the resale shop, some to the dump. The dishes and flat ware he would save till last. The drapes and curtains he would leave for the next tenant. The bathroom chose to be the biggest chore in cleaning, but it only took half a day.

The coffee shop meeting earlier that day had proven their identities. He didn't really believe them until...

"Hey, Ply. Will you join us for a cup of coffee? We'd like to present you with an opportunity about your acquisition from a previous place of employment."

The three of them looked normal enough as he followed them into the cafe. He had an uneasy feeling they were referring to the sword.

How did they know about the find? he thought.

"I'll get us what we need, you find us a seat." stated one as the other two headed for a booth in a back corner. Ply glanced around the establishment to size up his options. They were headed for a booth that had no windows for about six feet and the blinds were pulled on the glass behind them facing the party room in the back. One had what looked like a paper lunch sack in his hand which appeared to be about one third full of whatever was in it. They did not seem to be very big so if trouble aroused, he figured he might be able to escape. They stood talking small talk until the third arrived with the drinks and pastries.

Two scooted onto the back and the other slid close to the wall leaving Ply the seat on the edge so if he needed to bolt that was still and option.

Their opening proposition about his new possession had him curious. It wasn't often that Anothen made themselves known so blatantly. He promised himself he would keep his guard up and not let out any information unless he had to. What was this proposition that was to be given? Did they want the sword to do their dirty work? They never had need to prior to this. They settled down and introduced themselves.

"We understand that you have come across an ancient artifact that has been lost for some time."

"What artifact?"

"While exploring an old recently revealed cave your eye was caught by the glimmer of what appeared to be a piece of jewelry."

Ply stiffened. "How do you know this?"

The three looked at each other and after a long moment one of them said, "We are agents of the Master and there is nothing that escapes His notice."

Ply realized that these three were actually Anothen. Sometimes they referred to themselves as agents of the Master, but they were a strange being that actually had the power of the higher dimension within themselves. He did not know a lot about them but having now contact with them, and three of them at that, prompted a nervousness that he had not known before and a desire to do a little more research.

Ply thought back to the caves and the retrieval of the blade. Fighting the great beasts of a lower dimension was one thing, fighting these from a higher...?

Again, it was He who was looking at me as I fought the dragons, Ply thought. *It was He who noticed I had killed the dogs.*

"Yes," said the spokesman, "the cave and the barn."

Ply looked at the trio wide-eyed. They smiled back politely.

The talk had been low, and Ply had simply thought the statements and not voiced them. He looked around to see if anyone else had heard. He thought it was curious that there was an empty table between the four and anyone else in the restaurant. Most of the other tables were full of students and business people talking in a slightly higher than normal volume. He glanced toward the table and recognized that if these guys were actually agents, he didn't stand a chance against one never mind three. His mind flooded with questions and searched for options while his palms started to sweat.

"What is it you want from me?"

"Things are happening much faster than anyone would like to guess. We have been invited to offer you an opportunity that few in life get."

Ply thought about this for a few moments. *They still haven't mentioned the sword, but it seems that this is exactly what they are talking about* he pondered. "Tell me more about what you know?" he fearfully questioned.

"We know that you have discovered a sword that appears to have magical powers. The power it has is not magic. What is happening is simply a manifestation of physics that has been hidden from the human race for a very long time. A few of the principles have been revealed, so to speak, but not all that the sword can do has been employed since before the time of Noah."

"Noah?" inquired the owner of the blade. "You mean the old man with the boat and all the animals?"

"The same!"

This news sat Ply back on his seat for a few minutes. Quietly he eyed the three as the reality of the news about the real estate in the guitar case sank into his reasoning. "What if I decide to sell it?"

"We won't let you sell it."

"And how are you going to manage that?"

"If you accept our offer you will have enough evidence."

This all seemed like riddle talk to Ply. These characters seemed to know what they were talking about, but he wasn't fully convinced.

"We have been given instructions to allow you to think it over. You have some time to make a decision and we will meet at the exact spot where you found it."

The agent with the bag slid it over in front of Ply. "If you decide to accept the invitation to our next meeting you will need to indulge in a spoonful of these prior to your entrance to the cave."

Ply looked at the men. Slowly he reached for the bag. All three watched as he opened the mouth and looked inside. "They look like seeds."

"Chia seeds. The Mayans used them for a lot of reasons. They will give you extra stamina that will be needed if you decide to return to the cave and want to get back out."

"How am I going to get back in?"

"You're an intelligent lad Ply." one of them reported in a somewhat Scottish brogue. "The options to return to the cave are not yet fully extinguished."

Silence again for a few seconds. "When?" Ply interrogated.

"Tomorrow night."

"Friday?"

"Correct."

"What time?"

"Shortly after closing."

"What if I can't get in?"

The talkative one responded, "There is a new person working in your place. They will be alone to close up that evening. He will have conveniently forgotten that you are in the back room reading over some old maps and close up and set the alarms. Don't forget the case as you go into the cave. Leave the case on the tour side of the entrance through the pool. Do not take it into the undiscovered part or you will have to purchase a new one. The sword will render you invisible to the cameras and alarms as it has before. The case will not be noticed seeing it is between the visibility of the cameras and you will not have time or the desire to return for it if you take it into the new-found part of the cave." They said they would like to make him an offer that only he could refuse but it had to be at the exact spot where the sword had been found. Something about an ancient agreement that had to be confirmed.

Ply was astounded that they were familiar with all the ins and outs of what was going on at the cave. He blinked a few times and said, "Tomorrow night, closing time, old map room, and leave the case outside the new part."

"Chia seeds."

"What about them?"

Make sure you take a spoonful before you leave from your house and put a half a cup in a plastic bag that will stay dry and eat them before you end your conference with us. You will need them for the return trip out of the cave." The other two sat with hands folded on the table in front of themselves between sips of coffee and nibbles of pastries and watched as Ply took in all the information. "One more thing." said the speaker. "Don't waste all the seeds before tomorrow night."

"Just to prove to you who we really are we are going to go out the alarmed door and the alarm will not go off. Remember we do not need doors. If you try it, you will be asked not to return."

With that the three stood up and it was apparent that the conversation was over. Ply stood up and let them escape toward the alarmed fire door down the end of the hall past the washrooms. As they turned down the hall Ply decided he would watch them disappear. Quickly he stepped into the hallway only to find it empty.

"They ducked into the men's washroom." he muttered. Throwing open the doorway the light automatically came on revealing that this was not their hiding place. He opened the back door and the buzzer sounded bringing the manager immediately and a few anxious patrons.

"That is an emergency exit only, sir." stated the manager in an almost angry tone. As they ushered him down the hall the door to the woman's restroom opened releasing a frightened woman from the cubicle and revealing that this also was not the place the boys hid themselves.

That was Thursday afternoon. The next morning, he thought he would see exactly what might happen when a few chia seeds were ingested. He measured out a half a cup for the evening and placed another half cup into a plastic zippered bag.

"This leaves me with a little more than one cup left. If this stuff is as good as it is talked up to be, I may need to use it sparingly." He pulled out a teaspoon and dipped it into the seed. After shaking it down a little, he swallowed them with a glass of water.

"Now it is time for a little walk." The streets were still dark, and the sword was left at the castle. Seldom had there been any rousing on the weekdays. The worst that had happened is a few drunks would feel their oats on the weekend, so it was pretty quiet. The moonlight gave a good reason to enjoy the fresh air and soon he was jogging along.

"Wow, I feel great. How come these things never got advertised before?" He broke into a run with the wind in his face and did four rounds of the quarter mile track without getting winded.

He purchased a head lamp that fits him well so if he can move around with the sword if need be seeing he was warned that he might encounter some opposition.

* * *

About nine in the morning Ply arrived back at the castle and tried to sneak in to get the sword.

"Back already?" asked Mrs. Blythwood as Ply passed the open door at the top of the stairs.

"Just back to pick something up." said Ply and he passed her post.

I better go down the back stairs, so she doesn't see me haul out that old guitar case, he thought. Jane was in their room rummaging around for something when he came in.

"Wow." she said. "Done already? That was quick."

"Not quite yet." he answered. "I do need this though."

"What have you gotten yourself into?" she asked.

Ply stopped just at the door to the hallway, "It is going to take a lot of explaining, hon. Can I tell you when I get back?"

"Are you going to need me?" she asked. "There are things you can't do with that thing, remember?"

"This is pretty much one thing I have to do by myself." he stated firmly as he closed the bedroom door.

She ran to his side. "Ply what is it?"

"I have to make a very important decision."

"We are one now, can't you tell me what this is about?"

"I haven't made the decision yet, but you'll have to trust me".

"It's not just me now." she reminded him rubbing the bump in her belly.

"I know. So, pray I make the right decision." He opened the door to find his mother-in-law at the door. Ply gave her a disgusted look and walked past her down the stairs and out the front door.

* * *

The time had arrived. It was a dark and stormy night as he arrived at the caves one hour before closing time. He wandered around for a few minutes and then slipped into the map room. He placed the guitar case in the corner out of site of the door and moved a chair into the far corner with the back towards the entrance.

He sat and waited. Being loaded up with Chia seeds made the wait in the dark a challenge but with the sword in the case he spent it in real time.

"Man." he said after about three minutes and laid his head back in the chair and closed his eyes. What seemed like a few more minutes he heard the door creak and the light went on. He sat motionless. Shortly the light turned off and the door closed. He stayed in place till he was sure the staff member had fled. He turned the chair and saw the rest of the store go dark as lights were extinguished and alarms set.

How did those guys know that the door to the map room was not in line of sight of the motion detectors? he pondered. Waiting another fifteen minutes after the car had pulled out of the lot he arose and opened the case. Warming the sword, he shut the case and tucked it under his right arm. He turned and in the dim lighting coming in from the parking lot, he recognized he was not alone. He froze seeing a warrior from the past close to the window with his weapon drawn.

"Good grief, Ply, get a grip!" he said in a whisper as he remembered the artifact that was created for a promotion a number of years ago. "Whatever these guys have planned for me has really got me rattled." He stormed past the statue resisting the temptation to lop off its head.

At the pool he left the case in the toured area donned the head light and dropped into the other side. He checked his light against his clothing as he had before, this time with his forearm to block the light. New batteries were in order for whatever the agents had planned for him tonight, so it was very bright. He let his eyes adjust to the new light level then moved down the corridor towards the end of the hall as he munched the seeds, they encouraged him to devour.

"Do I cut the door a little bigger or not yet?" he questioned himself. "What if I cut a doorway that just fits for me?" He modified the door and kicked the rubble into the far corner never letting the tool out of his hand. "If I need to get out away from something, this just might work."

Entering the room with the pool apprehension grew. He knew his way around well enough now not to need the string and he needed two hands. The pool was like glass, but he kept his eyes there thinking...

There was a low growl behind him as he approached the

corridor the other side of the pool. Turning he saw a very large cat about the size of a lion, but it wasn't a lion.

"Well," he stammered, "Encounter number one." The beast crouched before the light and sprang at the intruder. The cat was faster than he had anticipated. Ply managed to cut off a paw as the animal fell into the water.

"Great!" reflected Ply. "Just what we need to rouse up whatever is there." He jumped at the wounded beast and cut off its head even as he had done in the practice sessions and dreams. The headless beast jumped backwards as its dying reflexes threw it into deeper water. Ply shone his light and noticed an enormous tongue consume the creature then re-submerge. Horrified, he hoped this might keep that one happy, as he knew he had to return this way.

"I sure hope that thing doesn't come in pairs?"

Not to disappoint him as he turned, he noticed another Cheshire crouched leaving him between the cat and the pool. Neither were smiling.

Ply lunged at the beast and it backed away a little but not enough for the swordsman to get by. The cat swiped at the blade and almost knocked it out of Ply's hand. Beads of sweat mounted on his brow. Now he needed his wits about him. The oversize tom noticed the fear and moved in for the kill. The brute jumped with claws extended. Ply imagined he was fighting against the fifty-millimeter gun and slashed the sword to and fro hoping to chop the thing into pieces. The action worked as the monster fell in a heap of chopped carnage at his feet. Quickly he jumped over the carcass and headed down the corridor to the meeting place wary of what might be before him.

The cut road was just ahead. Stepping onto the path brought no further surprises. Moving closer to the crevice he heard a noise behind him. Trapped between some super-sized cad and the bottomless pit was not a fortunate plan of action as far as he was concerned.

"Hi Ply." came a response from one of the agents. Ply turned to see one of the men he had talked to and the other two escape, from the room he had dug out earlier.

"You guys are just full of surprises."

"We have a contract to negotiate sir." the spokesman announced.

"A contract?" quizzed the armed one.

"Yes."

"And just what are your terms?"

"There is still time to turn from the plans that are developing."

"And what plans are they?"

"Some have been entertaining the notion to remove the Prince from His position."

"Oh, have they?"

"There is still redemption available but if you refuse this opportunity there may be no turning back."

"And how is that different from offers others have had in the past?"

"Few in the past knew when the final offer had arrived. They just glibly went on thinking they were in control."

"What is the catch?"

"You dump the sword into the well behind you and escape will be forthcoming."

" And what about Fido in the lake?"

"He can be distracted so you can get passed but you will have to be quick."

"How did all those creatures get there?"

"They have always been there, but you have not been ready to undergo their experience."

At this Ply thought for a few seconds but did not drop the armament.

The fact that the two cats were in the cave ran a chill down his spine, not to mention the house pet that slept in the drink as he spooned out some water to test for acidity. "How do I know this is not just some trick to get me eliminated?"

"We promised you safety. You will just have to trust us." They moved a little closer waiting for the response.

"Trust? On what grounds are you trustworthy? I don't even know you."

"You know us well enough and you know enough history to make an intelligent decision."

"Intelligent? Following the Master is the intelligent decision?"

"It has always been that way."

Suddenly Ply lunged at the spokesman and lopped off his head. The severed piece rolled down into the pit. The next agent picked up the torso and threw it past Ply into the hole. There was a rumbling at the mouth of the cave that led to the lake. Ply dared not look but did not like the sound.

The man-at-arms was not a little shaken that the live agents were not disturbed by the elimination of their companion.

"Consider the implications of you actions sir." pleaded the Scottish Anothen.

"Isn't it already too late seeing one has gone for a swim?"

"Not necessarily."

Ply stopped his advance but did not drop his guard. He stabbed his opponent in the heart, and he stumbled down the well.

"That just leaves you and me." said Ply.

"I guess so."

"So now that your friends are gone do you still have a plan?"

"The offer still stands."

"Still? How does it work?"

"It works this way. Right from the beginning man was tricked so there could be a choice. To some degree the choice is in man. Then there was the problem of the barrier."

"The barrier?" asked Ply.

"The dimensional barrier. It was God that was sinned against and it was man that had sinned. Therefore, the Redeemer could not only be man nor only God but had to be both. It was this very reason that man was created in the image of God, so he could be redeemed. If the God-man could die for the sins of the world then there would be opportunity for redemption for those who desired such. It did not end there. There had to be a place built that would only be temporary, so the dimension of eternity would not get, let's say, infected. This earth is that temporary place."

"So how do I fit in?"

"If you dump the sword and turn to the lead of the Master things will not change much but the outcome will be different for you."

"For me?"

"Yes. If you turn to His side it will be a bit troublesome for a while, but it will be more than worth it in the end."

During the conversation the agent maneuvered to between the crevice and Ply. Ply did not notice the changes to the pit that was now in front of him.

"And what if the end is NOW!" yelled Ply as he sliced the agent from top to bottom. Both sides of the Anothen fell into the fracture that had grown to stretch from wall to wall and the mouth was encroaching upon the murdered and the murderer. He backed up and turned to be confronted with large eyes that were almost forty centimeters apart.

"If I end up in the pit it will be over my dead body."

Ply warmed up the tool and lunged at whatever was in front of him. The eyes moved farther apart as Ply went between them. Slashing front and back the beast sat back and waited for the animation to calm down. Keeping the machine in peak mode he slowed and took stock of the situation. There seemed to be two of them, but what were they?

The entrance to the cavern with the lake was still ninety feet from his present position. What else was there to battle? For a moment he wondered if he had given the negotiators enough consideration. It seemed a little late now that they had arrived at Davy Jones' locker. A slimy substance touched him on the shoulder. He swung around and sliced up whatever it was only to be approached from behind again by what seemed to be more than one. In a few short seconds he was drowning in a bath of gooey spinach that clung to his outsides. He slashed and sliced till there seemed to be nothing left to chop and finally the agitation ceased. Covered with who-knows-what, he peeled off the mucus knowing that it might hinder his ability to maneuver. Even with the odor of the rotting mucus he refrained from plugging his nose. *I don't want that stuff up my snout and not be able to get it out,* he thought.

He tried to catch his breath and think but things were happening far too fast. He dared not crawl into the room he dug not knowing what might have taken up hibernation.

He remembered the second dose of Chia seeds. There was a small water packet in the leg of his trousers that helped down the energy bits. He rested for a moment to catch his breath but was not given much time. The way out was obvious, but it appeared that the gate to the lake was blocked.

"I may have to cut myself out of this." The excitement had dropped some loose rock above the opening to the lake blocking the exit. This was no problem for the blade, but it took up precious escape time to get out of there. Getting himself through, he looked around and found all things quiet. He noticed the place where the second cat had fallen. Now the animal was gone. All that was left was the trace of blood from the beast.

"Great!" he thought to himself, "Looks like there may be more fun."

Quietly he moved to about ten feet of the zig-zag door he had cut on the other side. Surprised at the progress, he had made he let down his guard, a little.

The lake boiled and foamed into a spout that cut into the rock in the ceiling. When most of the water had returned to the surface there were two of them, and they were enormous. The escape hatch was now in reach, but this miscreation was between Ply and the door. The mouth of one came to feeding distance in a matter of seconds but our hero had enough practice to catch the end of the nose with the tip of the blade. The beast roared and fell back giving Ply time to get to the gate. As he squeezed through the tongue of the second followed him through the door and right to the pool. He turned and rent the membrane to bits only to be covered with blood as he dove through to the other side. With the sword lit he grabbed the guitar case and ran to the exit at the back of the cave and made it to the car without any more nasty interruptions.

Arriving at his old apartment Ply cleaned the sword, set it in the case, and the case on the floor.

"Now what have I done?" he murmured to himself. "How much more trouble is this thing going to get me into?" He showered and tumbled trembling onto the mattress on the floor.

* * *

The next morning the only thing left to do was to dump the old mattress at the street, stuff the sheets into a large plastic garbage bag, and throw them into the trunk. He did notice the old Ford at the end of the street.

That car has been there all week, he thought to himself. *I wonder what that is all about?*

The spy had been instructed to follow anyone who had entered the apartment and note all that they had done. Ply tossed the guitar case into the trunk and headed for home. The Ford followed three cars behind him.

***

Ply arrived at the turn off from the highway and noticed the light blue mid-sized Ford. The old car hung back, but it apparently had followed him all the way home so far.

I just may need to take the long way into town, he said to himself. He was still a little shaken from the encounter from the night before and not ready to take any excitement to his wife with a little one on the way. He had lived there long enough to know the back roads and headed for the place Johnson used to work. He slowed at the gate as if ready to turn in then turned off his turn signal and kept on the road.

"Hopefully this will give this guy following me the idea that this is where I live at the moment." he breathed as he made his way back into town. Ply stopped in front of the hardware store and got out of the car. The old Ford passed him, and Ply tried not to look at the driver or show his face to the one pursuing him. He went inside a purchased three quarts of oil for the machinery he got to play with every once in a while. Ply walked to the back of his car and put the oil in the trunk. He watched the Ford through the front and back windshields of his own car and saw the one trailing him had turned left at the next intersection. The hood of the car was visible to but not the passenger compartment nor the steering wheel. Ply quickly looked under his car to see if there had been placed a tracking device behind the bumper. Nothing. He checked the wheel wells and found them empty also. He walked back to the driver door and noticed a small wire dangling from one side of the back door.

OK, he thought. *There it is.* He glanced around and found the nose of the Ford peeking from behind and old building just down the street from where it turned left. Ply got back into his car and started it. He sat there for a few moments surveying the situation and then made his move. The old horse was never a race car, so he pulled out slowly from his parking spot and meandered down the street until he was just out of sight of the Ford. He pushed the pedal to the floor and was very quickly up and over the hill and out of sight. There was an old warehouse that had been empty for as long as he had been at the castle and he pulled in behind it, hidden behind the building from the passing traffic. He jumped out, opened the trunk, grabbed the guitar case, and threw it in the front passenger seat so the sword would be easy to get to from his position at the wheel. The old buggy complained at the opening of the back door behind the driver's seat and then being slammed so hard. He threw the homing device on top of the warehouse sloped roof and it rolled into the gutter. As fast as he could, he jumped back into the car and fired up the sword holding on to the metal that was installed previously with the idea of flying the car. He disappeared three seconds before the old Ford showed up behind the warehouse. Ply put his car in gear and moved slowly out of the way to the far side of the parking lot. The old Ford moved into the position where Ply was few moments ago.

Man, I hate when thing get this close, he thought.

A very large man of about forty years of age lumbered out of the Ford. He checked his phone and scratched his head. Looking all around he appeared a little confused at where Ply and his car had disappeared to. He started to walk with his arms outstretched wondering if he might bump into something he could not see. The only things he bumped into were the building and his own vehicle. Ply wondered if the man was drunk, or even on drugs, or both. Finally, the car jostled as he flopped back into the driver's seat. He spoke something into what appeared to Ply as a radio microphone then the old Ford was put into gear and moved back onto the highway. Ply noticed that the marshmallow-man headed in the direction of the farm where Johnson used to work.

"I wonder if I actually convinced him that is where we live?" Ply mumbled to himself. Ply moved his car, still in invisible mode, to a place where he could see the adversary until he had driven over the hill and back into town. Ply put the sword back into the case and made his way back to the castle leaving the warehouse lot in the opposite direction the Ford had taken. When he arrived home, he drove the old white horse in the maintenance shed and parked in the back room. He covered the one shed window with a large piece of cardboard. He thought it might be a good idea to see if more than one homing device had been installed to trace his car but after searching for half an hour, he found nothing. Just to be sure, he covered the car in aluminum foil and grounded it to the metal posts of the building.

"There", he said to himself, "That ought to keep any

transmissions quiet for a while. Just might be time to sell the old girl." He was thankful Jane was not in earshot after speaking those words audibly. He didn't want to have to explain why he was getting rid of his mother-in-law.

* * *

Ply made his way toward the back of the house and let himself in through the kitchen door. Carol was at the stove making something for the gang. Ply walked over and gave her a kiss on the cheek.

"How is everything here?" he asked.

"Just fine." she replied happy to see him home again. "Did you get everything all cleaned up?"

"I most certainly did." he replied and then thought, *And then some.* "Jane around?"

"Upstairs preparing the baby's room."

"Thanks." Ply went around to the front stairs and hopped up two at a time. He glanced over his shoulder to see if 'Mom' had decided to make a 'listening appearance' and saw her shadow appear at the door to the hall. He saw Jane in the baby's room putting bumpers on the crib. He closed the door and ran over to her and started passionately kissing her with noisy slobbery kisses.

"Have you been gone too long?" she asked a little surprised at the advances made before a proper greeting was stated.

"Twenty minutes out of your arms is nineteen minutes too long," he replied. He grabbed a blanket from the big rocking chair and maneuvered her into the closet.

"What on earth have you got in mind?" she questioned him in shock.

"We need to talk where old elephant ears are not in a position to hear." he quietly whispered to her as he nibbled on her ear and shut the door to the closet with them inside.

"Who are old elephant ears?" Jane asked with her face scrunched up partly out of worry and partly because Ply was sticking his tongue in her ear.

"Are you two okay in there?" called Carol from the hallway.

"Exhibit A." stated Ply in his best lawyer's authoritative voice.

Jane threw open the door and yelled, "Yes Mother we are just

340

getting reacquainted after a long week of absence."

"Or abstinence." corrected Ply. Jane held back a smirk, or rather tried to.

"Can't you behave for two minutes?" she whispered as she turned and stomped down the stairs.

"We're married." he reminded her. "I'm not misbehaving."

"What is it we have to talk about?" she asked as she pulled the closet door and closed it as quietly as she could. She turned the handle so the latch would not click notifying 'the ears' that they had escaped into a quieter place.

"I was followed home by somebody from the apartment and it may be serious."

"Followed here?"

"No." he replied. "I led them to Johnson's old place of employment and then found a GPS homing device on the old white horse." Her eyes widened and her jaw dropped a little exposing her beautiful white teeth. Ply was tempted to... He looked away. "I ditched the GPS device at the old warehouse this side of town, hid from the guy chasing me, and when he left, he headed towards Johnson's and I came here. The white horse is in the barn and I wrapped it in aluminum foil just in case there is another device on it. I don't want them to know we are here. We will have to use your car for a while. Maybe we can sell the old horse!" he paused for a moment. "The car I mean".

She slowly shook her head. "Mother will only be here till we get stuff ready for the baby. What do you suppose they are after?"

"There is still a bunch of stuff I have to tell you, but it can wait until we are in bed. We may be in trouble with the Master."

"What happened?"

"Not a word until we are under the covers with the lights out and the door locked."

Dinner was quiet enough as Ply described how he got rid of all the junk from the apartment.

"I dropped my old coffee table from two steps up and it broke into a hundred pieces." he laughed. "That saved the recycle place from having to do it. I just dumped the pieces into the recycle dumpster out front and that was that. I took the bed frame to the used furniture store and even they didn't want it. As a result, most of the stuff I had got trashed or recycled."

When Ply was finished with the description of the apartment, Carol started in on all the new things for the baby's room and the nursery. Jane was quiet waiting for the meal to finish.

"Are you okay dear?" asked Carol to her daughter.

"I am really tired and now that Ply is back, I expect I shall sleep better." was her reply. "Thank you for coming to help in all the excitement of getting things ready for the baby."

"You're going to need us to help till at least a number of months after the baby comes." announced Carol.

Ply inhaled some of his potatoes but managed not to turn blue before he left the table and rushed to the bathroom in the hall.

Greg put his hand on his wife's. "Maybe we should let the kids call us when they think they need us."

"Ply already did call us."

"I better go see how Ply is doing." announced Jane and jumped from the table. Greg held onto Carol's hand, so she would stay where she was.

Ply was in the bathroom with the door shut trying to unload his dinner down the drain. Jane entered, quickly closed the door and gave Ply the Heimlich Maneuver. The lump of unchewed spuds popped out of his mouth and dropped into the toilet. Jane turned on the exhaust fan to drown out Ply's gasping for breath. It took almost fifteen minutes for Ply to get his color back.

"You going to be alright?" she asked with a very worried look on her face.

"Yeah, I think so." he responded in a shaky quiet voice. "Are they staying till the kid is six?"

"I sure hope not." she giggled. "I think Dad is talking her into leaving but we shall see what the morning brings." Jane flushed the toilet for the third time then swished the water around with a bowl brush and cleaned off the walls of the bowl while Ply regathered his composure sitting on a stool. Under the sink there were some cleaning supplies and she gave it a good cleaning. "That'll give the old septic a good workout."

"I feel like I just had one."

"You certainly did. I'm glad I got here when I did."

"Don't even go there, honey." encouraged Ply. "I think I need to lay down."

"Wait here a sec and I will tell the folks to clean up and I will

342

help you up to our room."

"Is he okay?" asked Carol as Jane came into the kitchen.

"He'll be fine. Can you two clean up and I will help Ply get into bed?"

Jane helped Ply up the stairs and down the hall to the first bridal suite where they had stayed since they were married. She kicked the door closed and flipped the lock. As Ply made his way to the bathroom to brush his teeth, she noticed the tennis ball on the nightstand by his side of the bed. Picking it up she noticed it was brand-new but did not have any markings on it. "Where's this from?"

Ply stuck his head out of the bathroom and nodded with his mouth full of toothpaste and brush. Jane set the ball back on the stand and wandered into the small room. Ply gargled and then kissed his bride. "Did that get rid of most of the odor?"

"Pretty much but maybe we can go without too much excitement until morning."

"I'll brush my teeth again." he stated rather firmly.

"And I'll get you a nice cold glass of milk. That will help wash down some of the stuff." Jane threw open the door and there was her mother with her ear very close to the door. "Mom!" she scolded in a disappointed tone. "We're married!"

Carol huffed herself down the hall towards her own room mumbling something about honeymooners, even after the honeymoon.

*　*　*

Jane returned with a good tall glass of ice-cold milk and some anti-acid to settle Ply's stomach. "The hall seems to be clear at the moment."

"You remember the tennis ball throwers at the court?" he asked her as she entered the room and locked the door again.

"How could I forget?"

"I had to buy a new package of tennis balls for the ones I chopped up with the sword."

Jane looked back at the door hoping her mother was not there with her ear plastered to the wood. "Go on"

"I only destroyed three balls, so I got one for a souvenir." he announced. "It has slept on my nightstand ever since." he grinned as he set the sphere beside his side of the bed on the little wooden stand, he made for it. "And I plan for it to stay there for a good long while."

Just as they crawled into bed Jane flipped off the light and checked the door once again. She opened it quietly and peeked out. Finding no one, she looked down both directions of the hall only to find it dark and all the downstairs house lights off. She closed and bolted the door. Ply tucked her in and slid in beside her. He pulled the covers over their heads and he said, "I think I am in trouble with the Master."

"Now what have you done?"

Ply told her of the meeting at the coffee shop, his testing of the Chia seeds, and the encounter with the critters in the caves. Every few minutes he would flap the sheets to get fresh air under the blankets. Finally, he told her.

"I killed three Anothen with the sword."

She looked at him aghast then threw her head into the pillow and laughed.

"I don't think it's funny at all." he rebuked her sternly. "If I have killed agents of the Master there just may be more on their way to get all of us here at the house." He considered what this might mean. "What if we wake up in the morning to find us all dead?"

This again was too much. Jane thought of the old King James Version account of the battle of Hezekiah, king of Judah and Sennacherib, king of Assyria where the early translation says 'they woke up in the morning and they were all dead' referring to the Assyrians. She wiped the tears from her eyes and said, "You can't kill the Anothen. They have already died and are in their resurrected bodies, so they cannot die again. Those who died before the Master returned to set up his physical reign came with him and now live in eternal bodies." She stopped to catch her breath. "I don't know what happens to those who die during the Millennium, but I expect something happens."

"I chopped one head off and cut another in half right down the middle."

"Did they bleed?"

Ply thought about this for a sec, "No."

"Did they seem upset that you had killed their friends?"

Ply thought about this for another second, "No."

"It's all part of the prophecy that we only get to die once."

"What about Lazarus?" he interrogated. "He got to die twice."

"He did not come back in his resurrected body the first time, did he?"

Ply thought about this for a few minutes. "But I chopped them up and dumped them down the shaft."

"Okay." she said. "Tell me exactly what happened as you remember it."

"I chopped the head off the first one and the second kicked his buddy down into the shaft."

"Was their water in the shaft?"

"I think so."

Did you hear him splash in the water?"

Ply tried to think. "There was a lot of excitement."

"Was the excitement sent to distract you, so you would not hear there was no splash?"

"Perhaps."

"You can't kill the Anothen. They can walk through walls and appear and disappear anytime they like. What is to say that they cannot let their bodies be apparently torn apart then reassemble themselves and pass through all the rocks in the caves?" She let this sink in for a few seconds. "Jesus tell us that we are unable to imagine all that we will be able to do with our new bodies and I can imagine that they can go through the meat grinder and reassemble themselves in a totally different location. Do you remember the movie from a million years ago about the iron giant that gets chopped apart the puts himself back together again?"

"I haven't seen that one yet."

"Well if man can think it, then it is considered able to be done plus all the things we cannot think about. You didn't kill any Anothen." she admonished.

"Then why did they make me believe I did?"

"Now that you just may have to ask the Master."

"I don't think I am ready to face Him yet." He leaned over and gave her a great kiss. "Thank you. I just may sleep a little tonight."

"Good to have you back home in one piece." she said.

"Seeing that I am unable to reassemble myself as yet."

The Stolen Sword

Ply dialed the thirty-six number to make an appointment.

"Reality Encounters." answered the pleasant voice.

"I need to make an appointment to see the Master." Ply informed the woman.

"What would you like to speak to him about?" the mild lady asked.

"I had some property stolen and I really would like it back."

"Stolen property is a matter of much lower courts, sir." she informed him in a business-like tone, the mildness in her voice slipping a little.

"This stolen merchandise may be referred to as top secret material." informed the young man getting a little upset at the stalling tactics of the girl.

Oh, boy, we have a real live wire once again. It seems we have been getting a lot of these lately. "Hold on I'll transfer you to my supervisor." There was a clicking of keys then a brief interlude of poor, rather hastily constructed, elevator music.

"Reality Encounters, this is 'Jones' speaking."

"I would like to speak to the one in charge about some secret weaponry that has been removed from my possession."

"This is a civilian number. What are you doing with a secret military weapon?"

"I found it in a cave..."

"Why have you not gone through the courts in the proper manner?" interrupted Jones.

"I think the police in this part of the world are part of the rebellion and I need to speak to someone who really has control." stated Ply.

"Okay, the waiting period at this time is about twenty-six months. We can squeeze you in for about fifteen minutes on the fifth of..."

"I don't think you understand the implications of what is really happening here." blurted Ply. "This weapon that I had I was using for the purpose of upholding justice but in the wrong hands it could possibly even take out the Master."

Right! thought Jones. *This one really has gone off the deep end. Should I call the men in white coats and the rubber truck or...? Not my job,* he mused. "I'll transfer you to the secret weaponry department." he droned, and Ply heard music that was perhaps one floor up from the elevator.

After about forty seconds Ply heard, "Reality Encounters, Smith speaking."

Ply had a little trouble believing he actually was speaking to those who ran the world. *Jones and Smith?* he pondered.

"Hello, Smith here."

"Yes, I lost a weapon that might be considered top secret and I would like to talk to the Master about the possibility of getting it back." Ply cautiously informed the gentleman.

"What were you doing with a top-secret weapon in your possession?"

"I found it while exploring a cave. I do believe that the tool has powers that have not been recognized in our present understanding of military experience. It may be able to overthrow the present government."

"Let me transfer you to a different section of security. Please hold." This time the music was not just computer generated but a classical piece by an orchestra.

"Reality Encounters, security, agent Jubal speaking."

"Yes sir, I had a piece of equipment stolen and I would like to report it missing but I would like to speak with the Master, so I might get it back."

"What type of equipment are you missing?"

"I had a sword that was stolen."

"There are lots of swords out there why not just purchase another?"

"I don't believe there is another like it and if there is, we just might be in a great deal of trouble." stated Ply.

"What kind of trouble?" questioned the officer.

"Maybe I need to talk to someone in a little more secure arena than the airwaves or telephone lines. Can we meet someplace to talk quietly?" petitioned Ply.

"Why do we need to do that?"

"It was not only unique in design but also in the properties it manifested."

What were the properties it manifested? Was it magic?"

"No, sir. I don't believe in magic. To every action there is an equal and opposite reaction, so the inverse is also true; to every action there must be a cause and to every physical action there must be a physical cause and this sword could change my personal time frame." There was silence on the other end for about eight seconds. "Are you still there?"

"Yes, we're here. Can we meet in Summerfield's Gardens at about two this afternoon? We will be by the daffodils sitting on the south bench."

"That is about twenty minutes from me. Yes, I'll be there at two this afternoon."

Thank you. We shall see you shortly." stated the agent. "Could you please bring along any evidence you have that you actually owned the sword?"

This request surprised Ply but he immediately thought of the guitar case. "Sure."

"Fine. We shall meet at two. Have a good afternoon."

The conversation ended on Ply's phone. "Man, these guys are weird."

* * *

Ply arrived at the daffodils and found the park bench. There was a parking spot about twenty feet from the bench, so he stopped Jane's car there but left the case in the trunk. He sat down on the bench and waited. It was two minutes to two and not a person in sight for as far as the eye could see. There was a tree that was about thirty feet away but in general there was almost a hundred-foot visibility that made it easy to see if anyone was walking or driving towards him.

He sat at the edge of the bench and at two o'clock on the dot two men walked from behind the tree. Ply looked around but saw no other people nor any means of the new arrival's transportation.

"Ply Gallant I presume."

These two did not look at all like any of the three he had encountered earlier so he relaxed a little, but how to relax in the presence of someone from...

"Yes." answered Ply. "Good choice of a quiet spot, men."

"Now tell us about this sword and what you have done with it."

The smile from the informal greeting slowly left the face of the mortal as he realized that he was really not in control of this situation. How much control did he have in any situation really?

"How much do you already know?"

"We are agents, remember? And we need to know that you are really who you say you are."

Ply walked over to the trunk and removed the case showing the boys where he stored the toy. He also produced the split tennis balls that he had dug out of the garbage and hidden at the bottom of his dirty laundry hamper in case he needed the evidence of the clean cut of the machine. At the time pitching them seemed a good idea but after some thought he dug them back out, put them in clean a plastic bag, and set them at the bottom of a place where most people might be afraid to look.

"That is nice but how do we know you did not steal it?"

"Because I am not a thief." he proclaimed.

"You stole a girl's heart did you not?"

Ply thought for a second. "No, I won it!"

"There are only a few who know what you really have done with the tool, if you really had it, and we have been informed of all that has happened, so you need to tell us, so we can be sure it is you who actually owned the machine."

A machine? thought Ply. If it was a machine, then there may be more parts than he and Jane had discovered.

He told them of the cave and how he was curious about the draft and it led to the discovery of the sword.

"Good." replied one or of the agents. "What else happened in the caves?"

Ply wasn't ready to go into this seeing that he was not yet sure that he had not sent the three other agents to a place that he was unwilling to go. His palms got sweaty and a telltale bead dripped from his forehead.

"I killed five rabid dogs that were holed up at the Whopplehorst farm but that was to protect the public. I burnt the farm barn to prevent the spread of the rabies."

"That is true." commented the other agent. "What else?"

Ply put the guitar case back in the trunk and then followed the two to the bench. "I practiced with the sword at a police firing range," he stated as they all sat down.

"Good."

"I helped Jane improve her game at Barb's mansion."

"Okay."

Jane and I retrieved the stolen lawn equipment and managed to get a conviction on all who were involved in the ring."

"Wonderful." stated one of the agents with his eyes partially rolled and an almost bored look on his face. "What else happened in the cave?" he asked attempting to suppress a noisy yawn.

"I had to fight horrible creatures and barely managed to escape with my life."

"Any other lives lost in the cave?"

Ply leaned forward, put his elbows on his knees and his head in his hands, closed his eyes, and stated in an almost inaudible voice, "I chopped up three agents and dumped them into a bottomless pit."

"You killed three agents with this sword?"

Ply stood up and paced a little to release some nervous energy. Admitting murder is one thing but being unarmed and admitting murder of agents was a totally different matter, especially in front of two that were in charge of security.

"And you want this sword back, so you can attempt to eliminate more of us?"

"That was a mistake and I need to make restitution but how do you make restitution for killing someone from..."

One of the two that were still on the bench stood up and glanced at Ply. He dropped his gaze and walked around the tree that the two had hidden behind. It appeared as if he just walked around the tree and returned to the bench by the flowers. "The Master says he will meet with you in two months."

"Two months?" complained Ply.

"Speaking face to face with the Master was not something to be taken lightly. The waiting period is normally twenty-six to thirty-six months. He is giving you some time to think about what has happened with this toy you have been playing with. You will receive a notice in the mail as to time, date, and location about two weeks prior to your appointment. We personally live in such a small world that we often need to be reminded that we are not the only ones with good ideas and important opportunities." With that the two walked behind the tree.

Ply rushed over to see what happens when they do whatever they do in situations like this but by the time he arrived they were gone. He looked all around the tree and then everywhere visible, but no one was in sight save an old man walking his dog coming over the far hill.

"They're not only weird but a whole lot of spooky." he mumbled to himself as he climbed into his wife's car and drove back to try to comfort Jane. Now he had to stand before the Master and give account for eliminating three agents. This was not going according to his plan at all.

* * *

"Sir, I need to personally report to you that my sword has been stolen." reported Ply before His Majesty.

"Tell me, young man," interrogated the Chief Magistrate. "Is there anything you actually own, or has it simply been given to you on loan as a stewardship for a period of time?"

"We could have reigned for another thousand years!" exclaimed Ply.

"What you mean 'we' *'Que No Sabe?'*" informed the superior. "Do you not see what tool has been doing to you?"

"Sir," reminded the minion. "Justice must be met. You of all people are aware of such things"

"Justice will be met, my son, and my purposes shall stand. Here, we have time and space that limit our opportunities. There, we have all of eternity to learn and play and love and..." the Master seemed to be looking to someplace that Ply had either lost perspective of or never really thought about.

"Indeed, there is much to learn and many opportunities to fulfill but this is no place to live forever." The Master opened the eyes of Ply to see just a short glimpse of what lay ahead. Immediately the human fell to his knees and put his face to the floor.

"Forgive me Lord, I have been proud in my rebellion of your purposes." he pleaded.

"I know." encouraged the Magnificent One. "That is why I allowed you to come. You and Jane are among millions of my chosen servants. I had the sword created so the hearts of men could be manifest as to their true desires. It was happening to you and I prevented it from destroying you, but you needed the lesson and a few other things that came with the discovery." He smiled.

Ply looked up into the most forgiving eyes he had seen yet not without the holiness of the Perfect One. It was both frightening and comforting.

"I will continue to lead you and soon enough you shall see the outcome of these things." informed the shaper of all history. Then standing, signaling the interview had ended he announced, "Anothen!"

Two people walked through the door, a girl and a boy, not appearing more than ten or eleven, holding hands. The seemed like Oriental in race. They bowed before the Lord.

"Oh, Ply," called the Master as Ply was staring at the two youths before him, "You might want to talk to Flannery about the Mower case."

Ply turned to the Lord, "Is there more?" The smile of the Master confirmed Ply's question.

Ply was ushered out of the immediate physical presence of the only one in history who is worthy of worship. The two, who appeared to be just kids, thanked Ply for coming.

"How old are you?" asked Ply to the guides.

"I was born in nineteen thirty-five." said the boy

"I was born in nineteen thirty-seven." said the young girl.

"This is thirty-one twenty-eight." stated Ply in confusion. "How come you seem like youngsters?"

"We graduated in nineteen forty-five." stated the boy.

"Chairman Mao tried to eliminate Christianity from China." announced the girl. "We were attending a school run by Missionaries when the Communists came, they set a Bible on the threshold of the door to exit the school. They said if we would spit on the Bible we could live. If we refused, we were to be shot. I was eighth in line, three of the students spit on the Bible, then one boy did not. He was shot and none of the rest of us spat on the Bible, but we kissed it and got to come home early."

"Only early by some standards." announced the young man and the two smiled at each other.

As Ply left the room and returned to the place he came from, the reality of all that had happened started to make sense to his very small and limited understanding.

"Wow." he thought while driving on the highway. "How foolish I was to even approach Him in such a manner of arrogance. But how grateful I am for His forgiveness, grace and provision."

* * *

Ply arrived back at the castle and found Jane feeding herself and the womb-bat.

"Are you two okay?" he asked.

"Why would we not be?" she responded. "How did the interview go?"

"Short and sweet."

"Sweet?"

"Well, short anyway. I wonder if a whole lot more people would accept His provision if He allowed them just to see Him?"

"I doubt it." she stated matter of factually.

"Really?" he asked in a surprised tone.

"If they hate Him already what would it be like if they actually saw Him face to face?"

"That's my question. Would they not recognize Him for who He really is?"

"He is the one who calls us, right?"

"Yeah, okay." he cautiously responded.

"So, if those who He has not called get to stand before His face would it not harden their heart?"

"But with me He was so forgiving."

"Of course. You are one of His called."

"He told me the sword was changing me in the wrong direction, so I had to get rid of it."

"I suppose attempting to kill Anothen is probably the wrong direction." she reminded him with a kiss on the cheek.

"I guess that is why He took it from me." Ply thought for a short moment. "He said it was built so the hearts of men might be demonstrated as to what they were really like."

"Jeremiah seventeen nine says, 'our hearts are horribly wicked and none of us know the potential of our own evil heart'." reminded Jane.

"I sure found that out about mine." said Ply
"Barb dying sure revealed to me a lot of my selfishness and pride."

"Did you get the drivers papers changed?"

"It is not three months yet since officially moving from the apartment. I don't want whoever it is that is looking for us to show up here with the sword asking questions that I do not want to answer."

"They have the sword. What more would they want?"

"What if they can't ghost out? What if they know nothing about the interior blades? What if they want the drone and the cabin?"

"Maybe you should dismantle them and get rid of the evidence." stated Jane.

"I guess you are right. Not everybody can do the things we did but it sure was fun while it lasted."

"In the wrong hands a lot of damage can be done," reminded Jane.

"I don't even want to think about it." Ply kissed his wife and headed out to the maintenance shed to dismantle and dispose of anything that might give evidence to having the sword. The grass had grown in nicely covering the bare spot the white towels left in the yard. He stacked the Plexiglass in one part of the shop and the metal pieces upstairs in another. The plastic he stuck in the recycle bin. The leather boson's chairs and the harnesses he burned in the burn barrel and then spread the ashes in the compost heap.

The next morning, he suggested to Jane that they look into purchasing a small cottage somewhere for a bit of a retreat from the monstrosity of the castle.

"Don't you have enough to do here?" she asked.

"Sure, but a place where I could boat, and fish would be fun, and we could teach the young one all the pleasures of adventure in the wilds."

"I just may have had enough of the wilds for a little while." suggested Jane.

"How soon are you getting back into the game?"

"Not for a while if all things work out okay. If we do have trouble, then it will still take some recuperation time."

"Are you okay with that? he asked.

"We should be if all our money is not spent frivolously on cottages and fancy cars."

"I resemble that remark!"

Author Albert Daniels started writing in third grade when he submitted an assignment about Spring. The poem is as follows:

"It is the morning of the spring
All the birds and Condors sing."

He thought it was hilarious. The teacher told him to never write again. He didn't. Until recently.
Albert now he lives in Missouri with his wife of 40 years who encourages him to write instead of talk at 2:00 AM!

CPSIA information can be obtained
at www.ICGtesting.com
Printed in the USA
LVHW012320271019
635508LV00014B/168/P